THIS COPY
SIGNED

7.00

In the Shadow of the Sun

by

Geoffrey and Elaine Meece

*Dick & Pat,
Enjoy your tour
of July, Elaine Meece
&
Geoffrey Meece*

D0905813

Copyright Page

In the Shadow of the Sun
Authors -Elaine Meece and Geoffrey Meece

Copyright ©2018 by Elaine Meece and Geoffrey Meece
Sassafras Publishing
686 Brinsley Cove
Memphis, TN. 38017

Published July 2018

ISBN- 13:978-0692125564
ISBN- 10:0692125566

Cover Art by Valerie Tibbs Design

Published in the United States of America. Publish date July 2018. All rights reserved. This book should not be copied or photocopied without written permission of the authors except in case of brief quotations embodied in articles or reviews.
This is a work of fiction based on the journal and notes left by Ressa Jenkins and interviews by Geneva Jenkins of their experience in the Philippines. The use of real people, places, and groups was to give it authenticity.

Acknowledgements

Geoffrey and I want to thank the Meridieth family for entrusting us with all their aunts' memoirs, government documents, and news articles. We also want to thank Beverly Marsh and Joanne Smalley for using their genealogy skills with research for the book and Valencia Keck and Alicia Feldman for their valuable help

The Meridieth Boys

The sense of patriotism that drove Ressa and Geneva Jenkins to fearlessly serve our nation under the harshest conditions is also characteristic of their two nephews.

John Meridieth joined the National Guard while in high school, then enlisted in the Army in 1955 and trained at several locations. 82nd Airborne, Artillery and Mortar Units, Classified Assignments in Military Intelligence. DA Civilian GS7, Vicenza, Italy and Warrant Officer, and Vietnam. In 1957, he received a rude awaking about WWII when he was assigned to Dachau, Germany (Hitler's crematory) and discovered there were still unclaimed remains, burning flesh stink, and a Displaced Persons camp. He retired with the rank of Sergeant First Class in 1975.

Sam Meridieth joined the Tennessee National Guard in 1957 while in high school, then enlisted in the Marine Corps in 1960, trained in infantry. Sam was wounded in Marble Mountain, Vietnam and received the Purple Heart along with Meritorious Medal, Vietnam Cross of Gallantry, and Combat Action Ribbon. Sam retired in 1987 with the rank of Master Gunnery Sergeant. Part of Sam's duty took him to Mindanao where unknowingly he retraced the steps his Aunt Geneva had taken twenty years earlier.

John and Sam have two sisters, Martha Ingle Sands and Liz Stigall. Liz and Martha went into nursing like their mother and two aunts. John, Sam, Martha, and Liz are the children of Univieve Jenkins.

Dedication

Geneva Jenkins (left) Ressa Jenkins (right)

In 1941, Ressa Jenkins and her sister, Geneva, joined others in the Philippines, looking for adventure and new experiences as nurses. On December seventh, paradise became hell.

Ressa Jenkins wanted to share her experience with the world. She wanted everyone to know the sacrifices made by both the nurses, doctors, and soldiers during the invasion of the Philippines by the Japanese Imperial Army. This book is in memory of Ressa and Geneva Jenkins and all the other men and women who faced the hardships and sacrifices of war with them.

It is also dedicated to the brave active duty military serving today. May our government never fail them and may God bless them.

Authors' Notes

We are honored to have been given this opportunity to tell Ressa and Geneva's stories. I write romantic suspense and comedy. A few years ago, Geoffrey took on this project. Seeing the magnitude of the task, I offered to help. I wanted Ressa's story told. We didn't want this to be just another factfinding book on the Angels of Bataan. We wanted to bring these angels to life.

Once home from the Philippines, Ressa wrote down her experience. She left a 266-page memoir. She also left radio scripts from three shows that includes the experiences of two other nurses along with government documents. We have interviews given by Geneva and some notes.

We tried to cover everything written in Ressa's memoirs and shaped it into scenes and dialogue. There are events and factual information we added to the scenes to round out the story. Our foremost goal was to tell the story Ressa wanted the world to hear. Geoffrey wrote Geneva's scenes, and I wrote Ressa's.

Some of the dates are exact dates given by Ressa and others are estimated dates based on our calculations using her journal and events listed in reference books.

Defenders of the Philippines and other government websites and these books: *Angels of Bataan, All This Hell, The Marcia Gates Story, To the Angels*, and *True Grit* were instrumental in helping with dates and events. If you wish to read more about these brave nurses, I highly recommend these books.

In one book, it has Helen Summers leaving for Corregidor from Hospital No. 1. Ressa left official documents showing Helen was with her and Geneva, leaving from Hospital No. 2.

Welcome to Paradise
Part One

GENEVA
August 1, 1941 Manila Bay

Something was different. I realized we were moving at a snail's pace. Quickly, I sat up with excitement shooting through me. I shook my sister. "Wake up, Ressa. I think we're here."

"Okay, I'm awake. Stop shaking me." She rubbed her eyes and yawned.

For the last two weeks, we had been roommates aboard the USS Coolidge, an ocean liner used by the government as a transport. We had departed from San Francisco on July fifteenth—destination Manila. I had suffered from seasickness during the first part of the trip. It had taken a while to get my sea legs.

I scurried around our quarters getting dressed. "Yellow or pink?"

"I like the yellow dress." Ressa grabbed her clothes and headed for the bathroom.

Ressa and I exited the cabin at the same time. Our hair combed, teeth brushed, lipstick lightly applied, and wearing our Sunday-go-to-meeting clothes.

Upon deck, I walked to the side and held the rail to prevent slipping. Ressa stood beside me. Her expression showed her disappointment.

A wave of apprehension swept over me. For the first time on our journey, we weren't greeted by warmth and bright sunshine. Instead, a gray overcast sky hid the sun, and an eerie fog hovered over the bay. Neither of us could see the land.

"I hope this isn't a bad omen of things to come."

Ressa, being the older by two years, always assumed the role of protector and surrogate mother. "Don't be silly. For Heaven's sake, it's not like you haven't seen fog before."

I hoped she was right. I sensed a slight doubt in her voice. Hopefully, all foreboding thoughts were due to the imaginations of my tired mind.

"I guess you're right. I'm starved. Let's find Winnie and see about breakfast."

We strolled along the deck toward the galley. We weaved our way around anxious passengers who had come out of their cabins. I stopped and stared into the mist. "Isn't that land?"

"Where?"

"Look there." I pointed through the haze.

"I see it now. Looks like a mountain. Wonder if that's Manila."

A crew member stopped and said, "No, Miss. That's the top of Corregidor, the island they call the Rock. The mainland is on the right side of it and farther back."

We stared in an effort to penetrate through the cloudy mist and get a glimpse of our home for the next two years. Boat horns blew, and sea birds flew overhead as if guiding the ship to port.

Ressa turned to me. "I guess we'll see it when we dock."

I nudged my sister. "There's Winnie." I waved. "Winnie."

Winifred Madden was a fair skinned Wisconsin girl with dark hair and soft eyes and a year younger than me. She'd been on the entire journey with us.

Ressa smiled. "Morning. You sure look lovely."

"Thank you. You both look lovely as well." Winnie waited for us to catch up with her. "Well, girls, we finally made it."

"We did." Ressa drew in a deep breath of the salty air. "It will be nice getting settled, but honestly, I've enjoyed the trip."

I placed a hand over my stomach. "Once I got past my stomach rolling with the waves, I enjoyed it. Ready for breakfast?"

"You betcha. As sure as God made little green apples."

I loved listening to her Wisconsin dialect. I'd always thought we southerners were the only ones with distinct accents. When I had nursed in New York before joining my sister in California, they had commented often about my accent.

Ressa forged through the people toward the galley. "Now that we're here, I hope we all get the same duty station," she said to us.

Winnie nodded. "I hope so too, you know."

We were almost positive we'd be assigned to the same hospital since we were sisters. We all walked down the long deck and entered the galley together.

The aroma of coffee and bacon filled the air, and it caused my stomach to growl. I only hoped I could eat without spilling anything on my dress. People sat leisurely sipping coffee, eating, and talking. We chose a table in the center. Two high-ranking United States officers sat next to us. Totally absorbed in what seemed to be a serious conversation, they didn't notice us.

Once our meal arrived, we doctored our food with salt and pepper and started eating. I placed the cloth napkin in my lap. Rather than talk, we ate in silence, making it easy to overhear the officers' conversation.

"Germany is pushing through Europe, taking everything in its path. Their troops are within two-hundred miles of Moscow," the older officer stated.

"War World I didn't accomplish anything. I hope we can stay out of it."

"We're up to our elbows in it. Giving Britain, France, and Russia supplies and equipment showed Germany who we're siding with."

"Roosevelt's Lend and Lease Pact was business."

"No, that was our ticket into the war. Then in March, when the U.S. captured the Axis vessels and in April fired on the Germany U-boat that sealed the deal."

I looked at Ressa and Winnie. They had been listening as well. "So long as the war stays in Europe, we should be fine in the Philippines."

Ressa and Winnie nodded and continued eating.

"Japan," the younger officer said. "I'm more worried about them than Germany."

"They've been too busy fighting China and seizing European colonies."

"They want to be a major power and obtain the resources and territories that come with being an imperial nation. The Japs want us to see they're superior in every way. I don't regret taking my wife and kids home. War with Japan is imminent."

The two men pushed their chairs back, stood, and left.

Rumors of war had overshadowed our trip. Most of the people we came in contact with were all of the same mindset; Japan will attack.

3

Ressa sighed. "Their conversation made my food settle like a rock in my stomach. Do you think he's right?"

It didn't help my digestion either. "I hope not."

"But everyone is saying it," Winnie said.

"They've been saying it for over two years," I reminded. "So, let's assume it's all talk that amounts to a lot of hot air."

"Let's talk about something else," Winnie said. "How many in your family?"

I smiled, looking forward to her reaction. "When we left, there were my parents and nine of us kids."

Winnie's mouth dropped open. "Cripes sake. That's sure a lot of kids in one family. I know an orphanage that doesn't have that many kids."

"I'm sure there will be one or two more by the time we return," Ressa added.

"It must've been tough making ends meet with so many kids," Winnie commented.

"It was," Ressa admitted. "That's why they let us four older girls attend the Normal School in Asheville, North Carolina. It's a boarding school. The Presbyterian Home Mission Workers arranged it."

"I attended there from second until I graduated as a senior." I sipped my coffee.

"Didn't you miss being home?" Winnie asked.

I nodded. "At first. We went home on breaks while we were in grammar school and helped with the farm, but as we got older we took summer jobs instead."

"What kind of jobs?" Winnie asked.

"We worked for doctors and lawyers doing odd jobs," Ressa said. "We were both nannies for a while. We made enough money to help with our tuition. So basically, we've always worked. Even when I was training at Knoxville General Hospital, I worked side jobs."

"We've always liked making our own money and providing for ourselves," I added. "Now here we are in our thirties setting off for a new adventure."

Ressa frowned. "Early thirties."

4

"I can't imagine being so independent," Winnie said. "My parents were overprotective. And believe you me, they were none too happy about my becoming a nurse and joining the Army."

"Our folks were mainly concerned with us being so near Japan." I glanced around us. "I guess we should hurry."

Winnie pointed her fork at us. "Well, girls, you's might as well take your time and eat slow, because I heard the pilot boat won't reach us for a couple of hours."

"You don't say? Well, I'll be. If that's true, we have time for a warm up on coffee." I waved my cup for a refill. "I'll be all wilted by then."

"I'll bring over a pot." Ressa stood and retrieved a pot of steaming coffee and poured us a fresh cup.

Shortly, we finished our breakfast and pushed our plates back.

Ressa pulled a pack of Lucky Strikes from her purse. "Care for a smoke, Winnie?"

"You know, nothing is better after a meal than a cigarette. Thanks."

Ressa held the lighter for Winnie before lighting her own. The embers glowed orange as the two inhaled, then exhaled. As they relaxed, a look of complete contentment showed on their faces.

"Geneva, have you ever smoked?" Winnie blew out three perfect smoke rings.

"No. It always seemed like a waste of time and money."

"Winnie, you never told us your opinion of Hawaii." Ressa flicked her ashes in an ashtray on the table.

Winnie blew out a puff of smoke. "I don't want to sound like a negative Nelly, but I'm starting to wonder if I made a bad choice. Honolulu was beautiful with clear sunny skies every day, and now I'm here in gloomy Manila. I'm hoping it's nice, but I can't say for sure until the fog lifts."

I wadded my napkin and set it on the table. "We all saw the same pictures and got the same information of our location choices before deciding. No hesitation on our part. It was the Philippines, hands down. It's a waste of time questioning that decision now."

Winnie smiled. "Now you're talking common sense. I needed to hear that. Thanks."

Ressa pulled the ashtray closer. "Like you said, sis, we picked Manila, but if I had it to do over, I'd choose Hawaii."

As sparks flew up, Winnie fanned them away. "Why?"

"Geneva's friend, Betty, gave us a tour of the island during our layover. We even attended a luau and tried to hula. It's a tropical paradise."

I nodded. "True, but we haven't given Manila a chance yet."

Winnie appeared uncertain. "The scenic beauty of the place isn't the factor I'm concerned with. Believe you me, after hearing all the talk around us, I'm more worried about war."

"Personally, I don't believe they're crazy enough to start a war with us," I declared, confidently.

Ressa sighed. "But if you're wrong, I'd rather be in Hawaii with our fleet where I know it's safer than here in Manila closer to Japan."

I shrugged off her concern. "I don't think there's anything to worry about."

"Why's that?" Winnie asked.

"We have General MacArthur to take care of us. Trust me, we're in good hands."

Ressa put her cigarette out. "I agree. I'm not going to worry about it. I'm going to have the experience of a lifetime and enjoy every minute of it."

We spent the next hour in light conversation, describing the hard farm life of Sevierville, Tennessee that our parents had endured while Winnie shared her cold Monticello, Wisconsin upbringing. "I'm going on deck to see if I can spot the pilot boat. You's wanna come?" Winnie asked.

"Why not," I said and stood. "Lead the way."

Ressa grabbed her purse and followed us. As we left, we waved at Dorothy Scholl, a young Army nurse from Independence, Missouri. She had ash blonde hair and lovely light green eyes. We giggled over how close she sat with a young military man, Harold Arnold, who had been assigned to the Philippines. They had met aboard ship and hit it off from the start.

On deck, a light drizzling rain made the air feel heavy, but the fog had lifted.

The pilot boat had finally arrived to usher the USS Coolidge safely through the treacherous Manila Bay.

The ship was safely maneuvered through the minefield. Several enormous battleships filled the harbor. Small fishing boats floated all around them.

Since the fog had lifted, Mount Mariveles could be seen in the distance as well as thick jungles. As the light filtered on it and its surrounding peaks, they appeared purple. The water we glided through sparkled like blue diamonds enclosed by the white sand of Manila. It surprised me to see the lovely homes circling Manila Bay. I'd expected to see bamboo huts.

A young adjutant from the Army had taken a smaller boat out and come aboard to greet us and pass out our orders. "Before I give you your orders, I have something else for you ladies." He handed us beautiful orchid corsages. Each corsage had three or four flowers. "These are a welcoming present."

"How thoughtful. Thank you. They're lovely." I sniffed mine and smiled.

"It's a really gracious gesture," Ressa added. "Thank you."

"Beautiful," Winnie added. "They smell divine."

We helped each other pin the corsages onto our chiffon dresses.

"And here are your orders," he said. "Have a pleasant day."

We thanked him, and he moved on to other nurses onboard.

I opened my paper and smiled. "I'm stationed in Manila at Sternberg."

Ressa beamed with joy. "Me too." She turned to Winnie. "Are you with us?"

Winnie frowned. "No, I'm heading to Ft. Mills on Corregidor. Looks like I'll be on the Rock."

"I was hoping you'd be with us," I said, truly disappointed.

"If I had my druthers, I'd rather be with you girls."

"Don't worry," said an officer, standing next to us. "It's lauded for its scenic beauty. And it is a fortress that can't be broken. You'll be fine there."

We introduced ourselves to him. With one hand left on the rail, Captain MacNeil turned toward us. "I'm assigned to Sternberg with you. I'll be working in surgery."

"We're nurses, so I'm sure we'll be seeing you," Ressa said.

As the Coolidge neared the dock, three Army planes streaked across the sky to honor the arriving ship, another display of welcome. I strained my neck back to see them.

The Army band who were dressed in white uniforms played a medley of patriotic tunes as we disembarked. She's a *Grand Ole Flag* began to play, one of my favorite G.M. Cohan tunes.

My heart swelled with pride and excitement. This had to be one of the most perfect days of my life. I whispered to Ressa, "I feel like the queen taking time off to meet my faithful subjects."

"I know what you mean. I expected a welcome, but nothing like this."

All the nurses walked down the gangplank. All of us attired in chiffon dresses, white gloves, and stylish hats. It looked more like a fashion show. We had been advised on what to wear.

A crowd stood on the dock, waiting for people to disembark. We saw Second Lieutenant Bliss, who'd we met onboard. He joined a group of men.

Dorothy and Arnold left the boat together, hand in hand, and when they reached the bottom, he pulled her into his arms and kissed her deeply.

We swooned, then giggled.

Several nurses leaving the ship would be taken to Stotsenberg about seventy miles northwest of Manila where Clark Field was located. A group of Navy nurses were heading to Canacao on Cavite Peninsula a very short distance from Sternberg. Another nurse would be taken to Ft. McKinley, seven miles south and even closer by ferry. Two nurses were going a hundred and fifty miles north to Camp John Hay in Little Baguio.

The band still played with gusto.

Welcoming parties held up signs with the names of nurses and doctors. We searched for our names. On the pier, a small group waited led by a woman of solid stature. She appeared slightly plump with white hair and ears that poked out. She held a sign with our names on it. It also had Captain MacNeil's name. Seeing Dorothy's name listed with ours, I assumed she'd been assigned to Sternberg with us or Corregidor with Winnie.

Dorothy caught up with us. Her eyes held a sparkle and her cheeks a tinge of pink.

"Welcome to Manila ladies. I'm Captain Maude Davison and this is Josie Nesbit, my right hand. I couldn't do without her." Her appearance and posture radiated with authority and the strength one would associate with a captain's rank.

"She gives me more credit than I deserve," the taller, lean woman said. "I'm only responsible for scheduling and filling out daily work rosters for the hospital."

"I see you already have corsages, but nonetheless, here are some more orchids."

The captain and Josie handed us more flowers of different colors—pale purples, pinks, and yellows.

"Thank you." A ripple of shock ran through me over the number of lovely flowers presented to us. I had my hands full. "Where we're from, orchids are expensive. You only see them around Easter time."

"We don't have these up Nort' where I'm from," Winnie said.

"They don't exactly grow around Missouri either," Dorothy added.

"Here they're abundant and cheap," Josie replied.

"I'm Geneva Jenkins. Thank you for our warm welcome."

"I'm Ressa Jenkins."

"Dorothy Scholl."

"Winifred Madden but call me Winnie. I'll be heading for Corregidor in a few days."

"Well, until you do, you're one of my girls," Maude Davison said. "And who is that young soldier who keeps glancing this way?"

The color in Dorothy's cheeks deepened. "That's Arnold. We met coming over."

"Will he be a distraction from your work?" the captain asked sternly.

"Yes, ma'am. I sure hope so."

We all laughed including the captain and Lieutenant Nesbit.

"Geneva, I think we're going to like it here." Ressa said, smiling.

"Who doesn't like being in paradise?" I asked rhetorically.

Captain MacNeil showed up and introduced himself. "I hope I didn't hold you ladies up."

9

"No, not at all." Captain Davison spoke up, "Lieutenant Nesbit, let's get these ladies and the captain out of the mist."

"Yes, ma'am. Follow me, please."

A large, dark car with a driver waited for us. MacNeil rode up front with Maude Davison. "I appreciate the ride. I'm meeting up with a group at the club. They'll take care of me from there."

"Glad to have you with us. We could use more like you," Davison said.

When we were all comfortably situated, Captain Davison addressed the driver. "Jay, take us to the Army/ Navy Club, please."

"Yes ma'am."

As we rode through the crowded streets, I couldn't stop staring out the window at the charming sights of the city. I felt sorry for Dorothy and Ressa crammed in the middle of the backseat without a clear view.

The Spanish influence was evident in a lot of the architecture. Cars along with pony drawn carts and rickshaws filled the street. Manila, a pleasant blend of modern and old, had tall buildings and smaller structures.

The aroma of our orchids filled the car with a strong sweet fragrance—pleasant, yet almost overwhelming to the senses.

"Thank you again for the beautiful flowers, Captain Davison." I said. "And you also, Lieutenant Nesbit."

"You're welcome, Geneva, our pleasure. One thing I might as well tell you before she does is everyone calls Lieutenant Nesbit, Josie. Most of the time she won't answer to anything else. Isn't that right, Josie?" Davison smiled.

"Truer words were never spoken," Josie affirmed.

It was around ten in the morning when the car pulled up to the Army/Navy Club. The driver quickly climbed out and opened the back door allowing us to exit. Our small entourage entered the facility.

The club entrance opened into a spacious lobby. Tall massive arches bordered each side. A balcony wrapped around the upper level looking down on the open floor below. Bing Crosby's smooth voice flowed like silk over the radio waves. Three off-duty nurses served as a welcoming committee. We joined them at a large table in padded comfortable chairs. A waiter served drinks to us.

Captain MacNeil joined a group of men at the bar. I was sure we'd be seeing him at the hospital.

"Ladies, I'd like to introduce the latest addition to our staff. These are the Jenkins sisters, Ressa and Geneva, and this is Dorothy Scholl. We also have Winnie Madden, who will be our guest for a day or two before heading to Corregidor," Captain Davison added.

"Welcome to Manila, I'm Juanita Redmond." The girl was pretty enough to be a Hollywood movie star. Her thick, dark hair contrasted with her blue eyes and fair skin. "Nice meeting you. I look forward to working with you."

She spoke in a refined and drawn out southern accent that one would expect from the affluent of the old south.

At that point, an attractive slender brunette lady, smiled at us. "Hi, I'm Francis Nash. You girls are going to like it here, trust me."

While her accent was also southern, it didn't have the refinement of Juanita's. She had more of a twang. "Where do you call home?" I asked Francis.

"I'm a Georgia peach. What about you?"

"We're from Tennessee."

"I've got a cousin there. Which part are y'all from?"

"Sevierville in the eastern part of the state."

"She's around Nashville. I always thought Tennessee was a beautiful state especially the part you're from. The Smokies are gorgeous in the fall when the leaves are changing."

"It's pretty enough," Ressa said. "Once those leaves fall it gets cold. Winnie being from Wisconsin knows about cold."

"You betcha. The snow gets up to my ears."

"We've had some large snows in Missouri. Probably not what you get in Wisconsin," Dorothy commented.

"That is one thing we don't have to worry about here." A slender sandy blonde girl said. "I'm Madeline Ullom, and like Francis said you girls are going to love the Philippines. You'll be sunbathing at the pool or playing golf while your friends back home are plodding through snow."

"Golf is a great way to meet officers. Do any of you play?" Juanita inquired.

"I like the game, but I'm not very good," Ressa admitted.

"Well, you'll have plenty of opportunities to sharpen your skills."

"Why's that?" I asked.

"Mainly due to the four-hour shifts," Francis said. "Honey, that's all you will work in the daytime because of the heat. Believe me, it is a long four hours."

"It is, but it still gives you ample time off to do whatever you feel inclined to do," Madeline said. "You can choose from tennis, golf, badminton, bowling, and swimming."

"I'm sure you'll find the schedule a lot less strenuous than what you had in the hospitals back home," Captain Davison said.

"How far is Ft. McKinley?" Dorothy asked.

"Close, very close," Josie said. "You'll be seeing your Mr. Arnold often."

"That's nice to know," Dorothy said, blushing because Josie knew exactly why she was so interested in Ft. McKinley.

Our apprehensions and thoughts of war were quickly dismissed and replaced with laughter and light-hearted conversation.

"I just came back from Corregidor. It's beautiful," Josie said to Winnie. The lieutenant had a long, thin face and wore glasses that hid her green eyes. Like most nurses, she wore her brown hair twisted in a bun.

Winnie didn't appear convinced. Concern flickered in her eyes. "Ya know, I heard it's a tunnel, not even a real building."

Josie laughed. "That's only partially true, but the hospital and nurses' quarters are Topside. The tunnel is mainly offices and used for storage."

Winnie offered Josie a smile. "Thanks for telling me. Believe you me, it made me feel a whole lot better hearing it."

"You will be working with a great group. Isn't that right, Captain?"

"Absolutely, and here's another little tidbit of information, they call it the Rock because it is an impenetrable fortress. If we end up at war with Japan like they predict, you will be in the safest place of all. Corregidor can't be taken, no matter what they throw at it," Captain Davison stated.

"That's what Captain MacNeil told us on the boat," I said.

Fans overhead and a slight breeze off the bay helped negate the hot humidity. Billie Holiday's *Strange Fruit* played over the sound system. A perfect setting to have a few drinks and enjoy the company of our new comrades. Everyone seemed fond of gin.

We hadn't been seated too long when I nudged Ressa. "Isn't that John Raulston, Joe's little brother?"

Both men had become doctors, but we didn't have a clue one of them would be here. It made the world seem so small.

"Well, I'll be. It sure looks like him. He's waving and headed our way."

Ressa flashed him a smile. "Look who's here."

"What are the Jenkins girls doing this far from Tennessee?" he asked.

"We were just about to ask you the same thing," Ressa replied.

"Just doing my duty same as you two. Are y'all homesick yet?"

"Not really. We've had such a nice welcome that I haven't thought about home. Speaking of which, I'm forgetting my manners. Captain Davison and ladies, I'd like you to meet Captain John Raulston."

"My pleasure, ladies." he said with a slight bow.

A slow tune by Tommy Dorsey, *All of This and Heaven Too* started playing on the radio. "Geneva, I'm a little rusty, but would you care to dance?"

"Sure, I'd love to." I looked back at Ressa and winked before placing my hand in his and letting him escort me to the center of the room. Several other couples were already dancing.

We moved gracefully around the dance floor. If he was rusty, it didn't show. I glanced over at Ressa and smiled. She waved from the table.

"Your sister said she's not homesick. What about you?" he asked.

"Not me. I don't get homesick. Besides, I like it here."

"I do too," he confirmed. "It's great for the time being, but I hope I'm long gone when Japan attacks."

"Do you really believe they will?"

"War with Japan is a certainty. Our government has been preparing for it."

"Preparing how?"

"Bringing in more soldiers and nurses."

"That doesn't prove anything."

"At the same time, they've been trying to get civilians out."

"With MacArthur here, I doubt they'll attack."

"They have spies. And they know, he's only been training the Filipino soldiers for six months. Not only that, the weapons our men are using were left over from the Great War. The Japs have us outgunned."

"I'm sure MacArthur and Roosevelt have a plan."

"The only plan they have is the WPO-3. Basically, we protect the bay and if that fails we retreat to the jungles and hills until Roosevelt sends reinforcements."

I stopped dancing and stared up at him. "Surely, they have something better than that."

"Nope. I'd appreciate you not mentioning it. I shouldn't have said anything."

"Trust me. Your secret's safe with me." I glanced back at Ressa. "Let's join the others."

"I hope I didn't spoil your day with my doom and gloom talk. Hopefully, you and Ressa will be safe at home when they make their move."

"Nothing could ruin this day. With the exception of the weather, it's been perfect."

He escorted me back to the other nurses who'd already had a round of gin and were starting a second drink.

"How's Joe?" Ressa asked John.

"Doing well. He's working at a hospital back home for now." He politely turned to everyone. "Ladies, it was nice meeting all of you, and Geneva, thanks for the dance. I'm sure we'll be crossing paths here."

After he left, they all turned their eyes on me.

Juanita smiled. "You two made a sweet couple."

"He's just a kid from back home," I said. "We were friends with his brother."

"Sugar, there's not a shortage of men here," Francis Nash said. "Plenty of Army and Navy guys."

"Any flyers?" Ressa asked.

"Lots of them," Josie said. "They come over from Clark Field."

14

"I've already found my man," Dorothy said on a dreamy sigh.

"Maybe you shouldn't decide until you've shopped around. Sweetie, this is like a smorgasbord of men," Juanita said in her refined southern accent.

"No, thank you. I knew the moment I laid eyes on Arnold, he's the one," Dorothy confessed.

"Suit yourself." Juanita swirled her ice around in her glass.

"Believe you me, I've never seen a couple fall in love as quickly as those two," Winnie commented. "From the moment they saw each other, they had eyes for nobody else."

"That's true," I said.

"She might change her mind. This place gets hopping on the weekends," Juanita added. "Ressa, do you like to dance?"

Ressa nodded. "I love to dance."

She grinned. "Get your dancing shoes ready."

My sister looked at me. "Geneva, looks like we came to the right place."

Though I nodded and gave her a light smile, I couldn't help but think about what John had told me. Sadly, it had overshadowed my happiness.

RESSA
August 1, 1941

On my way back from the restroom, I cornered the Raulston boy. Anyone who upsets Geneva had to answer to me. "Just what did you say to my little sister? You had her upset."

He put his hands up. "Hold up there. We were just talking about the possibility of war. That's it. I apologized for bringing it up."

I glanced toward our table. No one was there. "I'd better go."

As I exited the club, the others were walking toward the parked car.

"Don't leave me!" I waved and ran down the walkway. "For Heaven's sake. Wait for me." I caught up with them at the car.

"What were you talking to the Raulston boy about?" Geneva asked.

"I wouldn't exactly call him a boy. He's a doctor, you know. Besides, you need to mind your own business, little sister." I piled into the backseat of the car with Geneva, Winnie, and Lieutenant Josephine Nesbit. Since MacNeil had left with the other male officers, Dorothy rode up front. Good thing we were all thin.

Captain Davison turned to the Filipino driver. "Give us the scenic route back to Sternberg." She glanced back. "I can tell you girls are sisters. You favor one another, and you have the same accents and mannerisms."

I had always considered Geneva the beautiful one. Her hair and eyes were darker than mine. I considered myself petite and cute at best. Most people figured I was a high school student. Geneva compared to one of the orchids we had received, lovely but fragile.

The car whipped into traffic, stopping short to dodge a pony and cart. It hurled us forward, then tossed us back against the seat.

"Watch that calluses!" the captain shouted.

I twisted my neck to glance back at the pony drawn cart scurrying out of the way. Cars crowded the streets and shared the roads with horse-drawn trolleys and wagons pulled by horned cattle. Tall modern buildings formed a skyline.

"Jumping crickets, that cow is enormous," Winnie said. "What kind is it?"

"Carabao. It's in the ox family," Captain Davison said. She pointed to a streetcar. "The locals call it a tranvia. You'll pick it all up quicker than you think. But it's the easiest way to get around."

I loved seeing all the strange sights and sharing this adventure with Geneva. When she first left New York where she had been working and joined me in California, I took her sightseeing.

Since the day had become hot and muggy, we rode with the windows down, allowing an unpleasant odor in the car. I gagged. "My goodness gracious, what's that dreadful smell?"

Lieutenant Nesbit laughed. "It's the city."

"You'll get used to it," Captain Davison added.

I shifted my gaze to Geneva and mouthed the word, "Never."

"Hope it doesn't smell like this in Corregidor," Winnie commented.

Josie smiled. "Worse."

Sweat rolled down my back. Before we reached the hospital, I would be drenched. I figured sweating would become a way of life. Fortunately, we had packed enough hygiene products and cosmetics to last two years.

Geneva smiled, then pointed to several of the Asian style wooden buildings. "We don't have anything like those at home. The architectural design is downright amazing."

"I've never seen anything like it. Even in St. Louis," Dorothy said. "You got anything like that in Wisconsin?"

Winnie shook her head. "No."

"How close to the mountains did you live?" Lieutenant Nesbit asked us.

"Our farm was in the heart of the Smokies," Geneva replied.

"You'll find a lot of us were raised on farms. I was born in Butler, Missouri," Lieutenant Nesbit said. "We had a farm too. I was up before dawn doing chores until about the age of twelve when I went to live with my grandmother."

"Any particular reason you moved in with your grandmother?"

"My parents died."

"I'm sorry. I shouldn't have asked."

The nurse smiled. "It was a very long time ago. I'm all right with it."

Since I had put my foot in my mouth, I wanted to change the subject. "I hated chickens. I always hated gathering eggs because of all the mites."

Geneva grinned. "She sure didn't mind eating them. I just made one of our younger brothers or sisters do it. Chain of command."

"Big family?" Captain Davison asked.

"Yes," I said. "Univieve, Geneva, and I are in the middle. All three of us are nurses." She glanced at the lieutenant. "But our youngest sister, Mary Helsalee, wants to be a teacher. Sarah is determined to join the Navy and be a Wave."

Trying to get a better look at the city, I stretched my neck through the open window. The people, walking up and down the streets, wore colorful, bright clothes—yellows, reds, and oranges. Vendors peddled their wares on street corners, shouting out to the people passing by. Most of the sidewalks had covers to shade people from the sun.

We passed Filipino scout soldiers riding in the back of military trucks. They worked well with American soldiers under General MacArthur.

The area being so protected gave me a sense of relief. Not just by soldiers, but by the mines in the bay surrounding Manila. My parents had worried we wouldn't be safe and had wanted us to select Hawaii. When a chance arose, I'd write home and assure them we were fine.

Sternberg Hospital was positioned across from the massive Manila City Hall. The alabaster Spanish style building sprawled over a large area. I hadn't expected it to be so large.

Taking in the lush greenery and gorgeous flowers, I gasped in awe. "Lord-a mercy, this place is like the Garden of Eden." I twisted toward Geneva. "Are you taking this in?"

My sister nodded. "It's a real sight to behold. I wish Mom could see all these flowers."

"For cripes sake, this place is gorgeous," Winnie proclaimed.

"It'd sure be a lovely place for a wedding." Dorothy's dreamy eyes let it be known she was thinking of Arnold.

"If you think this is the perfect spot for a wedding, I can't wait for you to see the courtyard," Maude Davison said. She glanced at Geneva. "You're the quiet one."

Geneva smiled. "I don't have to talk. Ressa does enough for the both of us. She was born with the gift of gab."

I huffed. "She may seem quiet, but there's a lot of chattering going on in that hard head of hers."

Josie laughed. Even the stern captain smiled.

"Sternberg covers four acres," Josie stated. "We house four hundred and fifty beds."

"We'll take you to the nurses' quarters first," the captain said. She gave the driver some instructions. He stopped in front of a building. "This is the main wing of the hospital."

Josie climbed out from the other side. "Nice meeting all of you. I'll see you at the nurses' luncheon."

"Nice meetin' you," we replied in unison.

At the nurses' house, we entered into an enormous living room with black and white checkered tile floor. At the back, a wide staircase led to a landing where the stairs branched off to the left and right. The dark wooden banisters shined as though just polished. Elegant furniture filled the large area, giving the nurses plenty of places to sit and relax.

We followed Captain Davison up the steps, to the right, and down a hall. As we paraded by, girls poked their heads out the doors to get a look at us.

At the door to our room, the captain stepped back allowing us to enter. "Be sure you use the mosquito netting over the beds."

I nodded as I set my purse down on the bed. Our luggage sat in the center of the room on the grass mat rug. "I'm glad to see our things have already arrived."

Geneva turned back to the captain. "Thanks for keeping us together."

"Just made sense. Figured you two are used to one another. See you at 1300 hours in the dining room. There's a luncheon for you girls. See you downstairs." She turned abruptly and left.

"When is thirteen hundred hours?" I asked Geneva. We had no military training. We had come straight from a civilian hospital. So far, we'd only called each other Miss. We hadn't used our military titles.

"I don't know. I guess we'd better learn military time." Geneva stood between the two beds. "Which one do you want?"

I glanced at them. "They're both singles. I don't care."

"Then I'll take the one farther from the door."

"This one suits me fine. I'll have fewer steps to the bathroom." I sat on the bed, but it didn't bounce. "I'm not believing this. It's hard as a rock."

"As tired as I am, it's not going to matter."

Having so many sisters, I'd always shared a bed. At least this cot would be just for me. The room appeared very clean.

"I like the bamboo and wicker table and chairs," Geneva commented. "It's so tropical. It makes me feel like I'm on vacation."

"With this heat, I'm glad we have a ceiling fan."

"The window only has a screen on it." Geneva pushed back the curtain panel to show me. "See." She sighed. "Thinking of home, we didn't know when we were so well off."

"Oh, it's not so bad." I lifted my suitcase to the bed and opened it. "I wonder why there's only a curtain over the door."

19

"For ventilation," a voice from the hallway said. The lovely dark-haired woman with haunting dark eyes entered the room. "Hi, I'm Helen Hennessey."

"We're the Jenkin sisters. I'm Ressa."

"I'm Geneva."

She glanced at my radio. "You'll have to pay a small fee to use that."

"You're kidding?" I said. "Well, that's just great. I lugged this thing halfway around the world for nothing."

Geneva smiled. "Oh, just pay the fee."

"I'll give you girls a tip," Helen said. "Leave the closet light on so your clothes won't mildew."

Juanita, who we'd met at the club, entered. "I've learned to keep my gloves and stockings in a jar. It keeps them from rotting in this humidity."

"Thanks for the advice. We're fish out of water," I said.

"You'll love it here," Helen stated. "We only work four-hour shifts. The afternoons are yours to do as you please."

"That's what we heard," I said.

Geneva's right brow rose slightly. "So how do you spend your afternoons?"

"Playing golf, badminton, tennis, or sitting by the pool at the club," Helen said. "The streetcars can take you almost anywhere you want to go."

I smiled. "Tell me more about dancing at the clubs."

"There are plenty of guys to dance with," Juanita said, drawing out her words long and slow.

"There are several clubs in town besides the Army/Navy Club and the Manila Hotel. Someone's always having a cocktail party," Helen said. "Did you bring an evening gown?"

I nodded. "Two, actually. A glittering blue one and then a simple green one."

Geneva and I had been given a five day leave in San Francisco to shop before our deployment and bought enough items to last two years. Anyone heading for the Philippines knew to take formal wear. I also packed enough Pond's cold cream, Ivory soap, and Colgate toothpaste to last me a while.

"Good because clothes in town aren't cheap," Juanita added.

"That's because they're imported," Helen added. "But any service you need is cheap. You can get your shoes polished and clothes cleaned and pressed for peanuts."

I placed my hand on my suitcase and screamed. My hand flew over my heart.

A lizard stared up at me with beady little eyes.

After several minutes, my heartbeat slowed down. "I wasn't expecting to see wildlife this soon."

Geneva and the others laughed.

Helen smiled. "That's a gecko. It's harmless. They're all over the place."

I fanned my face with my hand. "Mercy me. That just about gave me a heart attack. I guess I should be glad it wasn't a snake."

Geneva shook her head slightly. "And we picked here over Hawaii."

We followed Juanita and Helen downstairs to the dining room. Long tables with white tablecloths filled the area. I counted about thirty nurses. Lordy, how would I ever remember all their names? Filipino boys worked as servers and brought food around.

Maude Davison glanced at the nurses sitting at the tables. "We'll let our visiting nurse introduce herself." She motioned at Winnie. "Go ahead."

"Winifred Madden, Wisconsin. I go by Winnie."

"Winnie will be stationed at Ft. Mills on the Rock." She glanced at us. "Now, our newest nurses please introduce yourselves." Maude Davison smiled at Geneva. "You go first."

My shy sister stood. "Geneva Jenkins, Sevierville, Tennessee."

Once she sat down, I stood. "Ressa Jenkins, we're sisters, so there's no surprise that I'm from Tennessee also."

Everyone laughed.

"Dorothy Scholl, Independence, Missouri."

"Even if you've already introduced yourself at the club, please do so again," Maude Davison requested. "They'd just stepped off a ship, so I doubt they remember your names." She glanced at us. "I'm sorry they couldn't all be here, but you'll get to meet the others later. Now, I'll go first. Maude Davison, Washington, D.C."

A tall, slim red-haired girl went next. "Ethel Thor, Tacoma, Washington."

"Francis Nash, Washington, Georgia."

The next lady stood, and I was glad to see someone shorter than me. "Doris Kehol, Pacific Grove, California."

"Sue Downing, Petersburg, Vermont."

"Madeline Ullom, O'Neil, Nebraska."

"Helen Hennessey, Leavenworth, Kansas"

"Juanita Redmond, Swansea, South Carolina"

"Adele Foreman, Masten, Pennsylvania."

"Willa Hooks, Renfrow, Oklahoma."

"Mina Aasen, Minot, North Dakota. And I like to paint."

Maude Davison frowned. "Keep it short."

"Sorry," Mina said.

"Ruth Straub, Milwaukee, Wisconsin." She glanced at Winnie. "Good having someone from my home state."

"Clara Mueller, Philadelphia, Pennsylvania."

"Anna Williams, Harrisonburg, Pennsylvania."

The women continued introducing themselves, but after this first group, I had trouble concentrating. I'd eventually learn their names while working with them. The one thing that struck me was that we came from all over the country.

After all the introductions were made, we feasted on baked chicken, mashed potatoes, several vegetables, and homemade rolls. I wondered if they did this each month when new nurses arrived.

I hadn't expected the food to be so good. "This meal surpasses my expectations."

"Most of our food is imported from the states," Helen said. "Except for the fruit. We're encouraged to eat at the hospital or club. You may find the local's storage methods different from ours."

Geneva reached for a roll. "I had enough stomach issues on the ship coming over. So, thanks for the warning."

Doris Kehol, the short, brown-haired lady with bright green eyes smiled. "I hope you girls like it here. There's so much to do, and we're close to everything."

"Are you a nurse?" I asked, noticing she wasn't in a uniform.

"No, anesthesia tech," Doris replied. "I get help from a civilian tech, Denny Williams, who lives in town with her husband, Bill. She comes in and helps us out. You'll meet her later."

I looked at Helen. "What do you do?"

22

"I'm in the ears, nose, and throat department. I end up treating a lot of children, but I love it."

There were so many names to remember and so much to take in that it overwhelmed me. I had a difficult time enjoying my lunch. I'd been hungry enough to eat a bear and now the excitement of the moment had stolen my appetite.

"Winnie, when do you leave for Corregidor?" Adele Foreman asked.

"Tomorrow afternoon."

"Be sure to do some sightseeing before you head for the Rock," Juanita advised.

Winnie smiled. "You betcha, I will."

Juanita focused on us. "You'll have a full day off before having to report for duty. You should go with her."

I nodded. "I'd like that. Right now, I'm still rocking from being on the ship so long." I glanced over at Winnie. "I'll go with you tomorrow. Maybe by then, the floor won't be rocking."

Geneva nodded between bites. "Count me in."

"Better see it before the war starts," Adele said.

"There's not going to be a war," Helen Hennessey retorted.

Doris stopped eating and looked up. "Don't count on it. The Japanese are very angry with the U.S."

"Oh, what has that hornet's nest stirred up?" Juanita asked.

Doris held up one finger. "One, the U.S. set an embargo against them for metal." She held up two fingers. "Second, they aren't pleased with the new immigration policy for Japanese citizens."

"They need to get over it," Ethel added. "Personally, I think they're just looking for an excuse to show their power. I came over last year on the U.S. Grant, and they were talking about war then. Nothing has happened."

"Enough of this depressing talk," Helen said. "We don't want these ladies chasing down the USS Coolidge and hitching a ride home."

We all laughed.

After the luncheon, we picked up our nursing assignments for Sternberg. We waited until we walked into the hallway to unfold the paper.

"What'd you get?" Geneva asked, holding the paper in her hand.

I gave her a sly smile. "Officer's ward. What about you?"

Geneva sighed. "Medical ward. I'll trade."

I grinned. "Not on your life. Give up the chance to be around a lot of officers."

Geneva rolled her eyes. "You're so lucky. Let's pick up our equipment."

At the supply room, the clerk handed us scratched up helmets and hideous gas masks with instructions on how to use them.

"These things are old." Teasingly, I placed the mask over my face. "I won't be meeting anyone tall, dark, and handsome wearing this."

Geneva smiled, then turned to the clerk. "Do we have to keep these with us?"

The serious female clerk shook her head. "You can leave them in your room. Read the directions on how to use them. You'll have periodic gas mask drills."

I stared at the gas masks we held. A chill ran over me. I hoped and prayed we'd never really need them.

RESSA
August 2, 1941

Geneva, Winnie, and I attended mass at San Augustine's in the Walled City. The inside wasn't like any church we had in Tennessee. Statues and stained glass enhanced its beauty. Though uncertain of what was said since it was spoken in Latin, I sensed a veil of holiness over the sanctuary. In a moment of silent prayer, I prayed.

Dearest heavenly father, bless the three of us. Protect us and keep us safe. In Christ name. Amen.

We stood in front of the church. The heat and humidity had already soaked the back of my dress. "Let's see the sights. I want to pick up postcards to mail home."

Winnie nodded. "I'd like to buy some as well. I might not get back over this way for a while, you know."

"Where to?" Geneva asked.

"There's a lot to see right here in the old walled city," Winnie replied. "But since I've got my bags, we may want to take a cab."

We took a cab and rode around the area. Its past Spanish domination showed in the stone walls and arched doorways with ornate gates. The twenty-five-foot wall appeared in good shape with vibrant flowers and plants growing in gardens along its base. Many structures sported reddish tile roofs and balconies that extended from the buildings, looking down on narrow streets. From what people said, little had changed.

The old city of Intramuros enchanted us. Tall coconut palms grew up to the clear blue sky and swayed in the breeze. Flowering plants and other trees thrived around the walkways. We stopped at Santo Tomas University. The magnificent building had stood since the seventeenth century and was built by the Dominicans. From there, we visited Tondo, a native district.

"Real quick, look at those homes," Winnie said, as she pointed.

Small thatched roof, bamboo houses on stilts lined the river.

"Nipa houses," the cabbie informed us.

"Those are so cute," Winnie said.

Wooden boats, housing families, anchored near the shore. I recalled seeing similar boats when we'd docked.

I glanced at my watch. Though we hated to part from Winnie, it was time.

"We'd better get you to the dock. You'd hate to miss the boat," I said. The quartermaster made a trip once a day to Corregidor. Winnie would spend the next couple of hours on the boat, making the trip across the bay.

Winnie wiped her eyes. "I've been with you for so long it's hard to say goodbye. Believe you me, I'm gonna miss you both."

"Corregidor isn't that far. I'm sure our paths will cross again," Geneva said.

"If I get a chance, I'll visit you," I promised.

Winnie hugged us both, then made her way onto the boat that would take her to the Rock.

My heart seemingly sank to my stomach as I watched her go. Seeing her alone made me all the more thankful I had Geneva.

Before returning to Sternberg, Geneva and I rode down Calle Rosario by the Chinese shops. Cabs and calezes lined up in front of the buildings. For our final stop, we visited Lineta Park, a gorgeous tropical paradise. We wanted to explore every section of Manila.

Like Captain Davison and Josie had said, the smell didn't seem as bad today. Maybe we were getting used to it. On our way back, our driver drove beside the Pasig River. Jone's Bridge loomed in the distance.

It wasn't until Geneva and I returned to Sternberg that we faced a dilemma. We didn't know anything about Philippine currency. The man said how much we owed him.

I stared at the money unsure which coins to give him. Instead, I let him pick the needed amount.

"I think he cheated us," Geneva said, as we walked toward the nurses' house.

"I think you're right."

In our room that evening, we spread Philippine money over my bed and practiced naming the amounts and counting it. Finally, I sighed. "He didn't cheat us. Now I feel better about it."

The first night, I couldn't sleep. I kept checking the bed netting, making sure it was closed tightly. We'd been warned the mosquitoes would drive us crazy especially at night. The mosquitoes buzzed all around the outside of the netting. Sweet fragrances drifted in through the window from all the exotic flowers.

I glanced at Geneva. She slept soundly.

I hoped we'd made the right decision to come to the Philippines. An overpowering sense of responsibility to protect Geneva came over me. I loved my younger sister more than anyone.

RESSA
August 3, 1941

I worried about Geneva. Sometimes, people misread her shyness and thought she was a snob, but my sister was anything but a snob. As for myself, I never had an issue jumping right into a situation. In high school, I'd always been in the center of everything.

The wards at Sternberg were large rectangular rooms with rows of beds down the long sides against the walls and a row running down the middle. I liked cheering up the men and laughing with them. It came easy for me to clown around as I administered their medicine and change their bandages. It made the four-hour shift pass quickly.

I met up with Geneva afterwards in the solarium looking out onto the garden. It gave a spectacular view of the flowers. "How'd it go today?"

"Not bad. We had a lot of Filipino wives and their children come in. It's amazing that some of them are no more than thirty with ten to twelve kids. Their husbands are with the Filipino scouts working with MacArthur."

I took a draw on my cigarette and blew it out. "That sounds like our family. Momma was young when she had us."

"Exactly, why I wanted to be a nurse." She fanned the smoke from my cigarette away. "What was your day like?"

I couldn't hold back the smile. "Wonderful. There are some really fine men in my ward. Officers. Several were banged up in a bar fight at the Pink Poodle. Nothing serious. A few of them have dengue fever." I butted my cigarette. "Dorothy asked if we'd like to go horseback riding."

"You don't ride. You've always been afraid of horses," Geneva said.

"I've always hated admitting we grew up on a farm with horses and never learned to ride. Maybe we should take riding lessons. Some of the girls said lessons are offered at Ft. McKinley. They take the ferry over. It's faster than driving."

Geneva's brows rose. "Is that so?"

"Yes, and they select just the right horse for you."

"Well, I think that sounds like as good a way to spend our afternoons as any. It'd really surprise everyone back home. I didn't bring any clothes suitable for riding," Geneva said. "Let's mosey into the city and see if we can find something to ride in."

The next day, we ventured into town to purchase riding clothes and boots. On the way back to Sternberg, I stopped at a corner vendor near the hospital and looked at the pearl jewelry from the Moro people who had come up from Mindanao. Some days, the people would lay out beautiful things on the lawn for the nurses to buy.

Geneva examined the pearl ring closely. "Doubt these are real pearls."

"They look real."

The man nodded. "Genuine pearls. Eight pesos. That's only four dollars your money."

I thought for a moment. "That's a good price." I slipped it over my ring finger. "It fits."

Geneva picked one up and tried it on. "They are beautiful."

We both ended up with pearl rings and the peddler sixteen pesos richer.

That night, I realized I'd gone to sleep with the ring on. I slipped it off, extended my hand through the mosquito netting, and set it on the nightstand between our beds. The next morning, mosquitoes buzzed inside my netting. Apparently, I had left it cracked after putting the ring on the table.

I swatted the vicious insects and finally stood.

Geneva woke up. "Why are you dancing this early? Save it for the club tonight."

"I'm not dancing. I'm swatting mosquitoes. The little devils got inside my netting." I wouldn't admit I was to blame.

"Check your netting for a hole." When Geneva sat up, she gasped. "My goodness. You're covered in bites. Oh, Ressa, that's not good. Rub some alcohol on the welts."

That day working in my ward, I tried to make my ten patients comfortable. My job kept my hands busy rather than give me idle time to scratch those bites. I made sure my patients received their medicine, were bathed, and their bandages changed. I spent time talking to them. This had to be the easiest job I'd ever had in nursing.

While restocking bandages on a shelf, I thought of the fun we'd have at the dance. A bunch of the nurses had asked me to go. It was pretty much a given that if you asked me, Geneva was included.

RESSA
August 1941 Manila Hotel ballroom.

That night we went with the off-duty nurses to the Manila Hotel Ballroom. The enormous room had rows of small dim lights running across its ceiling giving it an elegant ambience. Columns ran along the outer boundaries with arched doorways.

Enormous Asian lanterns dangled above the dancing couples. People crowded the club. They came not just from Sternberg but from all the other nearby hospitals as well.

The big band sound of Dorsey roared through speakers. The women appeared elegant in evening gowns while most of the men wore white dinner tuxedos. We also wore evening gowns to the theaters and formal dinners.

"I've never seen so many people dancing in one room," Geneva said.

"I've never seen so many men in one room," I replied. "Finding someone to dance with won't be a problem."

"Have fun," Adele said. "I'll catch you later."

Dorothy Scholl joined us. "Ladies, you remember Harold Arnold. Remember the Jenkins sisters?"

He nodded and gave us a wide grin. "Nice seeing you ladies."

"Same here," I said.

Dorothy was so smitten with the guy, it was almost funny. He seemed just as crazy about her. They made a cute couple.

"This your first time coming here?" Harold asked.

Geneva nodded. "We've been going to the Army/Navy Club."

"After dancing all night, your feet will hurt tomorrow," Dorothy warned. "Harold and I try to pace ourselves now."

Ruth Straub came up with a handsome man. "Girls, this is Glen Alder." She introduced us all to her boyfriend. Dorothy had told us Glen wanted to get married, but Ruth kept stalling. "Glen's a pilot at Clark Field."

I gave him a big smile. "You'll have to introduce me to your pilot friends."

Glen lit a cigarette. "I'll make a point to do that."

"Is that Francis Nash?" I motioned toward a thin lady wearing a beige and yellow swanky gown.

Dorothy nodded. "Yeah, that's her."

"Can't imagine her having fun," I said. "She's so serious at the hospital."

"Francis is rough around the edges," Ruth said. "If you can look past her profanity, she's a real softy."

Sinatra's *I'll Never Smile Again* played. I spotted petite Doris Kehol slow dancing with a tall officer. He was one of our doctors.

"Let's get a drink," I suggested to Geneva. I turned and didn't see her. I glanced around and found her dancing with a young man. "That sure didn't take long."

Before I made it to the bar, one of the officers who'd been in my ward, asked me to dance. Another Dorsey tune played. "You know the dirty boogie?"

He nodded. "Sure do. Let's give it a whirl."

The dance required you to step forward, then back and shake your rear which is where its name had come from. No sooner than the dance ended, another man asked me to dance. Fortunately, it was a slow dance giving me a chance to catch my breath. *Star Dust* by Artie Shaw played. I danced in his arms to the soft trumpet solo.

The Boogie Woogie Bugle Boy started up, and we did a dance called the Shag. It was a one, two step, and hop. No sooner than one dance finished, I moved on to another dance partner. The next dance we called Truckin' where the girl turned in a circle with her arm up and one finger in the air. By my last dance, my shoes had rubbed blisters on my feet. The officer I was dancing with encouraged me to give him one more dance.

Halfway through the song, I stopped dancing. "My feet are taking a beating. I'm going to find a drink and sit the next ten out."

He chuckled. "I'll go with you." The officer escorted me from the floor. "Since I insisted on doing the Lindy Hop, I'm buying."

"Thanks. I'll take you up on it."

While sitting to the side with him, I sipped on a gin and tonic and smoked. Helen and Juanita joined us with a couple of men. I studied the couples dancing and saw Geneva still with the same man she'd first danced with. She seemed to know him. So, I assumed he worked at the hospital.

When the dance was over, they joined us.

"This is my big sister, Ressa. Ressa, Jerry. He brought over some patients to my ward transferred from Stotsenberg."

"Nice meeting you," I yelled over the music.

"The pleasure is all mine," he said, in a Texas drawl. He stood taller than Geneva and appeared handsome.

Because of the noise and music, I couldn't hear but a small part of what was being said. I thanked the officer who'd purchased the drink. He spotted some of his friends coming in and joined them.

I walked to the edge of the buzzing dance floor, and a Naval lieutenant asked me to dance. I ended up demanding more from my feet and danced to several more songs. Juanita had mentioned visiting the Army/Navy Club next, but I didn't think I was up to it.

By the time we left, I wasn't feeling very well. Something seemed off. I hadn't had but the one drink. Hopefully, I'd feel better after a good night's sleep. Geneva and I had our first riding lesson the next day, and I wanted to be feeling my best.

The next morning, I woke with chills and a nasty red rash. Every bone in my body ached, especially my back. Revenge of the mosquitoes is what I called it. After discovering I had a high temperature, I reported myself as off duty and spent all day in bed with dengue fever, suffering with excruciating back pain and chills. I missed my first riding lesson.

Geneva returned late that afternoon. "How ya feeling?"

"Weak, but better. How was the riding lesson?"

"I enjoyed it. They gave me a gentle mare to start on. I'm gonna be sore." She fanned an envelope before me. "Thought this might cheer you up. Winnie sent it."

I ripped it open and read it. "She has a few days off next week and plans to come see us. She wants to go shopping." I looked at Geneva. "I've just got to get well."

"Then you'd better rest. Hopefully, you won't be left with any side effects from your bout with break-bone fever." She sat on the edge of the bed. "How does she like Corregidor?"

"She likes it. Seems she's been playing golf and has met someone she's interested in. She'll tell us about him when she comes to visit."

Visiting nurses were allowed to stay at the nurses' quarters while in town. Winnie would be able to stay the night and return on the boat the next day.

GENEVA
August 1941

After four days in bed, my sister conquered her dengue fever and returned to work. By the time Winnie arrived, Ressa showed no signs she'd been sick. I had been fortunate enough to stay well.

We shopped all day, then return to the nurses' quarters. Winnie sighed. "I haven't had this much fun in weeks. There's so much more to do and see here."

"Think you'll be up to going to the Army/Navy Club tonight?" Ressa asked.

"You betcha." Winnie turned to me. "You's coming, Geneva?"

"No," I said, hoping Ressa would leave it at that.

"Why not?" my sister asked, appearing disappointed.

"Jerry asked me to a movie. We're going to see *Shadow of a Thin Man*."

Ressa's shoulders slumped. "Well, I guess we'll go without you."

"You'll have a great time. This is my kind of movie. I'm looking forward to seeing it." I loved movies. With so many kids in one family and then being in a boarding school, we had never been able to attend movies.

"Behave yourself," Ressa warned.

"I'm always a lady. Actually, I should be telling you two to behave."

Ressa and Winnie giggled.

That night, I sat in the crowded theater, watching the movie. I enjoyed a good mystery, and this one had some humorous parts. During the movie, Jerry slipped his hand in mine. After the movie, we decided to walk back.

The Manila streets remained quiet with little traffic. We strolled toward Sternberg with our arms looped at the elbows. The big moon shined down on us, and the sweet fragrance of flowers rode on the night breeze. I thought about how romantic this was.

I talked about our riding lessons. "If I had known how much I enjoyed it, I would've been riding a long time ago."

He chuckled. "I've ridden a lot. Being in Texas, my grand-daddy always had horses. Hope you don't regret not being with your sister and your friend."

"Oh, Heavens no. That club with all the smoke grinds on my nerves after the first hour. I enjoyed this much more. Thank you."

"Do you bowl?"

"I have. I wouldn't expect to win a prize for it."

He grinned. "Me neither. Want to go bowling on our next day off?"

"Sure. I'd like that. Just don't expect much."

"You can even invite your sister if you'd like."

I laughed. "She can find her own date. Besides, she talks too much."

Outside the nurses' quarters, Jerry gently placed his hands on my shoulders and gave me a sweet little kiss. Simple and innocent. He smelled wonderful. But I warned my heart not to fall for him. I didn't want to end up with a broken heart if the war came and separated us.

I thanked him for the movie again and went inside. Ressa and Winnie hadn't returned, and I didn't expect them back for a few more hours. I used the alone time to write a letter home. I described our life at Sternberg and mentioned our riding lessons. I assured them we were well, not mentioning Ressa's dengue fever.

The next day, I found Ressa in the solarium. She sat alone drinking coffee and smoking. The previous night, I had never heard her come in, and when I left for my shift, she was still asleep. She and Winnie had stayed out dancing at the Army/Navy Club until late.

She glanced up and smiled. "Thanks for not waking me this morning."

"You were out of it. Has Winnie gone?"

"No, she had more shopping to do in town."

"How'd she like the club?"

"She loved it. We were both exhausted from dancing by the time we left. I promised to visit her next month."

The next day, Ressa and I took the ferry to Ft. McKinley to go riding. I thought we looked spiffy in our riding clothes and new boots. We each had our favorite horses we rode on the scenic trails.

RESSA
Late September 1941

We liked "boat days" because new nurses joined us. I attended the new nurse luncheon, and it reminded me of our arrival back in August. The one nurse that stood out was Helen Cassiani, who asked to be called Cassie. The dark-haired girl of Italian heritage was very attractive. Her family owned a large chicken farm in Bridgewater, Massachusetts.

I thought of my own love/hate relationship with chickens.

After lunch, I took the quartermaster's boat over and visited Winnie on Corregidor. I had hoped Geneva would be free to make the trip, but she had to work. I found myself fascinated by the strange layout of the island with its different natural levels. Fort Mills sat in a tranquil setting surrounded by blooming flowers like gardenias and honeysuckle. The hospital sat on what they called Topside and faced the bay.

I learned they actually had several stores, a well-supplied commissary, two theaters, golf courses, bowling, swim club, and tennis along with an officers' club. I placed my hands on my hips. "And here I was feeling sorry for you being stuck over here with nothing to do."

Winnie giggled. "Well, believe you me, it's not as exciting as Manila."

"Well, at least you don't have mosquitoes."

"That's the good part and it's quiet except for the crickets."

During my overnight stay, I was given a nice room with a connecting bath. The twelve Army nurses stationed here all had their own rooms with baths.

"We're the only girls left. They sent the officers' wives home," Winnie said.

"When did they do that?" I asked.

"I believe last March or April. Why?"

I shrugged. "No particular reason."

But it made me nervous. Many of the families in Manila had also been sent away. Apparently, our government had known for a long time that war was a possibility. "Do I get to see the tunnel?"

"Sure."

Two cars could easily drive side by side through the entrance of Malinta Tunnel. It had rails running inside for a street trolley. It was divided into long branches called laterals.

The air in the tunnel had a strange odor and the air quality poor. If I ever had to spend any time there, I'd go mad. The place was massive, and we only saw a small section of it. We met up with all of Winnie's friends at the military club on Topside.

"What do you think of the island?" Peggy O'Neil asked. She reached up and took the drink the waiter offered. "Thanks."

"The island is beautiful. The ocean is so blue. It's quieter here. We have too much activity going on around us." But I didn't think it compared to Hawaii. While it had a lot of shoreline, most of it wasn't suited for swimming.

"I prefer shopping in Manila," Inez McDonald said.

"If war comes, there's talk of moving everything inside the tunnel," Earlyn Black commented. They called the attractive girl, Blackie. She spoke with a Texas accent.

Winnie sighed. "It's insufferable inside."

"True," I confessed. "I don't think I could live in it."

"At least, we'd be safe there," Peggy admitted.

"If war comes, you could end up in it too," Louise Anschicks said. She had served during WWI and was much older than most of us.

Inez traced her finger around the rim of her glass. "It's the only place in the Philippines, they can't penetrate."

"It'd be overcrowded if they moved everyone inside," Winnie stated.

"MacArthur will never let it get that far," Peggy assured us. "Never."

I hoped anything the Japanese started wouldn't last long enough that we'd end up retreating to the Rock.

"A general who flew in from the states told us about Germany's aggressiveness in Europe," Peggy commented.

"That shouldn't affect us," I said, being naïve on politics and war.

Later at the dock, I turned to Winnie. "I enjoyed myself. Be sure to write."

"You betcha."

I went aboard the quartermaster's boat, turned, and waved. "Take care."

Winnie waved as the boat pulled away from the dock.

Several large ships had anchored in the bay. That made me feel safer.

I thought of our lives in this wonderful paradise. Evenings spent dancing at the Army/Navy Club, Jai-Alai Club, or at the Manila Hotel. We played tennis or badminton at least twice a week. I had been a little concerned over the time Geneva spent with Jerry. She claimed he was only a friend and enjoyed his company.

As for me, I had a thing for flyers. Something about pilots attracted me.

When I returned to Sternberg, Geneva was napping in our room. A tropical breeze blew in from the window, bringing in sweet fragrances.

Life had been good here. Neither of us had ever been happier. Hanging over our happiness had been the constant talk of war, and it never went away.

I tried not to worry. What good would it do?

GENEVA
October 1941

The U.S. Holbrooke arrived today bringing more nurses to the Philippines. I enjoyed 'boat days' and volunteered to help greet the nurses and pass out orchids. I met Eleanor Garen from Elkhart, Indiana, who would be joining Winnie at Corregidor. Phyliss Arnold would head to Stotsenberg. I briefly met Jean Kennedy, Leona Gastinger, and Millie Dalton, another Georgia girl. They glowed with happiness as they accepted the orchids.

It reminded me of the day we had arrived in August. We worked four-hour shifts, so why would they continue to bring over so many nurses?

I thought of what John Raulston had said about the WPO-3 plan.

RESSA
November 1941

"You seem down. What's that about?" I asked Geneva, who sat by the interior garden alone.

"In my ward today, there was more war talk. Japanese planes have been flying over Manila. The Red Cross is conducting drills on civilian evacuations. Mary Lohr claimed Nomura's clipper docked in the bay, and he entered the city."

"I had heard he was on his way to Washington D.C.," I replied. "So why stop here?"

Geneva shrugged. "Ever since Tojo became prime minister of Japan, there's been even more talk of war."

"As Josie says, why waste time worrying about it." I smiled. "Remember the major I met at the club our last visit?"

"Yes, the one you danced with all evening."

"That's him."

"He asked me out."

"Is that so?" Geneva asked, in her same smooth tone that showed little emotion or excitement. "You going?"

"Maybe. I haven't decided."

"Why wouldn't you? Juanita and Helen will be so jealous to know you're out with a major. That should be reason enough to accept. He sounds perfect."

I sighed and let my shoulders drop. "It would be if he were a flyer."

Geneva shook her head. "I declare, if you're not the pickiest woman I know. If he's a keeper, I wouldn't throw him back just because he's not a pilot."

I shrugged. "I'd rather wait and meet someone when I return to the states. If war comes, it'll be the hardest on the nurses who have boyfriends or husbands fighting here."

"Well, you should still go out with him."

Later that night, Geneva and I entered the Army/Navy Club ready to listen to the Army/Navy game on the radio. The games drew a lot of attention, and people flocked to the club. It was a piece of home transmitted thousands of miles. None of us wanted to miss the chance to capture a moment of normalcy.

Getting there early, we grabbed seats near the front and waited for the game to begin. All the off-duty doctors and nurses huddled around. Men from all the military branches came to cheer on their team. By game time, all the seats had been taken and those still coming in found a place to stand.

"Army's got this one wrapped up," an Army officer boasted.

A Navy man shook his head. "Sorry, to disagree, sir, but the Navy is sure to win."

The banter over who'd win continued. But when it was time for the game to start, everyone stopped talking.

A tall sergeant turned on the radio, but only static came through the speakers. He adjusted the knobs to make sure he had it positioned on the station, but again the eerie sound of white noise filled the room.

All the rumors of war entered my mind.

My stomach twisted, and I became queasy.

I assured myself it didn't have anything to do with the Japanese. But then why wasn't the program being picked up?

Geneva appeared very troubled, so I placed a hand on her arm. "We'll be fine."

But it wasn't just Geneva. The tension in the room could be sliced with a knife. My gaze moved from face to face. They all sensed it.

Our paradise could turn into Hell at any moment, and we all knew it. The war rumors hung over like storm clouds, putting us on edge even more.

"Don't let this get you down," one soldier said. "Let's make some music and cut a rug, ladies."

Geneva and I frowned at the young man. I sighed. "I don't think any of us feel like dancing tonight."

The soldier's smile vanished, replaced with a look of defeat. He also felt the impending doom the rest of us experienced. I really regretted snapping at him.

We all knew what was coming. It was a question of when.

RESSA
December 7, 1941 (December 6th in the USA)

"Sure, you don't want to come with us?" I asked Geneva. Jerry was on duty, so my sister didn't have any plans.

"And be a third wheel? No, thank you. It's not every day a girl goes out with a major."

"It's not like it's our first date. He wouldn't mind you coming. We're going to see the new Gary Cooper movie, *Sergeant York.*" Since meeting, Peter, we had gone to dinner and dancing several times.

"War movie?"

"I believe so. I don't care so long as Cooper's playing the leading role."

"Cooper's a dreamboat, but I don't care for war movies. I'm writing a letter to Mom and Dad tonight. I'll be sure to mention you're going out smooching." She gave me a sly smile. "I guess I should say "major" smooching."

"For Heaven's sake, don't you dare. Besides, the major and I are walking. I won't be out late. See ya."

Geneva smiled. "You go and have fun."

Inside the theater, many of the nurses and other officers from Sternberg sat around us. I liked sporting a major on my arm.

Before the movie, a news reel played. It talked about all the issues in Europe. To me it seemed like the world was falling apart. A chill ran down my spine.

While watching one battle scene after another in the movie, I realized I could never live through something so horrific. Though I figured I'd come closer to surviving it than Geneva. She was fragile. So, if one of us had to be subjected to it, I'd rather it be me.

The major placed his arm around me, and I sighed. "If we ever have war, I shall just die. I couldn't stand it."

"The only thing they'll do to us is try to starve us out."

His words didn't put my mind at ease. Instead, an imaginary veil of uneasiness settled over me. Even with his arm around me, I couldn't remove the icy chill of bleak uncertainty.

After the movie, we stood out front of the theater. Nurses and staff from the hospital spoke politely as they passed.

I smiled up at him. "Thank you for the movie."

"I'm sorry it left you uneasy."

"I'll be fine." But I wasn't. An ominous cloud of fear hung over, not just me, but everyone as we stepped out onto the street. I had never seen the traffic so heavy.

An eerie ambience had fallen over Manila. Overloaded cars drove by. Horns honked as their drivers tried to clear paths through the congested streets. Competing with the traffic, pony drawn carts full of people's possessions headed out of Manila. Frightened animals neighed. People walked hurriedly along the streets, carrying everything they owned, trying to leave town.

Where were they all hurrying off to? I knew the answer. The people sensed the calamity lying ahead of them. They were leaving Manila while they could. How I wished I could get Geneva out of this situation before anything happened.

"I hate to do this, but I think we need to call it a night," I said. "Don't you feel that something's very wrong?"

He nodded. "It's like standing on the edge of the earth and wondering when it will tilt slightly throwing you into oblivion."

I nodded. "That's how I feel."

"Let's get you back to the hospital." Peter looked as concerned as I felt. We had walked, and any chance of getting a cab was out of the question with the panic going on around us.

On arriving at Sternberg, a boom sounded in the sky. I jumped, causing my heart to soar. "A bomb!"

"It's only fireworks, my dear," Peter stated with a chuckle. "Remind me not to get in your way if we're ever bombed."

"My heart's still pounding."

The night sky lit with brilliant colors. It seemed odd. Since my arrival in August, there had never been fireworks. "What are the fireworks for?"

He shrugged. "I'm not sure. Probably the birthday of some Philippine leader who died a century ago."

I smiled. "Probably. None of the Filipino staff have mentioned any celebrations or holidays coming up."

"I wanted to ask if you'll attend the New Year's Eve gala with me?"

I knew Geneva was planning to go with Jerry.

"I'd be delighted."

Outside the nurses' quarters, we said goodnight. As I entered, I glanced back at him and waved.

Too bad he's not a flyer.

Stepping inside the living room at the nurses' quarters, my fears and anxieties melted. It was like I had suddenly stepped out of an eerie fog into a safe sanctuary. I talked to a few of the nurses. None of them knew the reason for the fireworks.

Sue Downing and Dorothy Scholl sat on a sofa, discussing their plans to marry. Apparently, Harold had proposed. Sue had been seeing a Naval officer, Robert Gallagher.

Ethel Thor, Adele Foreman, Willa Hooks, and Clara Mueller played cards.

"Who's winning?" I asked as I walked over to their table.

"Adele," Clara said. "The one I don't like to play against is your sister. You can't ever tell what she's thinking."

I smiled. "She was born with a poker face."

They laughed which made me smile. "Goodnight, ladies."

When I stepped inside my room, Geneva was asleep under the netting. My younger sister appeared so peaceful that I didn't disturb her.

After slipping into a gown, I quietly removed my makeup and put cold cream on my face. Then I pulled the netting back, climbed in bed, and made sure the net was secure. I didn't want to catch one of the other three strands of dengue fever. Something about being in my bed removed my uneasiness.

Despite the fear of war, despite the fear of being caught up in something so harrowing so far from home, my eyes grew heavy, and I fell into a deep sleep.

Paradise Destroyed
Part Two

RESSA
December 8, 1941 (December 7th in the states)

Geneva woke me up at 6:30 the next morning. "Let's go eat. I could use a cup of coffee. "How was the movie?"

"It made me proud to be from the same state as Alvin York. It was really good. I'd love to see it again."

"You don't say?"

"I wasn't expecting to like a war movie, but I did."

Geneva puckered her lips and made a kissing sound. "Any smooching?"

I threw my pillow at her. "No. He was a real gentleman. We called it an early evening." I sighed. "Something just seemed off when we left the theater."

"Off how?"

I explained about the traffic and panic in the streets. Then, I mentioned the fireworks. "No one knew why they were shooting them off. I can't think of any celebrations taking place."

Geneva shrugged. "Think you'll go out with him again?"

I smiled slyly. "He asked me to the New Year's Eve gala."

Downstairs, the aroma of freshly brewed coffee and bacon greeted us.

"How was the date last night?" Cassie asked.

"That's right, she went out with the major," Juanita said.

I smiled. "He took me to see the new Gary Cooper movie."

"I expected you to show up at the club with him," Cassie said. "Maybe show him off."

"We called it an early night." I didn't mention he'd asked me out again. They'd see us together on New Year's Eve. "We were both tired."

"Well, I didn't get to bed early." Juanita sighed. "And I've got to work today. I hope this coffee wakes me up." When the phone rang she pushed the paper she'd been reading aside and answered it. "Hello." She listened for a moment, then rolled her eyes. She covered the receiver and looked at us. "It's Rosemary Hogan playing a joke on me. "Listen, Rosemary, that's not funny." As she listened, a look of disbelief came over her face. "You're not joking." Fear shined in Juanita's eyes. She hung up the phone and turned to us. "The Japs bombed Pearl Harbor."

My stomach rose to my throat, and I gasped. A wave of fear and intense uncertainty washed over me. Geneva's face turned an ash white. We all sensed the impending doom. "Please tell me it's not true," I said. "Maybe it is a joke."

Dorothy and Clara entered the room, appearing anxious and troubled.

"It's true all right. Harold's already been called in," Dorothy told us.

Clara chimed in, "Little yellow devils destroyed our entire Pacific fleet in Honolulu."

Though it didn't show on her face, I knew Geneva was worried.

"Are you thinking about Betty?" I asked.

She nodded. "There's no way of knowing if she's all right."

"This shouldn't come as a surprise," I said. "I guess we should be more surprised they didn't bomb the Philippines first."

"I need to get a letter written to my mother," Ruth Straub said. "She'll be worried."

Adele, Helen, Cassie, Eunice and Anna's faces showed their concern and disbelief. We all spoke at the same time, speculating over what would come next. Sue, Ruth, and Dorothy worried about their sweethearts. The conversation didn't give us time to confront our individual fears.

Later in the living room, Josie came in and stood in the center of the room. "Girls, you've got to sleep today. There's not time to weep and wail over this. You'll be working all night. Now, get some rest."

War was no longer a rumor.

The Japanese would hit Manila.

GENEVA
December 8, 1941

Around 2:30 p.m., we were ordered to meet at the assembly hall. In the crowd of thirty-five doctors and thirty-seven nurses, I found Ressa and joined her. We waited, hoping we'd be told everything was under control and that we had nothing to fear.

Colonel Percy Carrol spoke, "War has been declared on Japan. This will be the third war I've been in. War is a terrible thing. For the time being, no one will be permitted to leave the facility without permission." An officer came in and interrupted him with an update. "I just received word that the Japanese are bombing Baguio in northern Luzon."

The Philippines were under attack. I wondered how long before they reached Manila.

"Damn, that's close," Captain McNeil said behind me.

"I have friends at Camp John Hay," Adele whispered.

Carrol continued, "Like I was saying, no one is to leave without permission and never go anywhere without your helmet and gas mask." Another officer interrupted, handing him a note. While he read it, his expression grew grim. "Clarke Air Field has been hit. They are in need of nurses. Please raise your hand if you would be willing to volunteer to go to Stotsenberg to help with the wounded."

Three hands shot up. Cassie, Phyliss, and Ruth volunteered. I didn't think Ruth would hold up to the pressure, but no doubt, she had taken on the mission to find out if her boyfriend, Glen Adler was okay.

"Thanks, I knew I could count on you." Colonel Carrol went into an in-depth discussion on different gasses and their effects.

Finally, Maude Davison stared out at us a few solemn moments. "Girls, we're at war. Each of us has a job to do. I have no doubt you'll do yours well."

We were dismissed and filed into the hallway. The seriousness of the news showed on our somber faces. Our leisurely life in paradise had come to an end.

Once we'd walked a few feet from the door, Ressa said, "This is the end."

"We'll never leave this island," I replied. A sea of hopelessness engulfed me. I wanted to sit down somewhere and cry, but we had so much to do. I glanced at my watch, then at Ressa. "I have about ten minutes before my shift starts. I'll see you at lunch."

"See you then, and Geneva."

"What?"

"Keep your chin up."

"I'll try."

Ressa headed off to set up new wards.

The ward I reported to buzzed with activity. Corpsmen brought extra beds in and set them up. The atmosphere was charged with nervousness and apprehension.

Patients constantly asked me questions. How many were killed? What was the damage? Are they headed our way? I didn't have any answers. I must have said *I don't know*, at least a hundred times. Truth be told, I was just as anxious to have answers to those same questions.

We all wondered what was going on back home. With the attack on Pearl Harbor, we were sure ships would be heading our way. We figured in a couple of weeks our forces would be here.

"Geneva, over here."

Jerry waited at the door. I smiled and walked over to him. "I was worried about you."

"We're heading to Clark Field. We'll have to reschedule our date."

"Oh, Jerry. It's so dangerous. I wish you didn't have to go."

"It's an order. Don't sweat it." He squeezed my hand. "You can't get out of our bowling date. I'll come back."

"You'd better."

When he left, I wasn't sure if I'd ever see him. I said a brief prayer for God to protect him, to protect us all. The news of who was dead and dying reached Sternberg, and nurses cried their hearts out over the death of husbands or boyfriends.

I stopped by the dining room for a late lunch and joined Ressa and the others at the table. Dorothy and Sue had both been crying.

"Bad news?" I asked them, hesitantly.

"No, we're just worried about them," Dorothy responded. "So many have died."

Sue nodded. "I'm so afraid for Robert." She blew her nose. "What about your young man?"

"Jerry has been sent to Clark Field. They're still bombing there."

My sister placed her hand on mine. "He'll be okay. Try to eat."

"Any news on when the wounded will start arriving?" I asked, hoping Jerry would return soon.

"Only to get ready for them. Sooner or later, they'll start coming in." Ressa lit a cigarette and inhaled it.

"We set up four new wards with twice the number of beds. Any ward that was closed is being reopened," Dorothy added.

"Have you seen what's going on outside?" I asked Ressa.

She flicked her ashes. "You mean all the digging?"

"Yes, it's kind of sad seeing grounds that were once beautiful dug up," I said.

Filipino workers had dug trenches all around the hospital grounds, ripping up the flowers.

"In the long run, it won't mean much. You know as well as I do, Sternberg is a huge wooden disaster waiting to happen, a firetrap. When it does go, we'll thank God for every trench we dive into."

"I know you're right. But it's still kind of sad. It always made me think of a beautiful green quilt with a thousand vibrant patches of color sewn into it. All that's left is dirt, not even the petal of a flower survived."

Ressa smiled and dabbed her mouth with a napkin. "Well, Geneva, which would you prefer, pretty flowers growing in the garden or green grass growing six feet above you?"

Some questions don't deserve an answer, and that was one of them. I merely nodded and said, "I need to get back. We have to get linens on all the beds. Walk with me."

As we walked through the hospital, we bumped into Anna Williams. "Iba has been bombed. They don't have a hospital."

"They'll bring all the wounded here," I said. Iba sat one-hundred-forty-four miles from Manila. With the road conditions, it could take up to six hours to reach Sternberg. Perhaps, more.

Ressa adjusted her nurse's cap. "That means we're going to be really busy. Prepare for a long night."

"I'm expecting twelve-hour shifts," Anna said.

"Thanks for telling us." When I reached my ward, everyone had heard about Iba. It's all anyone could talk about.

We worked like field hands getting things ready. I was on duty, keyed up and heart beating double-time, waiting for the wounded.

I finally headed for a dinner break around 7:00 p.m. I entered the dining room and cut my gaze to where we usually sat. Ressa waved back. She sat with other nurses and a few doctors. Dorothy followed me to the table and sat across from me.

"Anything yet?" I asked.

"No, but they're coming soon," Ressa said. "It's like the calm before the storm."

"Word is, all but seven or eight of our planes were destroyed at Clark Field." Juanita looked at the doctor who sat nearby. "Is that what you heard?"

Dr. Fox nodded. "I've been told it's bad. Seems the Japs flew in from China over the Zambales Mountains to avoid being picked up on radar. They hit without warning. There are a lot of casualties."

"Sneaky little yellow devils," Juanita said.

"They bombed the mess and barracks," Dr. Fox said. "The men were strafed as they ran for the planes. That went on for two hours. Since the hangars and oil drums were set afire, expect a lot of burn patients."

"Those damn bastards," Francis Nash said. Her language didn't shock us. We knew her choice of words could be quite colorful at times. "How the hell did they catch them on the ground?"

Fox appeared disheartened. "They were sitting ducks."

"I spoke to Arnold." Dorothy stopped eating and looked up. "Colonel Brereton had requested permission to bomb Japanese ships in Takao Harbor and their planes on Formosa. But he had to wait for MacArthur to give the order. They got the planes in the sky and were flying them around to keep them off the ground. After receiving the okay on the mission, all the planes landed to refuel. While that was being done, the pilots grabbed lunch in the mess. That's when they hit."

"I can't believe they got Baguio, Clark Field, and Iba so close together," Madeline said. "I'm expecting them to hit us."

"Thank goodness those trenches are finished," Ressa added.

I sat stunned over everything that was happening.

An orderly entered the dining room. "Ambulances are arriving! Get to your post!"

We scurried from the dining room. Outside the door, I hugged Ressa. As I headed toward my ward, I knew it'd be a night I'd want to forget but never would.

I stood with Ethel Thor watching the first ambulance arrive followed by a caravan of trucks and cars all transporting the wounded. I looked for Jerry but didn't see him.

Pure disbelief ran through me at the number of injured soldiers being brought in.

Immediately, we separated the wounded men using a triage approach. A large number of them were sent directly to pre-op while others were treated for less serious injuries. Many of them needed further evaluation.

The screams, moans, weeping, and cursing from these defeated men overshadowed the doctors' orders.

The smell of burnt flesh and blood filled the air. Torn limbs dangled by just a thread of skin. Some were missing either an arm or leg. Many had their skin ripped off their backsides, revealing raw bloody muscles.

I swallowed back my own discomfort and focused on these suffering men. I turned in response to a tug on my dress and looked into a face covered in dark oil and dirt. He had the bluest eyes I'd ever seen.

"Help me please. The pain." He tried to smile, but it turned into a painful grimace.

"Don't worry flyboy, I've got you." I administered morphine as fast as I could get it and helped clean him up after doctoring his wounds.

Doctors treated the more serious injuries. Anything that we nurses could attend to we did. But my main job consisted of stopping their pain and cleaning them up, until the doctors could get a good look at their injuries.

The Colonel was right. *War is a terrible thing*. Nothing you can imagine can prepare you for the stark reality of it. The only ones that understand are the brave, dedicated souls who have experienced it firsthand.

We had run out of places to put the injured men. They filled the halls waiting for their turn to be treated. Walking around them, I had to be careful not to step in the puddles of blood on the floor.

"How are you holding up, Geneva?"

I turned to the sound of Ressa's voice. "Might sound funny, but I don't know. I feel like a machine going through the motions, numb from the neck down. How about you?"

"I think you described it pretty well."

My sister's disheveled appearance surprised me. She looked older. I realized she was probably thinking the same thing about me. We were both worn out, physically and emotionally. It didn't matter. We were surrounded by people who needed us.

"Is it my imagination or has the number of wounded slowed down?" I asked.

"They're still coming, but I heard Carrol sent a number of nurses and doctors to open hospitals at the school of The Holy Ghost and the Jai-Alai Club. Maybe that's why the incoming wounded have slowed down."

That news was music to my ears. I let out a soft sigh of relief, "Thank you, Jesus. Well, sis, I guess I'd better get back to it."

"Me too. See you later."

"Ressa?"

"Yes."

"Thanks for checking on me."

"You're welcome. That's what big sisters are for."

That night we had our first full black out. All the blinds had been drawn, and all the electric white bulbs were replaced with blue bulbs. Only the enclosed operating rooms were afforded the luxury of white light. I didn't like the dim blue light.

"Phooey. I wished I'd purchased a flashlight," I told Juanita and Dorothy.

"I hear there's not a flashlight to be had in Manila," Dorothy said.

"Well, it'd sure come in handy. We'll be tripping all over each other. Think we'll be bombed tonight?" I asked.

"I don't think it'll be much longer," Juanita replied, in that slow refined southern drawl.

"Keep your helmets on and gas masks handy," Dorothy said.

RESSA
December 8, 1941

I tiptoed into the room trying not to wake Geneva.

"I'm awake." She sat up in bed and turned on the dull blue light.

"I'd rather stand in the dark than this pale bluish light. It gives me the willies."

"It's so dim I keep tripping over things. Dorothy and Juanita said they went all over Manila trying to buy a flashlight. There's none to be found. I guess we'll have to fumble in the dark with the others."

I shrugged. "Maybe not."

"You plan to run around with a lit candle?" Geneva asked.

"No, but I might use the flashlight I talked the quartermaster out of."

"Why Ressa, you little sneak."

"He sent one for you too. Cassie, Mary, and Juanita got one also." I folded my gown and tucked it away. "If they bomb us, I want to be ready. I'm sleeping in my uniform."

"I'm in my civilian clothes. They're cooler. Not to mention wearing white uniforms outside could make us prime targets."

I nodded. "You're right." I slipped from my nurse's uniform into civilian clothes and stretched out on my bed. "Goodnight."

"Night." Geneva rolled over and faced the wall.

The air had never been as hot and muggy. No breeze stirred with the blinds closed. Exhausted from that day's excitement, I dozed off immediately.

Bam, bam-bam-bam, bam.

Gunfire jolted me from a deep sleep. The piercing noise sent adrenaline shooting through my veins. Every muscle in my body reacted in a state of panic.

Geneva sprung up startled. "Holy smoke! They're bombing Nichols Field."

The siren blared warning us to head outside to our assigned places.

"Run!" Geneva handed me my helmet and gas mask.

"I'm right behind you."

Using our flashlights, we made our way downstairs with the other nurses. As we exited the building, we turned off the flashlights. In the dark, it took a moment to find our assigned trench for air raids.

The droning hum of the Japanese planes filled me with dread.

Geneva managed to get down first and yanked me down behind her. We were too terrified to be concerned with the fertile earth or the bugs and worms that shared the trench with us.

I quickly placed a pencil between my teeth and lightly bit down to secure it. This forced me to breathe through my mouth, reducing the possibility of a damaged eardrum due to blast percussion. It also kept a person from grinding their teeth. A good wooden pencil was a precious commodity in an air raid.

Outside, about twenty of us huddled down on the ground. I tried to find Mary and Dorothy. Not all the nurses came out. Those on duty had to remain inside with the patients.

My heart pounded, and my stomach tightened. I thought it odd that my mind could function and seemed separate from the fear in my heart.

The bombing continued. With each large boom, the ground shook causing my entire body to flinch. My stomach twisted in knots as their intensity grew. I worried more for Geneva than myself.

Several nurses mumbled incoherently or paced rather than sit or lay down. Each of us had our own reactions.

Between bombs, I fought my own battle with the mosquitoes. After experiencing one strand of dengue fever, I didn't want another. They also carried other diseases I didn't wish to catch. Despite my effort, I suffered many bites. I found myself in a double layer of hell; Japs attacking from above and mosquitoes attacking from below.

About thirty minutes later, the bombing stopped.

"All clear!" someone shouted.

The men also complained about the mosquitos biting them during the raid.

We climbed from the trench and dusted ourselves off. I drew in several deep breaths, trying to overcome the grip fear had on me. My heart rate slowed down gradually. I took Geneva's hand and squeezed it, wanting to reassure her we were all right.

"That was something I'll never forget for as long as I live," she said.

"Me neither."

Once back in bed, Geneva sighed. "I don't know if either one of us are cut out for this. I thought my heart was going to jump out of my chest."

"Same here. That one hit around ten. I doubt they're done for the night." I rubbed alcohol on my mosquito bites and passed it to Geneva, who'd also received several bites.

"I'm not sure I can go back to sleep."

"We need to try. Tomorrow will be a long hard day with all the causalities coming in from tonight." As I waited for sleep to come, I thought about what we'd just gone through. Though I knew there'd be more raids, that first one would be the one that would be in my dreams for years to come.

We finally went to sleep.

Boom! Boom! Boom!

The walls shook.

I just about jumped out of my skin again.

Geneva and I slipped on our helmets and grabbed our gas masks, then hurried back outside. Once again, we found ourselves down in the freshly dug soil.

The bombing lit the distant sky over Nichols Fields.

I closed my eyes and prayed for it to be over.

Finally, silence. We all waited a second before climbing out.

"Why bother going back to bed." Mary Lohr dusted the dirt off her clothes. "I'm staying downstairs. I won't have as far to run."

Adele put her hand up. "Me too."

I turned to Geneva. "I'm staying downstairs."

"Same here. If we're going to find a spot, we'd better hurry."

We staked out our little corner of the vast living room in the nurses' quarters. Juanita, Dorothy, Mary, and Madeline had taken time to snatch a pillow from their rooms. As for me, I laid my head on my arm. Geneva and I didn't have any cover. Though the floor was hard, I didn't care. A sense of numbness had consumed me.

"The floor is pure comfort," Juanita shouted.

"It'll make for a really good rest," Madeline added.

Despite our situation, we all laughed.

RESSA
December 9, 1941

The following morning, Geneva and I awoke early, ate a quick breakfast, and headed to our wards for duty. We both knew it'd be a challenging day.

Seventy beds had been set up in the ward. The other nurses and I spent the morning getting beds ready for more incoming wounded. As I returned from a restroom break, I paused at a nearby window.

Outside in the streets, people streamed by carrying their belongings in bundles, trying to get out of the city. Heavy traffic crowded the roadway. Manila had turned from a happy city to one somberly facing war.

I turned from the window and saw Mary, Dorothy, and Geneva coming toward me.

"It's chaotic out there," Mary said.

"I heard guns have been positioned around the wall," Dorothy added.

"Yeah, and the flag on city hall is flying upside down," Mary told us.

We knew the reversed colors of the Philippine flag indicated they were at war.

I looked at Geneva. "Suddenly, I'm wishing we were on Corregidor with Winnie. They'll never take the Rock."

"The Japs have been passing out leaflets trying to persuade Filipinos to join them," Dorothy said. "Japanese sympathizers shot off those fireworks the other night to let them know where to bomb."

"You don't say?" Geneva looked as troubled as I felt.

Mary nodded. "It's true. We heard it from one of the officers."

"I can't believe they'd do that. We're here to help them." My anger flared. It wouldn't have surprised me if steam had come out of my ears.

"None of our workers here or Filipino soldiers would betray us," Dorothy added. "I'm sure it was the Fifth Columnist behind it."

"I'd better get back." I hugged Geneva. "Stay strong."

She looked at the others. "She still treats me like I'm two."

They laughed.

Though the expected wounded hadn't arrived, the hospital kept us busy all day. A high pitch of nervous tension buzzed through me. There wasn't time to talk. Still, I'd hear little bits and pieces of what was going on in the city. There had been a lot of accidents with people leaving town. Panic never failed to cause injuries.

A siren and loud speakers positioned at Manila City Hall sounded off while we ate lunch. What I had already eaten threatened to come back up. I grabbed my mask and helmet and evacuated with the others. By the time we returned, our food was cold, but the air raid and the stress it caused had ruined my appetite. Still, I had to force the cold food down. It was important to keep a high level of energy and our strength up.

Geneva grabbed a roll and buttered it. "With all this tension and fear, I'm surprised none of us have gone into complete hysterics. Everyone is so somber."

I nodded. "None of us slept very well." I ate a few more bites of the potatoes on my plate. "I wonder what's happening back home."

Geneva shrugged. "Surely, with Pearl Harbor being bombed, they're sending ships our way. Our country wouldn't let us down."

I shrugged. Usually, I was the positive one and my sister the one who viewed everything with a negative outlook. "I don't know. Maybe."

"A convoy left California heading this way," Clara said to us. "This should all be over soon."

"It can't come soon enough for me. I told you they'd be coming for us," Geneva said.

All my anxiety faded away. Hopefully, they'd arrive before Manila was bombed directly. The news spread to others as well. The veil of despair and gloom that covered us lifted. That afternoon several of us took our breaks outside.

The dreadful sound put me on alert. Planes. I tilted my head back until I thought my neck would break. Seventy-five Japanese bombers flew over. It was a horrific sight. Immediately, fear turned my heart cold. Despite the planes flying twenty thousand feet overhead, the droning hum of their engines wreaked havoc on me. Our anti-aircraft guns couldn't reach them at that altitude.

The loud speaker from city hall shrilled with warnings.

Clear the streets. Get under cover. Clear the streets. Get under cover.

The intermittent warnings frazzled our nerves. The noise caused more stress than the threat of the planes overhead. We scurried to our assigned spots. Relief ran through me when I saw Geneva already there.

Those unable to walk very far took shelter beneath the beds.

The bombs dropped not even a mile from us on Port Area. Our laundry and commissary personnel lived and worked in the area. I could only pray they'd be spared.

At dinner, we were told the rumor of a convoy heading our way had been just that, a rumor. My spirit dropped to an all-time low. Geneva hadn't heard from Jerry, so she had a double dose of the blues.

Before we could finish eating, the siren sounded. They never failed to interrupt our meals.

We never went anywhere without our helmets and gas masks. We grabbed ours and left. We stormed into the courtyard to seek shelter from the air raid. We laid quietly on the ground while the squadron flew over.

Going back inside, I held Geneva's hand. "I think we should sleep downstairs again. It makes evacuating faster."

She nodded. "Let's grab our blankets and pillows this time and claim a spot."

"I'd love to find time for a bath. I feel so nasty."

Geneva smiled. "Only if you want to chance running out in front of everyone buck naked. I doubt any of our patients would mind the diversion."

"Looks like it'll be another sponge bath."

"Just like back home in the summertime when the well dried up."

With so many of us, baths at home had always been quick and to the point. In dry summers when the well was low, our baths were reduced to a wash rag and a bowl of water. Mom had called them spit baths. The thought made my heart ache for home. At that moment, I missed it and truly wished Geneva and I were back in Tennessee with our family.

Geneva handed me my comb and toothbrush. "I'm keeping mine with me in case this building is bombed."

I chuckled, but secretly thought it was an excellent idea.

That night we claimed our same spots in the living room. This time, I had my pillow and blanket. Lying in the dim, blue lights kept me on edge. At any moment, the sirens and warnings could blare warning us of approaching bombers.

Clara settled beside us. "I heard nurses from Stotsenberg are being moved to Sternberg. Our nurses who volunteered to help them are returning as well. I'm not sure when they'll arrive."

"We can sure use their help." I stared at the pearl ring I wore on my finger. It reminded me of happier times in Manila.

GENEVA
December 10, 1941

It was a long day. We were exhausted, but our sleeping habits had changed. I could come out of a deep sleep to a state of awareness in a matter of seconds. You never overslept when there was a possibility you might never wake up.

I hated the sirens, voices shouting over the loudspeakers, and the practicing drills of the Filipino soldiers marching out front. There was a constant shout of "Halt, halt." from their commander.

That afternoon, the commanding officer informed us to expect newly wounded. They were nearby and would be arriving within the hour.

I started preparing the blankets. Many of them would suffer from shock and need to be kept warm.

A half an hour later, the wounded arrived in ambulances, trucks, and cars from Nichols Field and Port Area. As they were brought in, I realized most of them would require surgery because of needing legs or arms amputated or to remove shrapnel. I did what I could to make them comfortable while they waited for surgery.

Another messenger delivered news that had us feeling defeated. A hundred more wounded men would arrive within the hour from Iba.

With the operating room backed up, we set up three emergency tables in the downstairs clinic.

Mary joined me. "Just heard Colonel Carroll is opening even more hospitals in the city. He's staffing them with Filipino nurses."

"That'll give us some relief."

"The nuns who run that little missionary hospital have turned it over to the Army."

"Maybe they'll be qualified to help as nurses."

Sue Downing shrugged. "They'll probably send some of us."

I didn't say anything, but I hoped Ressa nor I would be sent away from Sternberg.

It grew dark. The only thing we had were those dim blue lights to see by. I used my flashlight to move from patient to patient.

When I was off duty, I grabbed a bite in the dining room. Not seeing Ressa and the others, I went to the large living room. They sat in the depressing blue light talking and waiting for the raids to begin.

"Help has to be coming," Madeline whispered.

Juanita laughed. "If you believe that, I have some land to sell you."

We giggled.

"So, what do they expect us to do?" Clara asked.

I recalled the strategic plan the Raulston boy had mentioned. For us to keep retreating until help arrived. But I didn't say anything because he'd confided in me. I'd never mentioned it to Ressa either.

"There hasn't been any mail from home since November," Eunice said. "I wonder if my Christmas presents made it there."

"When'd you mail them?" Juanita asked.

"Early November."

"That's when we mailed ours," Ressa said. "Of course, when you have five sisters and two brothers you need a pretty big box. In the last letter from home, Mom said she's expecting again."

Boom!

The lamps and chandelier shook.

59

Josie rushed into the room. "Grab your gas masks and helmets and get outside."

We scattered like mice when the cat comes in.

I didn't know how many more jolts of pure shock my heart could handle without collapsing.

RESSA
DECEMBER 10 1941

I had worked all day.

That afternoon, I grabbed a cup of coffee and sat in the quiet solarium overlooking the hideous trenches. With so many people being sent to Sternberg, finding a spot for a little solitude became more difficult. At least, we had our room, but with the blinds kept closed, the heat made it unbearable in the daytime.

No sooner than I'd lit a cigarette and drew on it, someone came up the hall. My seclusion hadn't lasted long.

Dorothy joined me. "Did you hear about the B-17 that took off from Clark Field and attacked Japanese war ships over by Luzon? Someone reported it was the Natori along with the Aparri and Vigan. They sank one of them."

"That's great news. Did that happen today?"

She shrugged. "I'm not sure. Could've been yesterday. If I hear any more, I'll let you know."

"I'm surprised that we had a plane left to send up. That'd be something if this ended the war."

"I'm afraid it didn't go so well. On his way back to Clark Field, his bomber was attacked by a A6M2 Zero. Some of the crew parachuted and survived. Several weren't as fortunate including the pilot."

I shuddered from the tragic loss of life. "That's too horrendous for words."

She glanced at my coffee. "Think I'll go get a cup. It might help me stay awake. As soon as Ft. McKinley reaches capacity, they'll send patients our way."

"We're ready for them. Have you heard from Harold?"

"Not yet. But I've been doing a lot of praying for him."

It wasn't until later I learned more about the air raid on the Japanese ship. Colin Kelly Jr., a young pilot, and his crew had dropped three six-hundred-pound bombs on the ship and sank it and damaged others.

It was the first bombing mission in the Philippines to retaliate against the Japanese, but it had been intended for enemy ships anchored in Taiwan.

My heart went out to these men.

Around midnight, someone banged on our door. "The wounded from Iba have arrived. Everyone is to report. Hurry!"

Geneva and I quickly dressed in our uniforms and ran to help. Over a hundred patients had been brought in. With only one doctor to see them all, I knew it'd be a long night. Even worse, we didn't have any anesthesia to alleviate their pain and suffering.

For the soldiers, I first checked to see if they were in shock, then I gave them a smear test to test for gangrene bacteria. Sun stroke and dehydration made a few delirious.

The medics left wounded, young men scattered upstairs and down, some in serious condition. Many screamed out while others quietly suffered through their pain. Dirt and blood cover their tattered uniforms. Some had dried blood matted in their hair. It reminded me of the battlefield scene from *Gone with the Wind*. But this was real. Their pain and injuries were real. These men had mothers and wives back home who loved them.

"You're wanted in emergency," Maude Davison told me.

"I'm on my way."

I entered the operating room. The scent of blood hit my sinuses.

"Get your hands scrubbed," Captain Warren Wilson ordered.

"Yes, sir." I scrubbed my hands in green soap. As I turned from the sink, two young corpsmen brought in a wounded soldier. Blood had dried over his wounds.

"He's stripped and ready," Francis shouted.

Before bringing them in, the corpsmen stripped them down. Once treated, we gave them a thin gown to wear and carried them to a ward.

I stared at his ripped skin and lacerations, knowing he was one of the lucky ones. Many came in with dangling limbs or internal injuries severe enough to be taken into surgery.

"Wash that entire area," the doctor ordered.

"Yes, sir." I proceeded to clean his wounds with green soap to prevent any infections.

"Take me last," the youthful soldier pleaded. His dark eyes showed his sincerity. "There are others worse off than me."

"They're being taken care of," I assured him as I helped dress his wounds. "How much pain are you in?"

"I can deal with it. Save it for the others."

The next one hadn't been as lucky. He cried the entire time the doctor worked on him. After cleaning and treating his wounds, I administered morphine.

The wounded kept arriving well into the afternoon, and I continued helping the doctor care for them. Finally, I received a break and left the ward. "Clara, have you seen Geneva?"

"She and some others got the afternoon off. I think she's resting in her room."

"Thanks."

I managed to get a cup of coffee and found a quiet corner to sit in. I smoked a cigarette, then finished off the coffee. While I was on my break, Ethel came by. "Red Cross sent us about twenty graduate Filipino nurses and some civilian nurses married to military guys, living in Manila."

I butted my cigarette into an ashtray on the small wicker table. "We can sure use them. When they and the nurses evacuating from the other hospitals get here, hopefully, we won't have twelve-hour shifts."

"One can only hope."

RESSA
December 12, 1941

Yesterday, thirteen Navy nurses came to Sternberg because the bombing was too close to their hospital. Once the corpsmen set up smaller hospitals to catch the overflow of patients, these ladies would be reassigned. They wore blue dungarees like the men. Many appeared distraught and tired. I could only imagine what they'd been going through.

Mary Harrington, a Navy nurse we'd met while taking riding lessons, waved at us. We had gotten along very well. I could spot her red hair a mile away. She was a sweet girl from Elk Point, South Dakota.

Around noon in the dining room, Geneva and I had a chance to visit with Mary and meet some of the other Navy nurses. I found their conversation both interesting and disturbing.

"A radio equipped with a beam detector was found in the Navy yard," Peggy Nash said. "We were set up."

"Is that so?" Geneva asked, stunned. One of the few times my sister's face revealed her mood was when hearing news of the war.

Peggy nodded. "No doubt about it."

Mary Harrington frowned. "The Fifth Columnist pointed the Japs directly at us."

Their news angered me.

"I can't believe the Filipinos would betray us," I said.

"We were told it's not the native people but Spanish Falangists, who hope to make a coup in the midst of all the confusion," Mary added.

Because of what these nurses had endured, they were given the day to rest, but the raids kept them in a state of panic.

That afternoon, we had an air raid. I escorted several patients outside before taking my position. Some of the men refused to evacuate the building and crawled under their beds.

Planes flew overhead. Their target—Cavite, the principle Naval base. So, the Japs had targeted it.

With it being in a volcanic area, I wondered if people had been able to dig foxholes. Their hospital had started transferring their patients to Sternberg.

Later at dinner just as we started eating, the siren blared. The Japanese had perfect timing. I think it was a mental game they played. They deliberately deprived us of nourishment and sleep, a double whammy to both mind and body.

"Oh God," Madeline said. "I hope our ships are spared."

We stood and made our way to our assigned trenches. Geneva and I had become pros at climbing in and out. But sitting in a trench wasn't fun, and I hated my white uniform getting dirty.

The droning air raid continued much longer than any we'd experienced so far.

"This is the heaviest bombing yet," Geneva said.

I nodded. "They must be destroying every ship in the harbor."

It lasted so long that we finally ignored the bombs, climbed from our foxholes, and returned to our duties inside.

I hadn't been far off. The Japs had destroyed everything but two radio towers and the Naval hospital. One officer from that area informed us the entire Asiatic fleet had been sunk. This news left both patients and staff disheartened.

More wounded would be arriving. We faced the obstacle of finding a place to put them. Not only was every ward filled to capacity, our morgue stayed full of young men who'd sacrificed all.

Around three, casualties started arriving. Corpsmen carried men in on stretchers. Once every space on the hospital floor had been filled, they started leaving them on the stretchers outside the building until we could treat them. Many civilians had been wounded as well and laid among the soldiers.

Their voices quivered in excruciating pain as they moaned and screamed in agony. Not only did they have wounds from shrapnel but also burns from fires. The smell of burnt flesh and hair permeated the area, making my stomach churn.

Sternberg Hospital couldn't have been busier. Doctors and nurses scurried about in the wards, the operating room, in the halls and even outside. We worked at a fast pace. There wouldn't be time for dinner or breaks. I assisted in treating the wounded. Many of them remained unconscious, and some died while I attempted to help them. My heart filled with empathy, but I had to push my feelings aside and concentrate on the living.

"No dog tags on this one," I said to Dr. Fox. It saddened me to think he'd never be identified. His family may never receive closure.

"This one doesn't have any either," Dorothy said.

Many wouldn't have been burned so badly if they hadn't had beards, but the beards caught on fire and burned through to the chin and face.

There wasn't time to stop and take away the dead. We still had wounded we might be able to save. I didn't have time to cry. I knew that would happen when I finally had a break and time to reflect.

"You're spending the rest of the afternoon in the officer's ward. You're off at five for dinner," Josie informed me.

"Thanks." I hurried off to my next assignment. The work wasn't nearly as depressing or difficult in the officer's ward. Some of these patients had actually been treated at the Naval hospital in Cavite before being brought over, so while their conditions were serious, they weren't critical. Also, they had already been given morphine and weren't experiencing as much pain.

One officer, Second Lieutenant Donald Robert Robbins from the 14th Bomb Squad had been Colin Kelly's copilot and had parachuted out right before the plane had exploded. He suffered from minor burns and wounds from shrapnel. Fortunately, his face had been spared. He'd been lucky. From the neck down, he looked like Boris Karloff in *The Mummy*. I offered him water.

He lifted his head, sipped it slowly, then flung back on the pillow. His melancholy expression showed his regret. "Kelly was one of a kind. Damn good pilot. I can't believe he's gone. I thought he'd be right behind the rest of us. The entire time we were bailing out, the Japs fired on us. My parachute looked like Swiss cheese."

"From my understanding, he didn't clear the plane soon enough before it exploded."

He closed his eyes and grimaced. "I saw Delehanty's head blown off. One minute he's laughing and the next he was gone. The Zero swooped in on us before we could get away from it. Do you know if Joe made it?"

"He took a bullet in the ankle, but he'll be fine. I didn't tell him Sergeant Robert Altman, who'd parachuted with him, had survived only to be captured by the Japs. I figured he had enough to deal with without adding to it. "Try to rest. You've been through a lot. I can give you something to help you sleep."

"No, I'd rather stay alert." Again, his face showed regret. "Colin couldn't wait to get back to his wife and son. Now, they'll never see him. His kid will have to grow up without him."

"I'll be back later to check on you." Since I had a thing for pilots and he was easy on the eyes, this could be a problem. Besides, he was younger than me.

For the rest of my shift, I worked on charts as well as tending to the patients. All day my mind and body worked on automation without stopping.

I checked on Lieutenant Robbins again. He still hadn't come to terms with Kelly's death. "We left Clark Field around 0900 that morning with hopes of striking the Japs in Taiwan."

Though I knew the facts, I listened to him. "You're all heroes."

"I don't feel like one."

"Trust me, you are."

At five p.m, I headed for the dining room.

I sat with Geneva. I told her about the men brought in and their attack on the Japanese ships. Then I messed up and mentioned Lieutenant Robbins.

Geneva's brows rose in speculation. "Let me get this straight. Not only is he in your ward, he's a pilot. With your thing for flyers, he's in jeopardy of being showered with attention."

"He's a hero. Everyone is giving him attention. I don't give him any more than I give the others. Besides, he's not the only flyer in the ward. Not to mention, he's wrapped in gauze. Let me say, it'll be a while before he's ready to dance."

"I don't think Mom and Dad would mind us picking up husbands while we're here."

"As far as I know, he could be married. I looked on his chart, but it didn't say. He's a lot younger than me. Let me assure you, nothing will happen."

While we finished our dinner, we listened to the stories about Cavite.

"When I heard those Japs coming, I dug myself into the sand," a young Naval officer said. "Every time they flew my way, I dug a little deeper and finally dozed off. Some civilians weren't as lucky," he said. "They were standing against a wall. One of them grabbed an empty lard can and held it over his head. Damn thing saved his life. The other three were killed."

I stood and placed a hand on Geneva's shoulder. "I can't listen to any more depressing stories."

"You look exhausted."

"I am. My feet are killing me. I don't think I've ever been around so many people dying at one time. I'm going to the room. I need a shower. After being around so much blood, sweat, dirt, and body fluids, wiping off isn't enough tonight."

"Well, my dinner break is over. I'll be up when my shift ends." Geneva stood and gathered her dishes. "I'll take yours. Go on."

Upstairs, nothing had ever felt better than that warm water rushing over me. While I showered, I couldn't stop seeing images of the wounded and dead. Then my thoughts drifted to Robbins and his narrow escape.

GENEVA.
December 13, 1941

This morning more wounded arrived from Canacao Naval Hospital. Twenty nurses had been evacuated from McKinley and would be arriving at Sternberg soon. I wondered where we'd put them all. Most of them would be assigned to wards here or in some of the makeshift hospitals set up around town.

While I was in the dining room for a break, I had a real treat.

Jerry came up and sat beside me. "There's the prettiest girl in Manila."

"Jerry! When'd you get back?" He wore clean clothes and looked too groomed to be coming straight from the field. His bronze skin showed he'd been in the sun and contrasted with his blue eyes. Streaks of blonde highlighted his brown hair.

"Very late last night. And I've got to leave again. I have less than an hour. I couldn't think of anyone I'd rather spend that hour with than you."

"Well, phooey."

He appeared shocked. "You're not glad to see me?"

"No, of course I am, but I only have thirty minutes before I have to report back to the ward."

"Well, it'll be the best thirty minutes of my week."

After we talked about everything going on around us, he grew serious. "I think they plan to move everyone into the jungles. They've been working on two jungle hospitals and transporting supplies to them."

"Are the Japs that close?"

He nodded. "Fraid so. They landed in southern Luzon and are making their way on land." He chuckled. "Someone told us they ride bicycles."

"About these hospitals, they can't be very large if they're in the jungle."

Jerry grinned. "You realize they're outside. There's no roof or walls."

"So, we're just out in the open?"

"Yep. Pretty much. Bulldozers have already plowed down sections of jungle to use."

"Well, I'll be. I hope it's a rumor and a lot of malarkey. We hear so many things that turn out to be untrue. It's difficult to know what to believe."

"Eat your lunch. It's getting cold."

I took a few bites before I looked at him. "Please don't take any chances."

He smiled. "Trust me, I won't. I don't know when I'll return. You may not be here when I get back."

I sighed. "I hope I am."

He took my hand and squeezed it. "I'd sneak a kiss, but we've got a bunch of gossipers around us."

Before he had a chance to argue, I kissed his cheek. "You still owe me a date." I stood. "I'm going to be late. Stay safe."

Every day, more nurses with steady boyfriends learned of their deaths. I didn't want to experience that kind of pain.

RESSA
December 14, 1941

I checked in on Lieutenant Robbins. I found him looking much better. His bandages had been removed.

I wore my prettiest civilian dress. "It's my day off. I'm going shopping with a friend. Do you need anything while I'm out?"

He sighed while staring into space. "No, but thanks."

"Well, in that case, I'll be on my way."

Robbins nodded, then closed his eyes. The man had demons to deal with. Did he blame himself in some way for Kelly's death?

The orders to remain at the hospital had been lifted. The only thing we were told was not to wear blue. The Japanese wore blue, and the Filipino guards might shoot us assuming we're the enemy.

Mary Harrington and I caught a ride into the city. Not only did we carry our purses, we toted our gas masks and helmets. Only a few cars and pedestrians moved along the practically deserted streets.

"It's like a ghost town," Mary said.

"It's eerie," I replied. "Almost everyone has left Manila."

We stopped at the Army/Navy Club. Mary and I entered the club expecting to see a little gleefulness, but instead we found lines of people with dismal faces. I looked for Peter, but he'd been sent out with the other men. Someone mentioned he'd been put in charge of supplies.

I pointed to a wall of boxes and trunks. "I wonder what those are for."

"Those are the personal belongings of the officers. They're trying to get them out of the city," a young private informed me.

It saddened me to see the lovely ballroom turned into a storage facility. I recalled nights of dancing under the sparkling lights. This room that had been filled with happiness now appeared bleak.

Mary and I joined the crowd that waited in line to hear about friends who had vanished and hadn't been heard from. We asked about several men who we had treated or knew, but they had no information on their whereabouts.

Afterwards, we made our way to the Manila Hotel, another one of the places we had frequented often to dance and hang out with friends. We entered the cocktail lounge. Civilians sat at the bar and tables, drinking, talking, and even laughing.

We had stepped from a grim world where war was a reality to a world bubbling with glee and showed no signs of the horror we were living through just a stone's throw up the road. These people didn't wear helmets or carry gas masks. I thought of all the soldiers who had lost limbs. Lives forever changed. I thought of those carted out and wrapped for shallow graves.

My temper flared at the sight of these people who appeared not to have a care in the world. I had cried many nights over soldiers I had tended to. Our emotions ran too deep to come in contact with people who were oblivious to the pain and suffering we'd witnessed.

"Civilians can never understand what military personnel go through," I said. "They don't know what it's like, holding the hand of a dying young man and not even knowing his name because his dog tags are missing They would never be able to cope with it."

"I hate to tell them, but they're sitting on London Bridge," Mary said. "And it's about to fall."

Holding my gas mask and helmet, I couldn't have appeared more conspicuous than if I were a hornet in a bee hive. Though I didn't wish harm on any of them, it still left me feeling disgusted, angry, and frustrated over their sense of normalcy. Something, we couldn't afford to have anymore.

"I feel out of place."

Mary nodded. "Me too. We don't belong here."

"Nope, we sure don't. Let's get back to Sternberg."

Out front, we faced a dilemma. We hadn't considered how we'd get back. I looked in the distance for the blue lights of a cab. "I don't see a cab in sight."

"It never occurred to me we wouldn't be able to get a ride back."

While standing there, an official car pulled up. General Douglas MacArthur stepped from the vehicle. I nudged Mary, and she gasped when she recognized him.

"How are you ladies doing today?" he asked us. He stood tall with a sense of authority.

We stared at him with our mouths gaping open. Finally, I came to my senses. "Fine, sir. Except for the fact, we can't find a cab. I'm not sure how we'll get back to Sternberg."

"Cabs are scarce these days." He opened the passenger door. "Drive them to Sternberg. See they get there safely."

"Thank you, sir," Mary said, still looking at him as if President Roosevelt stood before us.

"Thank you, General MacArthur, sir," I said.

Once we were in the car, he entered the hotel where he stayed.

On the way back, we talked about the people in the hotel who had been relaxed and partying.

"I think they're all spies," I said. "Why else wouldn't they be worried about the Japs?"

Mary laughed. "You're right. They didn't seem worried."

As soon as the driver dropped us off at Sternberg, we squealed about what had just happened. "I can't wait to tell Geneva. She'll never believe it."

"I'm still pinching myself to make sure it really happened."

"I could kick myself for not asking him when help is coming."

Mary sighed. "We were so flabbergasted, we weren't thinking. To think we rode in MacArthur's private car."

"And he even held the door open for us."

We laughed and hurried up the walkway.

Entering the hospital, I was glad to be back with that special group who knew war as we did. The hospital was our sanctuary, and our work kept us sane.

I returned to the officer's ward and walked over to Robbins. I smiled at the lieutenant. "I brought you something."

Robbin's eyes reflected his surprise. "You didn't have to."

I handed him a candy bar. "Enjoy it."

I ended up sharing what had happened to Mary and me. For a while, he forgot about the demons haunting him and enjoyed my story.

"You sure look pretty today," he said, finally noticing I wasn't in my white uniform.

"Thank you. It's nice every now and then to dress up." Unable to think of anything else to say, I sighed. "Well, I'd better go. And don't think because I bought you a candy bar that I'm sweet on you. Though you are looking better without all the bandages."

He winked. "It's not every day I have a girl buying me candy. Your sister told me you're fond of pilots."

"She didn't?"

"Oh, yes she did."

"Well, the candy bar was to cheer you up. That's all."

"Yeah, whatever you say."

I huffed and left. I had a bone to pick with Geneva, my big mouth sister.

RESSA
December 16, 1941

Once again, Mary Harrington and I braved the city together. We had our reservations about going alone, so we asked two officers to accompany us. One was Father Cummings, the Catholic chaplain.

The sky remained overcast with black smoke billowing from buildings still burning from the bombs. Undesirable fumes filled the air. Most of the stores had covered their windows with paper to prevent the light inside from being seen during raids. Sandbags had been piled in front of most of the buildings.

As we drove across the bridge, Mary sighed. "I'll be glad when we get back to Sternberg."

"Why's that?" the officer asked.

"Because I know what to do at Sternberg when we have an air raid, but if one hit now, I wouldn't have a clue what to do or where to run."

"Let's pray we make it back before the planes come," Father Cummings said.

Like Mary said, Sternberg offered a sense of security. I didn't think I'd go into the city again.

"So why'd you come into the city?" the other officer asked.

"Shoes," I replied.

"You don't have any?" Father Cummings playfully asked.

"Plenty, but none that will go with the new khaki nurses' uniforms Mrs. Meyers had made for us. We couldn't keep the white ones clean, not to mention white stands out like a bullseye."

We didn't stay out long. Only long enough to pick up a few items. I purchased Geneva and me a pair of tan shoes. Unlike previous purchases, there was no bartering over the items. We were lucky to find a store still open.

Unlike the Europeans at the hotel, the Filipinos appeared anxious and in a hurry. Their expressions reflected their fear. I could understand how scared they were of things to come.

RESSA
December 17ᵗʰ 1941

At breakfast, we had to say goodbye to the Navy nurses. They would join Dorothy Still and some other Navy nurses who had been at the Jai Alai Club taking care of civilians or military. But now they were to open a hospital at Santa Scholastica in Manila. While they had been with us, they had been a big help.

I hugged Mary Harrington. "Take care, Red. I'm going to miss you."

"When this is over, we'll meet up in New York and go on a real shopping spree."

"I'm counting on it."

On my way to the ward, I saw Ruth Straub. She had been sent back from Stotsenberg and admitted as a patient. Once she had received news about her fiancé, Glen Alder, the pressure of the bombing and his death pushed her over the edge. From what I had heard, he had received a cracked skull and had been expected to make it. He had even called to speak to her. But shortly afterwards, she received the devastating news.

I patted her hand. "Ruth, I just wanted to check on you."

"I wish I could be brave like the others."

She was referring to all the nurses who had lost boyfriends, husbands, and friends and still continued to work day and night to save others.

"You've been through a lot. Rest."

"He wanted us to get married, so I might be sent back home. I wanted to stay here to be closer to him. Now, I wish we had married."

Clara entered the room and administered Ruth's scheduled dose of luminal to keep her calm.

Once she drifted off to sleep, I left. I feared Geneva was setting herself up for such a heartache.

After my shift, I found Geneva in one of the areas off to the side. I sat across from her. "Is Jerry back?"

"No, they expect him back soon with a load of wounded."

Though Geneva claimed it was just a friendship, I suspected there was more. "You're getting really fond of him."

My sister shrugged off the comment. "No more than you are of a certain lieutenant in your ward."

"He's a patient. That's all. He'll be returning to duty soon. He might not be as lucky next time around. Since there aren't any more planes, he'll be sent out to join his squadron and fight with the guerillas." Tears clogged my throat, so I changed the subject. "Did Jerry have any news?"

"He said they've been moving supplies to the jungles outside of Bataan. He's sure they plan to evacuate us soon."

"But with all the mines, the Japs haven't been successful at getting into Manila Bay," I replied.

"Jerry said they're coming through Luzon. They came through the Lingayen Gulf and Legaspi. Our Army is moving out of Manila for the sake of the civilians."

Mary Lohr approached us. "More patients just arrived from Stotzenberg Hospital. It's too close to Clark Field. They're afraid they'll get bombed."

"You don't say?" Geneva shook her head. "Well, I'm surprised they haven't transferred the nurses here. I wonder what they're waiting for."

"Lord-a mercy." I placed my hand over my heart. "They're getting closer all the time."

Mary sighed. "Help has to be on the way."

I grew weary. "It takes a couple of weeks to get over here. That is if they left right after Pearl Harbor was bombed."

"They should be arriving sometime this week or at least by the next week." Geneva stood and brushed the wrinkles from her uniform. "I've got to get back to the ward. I'll see you ladies later."

We all tried to calculate how long it'd take for ships to arrive to save us so all this madness would end.

RESSA
December 19, 1941

A few days later, I stood in the ambulatory ward upstairs, updating a patient's file.

Boom!

Boom!

My heart leapt in my throat. My hearing faded out from the deafening noise. When I regained my wits, I turned to evacuate my patients. They had gone. I locked down my ward and hurried outside to catch up with them. "Hey, wait!"

Outside, I finally caught up with them. "The alarm hasn't even sounded."

"I'm not waiting for no dang alarm," one sailor stated.

"Those bombs were warning enough for me," another soldier added.

The alarm sounded a good ten minutes later. I realized we had become so accustomed to the raids that we had become relaxed on our procedures. Part of it was from all the false alarms set off by the Fifth Columnist working with the Japs to break our morale. Most of our patients already suffered from shellshock, and the false alarms had an adverse effect on them.

"I'm more afraid of fire," one soldier said to me. "I don't want to burn up. I can't think of a more painful way to die."

"I understand." I couldn't think of anything else to say. My senses and reactions had dulled from all the fear of seeing so many brave men die. But one thing that was worse than fear, was waiting. It could take another week before help would arrive.

I hurried to my assigned spot and jumped in the foxhole. It scared me because Geneva hadn't come out. I knew she was on duty and with her patients. Afterwards, I crawled out, stood, and brushed the grass and dirt off. I'd given up on keeping clean. No sooner than I'd put on a clean one, I'd end up right back in the foxhole. At least the darker uniforms didn't show dirt like the white ones.

For the rest of the day, I jumped at my own shadow.

And when another air raid sounded, I hurried from the hospital. Normally, my first thought would be to find Geneva and protect her, but this time I panicked.

I froze in place and dropped to the ground. Lying on my back, I stared up at the planes flying above us and counted over eighty-four. I couldn't move.

Our anti-aircraft guns fired on the planes.

Without thought, I turned and was halfway under the building's foundation when I heard my name being called.

"Hey, Miss Jenkins," a young private shouted. "Where you going?" He started laughing and helped me up.

My cheeks warmed when I realized I had given into my fears. I'd have a good story to share with the other nurses that night in the living room.

In the ward, I looked at Dr. MacNeil as he entered. "I wonder what that was about this morning. It didn't last long."

He nodded. "Long enough to cause injuries. The quartermaster had his boys moving footlockers. Didn't hear the planes until it was too late. They're badly banged up."

"Geneva is working in emergency today. She'll probably be one of the nurses taking care of them."

Later that day, I hid a ham and biscuit in a napkin and carried it to a newly admitted soldier who complained of being hungry. "Don't let anyone see this. Here's some water too."

He smiled. "Thanks, Miss Jenkins. Gosh dog, I was out in the marshes for two days with no food or water. When my buddy rescued me, he wasn't expecting to find me alive."

I stood beside him redressing his wounds. "I'm sure he was delighted."

"He was. We were glad to see each other. He laughed when I grabbed an apple and ate it faster than termites on a toothpick."

I laughed, trying not to let my emotions get the upper hand. Because, truth be known, I wanted to cry. Once well enough, most of these boys would be thrown back into combat. Amazingly, most were eager to go.

"Shoot, we were finding all kinds of stuff blown from the stores and tossed into the streets. Even women's stockings. We buried a ton of whiskey at the beach, hoping we'd get back to it later."

"Anyone here seen my pants?" Sergeant Zimmerman asked, interrupting the soldier.

"You're wearing them," I couldn't resist saying.

"Not this pair." He frowned. "I had them hanging on the ward door."

I tossed a sheet over the soldier, then looked at the sergeant. "Remember that tall Marine who came in without any pants?"

His eyes lit with acknowledgement. "I'll see if I can catch him before he gets away with my pants."

I looked at the soldier, and we laughed.

Unfortunately, Zimmerman caught up with the Marine and took his pants. The Marine remained in his briefs until someone could find him some clothes.

I shared the story with Lieutenant Robbins. He actually smiled. He had a wonderful smile. Hopefully, it was an indication he was coming to terms with the death of his comrades. I still hadn't found the nerve to ask if he were married. Knowing he could have a wife back home kept my feelings at a professional level. I wasn't going to be one of those nurses who engaged in a wartime romance.

"When are you going to bring me another candy bar?" Robert asked, then winked.

"I'm not. I wouldn't want you thinking I'm sweet on you. Why just today, I gave a handsome soldier an extra ham and biscuit. Not once did he accuse me of being sweet on him. You're just full of yourself." I smiled. "But that's what I like a about you, flyboys. You're all so arrogant and self-assured."

I needed to distance my heart from these men. Any day they could be returned to battle and not survive. It was a hard fact of war.

That night, we had so many raids. Though the bombing had grown worse, none of them fell closer than Nichols Field and Port Area.

RESSA
December 23, 1941

We headed for the living room during the air raid and laid on the floor. Many of us had grown tired of running outside between the bombs dropping. It gave us a chance to visit.

"Eighty enemy ships were sighted off Lingayen Gulf," Juanita said to all the nurses in the huge living room of the nurses' quarter.

"Our forces are prepared for them," Helen countered.

"I'm not so sure we can hold the Japs off," Dorothy added. "They've been sweeping through the Philippines as fast as a Kansas grass fire in July."

Helen shook her head. "There's still no sign of a U.S. convoy coming our way. No officials have commented on it."

"Maybe the weather's been too rough to cross the sea," Mary Lohr suggested.

"It could be the production of new planes has been held up for some reason," Clara added.

The bombs started back shaking everything around us.

The phone rang.

"Jenkins, it's for you," shouted a Filipino boy over the noise of the shells and guns.

On my belly, I scooted across the room.

"I've seen snakes that couldn't move that well," Dorothy said, teasing me.

I continued wriggling on my stomach toward the phone.

"Go Jenkins! You're almost there," Mary shouted.

"I can't wait to tell Geneva about this," Anne remarked.

My face heated with embarrassment. Still, I made it to the opposite side of the room. The worker lowered the phone to me. I took the receiver and held it to my ear, making sure to remain on my belly. "Hello."

"This is Major Halstead from Fort Santiago. I need your serial numbers and addresses for the identification tags."

Over the horrific noise, I called out our numbers and gave him our addresses for our dog tags. A lot of the nurses were having them made fearful that if our bodies were burned severely, no one would be able to identify us and notify our families.

In the background, I heard him tell someone, "This girl's scared to death."

When he returned, I said, "Why I am not."

78

"Then what are you doing?"

"I'm flat on the floor. Sir, we're in the middle of our noonday raid."

After the call and the raid had stopped, we sat up and resumed our conversation.

When Josie entered the room, we grew silent. She stood before us appearing grim and concerned. "I just received orders to send twenty-four American nurses and twenty-four Filipina nurses to Bataan to open a thousand-bed hospital. I want everyone here to report to the dining room in one hour packed and ready to leave."

My heart sank. "Josie, Geneva's in the ward. I can't go without her. Please may she come too?"

"Yes, go get her now."

I hugged Josie. "Thank you. I can't stand the thought of us being separated."

She nodded. "Understandable. You'd better hurry."

"I will." I dashed off to find Geneva, but as I passed the officer's ward, I ducked inside the door and hurried to Lieutenant Robbins. "Are you awake?"

"Yes, I can't sleep."

"I'm not supposed to tell anyone, but I'm being moved to jungle Hospital No. 1. I won't be here tomorrow."

"I'll miss you. No one else will sneak candy in for me or is as interesting as you."

"I'll miss you too. Maybe our paths will cross again. I have to go now."

He lifted my hand to his lips and kissed the back of it. "Good luck, Ressa."

"You too. May God keep you safe." I squeezed his hand, then walked away. Just maybe I hadn't kept my distance as I'd planned, because my heart was breaking just a little.

GENEVA
December 23, 1941

I was in the process of charting when Ressa approached me. I could tell by her demeanor something had happened.

"Geneva, Josie just told me we're going to Bataan."

"Is that so? When?"

"Now, so put down what you're doing."

"How many of us are leaving?"

"Twenty-four of us American nurses and an equal number of Filipinos. We're going to set up a thousand-bed hospital. I don't know about you, but I am ready for a change of scenery."

"Not me. I've been dreading this. I knew it was coming. Jerry's not back. I wish he were here, so I could tell him goodbye."

"Leave him a note."

I nodded. "I'll write it now."

"We're going out just at the right time," Ressa said. "They're bringing in twenty more nurses from Stotsenberg tomorrow. It's getting a little crowded here."

We checked our suitcases. We fell into a routine of packing and reevaluating what we would take and what we could do without. This time we had the added excitement of knowing we were actually going.

Dorothy Scholl came in, "I was supposed to leave with the second group evacuating, but I got permission to leave with you. While I was asking, I learned we won't be leaving until tomorrow morning. So, you two can relax."

"That's good news." I hoped Jerry would return that night or early in the morning, so I could tell him goodbye in person.

"We'd better stock up on cigarettes, candy, gum, or anything else you like because you won't find any of that where we're headed. I'm going to make the trip into town. Figured you might want to tag along."

"Thanks, Dorothy. Give us a second, and we'll go with you."

"Take your time."

"Grab your money, Geneva. We've got some serious shopping to do." I turned back to Dorothy. "Do you still have room for my radio?"

"Sure," Dorothy replied. "I've got plenty of room. Like I told you before, I always pack light. I'll get it when we come back from the store."

Ressa smiled. "Great. Thanks."

Dorothy was a lifesaver. We beat the mad rush and had no problem buying what we needed. After stocking up on my favorite luxury items, I bought the limit on cigarettes. I had never smoked and never would, but Ressa and some of our friends did. I planned to hide several packs in case they ran out later.

Ressa purchased a certain lieutenant a bag of candy bars to last him. When we returned, she hurried to his ward.

I checked over and over to see if Jerry had returned. He hadn't. I was told he had gone to Nichols Field, where so much of the bombing was taking place.

Later, Ressa and I pulled out a map and spread it on the bed. She pointed to Bataan. "This is where we're going. It's a peninsula with Corregidor at its southern tip. It's separated from the mainland by Manila Bay on one side and the China Sea on the other."

My stomach twirled around. "I bet there's a lot of snakes there."

Ressa smiled. "Look at it this way, it might help you get over your fear of them."

I didn't find any reassurance in her comment.

That night, I laid quietly as did Ressa. I stayed lost in my thoughts. I had written Jerry a letter and left it with a nurse who promised to get it to him. I hoped he'd eventually be sent to one of the jungle hospitals. I flinched over what I'd said. I wanted him there as a medic, not a patient.

Neither of us seemed able to sleep. My sister broke the silence. "Geneva, it feels so odd."

"I know. I feel it too."

"Leaving is depressing."

"Yes, and sad."

"That's it exactly," Ressa said. "I was remembering when we first got here, the beauty of the place and the friendly people. I couldn't believe they were paying me to be here."

"I remember my first impression of Sternberg, the huge lobby and that massive staircase. I was thinking if the folks back home could see me now. There are a lot of things about this place I'm going to miss."

Ressa turned on her side facing me. "I'll always remember the fun we've had here, riding horses, swimming, and dancing at the club. Do you think we'll ever have it that good again?"

I remained silent for several minutes. Tears ran from the corners of my eyes to my pillow. I had the foreboding feeling the answer to her question was no. I didn't respond.

GENEVA
December 24, 1941

The wards each held seventy beds, and every single one was occupied. Usually, four nurses and four corpsmen worked a ward. So, every extra nurse would make life easier. Several of the nurses who'd volunteered to help at Stotsenberg had returned, along with the other nurses on staff there. They would be assigned where most needed.

We were up at 5:00 a.m. and gathered in the dining room for breakfast. We all ate a hearty meal, because we didn't know when we'd eat again.

I listened to Cassie's experience wondering if I could have been as brave. I sat at the table and sipped my coffee.

"When they finally loaded us on the train, an officer handed me a gun, I was shocked," Cassie said. "He showed me how to use it, and then told me I was to protect everyone on the train. He instructed me to shoot anyone who tried to stop it."

Ressa stared in awe at the young American Italian. "I would have fainted right there."

"You're not so bad with a shotgun," I said.

"So long as I'm aiming at a deer and not a Japanese Army."

"Exactly," Cassie said. "Like I could hold off the Nips."

We laughed, but we knew how frightened she must have been. I wondered if I would've been that brave if I had been in her position.

"Did you have to use it?" Adele asked.

"No, thank goodness. Words can't describe the destruction we saw," Cassie said. "Destruction to the buildings, the planes, and our soldiers. We were so afraid the Japs would return that we slept in a concrete bunker built beneath the pharmacy instead of one of the barracks left standing."

"It was cramped and just downright nasty," Phyliss Arnold added.

"Did you get bombed again?" Adele asked.

"You bet," Phyllis said. "I just knew we'd die."

"I was caught in the open," Cassie told us. "I had gone out for some air, and I saw the planes coming right at me."

"About seventy of them," Phyliss added.

Cassie scooted to the edge of the chair and leaned forward. "The Zeros started shelling us. I ran and jumped into an empty concrete swimming pool and huddled against the wall."

"I'm glad you're all safe now," I whispered.

"We heard some interesting scuttlebutt on our way here. Rumor has it, that MacArthur left Manila and moved his headquarters to Corregidor yesterday," Cassie said. "Seems like we're getting out just in time."

Other nurses talked about our evacuation. But I knew not all the nurses were going. Some had been told to stay and even be prepared to be captured. They had to remain behind with all the patients who couldn't travel.

"The Army Medical Department asked Tokyo permission to take the Mactan loaded with wounded to Australia," Willa Hooks said.

Dorothy's brows rose slightly. "Where'd you hear that?"

"I can't tell you. I promised I wouldn't say anything. I will say Florence McDonald is going to select a nurse to go with them."

We didn't probe more. Instead, I resumed eating. The merchant ship had been declared a Red Cross vessel, so I figured there was some truth to her rumor.

"Did Jerry make it back?" Ressa asked me.

I stirred the cream in my coffee. "No, but I left a letter with Francis. She promised to get it to him."

"I didn't go back to Robert's ward. I said goodbye when I carried the bag of candy to him."

"Was he thrilled?"

"Yes, very much so. He promised to look me up if he gets out our way." Ressa spread jelly on a piece of toast. "Though, I doubt he will. He'll probably join his squadron."

Before leaving, we were each handed a sack lunch for the long trip.

At 6:00 that morning, we lined up outside ready to climb into the car when I saw a military medic's truck pull up. Jerry rode up front with the driver.

"Ma'am, get in, please. You have a long trip."

Jerry turned just in time to see me. The most I could do was wave. He returned the wave. I drew in a breath as I lowered into the car. I knew he'd read my letter that morning. Hopefully, our paths would cross again.

We stopped at Jai-Alai where we picked up others being moved out. Our group consisted of a hundred corpsmen, forty-eight nurses, and twenty doctors. I had hoped Mary Harrington would be one of them, but she wasn't. I worried about her and the other Naval nurses left in Manila.

They assigned us to buses. As usual, Ressa and I were kept together.

Dorothy stepped forward with her bag. "Here comes our bus."

"It's a Pambusco," Ressa said. "This will be like sightseeing."

These sightseeing buses were popular in the Philippines and had two different seating arrangements. Seats either faced the front in rows or sideways. They were also open all the way around.

"Thank God, our seats are facing the front," Ressa said, fanning herself.

That was a great relief to us. We would still probably be filthy, but the poor souls who ended up facing the sides would receive the dirt head on. Not to mention riding on rough roads while sitting sideways would make me nauseated.

"Why are we the only nurses on this bus?" I asked.

"I was wondering the same thing," Dorothy added.

We both looked at Ressa, who merely shrugged her shoulders and added, "Don't look at me, you know as much as I do."

A soldier overseeing our transfer explained that every bus in the caravan was strategically loaded with similar combinations. Each carried a sufficient number of people and supplies to set up and maintain a hospital ward. If one bus was destroyed, it wouldn't kill the overall plan.

Our bus finally pulled out and headed toward the jungle.

"This is going to be a rough ride," Dorothy remarked, as the first cloud of dust swirled around us.

I fanned the dust from my face. "You can say that again."

As we reached the countryside, the damage done to barrios surprised us. The overall destruction to the land broke our hearts.

Crowds of local villagers cheered and waved enthusiastically, holding up two fingers.

"What does that mean?" I asked.

The driver held up two fingers and said, "They make a V. It stands for victory."

We shouted back, displaying the same sign. Their spirit boosted our morale. I never understood why Japan bothered bombing native villages. What could they do, shoot rocks out of a bamboo cannon?

Ressa nudged me lightly. "I'm hungry."

"Me too," Dorothy added.

I looked at the men with us. Not a one of them had brought anything to eat. "This puts us in an awkward position."

My sister nodded. "There's only one thing we can do."

Dorothy and I knew what she meant. I took out my bagged lunch. "Let's get it over with."

Ressa turned facing the men. "We didn't bring a feast, but I think we have enough to share."

"That's mighty generous of you," one soldier said.

"We don't want to take your lunch," another one added.

"Nonsense, we won't eat in front of you," I insisted.

We unpacked our lunches and started dividing them. Our traveling companions were hungrier than we were. Even though the portions were small the men were extremely grateful. The small act of sharing created a pleasant atmosphere of camaraderie.

I nibbled my boiled egg as I watched them divide my sandwich. I wish I hadn't been so hungry because I would've given my egg to them.

We didn't see another bus around. This was done purposely in case a Japanese bomber flew overhead. As we drove deeper into the jungle, dust blew up in our faces and covered us. I had dirt in my mouth and eyes. Fortunately, it didn't show on our tan uniforms.

Several civilians ran toward the bus, screaming and pointing upward. We immediately drove to the side of the road under a thick canopy to shield us from view. The driver slammed on the brakes. "Everybody out! Run for cover!"

The engines of Zero bombers roared above us.

We ran from the bus into the tall trees along the road. My heart rose in my throat, and I had a difficult time catching my breath. I laid on the ground sandwiched between Dorothy and Ressa. I closed my eyes and prayed they wouldn't see us or the bus.

The Zeros passed over without incident.

The soft underbrush had made a fairly comfortable refuge. Now, I probably smelled like plants. The vegetation held a distinct odor, not bad just odd.

One of the soldiers offered me his hand. "Let me help you up."

"Thank you. For Heaven's sake, I don't think I'll ever get used to this."

"No matter how many times you hear it, it's just as terrifying," he said.

"All clear! It's clear," several men shouted together.

We brushed leaves and twigs off our tan uniforms and walked back to the bus. The soldiers graciously helped us aboard.

I picked leaves from my hair. "I'm looking forward to the day when Japs are running for cover."

"I'm with you. It will be nice seeing those little bastards get a dose of their own medicine," Dorothy added.

I studied our surroundings. To the North, Mount Mariveles and the surrounding peaks ran across the land until they met the ocean.

We hadn't traveled far before stopping again. This time it was at a small barrio. Still hungry, I hoped they offered food. "Let's get out and stretch our legs."

"I'm more interested in something to eat," Dorothy admitted.

"Me too." Ressa stood and walked toward the back of the bus.

At the barrio, we purchased a variety of fresh fruit—bananas, papayas, mangoes, and a big bottle of gin.

Dorothy grinned slyly. "This might calm our nerves."

I winked. "I'm counting on it."

"Think one is enough?" Ressa asked.

"I should hope so." Dorothy giggled. "We won't be able to walk when we get there."

Once back on the dusty road, we started eating the fruit and drinking the gin. But we had only taken a swig or two before the men noticed we had it.

"You ladies gonna share?" a soldier shouted.

"Sure," I said and passed the bottle to him. By the time it made it back around, there wasn't a drop left.

The jovial atmosphere created from our companions drinking gin was contagious.

A deep voice of a corpsman, I think his name was Trigg, sang out, "Oh, don't sit under the mango tree with anyone else but me."

We helped with the chorus. He sang another verse. Again, we joined in on the chorus. "Don't dive in the foxhole with anyone else but me. Anyone else but me, anyone else but me. No No No."

Within seconds the entire bus sang along. It seemed strange that we were at war in the process of evacuating, yet we behaved like school kids on a field trip. We laughed so hard and so long our sides ached. Even our two doctors had joined in on the fun.

Driving through Bataan, we drove past a small barrio consisting of about a dozen buildings and a few stores strung out along the main road. A few natives congregated by the road in front. It took some time getting used to seeing these people relieve themselves in public. But it was the way of life for the villagers.

Despite the civilians evacuating, many of the stores appeared open. We passed Filipino scouts who'd taken up refuge in the area. The jungle consumed almost everything with thick undergrowth. Tall acacia and coconut palms with vines draped over them thrived in the humid climate and rich soil. The vegetation could take over rapidly. Since this was the dry season, very little water flowed beneath the bridges we crossed.

On the trip, my mind drifted to home and memories of past Christmases. Right now, Mom would be brining the turkey and cooking pies and cakes. My brothers and sisters would be there. They'd be wrapping gifts and popping popcorn. My heart ached for home and family.

Then my thoughts drifted to Jerry, and I wondered if I'd see him again. His job was dangerous. Sometimes, the Japs would lay in wait for the medics and the soldiers who returned for the wounded and dead and attack them as well.

Ahead I saw soldiers with rifles in their hands.

I thought of the Fifth Columnist and wondered if we were driving into a trap.

Jungle Life
Part Three

RESSA
December 24, 1941

Our bus stopped at the bridge. Fortunately, the soldiers were Filipino scouts and motioned us past them. We finally reached Camp Limay around five on Christmas Eve.

Several buses from Sternberg had arrived before us.

I looked around. "I have a bad feeling about this."

"About what?" Geneva asked.

"That." I pointed to a row of shanties on stilts. "I think that's Hospital No. 1."

"Good Lord, I think you're right," Dorothy added.

I frowned. "Well, if that doesn't beat all."

The people from the other buses had already unloaded and stood around talking. Our luggage that had been carried in a truck had arrived. We stepped off the bus, gathered our luggage, and joined the other nurses.

"It doesn't look like anyone is coming to greet us," I said. It was the custom to offer a greeting to arrivals at a new post.

"Apparently not," Geneva said. "Looks like we'll be roughing it."

Dorothy turned to us. "I heard this was the barracks for the 45th Infantry Filipino scouts, but they were ordered to move out. The only ones nearby are the America Quartermaster Corps."

Another nurse we didn't know joined us. "That's true. The scouts left things just the way they were. So, you might find your quarters in shambles. It's the luck of the draw."

Geneva placed one hand on her hip. "Well, that's just dandy."

We met nurses sent here from hospitals at McKinley and Camp John Hay. They were reunited with nurses who had transferred earlier from their hospitals to Sternberg.

The jungle had a distinct smell of undergrowth and rot. Thank goodness a nice ocean breeze blew over the camp. Colorful birds fluttered beneath the canopy, and monkeys scampered about in the trees. Wild flowers grew abundantly.

I couldn't believe this would be our new home. It reminded me of something out of a Johnny Weissmuller *Tarzan* movie. The buildings constructed of bamboo with thatch roofs of palm branches stood on stilts. They had windows with shutters but no glass, and doorways without doors-just long curtains.

Two long buildings stood parallel to the rows of nipa-covered barracks. Some of them faced the ocean and mountains. People strolled through a large grassy compound with trees scattered about. The barracks appeared deserted.

"What do we do?" I asked Geneva and Dorothy.

They shrugged. We stood watching more buses pull in.

An officer approached us. "Ladies, the nurses will occupy the old officers' quarters at the far end of the post. Gather your gear and head that way."

Carrying my belongings, I walked in the direction he pointed. Geneva lagged behind to find a latrine. Dorothy and I climbed the steps of the barracks to a large screened porch. We left our bags outside while we went inside to select a bed.

I came to two large rooms with four or five beds, but with further exploration, I discovered a tiny room with one bed. Nipa partitions separated the rooms and left gaps at the top and bottom for ventilation. The corner room had a full wall and a window that opened to the porch. I'd never had my own room. I had always roomed with someone. This suited me, so I went back for my luggage and staked my claim.

Nurses kept coming to claim their beds, but I didn't see Geneva.

"This is a pigsty," shouted Helen Summers, who'd been on another bus. Her Brooklyn accent distinct.

"No, I've seen pigpens that were cleaner than this," I said.

"There aren't any beds left," Juanita Redmond complained. "What are we supposed to sleep, the floor?"

Agnes Barre frowned. "The floor is disgusting."

She was younger than most of us and wore a flower in her hair.

Geneva found me. "I didn't get here in time to grab a bed. Why didn't you save me a spot?"

"I thought you'd get here in time to pick your own. I'm sorry. In my defense, I'm tired, dirty, and hungry. I wasn't thinking."

Geneva sighed. "I'd prefer to sleep on the porch anyway."

"You can keep your things in here. You'd better go claim a spot."

She couldn't depend on me for everything. Nevertheless, guilt edged its way into my mind for not snagging her a cot.

We were all disheartened at the filthy conditions of the quarters.

"This place is appalling," Earleen Allen shouted. "I don't think I've ever seen this much dust and dirt."

"The floors are covered in sand," Helen complained. "It sticks to my feet."

"The girls arriving tomorrow are in for a big surprise," Leona said. "I can hear them whining already."

I joined the others out on the porch. They wore long faces that reflected their disappointment.

"I just want to cry. I thought we were coming to a place that had been prepared for us," Jean Kennedy commented. "I don't need this now."

"Same here," Dorothy admitted.

"I'm so hungry it's hard to think about anything else," Agnes commented.

"My bed has soiled linens. There are soiled, mildewed clothes and trash piled in the room," Earleen grumbled.

"Mine too," Agnes added.

Dorothy huffed. "I bet there aren't any supplies or equipment here."

I didn't say anything. I had been fortunate. My room had been left in a decent condition other than the dust. The officer who had occupied it had even left clean sheets.

"One thing working at Sternberg taught me, war is never what you expect," I said.

"Amen to that." Dorothy scratched her arms. "This place makes me itch."

"What about bathrooms?" I asked. "Has anyone checked it out?"

"I did." Geneva frowned. "Only two toilets and two sinks for twenty-four of us to share. The Filipino nurses have the same. If you think this is dirty wait until you see those nasty toilets. And the outhouse is on stilts. So, whatever goes in has to drop a long way down and anyone passing by can see it."

"Just be glad we have them at all," Frankie Lewey commented.

92

An officer stepped on the porch. "Ladies, there are plenty of beds and mattresses in the shed. Follow me. We'll try to get you set up for the night."

I walked with Geneva to a tin covered storage facility. "You grab a headboard, and I'll get the footboard."

"That can wait. Help me with a mattress first. I want to pick one of the nicer ones."

"Aren't you the clever one."

We searched for the cleanest mattress in the pile and found one that looked like it hadn't had much use.

Jean Kennedy pulled another good mattress out. "Where'd these come from?"

"They're leftover from the Great War." The officer frowned. "Just like our weapons and equipment."

I didn't miss the sarcasm in his tone. Since no rescue convoys had come, we were all feeling bitter and deserted.

After several trips, we had Geneva's bed set up on the porch right outside my window. Now, she needed linens. The work had kept us busy and our minds off our stomachs.

A boy from the quartermasters joined us on the porch. "Report to the quartermaster's mess, ladies."

"Hallelujah," Dorothy shouted. "We won't go to bed hungry."

Earleen did a little dance and clapped her hands. "Don't you have a radio?"

"Yes. I was told generators provide electricity to the camp. I haven't tried the radio out yet."

"When we return from dinner, let's try it out. Music might just cheer this place up."

I patted my stomach. "Right now, I'm only interested in food."

All the nurses streamed to the mess hall and joined a line of people waiting to be served. The man serving gave us each a portion of beans and a piece of bread. I took my plate and stopped to grab a cup of coffee. I was glad to see the corpsmen who had traveled with us being fed.

We sat at long tables. My thoughts drifted to other Christmas Eves in Tennessee where life had been much simpler. "I figured Dad has the tree up and trimmed."

Geneva smiled. "Mom's fussin' that he didn't trim it enough. It's always too tall or too wide."

I laughed. "She's usually right. It's either leaning or bent at the top. I miss Dad taking us on sleigh rides."

"Then we'd make snow cream." Geneva sighed longing for home.

"Let's pray that none of them ever spend a Christmas Eve like this."

Geneva slapped her hand on the table. "Amen to that."

After dinner, I was still hungry. I'm sure the others were too, but not wanting to seem ungracious, none of us complained.

As we were leaving, we all thanked them for sharing their rations with us.

"Ladies, you're invited back for breakfast, but then you'll need to set up your own mess hall."

We found a nice surprise on the porch. The soldiers had left clean linens for our beds. We quickly made up the beds.

Lieutenant Rosemary Hogan, who'd been put in charge of the nurses, joined us. "At night, we'll have a complete black out. No lights. Don't even think of lighting up a cigarette. It's enough light to give a Jap a clear target from the sky."

"Where can we smoke?" I asked.

"You don't smoke at night. Not in the bathrooms or rooms."

I had planned to find a nice spot and smoke one before turning in, but that plan had just gone up in flames.

"Try that radio," Earleen shouted. "It might cheer us up."

"I know what would cheer you up." Juanita gave Earleen a coy smile. "Seeing your dentist, Dr. Francis."

"If you're dating a dentist, I guess you daydream about him checking your bicuspids," Evelyn Whitlow said.

"Having your teeth examined can be very intimate," Helen teased.

We all laughed.

I turned the radio on but couldn't connect with any stations. "I'm not picking up anything." After dragging that thing all the way into the jungles, it wouldn't do us any good. I figured the Japs had the signals blocked. "We'll try again tomorrow."

"I'd love to hear news from home," Lucy Wilson added.

After cleaning our rooms, we sat on the porch and talked. We shared some candy bars and talked about the nurses and doctors we'd left in Manila.

"The Duck has arrived," Whitlow said. "And he's not thrilled to be here without his favorite nurse."

"Quack, quack," several of us said. He was a surgeon from Sternberg and not our favorite doctor. She referred to Francis Nash. Though profanity spewed from her mouth on occasion, she ran a surgical ward like the captain of a ship. She had to be one of the best surgical nurses in the Army.

Dorothy Scholl held her hands palms up. "Listen. Isn't this strange? No sirens. No planes flying over or bombs going off."

"I like it," I said. "The noises were what wracked my nerves."

"I hated the constant smoke," Ann Wurts commented.

"Here we only have the waves crashing the beach, the birds, and monkeys chattering in the trees," Inez McDonald said.

Helen turned toward Inez. "At least the mosquitoes aren't a problem here."

A group of us walked toward the shore. Across the bay in the distance, flames shot into the sky coming from Cavite Naval Base. "Did they get hit?" I asked.

One of the Naval nurses we had picked up shook her head. "No, they're destroying the ammunition dump and burning all the fuel so the Japs don't get it."

Later in my room, I discovered a footlocker under my bed. I pushed it to the window and stood on it to peer out at Geneva.

She rolled on her back. "Why are you hovering over me?"

I laughed. "I'm dying for a cigarette."

"It'd be a good time to quit those nasty things."

"I know, but it's like the only pleasure I have right now. I'll quit when I get out of this mess." I changed the subject. "When you need to get in here, just come through the window."

"You'd better try and sleep. Something tells me tomorrow is going to be a long hard day of cleaning."

"I'm sure you're right." I finally settled in my bed. The night was soft and warm. The only sounds I could hear were small animals scurrying about, the flutter of nighttime birds on the hunt, and the swish-swish of the water lapping the shore. Quiet and peaceful compared to Manila's chaos.

I thought of my Christmas wish for everyone tonight. *Peace on Earth.*

RESSA
December 25, 1941   Christmas Day

Noise traveled through our quarters since the walls were only constructed of nipa. Christmas morning, we were all wide awake by seven. The day couldn't have been more beautiful with a warm welcoming sun to greet us.

In an open area not concealed by trees, the Filipino boys had put down white sheets with the Red Cross emblem in the center to say we're a hospital. Hospitals were supposed to be off limits from bombing. I wasn't so sure the Japanese followed the rules of war.

As we headed to the mess hall, a plane flew over, and we ducked for cover. My heartrate surged.

"Reconnaissance mission. No bomber with them," one of the boys shouted. "You're safe."

We thanked him. I'm sure he was amazed how quickly we could move. We made our way to the mess hall and feasted on pancakes and strong black coffee. Though bitter, anything going into my stomach helped ease the hunger pangs.

"Merry Christmas, ladies. This might be the most we have all day, so enjoy it," I said.

"Merry Christmas," other nurses echoed back. But after that we didn't mention it being Christmas. The memories it stirred caused a painful longing for family and home. No assignments had been given, so we spent most of our time cleaning our quarters.

This place held an ambience of solitude and peace. It almost made me forget the hell we'd gone through in Manila—the constant droning sirens and loud announcements accompanied by bombers roaring over us.

Wanting to smoke away from camp, a group of us hiked a short distance from the buildings and discovered a wire fence. Beyond the fence, a nice grassy meadow stretched across a wide area with the road to Manila running through it.

"Look, there's a barrio hidden over there in those palms," Juanita said.

"There are only a few villagers left," Geneva pointed out. "The civilians have gone."

"Seems that way." Dorothy plucked at her clothes that clung to her. "Anyone with half a brain is long gone from these islands."

From there, we strolled down to the ocean just behind our barracks. I expected to see a beautiful tropical beach and clear water, but instead, it was rough and dirty.

"Well, at least if we're bombed, we can jump in the water," Juanita said.

Dorothy examined an object washed ashore. "I guess that's better than burning to death."

Earleen Allen approached us. "Chaplain Father Cummings will be here around nine-thirty to hold a Christmas mass. Anyone interested in attending be at the officers' mess."

"Too bad Dr. Francis isn't here. Father Cummings could perform the ceremony. Just look at all the bridesmaids you would have," Nancy Gillahan said, wearing an expression of amusement.

Earleen sighed. "Well, he's not here."

Geneva and I along with the others made our way to mass. Though we weren't Catholic, we still attended. I hadn't seen Father Cummins since he'd gone to town with Mary Harrington and me. We waited to hear the Christmas story. We thought it peculiar he didn't wear his robe.

"Today, I thought I'd share about the robe of the priest. I will explain the purpose and use of the amice, alb, cincture, stole and chasuble. As he described each one, he put it on until he was fully robed.

The mass finished with us singing *Silent Night*. While singing, so many memories flooded my mind. I couldn't stop the tears from streaming down my face as that longing to be home hit harder than ever. Geneva wiped her teary eyes, then squeezed my hand. "Maybe if the war ends soon, we'll be home for Christmas next year."

I nodded. "I hope so."

Leaving the mess hall, the sight of soldiers digging foxholes greeted us. Any warm fuzzy feelings or the false sense of security left us immediately. We snapped back to reality. Prayers for peace could help our souls, but life is tied to physical preservation.

Our alarm sounded. My heart leapt. I drew in a deep breath and composed myself. The system consisted of a man standing upon the water tower, watching for bombers. We'd almost forgotten he was there, until he banged something metal against the tank. Though not as harsh as a siren, the message was just as nerve-wracking.

Planes headed toward Manila and Corregidor on a bombing mission. The roar of their engines buzzed in my ears like a thousand stinging hornets. Though they'd flown over us, we knew their mission meant trouble for those we'd left behind. They would bomb Manila.

That afternoon, we shared two brooms to sweep out our quarters.

"These tan dresses are going to be so dirty after we jump in a few fox holes," Dorothy said. "I wish we had something else to wear."

"I'm going to look like a mole coming up," I added.

The others laughed.

"Instead of tan, they should've used navy cloth," Geneva said. "Not only does tan dirty easier, it makes us stick out like pigs in the chicken coop."

Some of the women chuckled. My sister blushed. She had never been one to draw attention to herself. Unlike me. I threw myself in the middle of everything with gusto.

A short while later, we had everything scrubbed down and clean, not that it would stay clean with the open doors and windows.

Afterwards, Geneva and I took a stroll through the camp. Several officers ahead of us sat in a jeep, smoking.

"Ladies, merry Christmas," one said.

"Merry Christmas," I replied. Geneva remained tightlipped.

I pulled out a cigarette. "Got a light?"

"Sure." He held his to the tip of mine until the red glow formed.

"Thanks."

"I'm Lieutenant Daniels with the Quartermasters Corps."

"I'm Lieutenant Smith," the other man said.

"I'm Ressa, and she's Geneva. We're sisters."

"That's something you don't see every day," Daniels said. "Two sisters in the Army."

I drew on the cigarette, then exhaled the smoke. I tried to blow the smoke in a sophisticated way like I'd seen Ida Lupino do in her last movie. She'd appeared so glamorous. I ended up choking instead.

"How you girls adjusting?" Daniels asked.

"I guess our biggest complaint are our tan uniforms. They're filthy." I glanced down at my apparel. Geneva nodded but remained quiet.

"Some of the Filipinos left clothes in barrack bags. You're welcome to go through them to see if any fit. They're clean." Daniels removed his cap, wiped his forehead, and slapped his cap back on.

"We'd love to look. Did they leave any shoes?" I asked.

"Some," Smith said. "Filipinos have small feet. You may find some that fit."

"That'd be just dandy," Geneva finally said.

We walked with them to where the bags were stored. I think they got a kick out of us digging through them and holding clothes up to see if they'd fit. We looked like two shoppers at Macy's in New York. Some of the clothes, while clean, had rips or stained underarms. Anytime we found some that were in good condition, we set them aside.

"I think these trousers should fit you." I handed them to Geneva, who stood slightly taller than me.

She held the pants up. "They look long enough."

"I have three shirts and three pairs of trousers. Let's check out the shoes." We dug through the pile. Daniels was right. The men shoes were very small. "None of these would fit Josie."

Geneva giggled. "Not with her big size thirteen feet."

I'd never seen a woman with such large feet, but Josie was tall.

"What do you think?" I said, holding out my foot, to model the shoe I had on.

Daniels did a cat whistle. "Like those ankles."

"If you like them now, you should see them when I'm wearing heels."

"I wouldn't mind seeing your ankles," Smith said to Geneva.

She blushed. "I just bet you would."

He laughed. "You ladies done shopping?"

We nodded. Then we gathered our loot. We valued these clothes more than jewels. We couldn't have received a better Christmas present.

We entered our barracks with our arms full, still wearing the big stiff heavy shoes. Our shoes clunked the floor, sounding like giants stomping through.

"Hey, whatcha got there?" Dorothy eyed everything we carried with interest.

"Clothes. GI Government issued. America's finest." While I talked, I slipped into my new trousers and shirt. Then I modeled them for the others. "I've never been more comfortable."

"And we're wearing our new shoes." Geneva held out a foot.

"Those look sort of snazzy," Helen said. "I like the blue."

Juanita studied our clothes. "Where'd they come from?"

The others waited to hear our reply.

"Go find Lieutenants Daniels and Smith. They have bags of clothes the scouts left behind."

Frankie Lewey led the charge toward the men's barracks with Jean, Juanita and Dorothy right behind her. Geneva and I laughed.

"I'm glad we got first pickins'."

She smiled. "Me too."

Within the hour, they returned carrying clothes. They ran out of small sizes, and some of the women had to settle for baggy pants.

While they were gone another bus of nurses pulled up. Like us they arrived tired and disoriented. Once off the bus, Cassie and Hattie stared at the condition of our barracks.

"This place is a dump," Cassie said.

"If you think it's bad now, you should've seen it before we cleaned it."

We spent a little time helping them get settled. But clearly, all the good spots for a bed had been taken.

"Guess what I heard," Dorothy said, now wearing her own set of men's military issued clothes.

"What?" I asked.

"Some of the girls left the post without permission and just came back," she said.

"I didn't think we were supposed to go anywhere without asking."

"We're not. Get this. They dined with some officers and had turkey and the fixins'. Just the thought makes my stomach ache."

We were hungry, but I didn't begrudge the girls for eating. Hopefully, Lieutenant Hogan wouldn't find out. Since December seventh, we'd only had two meals a day. We sat around on the porch, hungry but didn't complain.

Earleen Allen talked about her wedding plans to marry Garnet Francis. Dorothy Scholl announced her engagement to Arnold. The war wouldn't deter their plans. For a moment, I envied them. They had someone to love. But then, I remembered we were at war. How quickly that could change their lives.

After making their beds, Cassie and Hattie joined us on the porch.

Hogan approached carrying cartons of tinned cigarettes and passed them out. "A little something from Lieutenant Josie."

"Cigarettes," Edith Corns said. "How considerate of her."

"She always puts others first," I said. We talked a moment about what a wonderful person Josie Nesbit was. No wonder the Filipinos called her Mama Josie.

Geneva took her share, then slipped them to me.

"I also have some candy bars for you." Hogan passed them out. "Please share with the person beside you."

"Thanks." Ann Bernatitis broke the bar in half and handed Dorothy half.

"Thank Josie next time you see her," Geneva said.

"Maybe this will help me make it until dinner," I said. "I'm hungry enough to eat one of those monkeys."

Everyone laughed.

"You'd have to catch one first." Juanita accepted half of a candy bar from Rita. "That'd be fun to watch."

Geneva and I split a large Baby Ruth. The partial candy bar did little to curb my appetite. I ended up drinking water to try and fill my empty stomach. Unfortunately, my stomach was too smart to be fooled.

At 3:00 p.m., our assignment was to sit on the porch and fold gauze for dressings. We talked about anything and everything. Officer Smith joined us, and he even folded gauze.

He talked about the WPO-3, Plan Orange. We were shocked to hear that retreat had been the only plan our government had offered. The only problem was they hadn't sent a convoy to rescue us.

"So just when is the rescue part of that plan going to happen?" Whitlow asked.

Hattie Brantley, who'd arrived earlier, stood. "Help is on the way. We still trust and have faith in God, in MacArthur, F.D.R. and the U.S.A."

"We've retreated as far as we can go. Why hasn't help come?" Agnes Barre asked, looking frustrated.

"Good question." Nancy rubbed the back of her neck.

Jean fanned a fly away. "I can't imagine what's taking our troops so long."

I was afraid of the answer. My faith only remained with God, not with MacArthur or F.D.R. Our government had pushed us to the back burner.

Smith stood. "I need to get back."

I figured he left in a hurry because he realized he'd said too much and had started a squall.

While we worked, planes kept flying over heading for Manila. Their engines droned loudly making one terrifying sound. A sound that meant death and destruction.

I set a stack of folded bandages aside. "I pray everyone in Manila survives these attacks."

"With so much bombing, I'm afraid many of them won't," Juanita added.

"I feel guilty that I'm safe and they aren't." I silently prayed for those being bombed. I prayed for Robert, wondering if he'd been released or what had happened to him.

Later that night, I tried to find a radio channel playing music. Again, I only heard static. A little music would have been nice. Though we all had the same fears and worries, we continued to talk about irrelevant things; things we'd already talked about. The conversations and knowing everyone sat in the same sinking boat kept me from going mad with worry.

When Christmas Day was almost over, some officers who were doctors joined us on the porch. They shared stories of their wives and children. For the first time, we spoke openly about home and Christmas.

"I wonder if the gifts we mailed in November have made it to Tennessee," I said to Geneva.

"Probably sitting in some dumpy post office. We might beat our presents home."

The others laughed and made funny remarks about the packages they'd sent stateside.

One of the officers grinned. "If I could get away with it, I'd ship a monkey home. My kids would love it. I'm not so sure my wife would."

We laughed. The one thing that kept our spirits up was the laughter we shared.

The moonlight illuminated the camp, painting everything in a silvery tint. Only the jungle noises could be heard. The night was quiet, beautiful, and romantic—the air soft and caressing. Geneva sat with a longing expression, and I knew she was thinking about Jerry.

RESSA
December 26, 1941

Today there would be no dilly-dallying or sitting around talking. This was my first experience at a field hospital. I had to disregard the sand and dust and convince myself it was as clean as the fresh air.

Rosemary Hogan addressed us. "If I call your name, you will work setting up the wards. If you thought your barracks were dirty, you haven't seen anything until you've seen the ones in back. Ressa Jenkins, Helen Summers, Jean Kennedy, and Ann Wurts. Head out."

I wanted to wait to see what Geneva would be doing. But when orders are given, you jump. I remembered to grab one of the brooms.

At our assigned barracks, we stood just inside the door, taking in the dirt and items left on the floors. Before I could sweep, we had to gather all their belongings and garbage. Sweeping the floor didn't bother me. It beat being in the heat of surgery while constantly worrying about air raids. Not only did we sweep, we scrubbed every inch of the place by hand.

Once we had cleaned it, we had wards to set up. Each one would hold twenty-four to twenty-six beds. With all the planes bombing Manila, the wounded would be coming our way.

After we finished, I found Geneva. We took turns with a shovel digging our foxhole. I glanced around at all the freshly dug foxholes. Being so hot, sweat soaked our clothes. "This isn't so easy," I said. "I wish we could hire someone to do it."

That night, Rosemary Hogan approached us in the mess while we were eating. "No more foxholes are to be dug until further notice. That's an order. Colonel Duckworth fell in someone's foxhole and broke his arm."

"Wish I could've seen that," Whitlow whispered.

I fought giggling.

After Hogan left, it sounded like a duck farm.

"Quack, Quack."

GENEVA
December 26, 1941

If idle hands are truly the devil's handmaiden, we nurses were Heaven bound. We toiled non-stop. Every nurse and corpsman worked together until the job was done. A steady ocean breeze kept the air fresh and the mosquitoes at bay. Overall conditions in this part of Bataan were pleasant.

I glanced up as trucks, ambulances, and buses brought in the wounded from Manila and its surrounding areas. I ran to the nurses' quarters. "They're here."

All the nurses hurried out to help. Medics unloaded and carried the wounded toward the wards. It didn't take long to fill almost every bed. The operating rooms stayed busy. The familiar stench of blood and burnt flesh filled the air.

Since there wasn't a Navy hospital on Bataan, a number of their wounded came to us. Many of them suffered from burns. Those poor boys suffered constant agony. We did what we could, but it was heart wrenching to witness.

One bright note was the arrival of Commander Smith, a surgeon, who was skilled and dedicated, a blessing from above.

It surprised me to see Francis Nash enter the surgical ward. "I thought you were staying at Sternberg."

"I was ordered to Hospital No. 2."

"Then how'd you end up here at No. 1?"

"Duckworth demanded I come here."

"Now things will run smoothly."

"I gave Jerry your letter. He seemed delighted to get it."

"Thanks. I owe you one."

As we worked on a young soldier, Francis talked about her trip from Manila to Hospital No. 2. "I managed to burn any important documents before I left, and I packed enough morphine just in case we were captured that we wouldn't have to endure any suffering at the hands of the Japs. That's between us."

I couldn't imagine killing myself, but I knew there were things worse than death. We all knew what the Japs had done to the Chinese women.

"Hand me more bandages," Francis continued. "We had a rough trip over. We crossed Manila Bay late yesterday evening, avoiding the mines. I fell asleep on deck wearing my helmet and gas mask. When I woke, flames were burning on Corregidor's Topside."

I thought of Winnie and hoped she was okay.

Francis continued. "We pulled up at Bataan's Lamao Dock. Jap bombers started strafing our little boat. I dove for cover." She laughed as she stitched the soldier's wound. "The only thing I saw to hide in was a chicken coop. Being an old farm girl, I shoved those chickens out and crawled inside. Believe me, they were none too happy, cackling and feathers flying."

I had to laugh as I imagined the scene.

She turned to one of the corpsmen. "Take this one to a ward. Bring in the next one in." She wiped her brow with her arm. "I was a lot more terrified than those hens."

That afternoon around 5:00, Ressa, Nancy, and I decided to go shopping. We walked to the small barrio we had passed on the day of our arrival. We found it occupied by a few civilians and some Filipino solders. We shopped in all three little stores.

"Wow, there's not much left," Nancy commented.

Ressa and I nodded in agreement as we scanned the bare shelves.

"We better buy what we can, because in a day or two this place will be closed." I studied the few items left.

Ressa found a comb and toothbrush. The shopkeeper informed us we missed out on the beer. The thought of drinking hot beer in this heat didn't appeal to me. We settled for Cokes. It didn't matter they were hot. I guzzled mine down enjoying the slight burn and sweetness. We nibbled our bananas as we strolled back to camp. Once back, we stored our items and got ready for dinner.

Within twenty minutes, I joined them in the mess hall and sat on the other side of Ressa. "Hope this taste as good as it smells."

"It does. This is the first real meal I've had in days," Dorothy stated.

The food consisted of salmon, rice, and coffee or tea. She was right, the food tasted great.

"After dinner, let's go down to the beach before it gets dark," Ressa suggested.

"You two can go," Dorothy said. "I'm at the end of a book. I think there's enough daylight left to finish it if I hurry."

"How about you Geneva, you want to take a walk on the beach?"

"Sure. Hey, Dorothy, can I borrow that book when you're done?"

"I'll put it on your cot."

"Thanks. I'll take good care of it."

"No need. When you finish it, pass it on."

I loved to read. Reading had always been a passion of mine.

As we walked toward the water, others joined us, wanting to get in that last cigarette of the day. Geneva, Helen, Cassie, Juanita, Ressa and I strolled casually to the edge of the tree line. Ressa lit a cigarette under the trees' thick canopy.

I breathed the salty ocean air. The rhythmic sounds of waves hitting the shore always caused a soothing effect. I could listen to the beat of the surf and totally relax. I thought of Jerry and wondered if he were safe. Dr. Smith had told me he was fine when he had left Manila. I secretly hoped he'd be sent to Limay.

When everyone put their cigarettes out, we left the protection of the trees and stepped into the warm sun. The sand under our feet produced heat also. Being warmed from above and below definitely gave us a pleasant sensation. After working around dying, bloody men, I needed this moment of peace. Because tomorrow, I'd be staring into the eyes of more young men facing death.

"Look, over there." Ressa pointed at some kind of printed publication.

We walked over to it. Of all things, a funny book was nestled in a pile of stones. We huddled around it and read the story of a grandfather telling a story to his grandson.

"Son," he said, "There is an Oriental country that is going to start a war. The first thing they'll do is attack the Philippines. Then when they accomplish that, they're going to launch an attack on America itself."

"That's amazing," Cassie said. "When was it printed?"

Ressa flipped it over. "In the United States in 1939."

"That's two years before Pearl Harbor," Juanita said. "I wonder if some Jap saw this and thought, that sounds like a good plan."

"I was wondering that myself," I admitted.

We kept it for the others to read. Although it's called a funny book, no one found any humor in it. On the way back, I remembered John Raulston talking about the WPO-3 plan. Now everyone knew about it. But still, I had never mentioned he'd told me about it our first day in Manila.

GENEVA
December 27, 1941

"Where are you two headed?" Dorothy asked, catching up with us.

Ressa stopped and faced her. "Geneva and I are off duty. We figured we would relax on the porch and check the supplies, fold gauze, and whatever else needs doing."

"I'm free. Think I'll join you."

"The more the merrier."

On the porch, we made ourselves comfortable and got to work. We checked the supplies and stored them for easy access. Then we sorted and folded gauze.

"Ever since the ban was lifted on digging foxholes, these new officers crack me up," Dorothy said, with a slight chuckle.

"You mean the way they take shovels and make a home away from home," I replied, laughing.

"Exactly."

Several of the newest officers had become the brunt of our jokes. They remained in their foxholes long after the danger had passed. When I say long after, I mean just that. We took turns going and asking if there was anything we could bring them. A cup of coffee or maybe some paper and pencil to write a letter. They kept us entertained and laughing for quite a while.

Today, we got word Manila had been declared an open city. This was done by General MacArthur on the day we were evacuated. It seemed sad news at first until we realized it had been done to stop the bombing and save lives. There was never any doubt the Japanese were going to take Manila. It was inevitable.

RESSA
December 28, 1941

In the afternoon, our first patients from the clearing station arrived. These first aid depots were positioned approximately fifteen miles from the frontlines.

No matter how many times I'd seen the mangled bodies of so many men in their prime, it left me hollow and sad. I could never get used to such horror. A lot of them also suffered from malaria, dysentery and dengue fever. We placed them in assigned wards. Suddenly, we found ourselves too busy to daydream or think of home. Several times, I also wondered which ward Geneva had ended up in. Though it sounded selfish, I wondered if we'd get a supper break.

RESSA
December 29, 1941

The droning sound of Jap planes had me running to my foxhole. The patients who could walk came with us. Those who couldn't either stayed in their beds or rolled under them. If on duty, you did what you could for your patients' safety before taking cover.

Fortunately, I didn't go on duty until later. I crouched down in my foxhole, my heart beating rapidly like automatic gunfire. My breathing remained winded and short. I glanced up and saw the red sun on the planes. The symbol seemed to flaunt their arrogance and strength. Once they passed, I took Geneva's hand and let her pull me up. I dusted off my clothes. "Thanks. If Manila's an open city, why would bombers be heading there?"

Geneva ran her hands over her clothes. "They're heading toward the Rock."

Not only was Winnie there, some of the Sternberg nurses had been transferred there.

Dorothy brushed her clothes off. "Keeping anything clean in this jungle is impossible."

We talked briefly before parting. Before the day was over, I had jumped into my foxhole over five times, but the bombers overhead weren't interested in us. As my daddy used to say, *they had bigger fish to fry*—Corregidor.

By supper, I was famished. I joined the others, and we talked about the events of the day—the soldiers who'd survived and those who hadn't.

The bodies piled up. The best that could be done for them was for the chaplain to say a prayer, then they'd be placed in a mass grave.

"Corregidor took a beating today," Lieutenant Colonel Frank Adam informed us.

Another doctor nodded. "Sure did, but the Japs can't penetrate the Rock."

Another officer shook his head. "I'm not so sure. They dropped 60,000 tons of bombs on it and took out Topside installation—barracks, hospital, and theater. The Japs racked up a lot of causalities today."

I drew in a deep breath. Worried about Winnie, I asked, "Do you know if any of the nurses were killed?"

"They all made it inside the tunnel. From what was reported, they had already moved the hospital inside."

It saddened me to think of it. I recalled how eerie and stuffy it seemed.

I returned to my little room and prepared for bed. With so much on my mind, I figured I'd have a difficult time falling asleep, but I dozed off quickly.

I woke from a sound sleep.

My heart pounded from the warning issued.

Gas.

Something we considered much more frightening than bombs. Thank goodness we'd had all the gas mask drills. We wasted little time grabbing them. In my panic and fear of breathing in deadly gas, my hands became awkward and clumsy making it all the more difficult to get the mask on and adjusted. I wasted a lot of precious time that could cost me my life. If a mask wasn't properly adjusted, there was a chance of suffocation.

We must have been a sight with the hideous masks, looking like something from a science fiction book. We made it outside, all the while wondering about our patients.

"False alarm!" a soldier shouted.

We removed the masks. All of us stood confused about the warning.

"Sorry, false alarm."

"Well, for Heaven's sake," I said.

"What the heck?" Dorothy stumbled around still wearing the hideous mask.

Helen ripped hers from her face. "What was that about?"

"It's like this," the soldier said. "One of the men started coughing, and another one thinking he was choking on gas panicked and shouted out gas attack. From there, everyone thought we were having a gas attack. Sorry, ladies."

"Is that so?" Geneva asked rhetorically. "Well, if that doesn't beat all. I was sleeping soundly."

Though agitated, we were all thankful it hadn't been an actual attack.

I returned to bed, but sleep wouldn't come. Instead, I listened to the waves lapping upon the beach. It sounded like a boat approaching and caused my nerves to grow taut.

Shortly after falling asleep, we were disturbed when someone entered our barracks.

"Get up. Get dressed," shouted the adjutant around 11:00 p.m. "Got five hundred patients being evacuated from the Army hospitals in Manila. Expect them to arrive any moment."

We joined the receiving officer where we waited over an hour before three hundred ambulatory patients came in accompanied by only three nurses. They had barely escaped Manila. They had left on a small ship and headed toward Corregidor to drop off Army personnel. With the Rock being bombed, they had hidden in a cove all day without food or water. Most of their injuries were superficial and required little care. We directed them to beds in the wards already made up. I looked but didn't see Lieutenant Robbins with them. From what I heard, his squadron fought the Japs in the jungles of Mindoro, another island. Had he joined them? If so, I'd probably never see him again.

RESSA
December 30, 1941

After breakfast, I had more wards to set up. The morning held a special surprise for me. I pulled a bed in line with the others and tossed the linens on it. I glanced up and gasped. Lieutenant Donald Robert Robbins walked into my ward. I immediately tried to brush my hair into place. I must've looked a sight wearing my navy pants, shirt, and clunky men's shoes.

He walked over to me. "You didn't think I'd forgotten about you already?"

"No. It's hard to forget a girl who brings you candy."

He grinned slyly. "You're a lot sweeter than that candy."

My cheeks heated. "I was worried about you. I figured you'd be back in the thick of the war."

"Considering the Japs destroyed every plane, I'm grounded. I'm helping bring the wounded over from Manila." He pulled me into his arms and gave me an affectionate hug. "Didn't think you'd get rid of me that easy, did you?"

Uncertain of what to do, I returned his hug, then stepped back slowly. "I'm really glad you're here. I had hoped I'd see you again."

It was true, but at the same time I wanted to distance myself. I didn't want to fall in love. Not here. And he had no idea I was in my thirties.

He glanced around the ward. "You look like you could use a little help."

"I never turn down help."

"There she is, the best nurse in the Philippines," Scotty, another former patient of mine said, as he joined us. "What can I do to help?"

Seeing Robert had a traveling buddy, I put some space between us.

Although Robert had never talked about family, for all I knew, he could have a wife and kids stateside. That'd definitely put an end to any romantic notions, because I didn't date married men. I had the idea he wasn't married since he hadn't mentioned it and didn't wear a ring. How would he react to the age difference between us?

My common sense reminded me life balanced on a thin thread that could break at any moment, so becoming romantically involved wasn't a wise thing to do. But somehow, my cold heart warmed when I was around him. I'd become fond of Robert. I knew our paths would turn in different directions soon.

Robert and Scotty ended up helping me prepare the ward.

"So, what's happening in Manila?" I asked.

Robert fluffed the sheet out over the cot. "Sternberg has been almost completely evacuated. No one is left but some Navy patients and nurses."

"What about Lieutenant Nesbit and Captain Davison?"

Scotty meticulously tucked the sheets around the cot. "Last I heard, Davison's at Corregidor, and Josie was sent to Hospital No. 2."

"The Red Cross ship, the Mactan, will be leaving for Australia," Robert added. "It'll be transporting about three or four hundred soldiers."

"Do you know if any American nurses are going?"

"Floramund Fellmuth left with Colonel Carroll. She's the nurse who rode the mule for the Army Navy game," Scotty said. "There might have been one other nurse who went with them. I'm not sure."

"Seems like they would've taken more than one or two nurses." I was thankful that almost everyone from Sternberg and the other hospitals had gotten out safely. At least Robert hadn't been sent to fight in the jungle.

Scotty grinned. "How 'bout I work with you fulltime?"

Geneva had worked with Scotty after he'd been released from the ward and only had wonderful things to say about him.

"Sure, I can always use an extra pair of hands."

Robert swept the floor while Scotty finished fitting sheets around the beds. While we worked Scotty told me about a group of nurses almost killed. "Figured they were heading into the jungles to open Hospital No. 2. They stood on a pier waiting. Only minutes after they walked off, a bomb hit it, destroying it completely. If they'd been standing there, they would've all been killed."

I shuddered. "That's nothing short of a miracle. Can you tell me anything about Ethel Blaine? We called her Sally."

"I believe she was in that group of nurses on the pier," Scotty commented.

I placed my hand over my heart and sighed. "Thank you, sweet Jesus for saving them."

It was much later before Robert and I had time to engage in a private conversation. We enjoyed each other's company. He had lived near the Pocono Mountains, and I was from the Smokies. We had some wonderful stories to share.

He escorted me to my quarters. He kissed me lightly and said goodnight.

RESSA
December 31, 1942

New Year's Eve seemed so uneventful, until some of the officers showed up with candy and a bottle of liquor. Robert and Scotty came with them. They passed the bottle around. When it came to me, I took a big swig and let it go down slowly, burning my throat. I didn't care. After all I had gone through, I wanted to feel numb from fear and uncertainty. But instead, I ended up singing an old tune called *Pig in a Pen*.

"I got a pig at home in a pen and corn to feed him on. All I need is a pretty little girl to feed him when I'm gone. Goin' on the mountain to sow a little cane. Raise a barrel of sorghum to sweetin' Liza Jane."

Geneva joined in on the second verse. At the end of the song, everyone clapped and whistled.

We ended up singing another old home tune. After a few verses, everyone joined in on the chorus. "I'm a Methodist, Methodist till I die. I'm a Methodist, Methodist 'tis my belief. I'm a Methodist 'til I die. Till old grim death comes a knockin' on my door. I'm a Methodist until I die."

Again, they applauded.

"So, you must be Methodist," Robert remarked.

I laughed. "No, Baptist. We just like the song."

"I thought it was wonderful," Scotty said. The others agreed.

I realized if we hadn't been nipping the bottle, we wouldn't have been so bold.

"One thing about Tennessee girls, we know how to sing and dance," Geneva said.

Our family had always been fond of music. The thought made me miss home, and I grew quiet.

We all sat on the porch, taking turns sharing stories about home. Robert leaned against the porch rail, and I sat beside him. Somehow, we ended up holding hands. I glanced at Geneva and realized she was missing Jerry.

Robert and I walked down to the bay and sat on a fallen tree. The moon shined over us, and the water ran upon the beach. A warm tropical breeze full of sweet fragrances swirled around us. He started to kiss me, and I stopped him. "There's something you need to know."

He appeared puzzled. "You're married?"

"No, are you?"

"No, or I wouldn't be trying to kiss you."

"I'm eight years older than you."

"You sure don't look a day over sixteen." He grinned. "I don't care."

"In that case, stop talking and kiss me." I knew that was the liquor talking. It didn't sound like something I'd say.

He drew me in his arms and kissed me. Yes, somehow my attraction had grown. I had feelings for him. Something about us had just clicked.

I pulled back. "I'm sorry. I don't want to be involved with anyone while this war is going on."

"Tell you what," he said. "When this war is over, I'm looking you up. I plan to take you on a real date. Am I clear?"

"Yes, sir. Just to give you a head start, I'll be in San Francisco."

Robert walked me to my quarters. He pulled my hand to his lips and kissed the back of it again. I loved the way he did that. It was so romantic and sweet. Darn it. I hate I had to be so wise and practical about matters of the heart.

RESSA
January 1, 1942

The first day of 1942, I woke to learn Robert had left with the others to fight in the jungles. He would be heading to the front. There hadn't been time for goodbyes. I feared he would be killed or captured. If he survived, I wondered if he would look me up once we were out of this terrifying mess.

Today became a repetition of any other day—work, planes flying over, and foxholes. I'd thought of home several times and of family that day. It'd left me in a dolorous mood. Mom would have a pot of black-eyed peas, ham, and cornbread to start the new year off right. Nothing would've been better than a big bowl of peas with lots of juice and buttered cornbread crumbled in it.

For the most part, we didn't believe help was coming, but we'd still look toward the bay in hopes of seeing a U.S. convoy heading our way.

RESSA
January 2, 1942

The news spread through camp. Japan had taken Manila and the U.S. Naval base at Cavite. Any personnel still there had been captured by the Imperial Japanese Army. Immediately, a loss in morale swept over us. Our friends that were left would be placed in concentration camps. Geneva worried Jerry might be one of them.

"What have they taken over?" I asked a young soldier.

"The Japanese officers took over the Army/Navy Club and made it their quarters. Jai-Alai is being used as a headquarters. "

"What about the roads?" Geneva asked.

"Controls all of 'em in Luzon," he replied.

I recalled Peter saying they'd starve us to death. If they controlled the highways, there would be no food or supplies coming our way.

Working in the ward that day proved difficult. A corpsman had purchased a hen from a Filipino man in the barrio and had tied her to a support beam under the porch. The thing clucked loudly all day. That night, he cooked it and gave me a wing. I guess it could be considered a feathered casualty of war. It sounded silly for a hungry country girl to feel guilty over a chicken.

A bunch of us sat in the mess hall at a bamboo table. Playing bridge had become our only source of recreation.

"Your deal," I said to Jean Kennedy.

Jean smiled. "I plan to shuffle the heck out of these cards. No more super hands for Geneva." She glanced over at my sister. "You quiet ones are so sly. You think you're gonna beat us again tonight. Well, we'll see, Missy."

My sister couldn't hold back a smile. "Just shuffle."

Dorothy laughed. "Maybe we should just throw our hands up and quit."

"You know why Geneva is so hard to beat?" I asked.

Dorothy and Jean shook their heads.

"Her face is unreadable. You can never tell if she's happy or sad."

Geneva rolled her eyes. "Suck it up and play."

While waiting for Jean to deal the cards, we shared the latest camp gossip.

"Did you hear about those Filipino nurses and the doctors sent to San Fernando?" Dorothy asked.

I shook my head. "Not really. What about them?"

"About twenty miles from the hospital, a Fifth Columnist shot up flares in a field near the town. Within minutes the town was bombed and a lot of people were killed."

Jean sighed. "Did they catch the traitor who did it?"

Dorothy nodded. "They did. He ended up wounded with the ones he betrayed. Serves him right."

"Lousy-no-good traitor," Francis Nash said, followed with some profanity.

"None of the nurses wanted to tend to him," Dorothy added.

"Who could blame them," I added.

"I have the feeling he didn't make it," Geneva remarked.

"Good riddance," I said.

We all shared the same sentiment about it. If any group was despised more than the Japanese, it was the Fifth Columnist. At least the Japs didn't know us. These traitors lived, worked, and even worshipped with us.

"Did you get any Navy boys in your ward?" I asked the others.

"We ended up with fifteen," Jean said, as she dealt the cards. "Some badly burned."

"We did too," Geneva said. "Those poor boys are in agony."

Dorothy sighed. "Let's talk about something not as depressing."

"Like what?" I asked.

"A group of us were almost run over by that herd of wild ponies."

Juanita smiled. "If one of them gets close enough to be caught, it could end up in a pot of stew."

We laughed.

With so many wounded soldiers and supplies dwindling, we had to ration the food carefully. Before this was over, we could very well end up eating the ponies or anything else that came near our camp.

GENEVA
January 3, 1942

A corpsman brought two young monkeys back from the jungle. One died, and the other became the camp pet, but we saw the creature more as a camp pest. It had kept me from sleeping. Of course, he had many names and answered to all of them.

"Ressa, you look tired," I said as she joined me for morning mess.

"I am. Who can sleep with that stupid monkey screaming all night?"

"Not me. I heard if you let him under the mosquito net he'll settle down and sleep."

"I'll try that tonight if he starts up his caterwauling. It'd beat him running across the tops of our mosquito nets."

"I'll tell you one thing. That little devil is smart. I saw him watching the boys brush their teeth. The next day I caught him brushing his teeth with a toothbrush he'd stolen."

"Are you kidding me?" Ressa laughed, trying not to spill the cup of coffee in her hand.

"No, I swear. If I hadn't seen it with my own eyes, I wouldn't have believed it. Here's another thing. He's an accomplished beggar. He has a memorized route he takes of staff and patients who regularly give him handouts. He eats better than we do."

Ressa sipped her coffee. "I'm glad you tipped me off. I'll be sure not to feed him, and I'll also hide my toothbrush."

Every once and a while the chance of a break in our routine would occur. Later that day, we had the opportunity to ride with ambulatory patients being evacuated from our facility and sent to

Hospital No. 2. Ressa, Grace Hallman, and I had the day off and decided to go visit our friends from Sternberg stationed there.

The large truck offered nowhere to sit, so we had to stand with the gasoline drums in back. The unpaved road jostled us around while dust flew up covering us. We passed soldiers who wore gas masks to prevent choking on dust.

"Whose idea was this?" Ressa shouted, getting a mouth full of dust.

"It was yours," I responded.

Grace nodded. "Sounded good when you suggested it."

The six-mile trip left us as dirty as three pigs wallowing in the mud.

Finally, the truck dropped us off at the Medical Supply Depot which consisted of two tents in the midst of a jungle.

"We're looking for the nurses' quarters," Grace said to a soldier standing guard.

He pointed down a jungle path. "Follow it to the end by the riverbed."

We thanked him and headed out. His directions sounded easy enough. We ventured down the narrow path surrounded by thick undergrowth, coconut palms, bamboo, and vines. I led the way, swatting low hanging branches out of our way.

After thirty minutes of not finding the riverbed, we admitted we were lost. Finally, we met another soldier who directed us to the right path.

"So, we just follow this path to the wards?" Grace inquired.

"That's right, Miss. Just follow it to the riverbed."

This time we were successful. We came to a small clearing and just beyond it was the riverbed. "I won't complain about our barracks anymore," I said, seeing how these nurses lived.

We recognized two nurses from Sternberg—Clara Mueller and Adele Foreman. It was wonderful seeing familiar faces. Both nurses were making beds that stood in an open space between the trees.

"Adele. Clara. Don't you know how to make up a bed yet?" I asked.

They glanced up and frowned until they realized who we were. Smiles lit their faces. "Well, if it isn't the Jenkins girls," Adele said.

"And Grace," Clara said. "What are you ladies doing here?"

Geneva walked over to them. "We came for a visit. We'll need to be back on the truck before it pulls out."

"We're setting up a new ward," Clara said. "What do you think?"

"I think this is really shocking," I said.

"Believe it or not, as soon as we get beds in place this is going to be a ward," Adele said. "We were told, any spot with trees overhead to protect patients from the sun and hide us from Japs is sufficient for a new ward."

Adele blotted the sweat on her forehead with her sleeve. "The bulldozers are already clearing out the brush and small trees for another new ward."

After several minutes of pleasant conversation, Ressa inquired about her good friend. "I'd like to find Sally Blaine. Know where she is?"

Clara gave us directions, and we followed another path. Jungle trails linked the wards together.

At the end of the trail, we found six nurses sitting on beds out in the open. If I ever thought conditions were bad at Hospital No. 1, I quickly changed my mind viewing No. 2.

Seeing us, Sally smiled and stood. "It's good to see you, Ressa. I've wondered how you girls were doing."

"Good seeing you too. It seems funny seeing you in G.I. garb with that long knife hanging at your side. Last time I saw you, you were a prim and proper nurse in white, and now you look like Sally Blaine jungle warrior."

We all had to laugh at the analogy.

"It's called adapting to war," Sally responded. She laughed as she said it.

I realized we were all adapting to war. None of us were the same as when we had first arrived.

We walked to their mess that made ours look like a five-star kitchen. We sat at a table and drank coffee. Sally shared her story about coming over from Manila and how close they had come to being killed.

Before leaving, we hunted down Josie and some of the others we hadn't seen. "Have you seen Jerry?" I asked Mary Lohr.

"Yes, he brought a load of badly wounded men to the hospital, then left to get more."

I didn't have pen or paper or I would've left him a letter. Just knowing he was alive lifted my spirits.

We arrived back at the truck right before it pulled out heading back to Hospital No. 1.

GENEVA
January 4, 1942

Every time an ambulance or truck brought in wounded soldiers, I watched for Jerry. Was he all right? Had something happened?

Needless to say, in war there are many dangers. Besides the obvious threat of bombs, we fought tropical diseases. But now we stayed on alert from another odd nemesis—ponies. The Filipinos had turned about six of them loose to run free on Limay. They were cute and enjoyable to watch at first, but now they had become a hazard.

I walked toward my ward. I'd been in such a trance thinking about Jerry that I didn't hear the hooves pounding the ground until the wild bunch of ponies were almost on top of me. I dove out of the way and avoided being trampled. It required a moment to catch my breath and dust off my clothes.

I stared at the ponies galloping away. I hadn't been the first nurse almost plowed over by them.

"Are you all right?" one of the men with the Quartermaster's Corps asked.

"Yes. After surviving all these bombings, I'd hate to be killed by these ponies. You guys should do something with them. Someone will eventually get hurt."

"We'll look into it." The men talked among themselves and left. By the time I had made it to the ward, I had calmed down.

I shared the story with some of my patients, and they had the gall to laugh.

RESSA
January 4, 1942

My day was like any other since being at Hospital No. 1. I spent the morning working hard, caring for the wounded, and wondering about Robert. In the mess that evening, Geneva shared her pony story, and I laughed.

"Why is it everyone thinks it's funny? I could've been killed."

"Well, you weren't, so it's okay to laugh about it. I wish I could've seen your face."

"I'm surprised my eyes didn't pop out of my head." She started eating. "I keep thinking Jerry might get over this way. If so, with him being from Texas, maybe he can rope them."

"I hope so. I'm glad he's all right. I hope Robert and Scotty are as lucky."

I didn't tell her the rumor Sally Blaine had mentioned about Jerry. Seeing how it was just a rumor, I thought it best my sister didn't know. But if true, any man who played with my sister's heart would eventually have to face me. And just because I was little, I had never been a pushover.

That night, we sat on the porch, telling the others about our visit to Hospital No. 2 when two men approached us. Lieutenant Noland J. Barnick and his friend, a captain, in the Air Corps came down from the hills.

"We're starving. You got any food you can spare?" Lieutenant Barnick asked.

Nancy nodded. "We might be able to scrounge something up for you."

"Anything," the captain said. "We'd appreciate it."

We walked with them to the mess. A short time later, our cook served them fish cakes. They made a joke about the fish looking like doughnuts without the holes. They gobbled down the food faster than I could blink my eyes.

The captain shared some bad news with us. On December twenty-ninth, the S.S. Panay had been bombed and sunk. Her sister ship the Mayon had also been attacked but narrowly escaped. Then the captain also told us news that left us in the doldrums. When the Japanese had taken over Manila, some Navy nurses had surrendered.

Guessing, he figured it was around eleven or twelve of them. I realized Mary Harrington was one of them. Also, Peggy Nash and Edwina Todd who'd spent time with us. I'd make sure I prayed for them.

GENEVA
January 6, 1942

The men in the Quartermaster's Corps invited the nurses to an amateur rodeo. They called it Texas on Bataan. The men realized they had a use for the ponies and rounded them up.

They had the feisty animals boxed in and proceeded to catch them. It was a combination of cowboy and Keystone cop as they tried to get ropes around their furry necks. The ponies jerked away and kicked as the soldiers chased them. They trotted around neighing. Some of the men tried more of a bulldogging technique of tackling the ponies. We laughed until we ached. Finally, the men had the ponies caught and tied up.

"I haven't laughed that hard since our bus ride from Manila," Ressa said.

"Me neither. Seeing those big men outsmarted by those ponies had me in stitches."

"I hope they don't eat them," Dorothy said on the walk back to our quarters. "They're so cute."

"At least none of us have to worry about being trampled again," Cassie added.

"I've had to jump out of their way several times," Jean said. "I won't miss them."

Rita Palmer met us on the path. "Listen up. Everyone is needed. General Wainwright was fighting in northern Bataan today. He along with our allied forces put up a good fight but couldn't hold the line. The Japs were ruthless, so we're expecting more causalities than usual. Nash said expect to work through the night."

Our laughter stopped, and we hurried to the hospital.

As we worked, the wounded steadily increased. That night shifts stretched out for eighteen up to twenty hours. Time seemed to speed up as things became more hectic. By now, we had grown use to the stench of blood and burnt flesh. Though just as horrific, the wounds inflicted didn't shock us as in those first days at Sternberg. Still each death of a young soldier who would never return home tore at our hearts.

As more were brought in, I kept hoping Jerry would be driving one of the ambulances.

Later that evening, we learned why today's defeat was so devastating to all of us. The Japs gained control of the road used to bring in our supplies and food from Manila. With the number of wounded and sick soldiers growing each day, how would we take care of them without medicine and supplies? And food, how would we feed so many? I recalled Dorothy worried the ponies would be eaten. Sadly, there was a good chance, it'd come to that.

GENEVA
January 10, 1942

Our hospital constantly admitted more severely injured patients while evacuating others to Hospital No. 2. I learned the trip between the two hospitals had become perilous with the Japanese advancing on us. We had worked into the early hours of the morning and part of our day off. Around 10:00 a.m., bombs dropped and bullets sprayed the hospital. Half asleep, I left my cot and in a state of panic, I rushed to a car instead of jumping in our foxhole and wriggled underneath it.

I realized immediately what a foolish mistake I'd made. The car was a sitting target. Someone pushed their way under there with me. I glanced back and saw Ressa. As the pings from shells hit the car, I thought my heart would burst. I held my breath and prayed we wouldn't be hit. We hadn't chosen the best place to take cover. I had been caught without my helmet and mask. I had to be more careful in the future or I might not have a future.

In a moment of silence, we crawled out from under the vehicle and ran for our foxhole. Odd, how both us had made the same mistake. But mistakes could cost you your life. After the raid, we crawled back on our cots and fell asleep from exhaustion.

Later that morning, we learned flares had been sent up by traitors to alert the Zeros where to bomb. The barrio at the entrance of Camp Limay had taken a direct hit and had killed many civilians and villagers. A corpsman found a five-month old baby whose mother and grandmother had both been killed during the attack.

Geneva and I sat in the mess hall drinking coffee and eating toast. The men wouldn't stop fighting over who would hold the baby next.

"Okay, enough," Leona Gastinger shouted. "Give him to me."

The men reluctantly handed the child over.

On our way out, Ressa stopped and made baby-talk with it. I thought he was cute and empathized with the little guy. But we had to be in the wards, so we wished Leona good luck.

All that week, a corpsman looked after Benji at night while Leona tended to him in the daytime. She'd been given some slack in her duties to care for the baby.

RESSA
January 1942

I woke in the night. Hearing noise coming from the beach, I left my room and quietly walked down the beach path. I came upon a group of soldiers camped out. "What's going on?"

"We're waiting to catch the traitors setting off flares," one said.

"Then you might want to be a little quieter. It sounds more like a beach party."

The next day, I worked receiving the arriving wounded. I evaluated each case to determine if they were serious enough for surgery or whether they needed to be assigned to a bed.

In most cases, corpsmen ripped or cut off their bloody clothes, but sometimes, we had to do it. A younger nurse reached in a soldier's pants pocket and pulled out an object. From where I stood, I couldn't get a good look at it until she held it up.

In the middle of my conversation with another nurse, my heartbeat skyrocketed.

"Stop. Don't pull that!" a doctor shouted.

Several other people were yelling also.

"You want to blow us up?" Lieutenant Smith, one of the surgeons, asked.

"What is it?" the young nurse asked.

He scowled. "A damn grenade! Are you crazy?"

The girl's eyes grew large. "Take it. I don't want it."

Everyone backed away. Suddenly, it looked like a game of hot potatoes.

Finally, one of the ambulatory soldiers took it and left the hospital area.

It required several moments for my heart to stop its marathon through my chest.

At lunch that day, I had a good story to share. Though they realized the severity of the incident, they laughed.

"And she was about to pull the pin," I restated. "Can you believe that? We could have been blown to smithereens."

Geneva and Dorothy laughed.

"I can't top that, but this one is pretty good. I spotted two Filipino soldiers crawling across the floor carrying weapons. I don't know where they thought they were going."

"How'd they get past security?"

Dorothy shrugged in a nonchalant way. "Damned, if I know. Fortunately, they lowered the weapons before anyone was seriously hurt."

Captain Milton Whaley, who we called doc, joined us at our table. "You mind me joining you ladies?"

"Not at all," I said.

Dorothy scooted over to make room for him. "We were sharing war stories."

Geneva aimed a fork at him. "Personally, I think they made them up."

"We did not," I insisted.

He grinned. "I reckon we'll all leave here with a bag full of war stories."

I recognized his accent. "Where are you from?"

"Sevierville, Tennessee."

"You don't say?" Geneva asked.

"So are we," I said.

Geneva smiled. "Good meeting someone from home."

For the next ten minutes, we talked of home. Funny, but we knew some of the same folks.

"What I miss the most is the music," he announced. "I miss sittin' on the porch and pickin' on my geetar and singing my heart out."

"Sing us a good old hillbilly song."

"I'll give it a go. Too bad I don't have my geetar."

He sang my favorite *I Left My Gal in the Mountains*. Then he sang *Hop Along Mary*. We joined in the chorus each time.

For just a short time, we forgot about the war and all its horrors.

"Got a story for ya," Dr. Whaley said. "Some of the men started screaming they'd seen dead men come out of the grave and walk." He chuckled. "Turned out to be wounded soldiers who'd taken shelter in freshly dug graves. When they stood, the men saw them and ran."

We had a good laugh over his story.

"I have a story," Geneva said softly.

We all glanced up at her. It surprised me since she was usually just a listener.

"A few weeks back, Captain MacNeil needed some coveralls. I shared a pair of the size 42 coveralls with him we'd been given."

"You sure couldn't wear clothes that big," Dorothy stated.

"No, but that's not the point of my story."

Dorothy gave her an apologetic look. "Sorry, go ahead."

"One day after that, the captain was coming down the street wearing those coveralls when a bomb hit. When he stood up, he was as naked as the day he was born. His clothes had been blown right off him, and he hadn't received a single scratch. I can't say as much for the coveralls."

Dorothy and I laughed the hardest since we had met MacNeil on the Coolidge. Doc Whaley had been right about each of us going home with a bag full of war stories.

RESSA
January 16, 1942

Things started picking up. We could see flashes in the distance, and we could hear the faint sounds of explosions. Our shifts varied from twelve to twenty hours. We cared for patients by using flashlights. Leaning over the very low cots was grueling and left my back aching.

We worked diligently on the steady flow of wounded men that included Navy, Marines, Army, and civilians. We tended every kind of wound known to man.

I guess keeping busy was good therapy. If I'd had time to dwell on the pain these innocent, young men suffered every day, I would have lost it.

A person can only empathize and cry so much before the spirit becomes numb. It never got to the stage of being cold or hard, merely numb. A metamorphosis we succumbed to for our mental and spiritual preservation. *God help us all.*

"Not again," I moaned as the air raid warning sounded. "Get up, Geneva. They're playing our favorite song."

We ran outside together and jumped in the trench reserved for us. The rule was, if you dig it you own it.

"Well phooey."

"What's wrong?" I asked.

"I grabbed my helmet and gas mask, but I left my pencil."

"Don't worry. I have an extra, here." She retrieved a pencil from her pocket and handed it to me.

Later that night, a message from MacArthur on Corregidor lifted our spirits.

Help is on the way from the United States.

He promised thousands of troops were headed our way.

We all shouted and clapped. The wave of relief and joy moved through our camp. At last, we would be saved from the starvation or captivity we thought lay ahead of us.

GENEVA
January 17, 1942

As Beth Veley and I walked toward the ward, we heard an argument and hurried to stop any fighting from happening. We found our favorite patients—Lieutenants Hennesey and Garth. I frowned as they bickered back and forth. One had been wounded and thought dead by the Japs while the other had been shot in the hip by a sniper.

Garth snarled. "Oh yeah, well I'll tell you one thing."

"Tell me, Garth, I can't wait to hear it," Hennesey responded.

"If that damn Nip hadn't put a bullet in my hip, I would kick your ass."

"On your best day if you tried it, you would end up right where you are now—in a hospital."

Those two carried on like that non-stop. They thoroughly enjoyed the continual banter and would have been miserable without each other. It was good therapy. I'm sure it was their way of coping with this damn war.

GENEVA
January 18, 1942

"Miss, could you help me?" a soldier asked as I walked by.

I stopped and faced him. "What can I do for you?"

"I'm Lieutenant Osborne. I'm in charge of evacuating some of our boys to Hospital No. 2. Are any of these men in your ward, Miss..."

"Jenkins, Geneva Jenkins." I glanced at the list of names. "Kincaid, Andrews, are those two." I pointed to two men in beds. "Thomas is in the bed to your right."

"Can you get them ready to travel?"

"Yes. I'm glad you're taking them to a safer place," I said while preparing them to be moved.

"To be honest, as fast as the Japs are advancing, there aren't any safe places, with the exception of Corregidor. Even the road to No. 2 is dangerous."

"True, but we've had Japs flying over since day one. That's nothing new. Have you heard what MacArthur announced the other night?" I asked.

"I did, but no one has seen hide nor hair of any help. Until they get here, we got to keep dodging the Japs."

I packed Kincaid's gear as two corpsmen quickly removed him under Osbourne's direction.

He helped me prepare Andrews for the move. "The Zeroes aren't our biggest threat at the moment. It's the snipers we have to watch for now."

"Snipers?"

"Yep, they've been sneaking through our lines. They wear camouflage uniforms and tie themselves in the tree tops. Hard as hell to spot. Sneaky little bastards play a game of wound and wait. They know we won't leave our wounded. The plan is to pick off anyone who attempts to rescue their buddy."

Osborne seemed like a nice man. I said a quick prayer asking God to protect him, then I returned to work. After I changed the linens, immediately, newly admitted men occupied the three vacant beds.

The emotion of love was part of my upbringing. Instilled and nurtured by family and church. It was as natural as breathing. On the other hand, the feeling of hate was unnatural to me. It was something I had learned, and the Japanese were excellent teachers.

I believe one factor that kept me from becoming bitter were the Filipino people. They were unbelievable. It didn't matter how bad conditions became or the pain they suffered, they never uttered a complaint. They met every obstacle with courage and an undaunted optimistic spirit.

RESSA
January 20, 1942

Earleen Allen had finally returned late that evening from the frontline where she'd been driven by Captain Garnet Francis. She approached us in the mess hall. Her cheeks glowed pink, and she appeared so happy.

"So, tell us all about it," Geneva said.

Rosemary Hogan, Rita Palmer, Helen Summers, and Ressa gathered around the new bride.

"She's still sparkling with love," Rita said, who was also in love with Captain Nelson.

"Who performed the ceremony?" Ressa asked.

"Father Cummings. Some of Garnet's men built us a nipa hut and even had an old phonograph playing romantic music."

"How long did you have to honeymoon?" Rosemary asked.

"Three hours. The most wonderful three hours of my life."

"Congratulations, Earleen. I wish you and Garnet all the happiness in the world." And I truly wished they would both make it through the war.

Nurses with sweethearts back home found themselves jealous. I thought of Robert. But then I saw the sadness of their situation. More than likely, they would be separated until the end of the war.

God only knew how long that'd be. I know Geneva thought of Jerry often.

"Anything happen while I was gone?" Earleen asked.

I smiled. "Well, that foul monkey disappeared. The guy who owned him has searched everywhere for it."

Earleen smiled. "Good. Now maybe we can sleep. Anyone know what happened to him?"

"Well, the night after he came up missing, the cook served a stew made with a new meat. Claims it was chicken, but it wasn't. At the time, the monkey hadn't been missed, so I didn't even consider it could be monkey meat."

Earleen laughed. "Was it any good?"

"Not bad," Geneva replied. "Maybe a little stringy."

Dorothy nodded in agreement. "I heard an old soldier who'd been stranded in a jungle say, to survive, you watch the monkey and eat everything it eats, then eat the monkey."

Though we felt sorry for the monkey, we couldn't help but laugh.

Earleen sighed. "From what I heard, a group of us are being transferred to Hospital No. 2."

Cassie and Dorothea Daley had already been transferred. If they sent me, I hoped they'd send Geneva and Dorothy Scholl also.

That night in case my name was called, I crammed my things in my bag. I scanned the area, making sure nothing was overlooked. The sounds of battle could be heard in the distance. The Imperial Japanese Army moved closer every day.

Hospital No. 2
Deeper into the Jungle
Part Four

RESSA
January 23, 1942

Nancy Gillahan, Earleen Allen, Evelyn Whitlow, Jean Kennedy, Ann Wurts, Helen Summers, Grace Hallman, Leona Gastinger, Beth Veley, Edith Corns, Geneva, and I had been called together.

When Lieutenant Hogan joined us, my stomach sank. I didn't think this would be good. She appeared grim with a degree of hesitation in her eyes. Whatever it was, she dreaded telling us. "Ladies, you're being transferred to Hospital No. 2. The frontlines are getting too close to Camp Limay. Pack up. You'll leave sometime tomorrow."

Leona Gastinger raised her hand. "What about Benji? Can I take him with me?"

Rosemary's expression said it all. "No. I'm sorry, Leona. He'll be placed in a nearby civilian hospital. The interior jungle is no place for a baby."

"But he's so attached to me. Let me stay and take care of him."

"I'm sorry. The orders have already been approved. He will receive good care there."

Leona's shoulders drooped, and her face grew forlorn. She treated Benji as though he were her own. Tears formed in her eyes, and she nodded. "May I go with them to take him?"

Rosemary nodded. "Sure. Get him ready. You'll leave within the hour."

The rest of us grumbled and groaned about our new assignment. Living in the middle of a thick jungle without the ocean breeze to fend off the humid heat and mosquitoes would make life almost unbearable, but the soldiers needed us. I said goodbye to Dorothy Scholl, who hadn't been reassigned with us. She had become like a sister to me.

"Well, I'll be. It just keeps getting better," Geneva said. "But at least there, I stand a better chance of seeing Jerry."

After what I'd heard, I hoped she didn't see him, not that I wished any bad luck on him.

"I had hoped we'd stay with the group in Limay," I said. "Hospital No. 2 doesn't have the conveniences we have."

"Like showers," Edith Corn said. "They bathe in an offshoot of the Real River."

"We'll have plenty of mosquitoes to keep us company," Whitlow said. "I also hear they have tree rats that bite. Lucky us."

"Talk about some people having all the luck," Grace added. "Guess, we'd better start packing."

It would be difficult once again to leave all the patients and people we had become fond of.

Back in my quarters, I pulled out my personal belongings. "Can you believe I still have seventeen white uniforms?"

"Me too," Geneva said. "I don't know why we kept them? Sure can't wear them around here. They'd make us an easy target."

I hated giving up my little room, but I was glad to see Dorothy move into it.

RESSA
January 24, 1942

A truck picked us up around two in the afternoon. It generated a lot of heat on an already hot, muggy day. We hugged and said our goodbyes to everyone remaining behind.

I had hoped Robert would return in time, but he didn't. If he made it back to Camp Limay, I wouldn't be there. Again, I reminded myself why it's best not to fall in love with someone during wartime. Love in wartimes could best be described as two ships passing through the night going in opposite directions.

Riding in the back of the truck with so much dust flying up in our faces, breathing became a challenge. Jean tore off pieces of gauze and passed them out. I held it over my nose so I could breathe.

As the truck traveled along the bumpy road, our heavy suitcases kept falling on the back of our necks and shoulders.

Finally, around 3:00 p.m. we reached Hospital No. 2 that sat on what could be described as an inland island etched into the middle of a jungle surrounded by streams and creeks. After crossing the stream, a burlap screen stretched out on bamboo poles formed a seven-foot-tall privacy screen. It ran down both sides and isolated one section where a clear pool of water was used for bathing. The high bank on the other side shielded the area from anyone seeing in. The clear water flowed fast and looked inviting. We were warned the tepid stream had a rocky bottom and was shallow in some spots while deep in others.

"Hard to believe this is the same place we visited earlier," I commented, seeing an improvement.

Geneva wiped sweat from her forehead. "You're right. These folks have been busy. Let's store our gear and check out the duty roster."

The fragrance of the musky jungle filled the air. The drone of mosquitoes constantly buzzed in my ears. It required too much energy to swat them. I merely brushed them off. All the nurses took quinine pills every day to prevent diseases.

Geneva and I along with the others followed a little path that crossed a plank bridge and found our quarters located at the far end of the encampment. Again, burlap walls overlapped and shielded the area.

"This is it," Helen said, "nurses' quarters." She rang the bell by the sign.

A small bamboo summer house sat in the middle and had benches and chairs where we could gather to rest and talk. Just inside, we found a lister bag.

"Better refill my canteen," I said, then turned the faucet of the heavy bag that contained chlorinated drinking water. "It might come up empty later."

Geneva nodded and filled hers also.

"Glad you're here. I hope you ladies brought mosquito netting. You're gonna need it," shouted a nurse I didn't recognize.

Mary Lohr whispered, "Secure a bed first. They're in short demand. We'll talk later."

"Let's go. I don't want to end up without one like I did in Limay," Geneva whispered. We walked to the beds and studied our choices. The two beds we selected stood side by side with newer mattresses. "Mary saved us."

"Yes, she did." I set my things on the bed to claim it.

"Now I've seen it all," Geneva said.

"What?"

"Beautyrest mattresses in the middle of the jungle."

"Praise the Lord for that small luxury," I replied.

No sooner than we had staked our claim, the others headed our way.

Geneva and I made up our beds, then shoved our suitcases on the bare ground under them.

"Home sweet home," Leona proclaimed.

"Hey, I didn't get a mattress," Grace complained.

Around 4:00 p.m., some nurses who were off duty joined us. "Follow us to the mess hall," Cassie said. "I figured more of you would be joining us."

After the long day we'd had, food sounded good. Of course, we never knew what we'd be served or if there'd be enough to fill our stomachs. It was one of the uncertainties we faced daily.

Geneva asked about Jerry and was told he was out picking up wounded but would return. After that, she kept her hair combed and a touch of lipstick on.

The path to the mess hall led through some undergrowth. The dining area consisted of long bamboo tables and benches in the center of the small clearing. About twenty feet from the tables, a makeshift kitchen had been set up.

Another long table held the food offered in a cafeteria style arrangement. At the opposite side of the tables, a fire trench had been built. The large metal drums set over the fire. One contained soapy water while the other two held clear water for rinsing.

We joined the line at the serving table, but then realized we hadn't brought our mess kits. The workers loaned us each a tin plate and fork.

Later that evening, I decided to hunt down Sally Blaine while there was some daylight left. I hadn't seen her since our visit to Hospital No. 2. She'd been here for some time. I found her with Anna Williams by their cots all the way over by the burlap wall.

"Sally," I shouted.

She glanced around. "Ressa Jenkins. Are you visiting us or assigned here?"

"The Japs were too close for comfort. They're closing it down and reopening Hospital No. 1 around Baguio."

I studied the burlap wall that had been pushed back to the other side of the bank, allowing them to dam the stream with rocks. "You made your own pool. That's clever."

Sally smiled. "It's luxury in the jungle. Trust me, out here we get very little of it."

We talked about our trip and things that had happened at our jungle hospitals.

Sally stood. "Well, I've got to open a new ward. Care to help?"

"Sure. Should I check it out with anyone first?"

"Check it out with Josie and catch up with me." I found Josie Nesbit, and after hugs and informal greetings, I asked if I could help Sally. She agreed and gave me directions to the new ward.

That night, we all gathered in the summer house and talked and smoked for hours. It was the first time I'd been able to light up without worrying the glowing red flame would draw Japanese planes. Some nurses had lanterns on or candles burning, but the thick canopy of the trees kept the lights hidden.

Geneva had turned in earlier. She had hoped Jerry would return that night, but he didn't. I walked down the path toward the sleeping area. Seeing Geneva asleep next to me gave me a sense of comfort. I quietly undressed trying not to wake her.

On my cot, the mattress gave a feel of comfort I wasn't used to. I made sure my netting was fitted around me not leaving any openings. Then I shined my flashlight around the inside of my netting to make sure no lizards or insects had slipped inside it. I turned off my light, but instead of closing my eyes, I stared through a slight hole in the canopy and looked directly up at the night sky.

I had never seen anything so lovely. The moon shined brightly. White iridescent clouds filled the dark blue sky. They kept drifting out of my sight with others following in the never-ending kaleidoscope of shapes and patterns. The moonlight seemed to envelop everything in an ethereal aura that shimmered through gently swaying trees. In the distance, I heard a monkey screaming, and nearby, Gecko lizards called back and forth. *Gecko, gecko.*

The next morning, I woke to find Geneva already dressed. "You're up early."

"I don't plan to be at the end of the mess line."

I sat up and started dressing. "I hope they have hot coffee. I was dreaming of Mom's homemade biscuits and white gravy. I'd kill for some."

"Nothing ever tasted better. When I get home, that's the first thing I want to eat. And maybe some chicken and dumplings."

While we waited in the mess line, we learned a lot about Hospital No. 2. It had four mess halls—three for the men and one for the officers and nurses. Fortunately, if Robert made it here, he'd be dining in the same area. We were all given a ticket that allotted us one meal a day.

"Some of the corpsmen are willing to trade their tickets for cigarettes," Whitlow whispered.

"As much as I like to smoke, I like to eat even more," I said.

Geneva gave a piercing look, then rolled her eyes. She wanted no part of smoking and often begged me to quit. After a small breakfast, we carried our clean clothes to the bathing hole. As far as modesty, Geneva and I had been raised with sisters and didn't have an issue with other women seeing us naked. Neither of us had bodies to be ashamed of.

But one thing I noticed was how much thinner we were than when we had first arrived in the Philippines. We could eat a banana split every day for a year and still be considered too thin. A corpsman informed us the sergeant who cooked had to be creative with our meals. I didn't want to know what that meant. But any creature that crawled, flew, or slithered into camp could end up in a pot.

We worked on our living space. We crossed bamboo poles to form a shelter over our beds, then covered them with palm leaves. One of the corpsmen even built and nailed us a little shelf into the tree, so we'd have a place to set things. Assuming we might need to roll under our beds during a raid, we pulled the grass and replaced it with bamboo mats.

Afterwards, we strolled slowly to headquarters to check our assignments.

"What's that up ahead?" Geneva asked.

"Otolaryngology." I smiled. "If you need your tonsils yanked out you'll know where to go." It consisted of a room with walls. Nearby, we discovered a dental clinic that had chairs but no walls. We finally came to the only completed building that housed the operating room, only large enough for three operating tables. From what we heard, they stayed in continuous use from early morning until late into the night. Two large tents each holding ten beds for postoperative patients stood behind the building.

Hospital staff sterilized everything with an autoclave, a mobile sterilizer. The large metal contrivance had been mounted onto a truck.

"I know we have it rough," I told Geneva, "but those girls in surgery have it rougher."

"You've got that right. I wouldn't want to be in their shoes."

"So, what do you think of the place?"

Geneva glanced around and sighed. "It's bigger than I thought. It sprawls all over the place. Honestly, I miss Limay."

"I do too." I missed Robert and all the nurses we left behind. There had been only one constant presence in my life here and that had been Geneva. I don't know how I could bare it if we were ever separated.

Headquarters also had walls and a roof, containing several desks, chairs, and a table with a book where we signed in and out. This room had a telephone that kept us linked to Corregidor and other parts of Bataan.

Inside the office, we greeted the people, then searched the bulletin board for our names. "There you are," I said. "You're in ward four. Do you see me?"

"You're in ward two. It doesn't say when to report."

"I'd better run talk to them."

"Mine doesn't say. I guess I need to stop by ward two. I'll see you at dinner."

Geneva hugged me. "See you."

We parted ways, and I started looking for ward two.

"Morning," Denny Williams said. "Good seeing you again."

"How's your husband? Have you heard from him?" I asked.

"Bill's good. When he can, he comes to see me."

I asked for directions, then followed the path until I came to ward two. I spotted a clearing with beds set up under the trees.

"Hey, Sally. I'm in this ward, but I'm not sure when I'm to report."

"How 'bout now? We're shorthanded."

"Sure. What do you need me to do?"

"Grab a pan and start bathing these patients," Sally instructed as she continued going over reports.

I saw a soldier trying to reach his cup, so I helped him. Each bed held a tin can to catch the rain for drinking. "Thanks, Miss."

Seeing he had lost both legs, I nodded and forced a smile.

RESSA
January 25, 1942

Bataan was dry. There wouldn't be anyone passing around a bottle at Hospital No. 2. Cigarettes were at a premium, and if you had some to spare, you could buy anything you wanted. I actually paid a soldier to dig a foxhole between mine and Geneva's beds.

With the ground being rocky, it was more difficult than the sandy ground at Hospital No. 1. While he worked, I dozed off on top of my bed.

"Nurse! Nurse!"

I awoke with a start and sat up. "What's happening?"

I figured a patient was calling me. Instead, the boy stood in the middle of an enormous foxhole, large enough for Geneva and me.

Sweat ran down his face, and he grinned. "Is this big enough, Miss?"

"It's really nice."

He hopped out, and I paid him with cigarettes, and he couldn't have been happier.

Geneva walked up. "Well, if that ain't one luxurious foxhole."

"Ain't it?" I replied, exaggerating my Tennessee accent. We giggled.

Later sitting around the summer house, trying to stay cool, Earleen talked about her new husband, Garnet Francis, and how she wished she could see him if even for a moment. "I'm trying to save the rest of my makeup to wear when he returns."

"I'm out of foundation. All I have left is powder," Jean Kennedy said.

"I have extra powder and powder puffs if anyone needs them," Josie Nesbit said. She glanced over at Earleen. "I'll save one for you."

"If my foundation isn't too dark, you can have one of my bottles," Geneva said. "I stocked up in Manila."

"Me too," I said. "Out here, it feels better to have a clean face and my hair short or pinned up." Bobby pins had become a valuable commodity.

Helen Summers placed a hand on Earleen's arm. "When you get a visit with your hubby, we'll make sure you're all dolled up."

Josie smiled as she stood. "I was saving this for later, but I received a box that was salvaged from a sunken ship in the harbor, and it contained some interesting cargo."

"Don't keep us in suspense." Cassie's dark eyes widened with intrigue. "What's in it?"

Josie smiled. "Girdles. All sizes and colors. After dinner you each get to select one."

After dinner, we ran to the box of girdles. Eleanor, Cassie, Mary, Denny, and Minnie led the way. That night, I picked a white one with little pink roses on it. I'd never needed one. I still took it and added it to the treasures in my suitcase. Geneva did the same.

I don't believe anyone wore the girdles, but they lifted our spirits out of the pits of depression for just a little while and gave us something to smile about.

For the most part, we nurses are calm people, but at this point it would've been nice to let out a bloodcurdling scream to relieve the tension in my nerves.

In bed that night, I tried to deal with my frustration and the chaos surrounding us. The sounds of nocturnal animals kept us on edge.

Bats fluttered through the trees. Geckos continued crying out most of the night. The rats bothered me the most. Despite that we were scrupulously careful in not leaving any food out, they came through the camp every night. Their rustling sounds terrified us at night, while their horrific odor overpowered our sinuses. It was a nasty smell. One that even in the daylight hours faintly lingered in the camp.

The next day in our quarters, Earleen screamed.

I assumed she'd received bad news about Garnet.

"What's wrong?" I asked.

Geneva and the other nurses gathered around her, waiting for the gut wrenching news.

"Termites have eaten my suitcase!" She held up what had been expensive luggage. "It's ruined." The bag literally turned into powder and poofed into thin air. Her belongings were piled on the ground. "All my stuff is going to ruin."

Geneva stared with a look of bewilderment. "Well, if that doesn't beat all."

"The little beasts have good taste," Whitlow teased.

"That's what you get for having expensive luggage," Helen added.

Anna's eyes lit up. "We'd better check our bags."

Anna, Marcia, and Sally ran for their luggage. We were right behind them.

Geneva and I headed for our beds and jerked our bags out from under them. Sure enough, we also had little white larvae. I picked them out and then doctored my leather bag with kerosene. "At least we caught them in time."

Later that afternoon a group of us walked to the community clothesline. All our rayon and silk stockings hung on the line from being washed earlier.

Geneva pulled hers down and frowned. She gave them a closer look. "Am I seeing things?"

"Seeing what?" I asked.

"Little holes."

"I see them now. They're ruined."

Geneva sighed. "Well, phooey."

I spotted flying insects fluttering away as I jerked mine from the line. I glanced at the other nurses. "Better check your laundry."

Marcia, Helen, Jean, and Ann ran over. Their stockings and dresses had been ruined. Soon others arrived to examine the damage.

Fortunately, mine and Geneva's civilian seersucker dresses had been spared. Sometimes, we'd dress up for dinner. We called it going feminine. It lifted our spirits. And now some of the ladies had lost even that.

"There goes our last vestige of femininity," Cassie said.

"Now we've nothing but those damn girdles," Helen whined with a sigh.

The ladies moaned and groaned. Several cried. I knew it wasn't just the stockings and clothes that caused the tears to surface. It was everything. We were at our wit's end. I didn't dare wonder how much more of this we had to endure.

We worked long hours in the jungle not knowing what was going on in the rest of the world. Our world consisted of suffering and death. Rarely, did we hear a radio. There were no newspapers to keep us updated with the war. At best, we had a jungle newsletter.

GENEVA
January 26, 1942

I stopped by the mess hall and grabbed a corned-beef hash sandwich and a cup of coffee. I had to work and didn't have time to sit and enjoy my food. Once in the ward, I sat my dinner down on a bamboo bench at the entrance. I checked the charts to see what needed to be done.

Three hundred men needed my attention in one way or the other.

"Hey, Geneva. I'm working with you," Cassie said.

"You start on that side, and I'll cover this one. We'll meet up in the middle."

"Sounds good."

I first administered their medicines. I realized before long we'd be out of drugs. What then? Once I had that done, I changed dressings on wounds. Unfortunately, gauzes were low, so we ended up washing and sterilizing used bandages. Sometimes, we removed them from the dead.

I stopped at the bed of a young Filipino. "Looks like you've seen some action. Let's have a look under those bandages." I realized he was serious. "Not too bad," I lied. The extent of damage was brutal. I read his name on the chart. "So, tell me about it, Daniel. How'd you get banged up."

"I was on my way home when I heard men coming toward me. I laid hidden in a cane field close to a low footbridge. I couldn't tell if they were Japanese or ours. One talked to a wounded man. They were Japs. When they got right next to me, I attacked."

"How many were there?" I asked.

"Five, counting the wounded one, but even he put up a fight."

" Five!" I expected him to say three at most. "You attacked five Japs! Daniel, you are either the bravest man I know or the craziest."

He smiled and replied, "A little of both, I think."

"Looks like you paid a heavy price. How did you get away?"

"Getting away was easy. I killed them all and walked away. Getting here for help, not so easy."

I gave him a drink of water and wiped the sweat from his face. "With men like you, this war will be over in no time."

He smiled appreciating my words of praise. Neither one of us believed it, but it didn't hurt to bolster his spirit. Many Filipino men were devastated by the treatment from the Japanese. Japs treated them as slaves and raped their women.

Daniel had a nasty wound that was draining. I left the maggots to eat away the dead tissue. It hastened the healing process.

The soldier across from him didn't have maggots, so I washed out the wound with water and green soap, then poured peroxide over it. One doctor also used Vaseline and sulfanilamide powder when we had it. But once we ran out of something, we couldn't get anymore. I'm surprised we didn't have more infections with us being in the thick of the jungle.

"I'm going to grab my sandwich and coffee. I'll be right back."

Cassie nodded. "Take your time."

Due to the unsanitary conditions and outhouses, flies swarmed us all day. I had wrapped my sandwich in some wax paper to prevent them from landing on it. I stopped at the bench where I'd left my food and cold coffee. All I found was a turned over empty cup and the wax paper.

I glanced up in the tree and wondered if a tree rat had taken it. I returned to the ward with my stomach aching for food. I hadn't eaten all day and had been lightheaded for the past hour.

"That was fast," Cassie said.

"It wasn't there."

"More than likely a tree rat or monkey ate it. You can't set anything edible down. And be warned, the monkeys like shiny things."

I worked without eating. If I caught the creature that had taken my food, it might end up being my dinner. I worked in the ward, using my flashlight to see. When my duty ended, my back ached, and I was too tired to think of food. I'd eat tomorrow.

RESSA
January 29, 1942

We joined a group of nurses sitting in the mess hall for hot tea. We talked about everything going on. Marcia Gates sighed. "I tried to get a letter out to my mother. She worries herself sick over me."

Anna Williams glanced up. "Minnie has malaria again."

"Damn mosquitoes," Denny Williams said. "We're running low on quinine pills. Over half our patients suffer from malaria or dysentery."

Geneva had been rather quiet. I was sure her quietness was a result of her concern for Jerry. Each day she walked around to where the wounded came into camp and watched for him.

A cute little nurse offered us a smile. "Today is going to be a wonderful day."

"I can't imagine any day in this jungle being good," I said.

146

"Well, my boyfriend is heading back this way. He wanted us to get married the last time he was here. By the time I made up my mind, we couldn't find the chaplain."

We continued eating and smiling politely at her.

"I've decided if Jerry still wants us to get married, I'll marry him. You ladies are all invited to our wedding."

Geneva choked and had to drink her water. Other than that, she remained unreadable but stopped eating.

Apparently, the rumor Sally had told me was true.

"Jerry made us a stove," Ethel Thor commented. "Such a clever man."

"He's real handy around here when he's in camp," Marcia said.

Geneva stood. "I need to run. See you later, sis."

I followed her. "Listen, maybe it's a different Jerry."

"Sis, I had already sensed something wasn't right. He's never made any attempt to see me at Hospital No. 1. You're the first person Robert found once he reached the jungle. Jerry could've found me. I'm all right with this."

She left for her ward before I could hug her, but I think if I had hugged her, she would've cried.

Though I hated to see her suffer emotional pain, I smiled over what she'd said about Robert. Just maybe, if we both survived this war, I'd open my door in San Francisco one day and find him on my doorstep.

GENEVA
January 30, 1942

I worked in the operating room today. My main job had been sterilizing and making sure the doctors didn't run out of bandages. It kept my mind off Jerry and his sweetheart.

"Nurse, take that bucket out and dump it," the doctor ordered.

I grabbed the blood-filled bucket and walked a little past the ward when an ambulance pulled up. I stopped and stared at Jerry as he climbed from behind the wheel.

Despite everything, I felt a sense of relief he hadn't been killed. I started to approach him, but the young nurse beat me to it. Their greeting seemed more like that of friends than sweethearts.

Rather than interrupt, I dumped the bucket and returned inside.

Lord help him if Ressa caught up with him. He'd be begging for the Japs to take him prisoner.

In this environment, there wasn't time to cry over a lousy two-timer. It wasn't the first time I'd had my heart broken and wouldn't be the last.

Later that night, Jerry found me as I left the mess hall.

"Geneva, I heard you were here. Seeing you here has made my day. I didn't think I'd ever see you."

"Apparently."

He appeared worried. "You know?"

"About your fiancée'? Yes, I do. Sweet girl."

"It's not what you think. We're just friends."

"Did you ask her to marry you?"

He appeared guilty. "Yeah, but there's a reason."

"I don't want to hear it. So, if you'll get out of my way, I have things to do."

"But, Geneva. Let me explain."

Ressa happened upon us. Her timing couldn't have been more perfect. She stood in front of me and shook her finger at him. "Stay away from my sister. Don't come near her. You may find yourself fighting on the frontline instead of bringing the wounded in."

His face paled, and I wanted to laugh. Ressa didn't have any strings she could pull to back up the threat, but obviously, he didn't know that. He walked off like a dog with its tail between its legs.

"Thanks," I said. Then I thought of something funny. "If you have that kind of powerful connections, get us booked on the first rescue ship out of here."

We both laughed at the frivolous thought.

RESSA
February 5, 1942

148

Five nurses arrived today from Corregidor. I hoped Winnie might be with them, but there again, I wouldn't wish this on anyone. It was good seeing our old friends. Beulah Putnam, Hortense McKay, Phyliss Arnold, and Ruby Motley waved as they entered the camp. Surprisingly, Ruth Straub came with them. I was careful not to bring up Glen. She still came across as frail. I wondered why they had sent her here. Maybe, they thought the fresh air or change of scenery would help.

"Welcome to Hospital No. 2?" I shouted.

"We're not thrilled to be here," Ruby shouted back.

"I'm not looking forward to sleeping in a jungle," Hortense added.

"Trust me, the worst part is the food," Denny said. "We've been eating carabao and horses. I try not to question what the meat is. It's best if you don't know."

"Anything else we should know?" Beulah asked.

Whitlow grinned. "Watch out for the tree rats. They bite."

RESSA
February 8, 1942

I attended service at one of the makeshift churches. We sang hymns that we knew from memory and prayed. Afterwards, we all stood around talking and catching up on the rumors passing through the camp.

Everyone talked about the government evacuating some of us to Australia. We laughed at the ridiculous rumor. No one would be able to get us off this island under the nose of the Imperial Japanese Army.

GENEVA
February 9, 1942

The vegetation grew abundantly, and its tangled mass reminded me of ogres, witches, and fairies I had heard of as a child. Philippine mahogany, great banyan trees rose skyward with dao and nana vines climbing through their branches and around the trunks of all the trees. The natives cut the tubers from the vines and cooked them, but we never tried eating them.

Plants flourished in the lavish jungle with edible fruit, but it was out of season. We could only admire the sight and dream of its future flavor.

I ate a quick breakfast and headed toward ward one. I talked to Leona before starting my rounds. She looked exhausted. "You look like you could use a nap."

"Maybe later. I can't stop now, we have to set up a new ward with two hundred beds for the incoming."

"I saw the boys clearing the brush for it. Two hundred beds means our already long days are about to get longer. I hope they send us help. Lord knows we'll need it."

"I hope so too. My energy level bottomed out days ago. I wish I had the stamina of Nash. She's been a dynamo from the day they put her in charge."

"You won't catch me sassing her. That Frances Nash is one tough cookie all right," I said. "Have you received any news about Benji?"

Her shoulders drooped. "No, I haven't. Hopefully, someone will take care of him. I truly loved that little boy."

After she left, I started moving from bed to bed, treating each man to the best of my ability. Checking wounds and cleaning them, wiping sweat from the patients with dengue fever, trying to tend and comfort malaria patients.

"Beth, have you noticed our native, the Igorot?" I asked.

"I know the patient, but what are you talking about?"

"Look at him. Every time I see him, he's staring at those coconuts at the top of that tree, just like now."

"I see what you mean. You don't think he's thinking of climbing that tree, do you?"

"That's exactly what I think. I'd be willing to bet in a day or two those coconuts will come up missing."

"If by chance you're right, I would say he is in good enough shape to check out and leave that bed for someone else."

Later that day, I found his bed empty. I called Beth. When she arrived, I pointed to the tree.

"I don't believe it."

We both watched the progress our bedridden Igorot native was making. He climbed with a bolo-knife clenched between his teeth. Seconds later, two coconuts fell to the ground followed by a smiling native.

"What in the world do you think you're doing out of bed in your condition?" I scolded.

"I get this for you, Miss Geneva. You always take care of me so I brought you food."

Even though it was a crazy stunt to pull, I didn't have the heart to reprimand him further. It was such a sweet gesture.

He eagerly hacked the coconut open and stared at the green, unripe interior with a displeased expression. "No good."

"It's the thought that counts. I appreciate your effort."

He paid a price for his escapade. He suffered so many scratches and bruises, that it took days of care to get him back to where he was before his tree top adventure.

RESSA
February 13, 1942

The planes kept bombing Cabcaben, and many people died including women and children. Some men returned with another orphaned baby. This one wasn't as young as Benji. It didn't take long for Leona to claim him.

Life in the hospital became routine even during bombings. We had turned into professional foxhole divers. We cared for wounded as best we could under fairly unsanitary conditions. Our spare time consisted of rolling gauze and preparing bandages while fighting the never-ending battle of dirt and dust in the wards. On top of the dirt, thick yellow pollen covered everything.

Geneva and I hadn't seen each other since that morning. I sat by my sister and glanced over at Ruth Straub.

She sat picking at her food. "I can't eat this."

I stared at the fish and rice. "It beats that carabao they served the other night. You need to eat. Ask if they'll give you a jam sandwich."

She hadn't been the same since Glen had died during those first attacks.

She sighed. "I just keep hoping help will arrive. Surely, it will. I'm not sure how much more of this I can take."

I didn't have the heart to tell her what I thought.

Help wasn't coming.

GENEVA
February 1942

They shortened morning mess. We no longer had time to leisurely sip coffee. The flow of wounded soldiers had increased significantly. We quickly adapted to eating on the run. I joined Grace Hallman, Sally Blaine, Helen Summers and others at the table. I ate while listening to their conversation.

"I wonder when ward ten will be finished," Grace commented.

Helen set her cup down. "It's going to be a while. Clearing the heavy brush is a slow, hard job."

"The sooner the better. Lord knows we need it. How are you holding up Geneva?" Sally Blaine asked.

"One step at a time and one patient at a time," I responded. I was a much better listener than a talker. Actually, Ressa was the social butterfly of our family not me.

"To me, the worst of all are the boys with gas gangrene," Helen Summers said.

Sally nodded. "Those poor boys are the saddest of the bunch. They're rotting away from the inside out and the smell. Jeepers, it's bad."

"We're out of sulfur power," Grace said.

"They're isolating them from everyone," Helen informed us. "I'd hate to be assigned to the contagious disease ward."

Francis Nash had joined us. "Well, Colonel Adamo is trying something with them. And it seems to be working."

"But we don't have any medicine that stops the bacteria," Grace said.

"True, but he's opening up their wounds. The air and sunlight kill the bacteria. It's truly just short of a miracle."

I stopped eating. "You don't say? That's amazing."

Gas gangrene was an anaerobic bacterium that lived in the fertile soil.

Francis Nash appeared distraught. She blew out a long shaky breath. "I had to collect the dog tags off the dead soldiers before the bulldozers covered them. The chaplain was out there saying a blessing over them." She bit her lower lip, but still it didn't stop a tear from rolling down her cheek. "I can't go back out there. I don't think I'll ever forget the sight of those young, dead men thrown out there like trash in a landfill."

Sally, who cried over all the men who died, teared up. Her tender heartedness is one reason we liked her so much.

There was a time when none of us could have talked about such things as decaying flesh and dead soldiers while eating, but those days were long gone.

"I'm sorry," I said. "Next time, get one of the men to do it."

We rose and separated, all wondering how long this would continue before we starved to death or were captured. Surely, our leaders knew what we were going through. Why hadn't they sent ships and planes?

Sally joined me as I walked toward our quarters. "When are you due back on duty?"

"I've got about an hour. Just enough time to dip in the creek and give my soiled clothes to a soldier to wash," I responded.

"I think I'll do the same. My trousers are filthy. Setting up beds in the jungle is a dirty job. Geneva, are the boys charging you cash?"

"No luckily, I kept several packs of cigarettes in case Ressa or others ran out. I never thought I'd end up using them to pay my laundry bill."

We stopped to get a clean outfit and soap before walking the short path to the stream. This section had become the nurses' public bath. After disrobing, we placed our clothes in the dirty pile and dipped in the flowing water. We used our helmets to dip water to pour over us. The feeling of being clean was always pleasant but short lived. It wouldn't take long working in the wards or clearing brush to become drenched in grime and sweat.

"I'm sorry about Jerry."

"I've already put him behind me," I lied, still feeling the sting of betrayal.

"Well, good for you."

I could have relaxed in the soothing current for hours, but duty called. I quickly donned my clean clothes and gathered up the dirty ones. I left them with a soldier and paid him with cigarettes.

"You do realize our little laundry man has hired help," Sally said.

"What do you mean, help?"

She explained for every three smokes he earns he pays one to a Filipino boy to guard our clothes while they dry."

"Talk about an enterprising chain of command," I said.

"I guess everybody comes out happy," Sally replied. "I have clean trousers. He and his lackey both have cigarettes."

I reported to my ward where so many gravely injured suffered. I did what had to be done. I cleaned wounds and dropped the bloody wrappings in a bucket for washing. Feverish foreheads, chest, and arms had to be wiped and cooled. I constantly monitored amputees for infections and administered morphine as needed.

Due to several evacuations, our medical staff had become depleted. Ward ten was close to completion. As fast as they set up beds, patients occupied them. Often the men who weren't as ill or injured as the others would pitch in to ease our workload.

"Miss Jenkins, I can sterilize those for you," one soldier said.

After the doctor ordered a bucket to be dumped, another soldier stepped in. "I'll get that for you."

I looked at Captain Riemann, an awesome doctor from Florida. "These soldiers are a real Godsend."

"They're real troopers. I'm thankful to have their assistance. It makes everyone's job easier."

The only sad part was if they were able to help, they'd be considered able to return to the frontline to fight.

GENEVA
February 19, 1942

We had a jungle wedding. Dorothea Daley and her boyfriend, Boots, tied the knot with Father Thomas Cummings performing the ceremony. He had married many of the nurses and soldiers since the war had started. The two had fallen in love in the autumn and had been separated until recently.

I wondered if Dorothy Scholl and Arnold had married at Hospital No.1. Ressa would be upset if she'd missed it.

Dorothea glowed with joy. "I figured it was now or never while we're both in Bataan."

"When we ended up in this godforsaken jungle at the same time, I knew it was meant to be. I've loved her since I first laid eyes on her," Boots said, then kissed his bride.

I glanced over at Ruth Straub and recognized the sadness in her eyes. I knew she had to be thinking of Glen. Still, she congratulated Dorothea.

In war you could go from a blushing bride to a grieving widow in the same week. I thought of Jerry and the dreams I'd had for us, but now, that would never happen.

RESSA
February 20, 1942

Our commanding officer, Carlton L. Vanderboget made every effort to separate the wards—ambulatory, dysentery, malaria, and so on. The jungle had filled with pockets of beds. But malaria and dysentery attacked practically every patient which added more discomfort to whatever disability they had. A new disease showed up in our patients—tuberculosis.

Jean Kennedy waved her arms motioning us over. "We need more beds!"

"Stop flapping your wings, Jean. We've already snatched the mattresses right out from under our patients."

Their mattresses had been tossed on the ground for incoming wounded. We didn't have anywhere to put them.

"Take the covers off the mattresses and stuff them with leaves," Lieutenant Nesbit suggested. "Watch for snakes."

"I spent the morning removing the covers and stuffing them. But while working, I became weak and feverish. I'd made it ten days at Hospital No. 2 without coming down with anything, but now, I too had fallen victim. I finished what I was doing before reporting I was ill with dysentery.

"You don't look well. You shouldn't have pushed yourself," Lieutenant Nesbit scolded.

"I know, but there's so much to do."

"I'll add you to the list. Lieutenant Comstock will come around with some sulfa. And I'll check on you in a bit when I make my rounds."

"Thank you," I said, then dragged myself to bed and collapsed. I thought of how hard Josie worked and never slowed down, always putting us first.

It wasn't until the next morning, Lieutenant Jack Comstock gave me the sulfa.

Geneva fretted over my illness and checked my temperature. "I wish I could stay and take care of you all day."

"I'll be fine. I feel guilty I'm not able to do my job."

"Don't. Eventually, we'll all get it," Geneva said. "You stay put until your fever breaks and you're over it."

By the third day, I was better but still unable to stand without being dizzy and weak. I pulled out my radio and tinkered with it. Suddenly, it started working. I couldn't believe my ears. All day, I listened to it while lying there. This was the only time it had worked my entire stay in Bataan.

I picked up Japanese news from Manila. It was given in four different languages, one being English. They also played popular American music and cunningly dedicated each number to the poor starving soldiers on Bataan and told them to go home to their wives and children who needed them. They even had the effrontery to dedicate songs to American soldiers who waited for ships that never arrived.

Listening to all the propaganda made my fever rise.

Twice a day, *The Voice of Freedom,* a secret station operated by the Americans and Filipinos aired. They said it operated from various parts of Bataan, but we strongly suspected it broadcasted from Corregidor. They exposed every Japanese lie and told the truth.

All the nurses gathered around my bed to listen to President Roosevelt's *Fireside Chat.* While the President talked, the program was interrupted. A news flash blurted out.

"We shelled Santa Barbara today."

Instant shock ran through me. They had attacked the mainland as they had promised they would. Why Santa Barbara? It had a smaller population.

I sat up and looked at the others. "They hit Santa Barbara!"

Concern showed on their faces.

I took out my notes and jotted down the date, February 23, 1942 and wrote about what I had heard.

"I don't believe it," Anna said.

Jean waved it off with a slight hand gesture. "It's just more propaganda."

All day I waited for the *Voice of Freedom* to come on. They confirmed that it had been intended to affect our morale. Though I knew it wasn't true, I still worried about the people at home. What if the Japs invaded the west coast? Could it happen? No one would be prepared for the attack. The thought left me upset and trembling.

RESSA
February 24, 1942

When I returned to work, I'd been assigned to ward seventeen, an orthopedic ward. There were over three hundred patients.

I waved at Katherine Nau and Mr. Graybill, our Red Cross workers. They moved from patient to patient helping them write letters to send home. Truth was the letters rarely made it out.

"Jenkins, you're taking care of those fifty patients today," Gwendolyn Holmes said, as she motioned in their direction. "You've got a few in full body casts."

"Yes. I'll get started." I turned to the corpsmen, an American and a Filipino. "I'll need both of you helping me lift some of these patients."

"Yes, ma'am," the larger American soldier replied.

"While I check their bandages, go ahead and give them water."

"Yes, Missy." The Filipino smiled, then headed for the water bucket. The American helped me raise patients from their beds.

As I walked around looking at the condition of the patients, I spotted one with a foot that had turned black. I did a smear test for gas gangrene but didn't see any signs of it. However, the foot looked limp and dried up.

When I saw Captain Whaley and Captain Roland, I walked over to them. "I have a patient whose foot is black but doesn't have any swelling."

Captain Whaley looked sorrowful. "Yes, it has to be amputated. It's basically dead. There's no saving it. We're waiting for Major Schwartz to have the time to get him to the operating table."

"Will he be able to hold out that long?"

"He's not in any immediate danger. We remove a ton of scrap metal from these boys." Captain Roland frowned. "The automobile that doesn't hit you at home, will get you in Bataan."

The Japs melted old cars and machinery down to make their bombs and ammo.

I looked back at the young soldier and shuddered at what lay ahead of him. An immense strain had been placed on these doctors in the operating room with the decisions they had to make.

That morning, I managed to change the linens for some patients, especially those with wounds that were draining. Many with open wounds had maggots eating at the dead skin. We didn't have the facilities to launder the linens as we should. I swatted flies away as I walked through the ward. Unfortunately, the dried blood from all the wounds attracted them. I tried to keep nets over many of the patients, but there weren't enough of them to go around.

Some of my patients could bathe themselves while others needed help. I bathed a few of the patients. I rolled the ones too injured to have a bath and rubbed alcohol on their backs to prevent infections. But only a few of these patients were seriously ill or died while in our care.

During our normal air raids, I didn't take cover. Most of my patients were immobilized and had to stay in their beds. I didn't feel right running out on them.

A Filipino we called the fox because of his clever business deals stopped and saluted me. I laughed because he saluted everyone. "I'll give you three cigarettes if you'll make me a palm leaf broom."

"Yes, Missy."

Hours later, he returned with my broom complaining the job had been worth more. "You, Missy, outfoxed the fox."

I laughed and took my broom.

The next day, Captain Robert Benson sent twenty-five pounds of nuts and raisins. I put the wormy raisins in a large can and sealed it. We ended up making pies out of them. I sat with Captain Whaley, Captain Roland, and Nancy Gillahan eating the delicious pies, worms and all. I shared the rest of the raisins and nuts with the soldiers.

"Whatcha got there?" Whaley asked me.

"These bundles arrived, and I managed to get one."

"Me too," Nancy said. "Let's open them. I hope it's something I need."

I peeled back the burlap and frowned. "What is this?"

"Flannel pajamas," she said, staring at them in disbelief. "And they smell like mothballs." She looked at the men. "Want 'em?"

Captain Roland laughed. "Not in this damn heat."

Though I worked long hours and found myself exhausted, this had been one of the easier wards. Unfortunately, I would be moved. They shifted us from ward to ward to make it fair.

RESSA
February 24, 1942

I sat with others listening to Major Teasineau in our mess hall.

"We came across a Japanese grave," he said. "That's not so uncommon, but this one had been decorated to the hilt. We figured it had to be a general."

"Did you dig it up?" Helen asked, with enthusiasm.

"We did."

I sat on the edge of my seat eager to hear. "Who was it?"

He grinned. "Not a who but a what. It was a damn field gun and ammo. They really outsmarted themselves on that one. It helped our arsenal out."

We laughed with him.

"I bet they were surprised when they found it missing," Jean said.

Navy doctor, Lieutenant Max Pohlman, started the next tale. "I heard some Marines had let their beards and hair grow out. They weren't in uniform and looked like a bunch of brutes. They ran screaming bloody murder toward a group of Japs coming up a hill. The Japs thought they were wild men from the jungle, turned, and ran."

I imagined the scene in my mind and laughed the hardest. But we all knew what merciless killers the Japs were. They wanted to make the men suffer greatly before they died.

MacNeil told about a soldier who had an incident with a python. "He said the thing swung its body down from the tree knocking him over. Then it dropped and curled around him trying to squeeze him to death. His buddies saved him."

"Snakes have got to eat too," Pohlman said. We all laughed.

I swore I'd never walk under the trees without glancing up. A snake had also dropped down on a nurse, who managed to kill it.

"One of our boys jumped in his foxhole and then jumped right out," Blanche said. "He didn't care if Japs were flying over. The other guys ran over to see what the problem was. It turned out that a python was in his foxhole."

My skin crawled from the thought of it. While I knew snakes lived in the jungle, I'd never seen one. Our jungle not only had pythons but a variety of venomous snakes including the king cobra. With so many people around, most of the reptiles had moved deeper into the jungle. Snakes terrified Geneva. It was a good thing she was on duty and hadn't heard these stories.

That night while on my bed, I glanced up at the nearest tree and spotted a slight movement. "Earleen, I saw something coming down from that tree. Do you see anything?"

I figured after the python stories I was being paranoid.

We both stared at the tree for a good minute before something moved. As it slithered down the tree towards my bed, I screamed.

"Help!" Earleen shouted. "Someone help us!"

Sally came with her machete. "Did you see a Jap?"

Beth showed up with a stick. "What's wrong?"

We pointed to the huge snake still making its way to my bed.

We outnumbered the snake, so we killed it.

The following evening, I managed to get something on my radio. I had to ignore the static and listen to the announcer. "It's from Washington D.C."

"Sit next to me," Beth said to Blanche.

Blanche sat and stared at the radio, concentrating.

The announcer discussed an upcoming formal banquet in D.C.

"Oh Lord," Blanche said. "Just think of all the good food they must be having. It makes me want to cry."

We all had a good laugh over her exasperation.

One of the nurses started singing a song someone had made up, and we joined in repeating it over and over.

We are the battling bitches of Bataan, no mommy, no poppy, no Uncle Sam. The men's version went: *We are the battling bastards of Bataan, no mommy, no poppy, no Uncle Sam.*

GENEVA
February 25, 1942

Ressa's voice woke me. "Let's go."

I sat up, disoriented, then realized a shot had been fired. It served as our alarm for raids. I lunged from bed and grabbed my helmet, gas mask, and pencil. I dove head first into the foxhole. I wasn't alone. "Aaaah, what the heck?"

Something smooth and cold moved by my arm. As Ressa lowered inside, I passed her climbing out.

"Where are you going?" she yelled over all the commotion.

"Not in there."

"Why? What's wrong?"

"There's something in that hole." I shivered as I pointed down. "It felt like a snake."

Ressa laughed at the harmless iguana when it ran from the foxhole. After she shooed it away, I joined her for the remainder of the raid. To me, it was no laughing matter. Anything reptilian terrified me. From now on, I'd never dive into another foxhole without checking first or better yet, letting Ressa lead the way. Though she'd tried to keep it from me, someone told me about the snake they'd killed.

The next day, I greeted Ressa as she entered my ward. "How's your day going?"

"Same as yesterday. I'm tired and hungry."

"Well if you're hungry enough, the Filipino boys offered to share their balut."

"Heavens no. I don't think I'll ever be hungry enough to eat a duck egg that's been buried for weeks."

I couldn't resist teasing her. "Oh now, Ressa, don't be so picky. Think of it as the middle of the road between an omelet and a duck dinner."

"Not even close. They eat it raw. Disgusting. Have you tried it?"

"No, but who knows what the future holds. A month ago, the thought of eating a horse would have made me sick. Now, I don't give it a second thought."

"Has Jerry tried to talk to you again?" Ressa asked, changing the subject.

"No. I avoid him when he's in camp. Heard anything from your flyer?"

"Nothing. No one has seen or heard from him. I've been checking some of the dead to see if he's one of them."

RESSA
February 26, 1942

The following day, I stood outside my ward, mentally preparing myself to go inside. Adele Foreman and several doctors walked past me. It literally took from early morning until late at night to dress all the wounded and injured soldiers. They had few breaks. I couldn't help but notice the transformation in Adele. She'd been a picture of health and vitality, and she had faded away to just skin and bones. Her eyes had a haunted expression, and her lips drew into a tight, thin line. She never complained about her growing fatigue. Despite her workload, Adele remained kind and considerate of everyone.

Had I changed? Had living and working in the jungle taken a toll on me? My job wasn't as stressful or demanding and for that, I was thankful.

I snapped from my thoughts when P040s flew over.

A bunch of Filipino soldiers became excited. "Those are our planes," one said proudly.

I gritted my teeth to prevent crying. Could this be it? If only enough help would come to stop the Japanese and end the war. We felt loyal to the United States and to the Filipino people. It had become a personal obligation to save them and their country from the Japs.

Later, I sat with Colonel Ronald Craig from Tennessee. His country way of talking made me smile.

"My, I sure wish I had my squirrel rifle with me," he said, grinning.

"It'd be nice to have something different on the table," I replied. "I'm tired of horse meat." Anytime we ate it, I thought of the old cavalry horse I had ridden. I had become very fond of him, so it made me sad to think I might be eating him.

"I need a damn toothpick," Major Lewis of the Medical Corps called out. "My oatmeal is full of worms. Got one stuck in my hollow tooth."

"Think of all the extra vitamins," Clara Mueller said, smiling.

We had become so used to the worms, we didn't think twice about eating them.

"If Captain White would bring me mustard seeds from Cebu, we'd have us some greens," Colonel Craig said.

I smiled. "Being a good southerner, you know greens aren't any good unless you've got some pork to throw in the pot."

He grinned and winked. "You got that right. But don't forget the cornbread."

Mrs. Franz Weisblatt, a civilian whose husband was a prisoner, oversaw our diets. With what she had to work with, she did a fine job feeding all the staff and patients. Turnip greens and lettuce weren't a part of our diet.

On the way back to my ward, a shot fired into the air. I heard the planes coming from a mile away and rushed to my foxhole.

Geneva didn't join me. Hopefully, she had taken shelter near her ward. We had so many foxholes, it looked like a giant mole village. I poked my head out but didn't see her among those scrambling for cover.

At dinner, Edith told us about Ruth Straub's cobra experience. The thing had lunged at her. Fortunately, she hadn't been bitten. Some soldiers killed it.

I wouldn't take any more shortcuts through overgrown areas.

GENEVA
February 1942

Hospital No. 2 stayed busy. A steady flow of wounded kept us all hopping. The mental ward was no different. Sad to say the horrors of war can't be witnessed by anyone without leaving scars, both physical and mental. Colonel Carroll's words, *war is a terrible thing,* was an understatement.

Ward one stood about a quarter of a mile from the nurses' quarters. I had been assigned to work in the psychiatric ward. Captain Katz and Lieutenant Gonzales oversaw this unique ward containing one hundred and ninety patients.

Ward one stood at the edge of a stream with a path that came over a hill and cut through it. People came and went all day. An enormous mango tree grew in the center. Its fruit covered branches spread out over us. We sat on its trunk and rested against it.

The medical cabinet had been constructed from the roof of a bus supported by four posts. Bamboo shelves had been built inside it to store medical supplies and blankets.

Ressa entered the ward. "Josie sent me over. What do you need me to do?"

"You'll be administrating medicine. Miss Cruz will change the linens and tend to the men while I get our books done."

My sister appeared apprehensive. "Any words of wisdom about surviving the mental ward?"

"It gets pretty bizarre. Best thing I can tell you is be ready for anything, and that goes double during an air raid." I smiled at her. "Welcome to the loony bin."

"Really?"

"Oh yeah, and even though this is basically a mental ward, we still have a few wounded and some malaria cases. We even have a leper."

Ressa's eyes widened. "A leper! Like the Bible kind?"

"Yeah."

"I've never seen one. What does he look like?"

"He's right over there. Come. I'll introduce you."

Ressa's enthusiasm surprised me. Her face grew stern as she tried to look professional. "Of course, I'm only interested from a medical standpoint."

I knew better. She reminded me of a kid at a county fair headed for the freak show. "How are you feeling today?" I asked him.

"I'm fine, Miss Geneva. I've been sweeping the floor, trying to help with the cleaning."

"That's really good. Just remember the rule about not touching anything that doesn't belong to you."

"I know. I only touch the broom handle."

"That's fine. We appreciate all your hard work. The ward looks a lot better since you've been here. This is Miss Ressa. She's the new nurse."

"Miss Ressa." He bowed slightly. "I'm Mandy."

Ressa acknowledged him with a nod. "Nice meeting you."

We left him and continued on our rounds. "Well, now you've met a leper. Don't worry about him. The rule of not touching anything is only for the peace of mind of our patients. He isn't contagious and won't be for quite a while."

"He wasn't what I expected. His skin was leathery looking but other than that, he seemed normal. He was pretty cheerful for a man with leprosy."

I was about to respond to Ressa's observation when a single gunshot fired a warning. Screams of panic rang through the ward as chaos ensued. Men fell out of beds and quickly wriggled under them.

Several ran out of the ward and dove into the underbrush. One ran naked into the jungle yelling at the top of his lungs with a Marine in hot pursuit. Malaria victims lay where they were, moaning.

Ressa stood with an incredulous expression of disbelief. She turned and faced me, "Good gravy. Is it always like this?"

"Pretty much. You'll get used to it. Most of these boys have foxholes under their beds. A few will venture out in time, but the majority will stay down until mess call.

Hours passed before the Marine caught our naked runner and coaxed him back. Ressa soon learned ward one was many things, but boring wasn't one of them.

GENEVA
February 27, 1942

The occasional break in the daily routine was nice. One of those was a visit from nurses on Corregidor. They had been underground in the Malinta Tunnel for quite a while and wanted to experience the great outdoors. They missed the fresh air and the warming rays of the sun, or so they thought. Our friend, Winnie Madden, was one of them.

"Winnie, it's good to see you." Ressa said, as they hugged.

I greeted her in the same manner. I couldn't help but notice her pale skin, evidence of months underground. We looked like Indians greeting the pilgrims to the new world.

"Come on, we'll give you the grand tour," I said.

Something was a little off. They were nervous.

"What was that?" Winnie demanded.

"What?" Nancy asked.

"I thought I heard something."

Nancy looked at me. "I didn't hear anything, did you?"

"No," I responded, "nothing."

We gave them a tour of our jungle hospital.

"This is so primitive," Peggy O'Neil said. "I can't believe you just sleep out in the open like this."

"You get used to it."

When I had Winnie alone, I told her about Jerry.

"Well, believe you me, you should hear the boy out."

"I don't like leftovers."

Every sound made the Corregidor nurses jump and at times dive for cover. It was both sad and comical. Working underground the sounds of nature didn't exist. I prayed we wouldn't end up there. Nevertheless, it was still nice seeing Winnie again.

Maude Davison visited us a few days later. She said she was ready for an outing with her girls above ground. Her time with us was enjoyable. It also reassured us that a person could work in the tunnel and not end up jumpy. Maude seemed to be made of sterner stuff. Nothing bothered that tough, ole girl.

RESSA
March 1942 (early in the month)

I stood with Dorothea Daley and watched the MPs drag back one of our Filipino patients who'd run off during a raid wrapped only in a towel. The man panted to catch his breath.

The officer looked at the man. "Who do you think you are? Dorothy Lamour?"

The small soldier shook his head. "Just scared."

"If you're scared, you get your ass in a foxhole. You don't run half-naked through the jungle," the officer said, sternly.

"Thanks for bringing him back," I said. "We'll take him from here."

I couldn't blame the guy for being terrified. The raids happened more frequently.

We could keep up with time by the daily scheduled Japanese reconnaissance plane flying over each morning. We called the pilot Photo Joe. Then the air raids would start, one at noon and another at 4:00 p.m. The roaring of their engines sent chills through us and kept us on edge.

That evening, I sat with Geneva at the mess table. I was delighted we had fish and rice instead of carabao or horse meat. I quickly learned that if you're hungry enough you'll eat anything regardless of its source. What I really missed were onions. I figured I'd lay down and die if I could just have one succulent onion.

I glanced over at Geneva, "Did that corpsman ever find who had stolen his shoes?"

"No, but he finally got a pair from somewhere."

Shoes were a valuable commodity. The poor guy had gone barefoot for a day.

Dorothea pointed her spoon my way. "I like what they did in ward one."

"You mean our park?" I asked.

"Yes, indeedy. It's nice," Dorothea commented.

Nancy glanced up from her food. "What park?"

I swished my coffee in the cup, trying to get a drink without the grinds. "Captain Katz put in a park. It's called MacArthur's Square."

"Why'd the tiger do that?" Nancy asked. He'd earned the nickname because of his freckles and red hair.

"It's a shrink thing," I said. "It helps keep up morale."

Helen joined us. "You must be talking about the park. It's right in the middle of the ward. All the guys are busy building benches and swings."

"I was skeptical at first, but it's nice," Geneva admitted.

We were so busy talking we didn't hear the planes until they flew almost on top of us.

"Raid!" I shouted. "Don't forget your helmet!" I tried to figure out how to take my dinner with me. Instead, I grabbed my helmet and gas mask, then ran for a foxhole. I just hoped some creature didn't eat my dinner before I made it back.

I jumped in and lowered my head. I held my breath as shells rained overhead. They thudded the ground around me, and I prayed we wouldn't be hit. Finally, it stopped. "Thank you, Lord."

Fortunately, I had my helmet on. You had to wear it to prevent someone from stealing it. After I climbed out, I searched for Geneva.

She was brushing the dirt off. "Well, phooey. I'm dirty again."

Once I knew she was safe, I returned to my fish and rice.

The next day, I was changing linens on several of the beds when soldiers from medical supplies came up the hill toward us.

"They're here!" I shouted to the other nurses. We dropped what we were doing and ran out to greet them. "Got any paper?"

"Not today."

"Just a few extra pages," I said. "My journal is running out."

Dorothea ran up. "I don't have any paper to write letters to Boots. Surely, you have a few pieces for me."

Nancy stood looking disappointed. "I'm out too."

They turned their palms up to show they were empty. "Not today, ladies."

"Save us!" a soldier shouted. "We're being attacked by wild jungle nurses."

The guys all shouted similar things and pretended to run away. One stopped before us. "You the Jenkins sisters?"

I gave him a curious look. "Yes, we are."

"Major Kemp wants you ladies to join him for dinner tonight. Someone will come by to escort you."

"We'll be ready." I smiled. I hadn't seen Peter since we'd gone to the movie the night before Pearl Harbor had been hit. I only hoped he had real food to eat.

Geneva glanced at me and grinned. "We'll definitely be eating good tonight."

That night, we dressed like ladies in our civilian dresses and walked to the smaller mess away from our camp with a young soldier as our escort. We dined on delicacies. Pickles and good white bread. Things that never made it to us.

After dinner while sipping coffee and finishing our pound cake, we talked. "I guess no one is coming to rescue us."

He sighed and sipped his coffee. "When we do hear something, it's bad news. Just learned about the Houston being bombed on March first. It was our largest war ship. The Japs sank it."

"Where?" I asked, wondering if they had been trying to reach us.

"In the Java Sea. They're claiming it's their biggest victory."

With only depressing news, I stood and thanked him for the dinner. Geneva and several of the other officers strolled ahead. I lingered back to thank Peter. "Thank you for a wonderful evening. We don't get many."

"It was my pleasure." He took my hand. "We never made it to the New Year's Eve gala."

"No, looks like fate had other plans."

He chuckled. "Life has thrown us a curve ball."

I rose on my tiptoes and kissed his cheek. "Thank you for a wonderful dinner. Stay safe."

Though Peter was a wonderful man, Robert was the one I thought of.

Peter had a soldier escort us back. One couldn't be too careful. There could be Japanese hidden around us. The most likely obstacle would be a carabao that blocked the path or wild pigs running free. Trust me, I'd prefer the ponies over anything with tusks.

Later that week, a friend of Josie's, Major William Latimer, of the Ordinance Department, invited us to the mess hall near the new Hospital No. 1 located in Little Baguio. They had good coffee and pie made with real canned fruit. At this rate, we'd finally put on a little weight. We were both thin as toothpicks.

I met Captain Anderson of the Medical Corps. We poured our hearts out about how bad the food was at our hospital.

"I've had nothing but rice for four days," Captain Anderson added.

"Is that so?" Geneva asked. "And I thought we had it bad."

"That's the truth," he replied. "Times are tough, and food is scarce. "

"My biggest complaint is with the underwear they gave us. They're too big," I said without giving it any thought. Then I realized I was talking about our panties. My cheeks warmed. "It's just that they're so big they rub us in the hot muggy places."

The entire group exploded into laughter.

It hadn't come out as I had planned. I had intended to say *this* not *the*. My cheeks burned with embarrassment. "I'm referring to the jungle."

Geneva's mouth remained opened, and her eyes bulged out as she stared at me in disbelief.

"Oh, close your mouth. You know what I meant."

"What you said could be translated another way."

He laughed and laughed for a good two minutes. "Tell you what, I know where there are a couple of small pairs of G.I. underwear. If I find them, I'll bring them to you."

"That'd be really nice."

Though he'd offered, I didn't expect him to remember.

A few days later, Captain Anderson motioned for me to follow him. "Gotcha something."

I didn't question him and walked with him up the hill.

"I found two pairs of size 28 GI shorts. But you've got to promise you won't tell anyone. They wouldn't be happy with me passing them out."

"I promise. Oh, thank you so much." I gave him a light hug. "I really appreciate this. I will gladly keep it a secret."

The only person I told was Geneva when I gave her a pair. She also promised not to mention it.

While working in ward one, a man walked in. "Ladies, I'm Lieutenant Commander Frank Davis of the Pigeon. It's a mine sweeping vessel. For now, we're docked at Seaman's Beach just below Baguio."

"Welcome to Hospital No. 2," I said. "Is there any particular thing you're looking for?"

"Actually, I heard about MacArthur's Square and walked over to take a peek at it."

"Well, did you like it?" Nancy asked.

"Nice little spot." He glanced around him and chuckled. "You think you've got enough foxholes. I've never seen this many. You got more foxholes than these monkeys have fleas."

"When those planes fly over, you want to be able to find one quickly. Around here, we don't think we can have too many," I said.

He grinned. "You ladies care to join me tomorrow night for dinner on the Pigeon?"

One thing about us, we never turned down a chance to eat.

Geneva nodded. "Sounds really good. What time?"

"Six okay?"

Nancy smiled at him. "Six it is."

The next night, we cleaned up in the bathing area and changed into our civilian dresses. Lieutenant Davis sent an escort to take us to the boat.

We entered the dining galley onboard and took an emotional hit. The place reeked with an ambience of luxury with clean white linen tablecloths and shiny silverware. Ice sparkled in crystal glasses filled with water.

After living in the jungle eating rice and fish, sometimes with our hands, this knocked us off our feet. It's a sight I'll never forget.

We ran our fingers over the tablecloth and touched the glasses. The chill of the water felt so wonderful, something I hadn't felt in a very long time.

Lt. Commander Davis looked at one of his crew. "Tell them we're ready to be served."

The sailor saluted. "Aye, aye, sir."

I could already smell the aroma of the food, and it made me want to cry.

While we dined on fried chicken cooked to perfection and biscuits with real butter, I couldn't help but think, *Ah me. For the life of a sailor.* I had to force myself to use good manners. I was so hungry I just wanted to wolf it down.

"That's a very ingenious bamboo air raid shelter you built against the hill," Nancy commented.

"Built that for my men. Figure they could take shelter under it while the officers and I stay onboard. So far, they shoot all around us, but never seem to hit us. I pray to God, he continues to look out for us. You ladies enjoying your dinner?"

"More than I can say," Nancy said. "This is the best evening I've had in a long time."

"Me too," Geneva agreed.

"It's like suddenly living in a fairytale. It's so magical," I added.

"The other day," he said. "Those Japs fired all around us and killed every fish out there." He chuckled. "Once they left, my crew dove in and reaped the harvest, then had a fish fry."

We giggled politely.

"My cook can fix anything," he said and smiled up at the man who'd prepared dinner.

"My birthday's coming up," Nancy said. "Too bad you can't bake me a cake."

His cook smiled. "You come up with some baking powder, and I'll bake you one with white frosting."

The thought made my mouth water. But I knew there wasn't any baking powder to be had.

"I'm going to see if I can beg our mess hall cook for some," Nancy said.

I looked at Lt. Commander Davis. "Exactly what is the work you do on the Pigeon?"

"We're a submarine rescue vessel. We're a tremendous aid to the PT boats. We carry equipment for repairs that none of the other ships have. One of them had my men diving down to a sunken boat for bags of flour, of all things. But it had gone too deep. Fortunately, they called it off before any of my crew were injured. There's two other tenders, the Quail and the Canopus. We often work together."

"Seems dangerous making yourself a target," Geneva said.

"We rendezvous with submarines after dark. We slip through the dark sea and go undetected. That's how we bring food and medical supplies in."

I wanted to say, it'd be nice if more of this food made it to our mess, but I didn't.

"Well, we could sure use some quinine," Geneva said. "Our supply is dwindling."

"We use it for malaria. Each patient gets about twenty grams of quinine when they come to us. After that, each one needs it every four hours. Not to mention, all of us get one dose a day to prevent us from catching it," I added.

"We're down to only liquid quinine. Each day we have more and more malaria patients," Nancy stated.

"I'll see what I can get you," Lt. Commander Davis said. "I don't know a lot about the disease."

"It's difficult to treat," I said.

"The strangest reaction is the disintegrating of the nervous system," Geneva commented. When they first come to us, they're in shock, but after a few days a nervous breakdown occurs. They lose all hope to live."

"Damn Japs know what they're doing. They know how to take advantage of the psychological factors. Mental and nervous collapse caused by continuous night attacks," I said.

"Interrupted sleep brings on mental anxiety and stress," Nancy stated.

"It's as effective as direct bombing," Geneva added.

The commander listened to us. "You ladies are brave. I just hope the rest of the country discovers what you've gone through and the sacrifices you made for our men."

The next day, I worked in ward one. Sergeants, Graham and Messer were Godsends. Graham had been an accountant and did wonderful work on our books. He kept up with all the patients' information. We paid them with soap and cigarettes.

I heard the familiar sound of Jap planes heading our way. "Raid!"

Everyone jumped into foxholes, all but Graham.

He stood in the center and shook his fist at the planes while cursing loudly at Japs and calling them names.

"Sergeant, stop that," I shouted.

"He's too stupid to take cover," Messer shouted. "Leave him."

Graham continued his ranting. Fortunately, he wasn't hit. One soldier who'd done something similar hadn't been as lucky. He'd been killed during a heavy raid.

I wondered if Geneva had taken cover. My concerns always centered around her. Hopefully, she was safe.

GENEVA
March 7, 1942

It's odd to think a world consisting of bedlam and chaos can become normal. I had adapted to people screaming, diving into trenches, or running naked as a regular daily routine.

I was making my rounds, talking to patients, and caring for their needs when the gun shot went up, resounding around the hospital. Every one reacted as expected, except for one Filipino soldier. He casually stood by the desk out in the open.

"What do you think you're doing?" I screamed. "Take cover!"

He waved with a smile. "I'm as safe here as I would be in a dirty hole."

"Like heck you are. That dirty hole might save your neck. I suggest you find one and be quick about it."

"Don't worry, I've seen a lot worse action than this. I wouldn't even be here if I hadn't caught malaria."

"Please," I begged, "Humor me and get under cover."

There is a huge gap between bravery and bravado. His aura of invincibility got a reality check when a piece of shrapnel struck him in the head; the fact that it was from our own anti-aircraft guns added insult to injury.

"I'm hit, I'm hit!" His eyes grew wide.

"Here, let me have a look," I said, after the raid. "It's not too bad. This time you were lucky. Next time I tell you take cover, do it." I cleaned the wound with antiseptic and bandaged it.

"I can't believe I got hit."

"Well, now you know."

"What?" he asked.

"Even a man of steel like yourself can be wounded. Next time, don't tempt fate."

He grinned and returned to his cot.

I couldn't hold back a smile as I continued with my rounds, tending to my patients. Another warning echoed through the camp, but this time, he jumped in a foxhole in record speed.

That night it started to rain. The rainy season had started. Even in the tropics being damp could cause you to shiver. It only added to everyone's discomfort and misery. The next morning, all the mattresses had to be set out to dry. Our little roof had shielded our beds for the most part.

The water seemed to bring out the snakes, and the thought of running into one terrified me. It wouldn't be long before our hospital was under fifteen feet of water. They had started scouting for a new location.

RESSA
March 10, 1942

I had a little time, so I decided to pay a visit to the officers' ward. Most of the men hated the time they had on their hands. They wanted to heal so they could head back to the frontline. I visited and passed on rumors. Within Hospital No. 2, we ignored the *button your lip policy.*

On my way, I was asked to take some quinine and cigarettes to Lieutenant Herman Garth, who'd been in the hospital since January and had come down from Limay with us. By the end of the day, Hospital No. 2, would be out of quinine. How would we fight off diseases caused by mosquitoes?

I started my walk down the path only to suddenly leap into a foxhole. A Jap plane flew over shelling us. I climbed out, and as I dusted my clothes off, another plane approached. I leapt into a second foxhole. By the fifth foxhole, I figured I had smashed his cigarettes and spilled the quinine.

When I arrived in the officers' ward, I found him in a foxhole. He frowned. "We're slewed, stewed, and tattooed. The damn Japs are going to take this place."

I tried to calm him down. But I secretly agreed with him.

After visiting him, I visited Colonel Carlton Vanderboget, who was in the hospital with several shrapnel wounds and a severe head injury that had left him deaf.

He'd been out looking at new hospital sites with Major McClosky when Jap planes flew over and dropped a bomb. The major was killed. His death was a great loss for he was a very competent surgeon who did outstanding work in Bataan.

Colonel James O. Gillespie would be taking over Hospital No. 2 for Vanderboget, who would be transferred to headquarters once he was healed. Gillespie had come from Corregidor. Major Barry, who was a sanitary inspector, accompanied him.

That night at dinner, Colonel Gillespie and Major Barry joined the nurses in the mess. Needless to say, they ate the same horse meat we did that night.

"So, inspector," Edith said. "Do you think this place should be condemned?"

"No. I plan to bring it up to code. By the time I'm done, the toilets will have plush seats."

We laughed, because we knew there was no hope to make this place better.

"As bad as this place is, it's a wonder we don't all get sick," Sue Downing said.

Minnie Breeze fanned the flies away. "I stay sick."

"Well, people from Brooklyn never get sick," Helen Summers boasted.

"That's interesting," Major Barry said. "What's their secret?"

"Don't get her started," Blanche said. "She'll talk all night about Brooklyn."

Sally shook the tea grounds out of her cup. "Instead, sing your new song for us."

"Well, if you insist," Helen said with a gleeful smile. "I thought this would cheer everyone up. I set it to the tune of the *Missouri Waltz*."

Way out in Bataan when we were in the A.N.C.
We ate but twice a day and drank diluted ginger tea.
We sweated the chow line after a day's grind.
Carabao stew was our daily menu.
Sitting on a rock and bathing in the mountain stream.
Wished we could wake and find it just an awful dream.
But for the duration we'll pretend it's a vacation,
And see it through.

We clapped and whistled. For a moment, her song brought us a brief moment of joy.

RESSA
March 11, 1942

I found Geneva and pulled her aside so her patients didn't hear me. I was sure my news would hit them as hard as it had me.

"What's so urgent?" she asked.

"I just heard. MacArthur was ordered to Australia." The general was a symbol of hope and security. With him gone, despair would consume us.

Her face remained dauntless, but her eyes revealed fear and concern. "Without him, what hope do we have?"

"I'm sure they considered it the wisest move to make," I said. "Still, it makes me think the end is near."

"Are they sending someone to replace him?" she asked.

"General Jonathan Wainwright, ole skinny."

"That's a good choice. His men all adore and respect him."

"I know." I helped Geneva make up an empty bed. "I also heard buses are coming to move us to another hospital."

"Where did you hear it?"

"It's spreading all over camp. And Josie Nesbit heard it also, so it must be true. They'll move us out in a moment's notice. You'd better keep your bags packed and ready."

On March thirteenth, boys started clearing a road through the brush. Now we knew the rumor had been true. We were being transferred. It would be even harder to leave our patients now than it had been before.

RESSA
March 16, 1942

When we came off duty, Geneva joined me, and we walked back to our quarters together. "What the heck? Where are our beds?"

178

I stood stunned. "Our beds are gone. Look, all our belongings are on the ground."

A small bus was parked near where our beds had been. Two large buses and six or seven smaller ones filled the area. All the seats had been removed, and only a few had the luxury of lights. Thinking we were being evacuated, we gathered our belongings. "When do we leave?"

Dorothea laughed. "We're not. Welcome to our new quarters. Ruth and I are on that big bus. We named it Shangri-La."

"Where are we?" Geneva asked.

"Over here," Earleen shouted. "We're on a smaller one."

We joined her inside, and immediately sensed a blanket of false security that a roof and four walls gave us. Our homing instincts kicked in, and we were ready to put up ruffled curtains. We wanted to make it ours.

Beulah Putman and Hortense McKay shared a tiny bus. Beulah stood in the doorway sweeping the dirt outside.

Sad how desperate we were to have a home no matter the size or how long we'd occupy it.

RESSA
March 22, 1942

Many of the soldiers, doctors, and nurses updated or filed their life insurance policies today. Wainwright had restricted any radio use all day to make sure everyone filed their insurance information. Anything Geneva and I had in the event of our deaths would go to our family.

That day heavy bombing continued as Japan tried to finish us off.

RESSA
April 1, 1942

Major John Raulston approached me. "Heard you wanted to see me."

I smiled. "I have something for you."

"What's that?"

I pulled four packs of cigarettes from my pocket. "I'm giving you most of my stash."

His brows rose in surprise. "You quit the smokes?"

"No, but the rumor is we'll be moved to the Rock soon. I'll be able to buy more there." Most of the men had run out of cigarettes.

"Nah, this is too much. I can't take them."

"You know how scarce cigarettes are in the jungle? Besides, being from home, you're almost family." I held out four packs.

"It's tempting. It gets tiresome looking for butts on the ground."

"I really want you to have them. I have a few packs left, and I'll be able to get more on Corregidor."

"Thanks." He finally shoved them in his pockets. "Everyone here has been so nice to me."

John had returned from the frontline without any clothes. They'd been blown right off of him. Major Edwin Keggie had given him coveralls and other clothes. But they hadn't been able to find a cap, so he'd made one out of an old pair of britches.

After John left, I ran into Major Keggie. He had that distant homesick look that he often got. I knew he was thinking of his family. He stood talking to two civilian refugees who had two little blonde-haired children. Apparently, seeing the children play made him miss his own child.

After the people left, I approached him. "Homesick?"

"Oh yeah. But if my being here helps keep my son safe, it's okay."

I felt even more sorry for the civilians stuck in this hell with their children.

That evening, Major Keggie sang songs for us. He had a gorgeous voice, and we all enjoyed listening to him.

"I'd better turn in," Keggie announced.

"Oh, no you don't," Helen said. "You haven't sung your full repertoire."

He grinned. "Two more."

The silky smoothness of his voice and rich tones made us forget we were sitting in the middle of a jungle with the nastiness of war all around us.

We finished up the night by all singing Helen Summers' parodies that was a favorite to us all. We sang it to the tune of *The Darktown Strutter's Ball.*

Dig those foxholes deeper, boys.
The Nips are on their way.
They're going to bomb all night,
They're going to bomb all day,
So, dig those foxholes deeper, boys.
The Nips are on their way.
When's that convoy coming in, Franklin, Franklin?
When's that convoy coming in Franklin D. old man?
We're going to sweat all night,
We're going to sweat all day,
We're going to sweat that convoy in
Until it hits the bay.

The major excused himself and left for his quarters.

Whitlow looked at us. "We'll be receiving wounded from the frontline in the morning. I guess we should call it a night."

"Where are we going to put them?" I asked.

Nancy tightened the ribbon holding her hair up. "They marched over two hundred of our ambulatory Filipino patients to Indora."

There would be many more to take their place. The flow of the injured and severely wounded continued as the Japs pushed our frontline back.

With Easter approaching, once again our hearts longed for home. Holidays had a way of reminding us of family and how far from home we were. Sunday, I attended Chaplain Dawson's service. He'd constructed an outdoor chapel located across from our quarters with the deep blue sky for a dome and the greenery all around to form the walls.

Right in the middle of his sermon, Jap planes approached.

He closed his Bible and stuck it in his pocket. "You may all get down in your foxholes. I'll finish the sermon when it's over."

We all dove in the closest foxhole and waited for the raid to end.

Later that week, Father Talbert, the Catholic chaplain, stopped me in front of his chapel located on the main road opposite the hospital. "Morning, Ressa."

"Morning, father."

"Want to see my new altar? I had to be creative."

"Sure. I'd love to see it. How are your masses going?"

"Well attended."

Inside, my gaze fell on the altar constructed from cardboard boxes with a large cross in the center. He had a split rail made from bamboo running across the front.

"It's very nice. I'm sure God doesn't mind part of it is made of cardboard. I haven't seen you in the hospital lately."

"I'm afraid it required all my time to build my church, but I'll be back to help you ladies soon."

"Well, we all miss you." I flashed him a smile. "And your extra pair of hands to help us out. If I want to eat today, I'd better head to mess."

"Ressa, our Holy Week is coming up. It'd be nice to have real wine to use for communion. You don't by chance have any you could donate?"

"No, I don't. I'll see if I find some."

"I'd appreciate that."

On my way to the mess hall, I ran into Frank Davis, commander of the Pigeon. "Ressa, you look like a lady on a mission."

I laughed. "I'm hungry. I get serious when my stomach starts growling."

He chuckled. "You girls need to come dine with me again."

"We'd love too." I offered him a sweet smile. "Do you by chance have a bottle of wine Father Talbert can have?"

"I have half of a bottle left. I gave the other half to the Navy chaplain. I'll send it to you."

"Thank you so much. I'm sure he'll be delighted. "

I went on my way. In the mess hall, Evelyn Whitlow, Helen Summers, Nancy Gillahan, and Geneva sat together at a table. I waved, grabbed my food, and joined them. I told them about Lt. Commander Davis donating his wine to Father Talbert.

"Davis is one sweet man," Geneva said. "He's so considerate."

Whitlow glanced up at me. "We're planning our Easter parade."
"And Helen has written a song we can sing for it," Nancy added.
Geneva didn't appear interested.
I smiled. "I can't wait. Sounds like fun."
Nancy placed her hands on her head. "We're having a bonnet contest too."
"We're giving a prize for the most creative," Helen added.
"I can't even start to imagine what to make my hat out of." I turned to Geneva. "Are you making one?"
She shook her head, looking bored. "Think I'll be a spectator."
"Party pooper," I replied.
The others laughed and returned to ideas for their bonnets.
The following day, I received the wine from Davis and carried it to Father Talbert. He wasn't there, so I left it with a brief note.

GENEVA
April 3, 1942 Good Friday

I came upon the nurse who Jerry was engaged to. She was a surgical nurse, and I was there to do whatever she said. I couldn't walk away.
She smiled. "I haven't seen much of you."
"I've been busy." I sighed a frustrated breath. "So, where do you need me to start?"
"Sterilize that surgical equipment and bring in more bandages."
"I'll get those to you right away."
"Wait. I need to tell you something."
I didn't want to hear it, but not having a choice, I stayed.
"Jerry was never my boyfriend. He doesn't love me, and I don't love him."
"But he proposed," I said. "There had to be something between you."
"He'd been so sure he wouldn't come back that day. He hated dying with no one to receive his insurance money or pay. As his wife, I would receive everything if he died."

I considered what she'd said. "He just wanted to make sure someone received his insurance and pay?"

She nodded. "He doesn't have any family left. Actually, he told me there'd been a girl at Sternberg he should've married before she moved out, because they really cared about each other."

"You don't say?" I yearned for what she said to be true.

"Yes, I promise. He told me you were that girl, but now after hearing about us, you won't give him the time of day. If you'll at least hear him out, I think he'll tell you just what I said."

"Is he in camp?"

She shook her head. "No, he's not."

If he didn't make it back, I'd feel terrible for not letting him explain. I turned back to her. "Thanks for telling me."

We worked well together for the rest of the day.

At dinner, I told Ressa what she'd said.

"For Heaven's sake. Are you giving him a second chance?"

I shrugged. "Maybe. If he makes it back."

That night, we all attended a Good Friday service at the small jungle church. I prayed Jerry would be spared and brought back safely.

RESSA
April 5, 1942

Easter, we were acutely aware of the religious significance of Holy Week. It brought us closer to understanding Christianity, its essence and origin more than ever before. We knew what Christ had felt at Gethsemane, for we had seen so many strong young men bravely die horrific deaths as a sacrifice to others. To us, Easter in 1942 meant saving the Philippines and its people.

After the Easter service, our parade started. All the ambulatory patients, nurses, and doctors participated. Many of us wore silly hats made from tree leaves to trash we had gathered. Regardless, we all looked ridiculous. We made enough noise to be heard for miles.

Geneva eyed my Army helmet decorated with wild flowers and leaves. "It looks as ridiculous as the others. See now why I didn't want to make one?"

"You're missing all the fun."

"Any Japs that stumble on all of you will think you've gone mad and run."

We marched around the jungle while singing Helen Summer's new song to the tune of Irvin Berlin's tune, *Easter Bonnet*.

This year's Easter bonnet is an Army helmet, darn it.

With olive paint and chin straps,

They will give us the eye.

For we will be self-conscious at the Easter parade.

On the jungle trail, in the sun,

That dusty trail, ain't no fun.

No photographer to snap us.

For glamour is something the war has undone,

Oh, I could write a sonnet about my Easter bonnet, but what's the use, when bonnets are so common today.

Even those on duty found time to slip away to one of the chapels and pray. That Easter Sunday, whether American or Filipino our prayers were selfless, praying that others would be spared the ordeals and the suffering of war.

I thought of home and family. Japs flew over and dropped bombs interrupting my memories. Today, the bombing had been unusually heavy.

I ran to the foxhole with the others and dove in. Geneva made room for me. This raid seemed to go on forever. My heart beat rapidly, and I found it difficult to breathe. Insects of all kinds called these foxholes home. I didn't like sharing it with them.

RESSA

April 6, 1942

I entered the ward that morning and immediately noticed the somber expressions everyone wore. Helen and Nancy looked on the verge of tears.

"What's going on?"

"Hospital No. 1 was bombed early this morning." Nancy wiped a tear.

"How badly?" I asked.

"It's been wiped out," Helen announced. "Rosemary Hogan and Rita Palmer were both wounded. Juanita Redmond barely escaped injury."

My heart dropped to my stomach as I thought of our dear friends. Suddenly, I was thankful for being sent to Hospital No. 2.

Thousands of wounded soldiers started coming in.

At dinner time, we entered the mess and sat together. We continued to talk about our friends wondering if they were still alive.

"Ladies," Major Keggie said. "Just spoke with someone from Hospital No. 1. During the massive artillery attack, the Japs targeted an ammunition dump, and by mistake hit a truck loaded with explosives. The explosion wiped out a truck full of wounded men being brought in."

My heart sank at the absolute horror of those men who clung to life obliterated instantly in a ball of fire.

"Do you know how Rosemary Hogan and Rita Palmer are?" I asked, hearing my own voice quiver.

"They were hit but taken to surgery immediately. They'll make it."

"Captain Nelson must be devastated since he's engaged to Rita," I said. I had worked with the Navy doctor before.

Whitlow joined us and heard what I had said. "Word has it, he was pulling the shrapnel fragments from her wound when another air raid happened. He carried her to a foxhole. Once it was over he finished caring for her." She swooned. "How romantic!"

"Now that's true love," I said.

Our idea of romance had been sadly distorted. I thought of Robert and wondered where he had gone. Was he alive?

The tension and pressure continuously increased all of the time, but still no help arrived.

The ambulances and trucks carrying the wounded from the frontlines came in and out all day. The continuous air raids made it practically impossible to make the patients comfortable.

We were thankful ten nurses had come over from Corregidor. The journey was perilous, yet they had volunteered.

After seeing our wards and how we lived, Louise Anschicks, the oldest nurse and a WWI veteran, shook her head. "Girls, the Great War was a picnic compared to this."

As more stretchers with wounded were brought in, I wanted to sit and cry. There wasn't time for hysteria. Seriously injured men covered the jungle floor. The men cried and moaned while suffering intense pain. Some begged for relief.

One of the boys stared with an expression of horror. "This situation is impossible. Frontline is bound to give way entirely any time now."

"Stay calm. I want you to relax and not think about it," I said. But others came with the same fears and thoughts. Nothing we said helped.

We all knew we had been abandoned by the very country who'd promised to rescue us if war with Japan came.

"Orders are not to leave the hospital grounds," Lieutenant Nesbit said.

"I'm too tired to even think about leaving," I replied.

"You won't catch me outside," Helen added. "I'm afraid the Japs will grab me and throw me in a prison camp."

I rinsed my hands. "Or worse. They could shoot us on the spot."

"What's to stop them from marching right into the hospital?" Geneva asked.

"Nothing," Louise said. "We can only hope they don't think we're worth the trouble."

"Back to work, ladies," Josie said. "There's more coming. We don't have time to sit and worry about what could happen."

That evening, we puttered around our bus. Our musette bags had been packed in case we were evacuated in a hurry. Silly, but every night we unpacked them and repacked them. It was imperative that we stayed busy. If our minds became still, fear would creep in and overtake us.

Later at dinner, I saw Earleen. Her drawn face showed her anxiety.

"Penny for your thoughts," I said. "What's bothering you?"

"What I worry about all the time. I'm afraid I'll never see my husband again. He's at the clearing station near the frontline."

"God will get your Captain Francis through this," Whitlow said.

"You just keep praying for him," Helen added.

Again, I thought of Robert and wondered what had become of him. Each time I walked up to a patient, I expected to see him. Many times, I worked on a soldier I had danced with at the club. Seeing these men reduced to mangled piles of flesh and bones broke my heart.

RESSA
April 7, 1942

I shuddered each time bombs exploded around us. It started early and continued most of the day. In the ward, the mental patients ran around the beds with their hands over their sensitive ears to block the sound of Jap planes flying over. They flopped on their beds, then jumped into foxholes. It was impossible to calm them when we were just as excited.

The doctor glanced my way. "We're all nuts in here."

"And it's about to get nuttier," a nurse shouted in the confusion. "We've got an unbroken chain of soldiers heading our way."

Since the front had given way below Limay, men headed to Mariveles, trying to escape.

Even though our ward was for patients with mental issues, they started bringing wounded soldiers in to fill the empty beds. As usual many of them suffered from our old nemeses—malaria, dysentery, and beriberi. Most of them needed vitamins and a quiet place to rest. This ward wasn't exactly quiet.

"We'll be out of medical supplies before the day's up," I said.

"Just do the best with what you've got," Dr. Fox replied.

I finally stepped out of ward one a moment and noticed that surgery was swamped with people. Ward 27 had been filled to capacity and had more men covered in flies, waiting on the jungle floors. Some of the soldiers brought to our ward hours earlier stood and started leaving.

"Hey, where do you think you're going?" I hollered.

One of the men shrugged. "This is taking too long."

His buddy nodded. "We're good enough to fight."

"We're heading back to the frontline," the third guy replied.

I stepped aside. "God bless you."

On my way to the nurses' quarters, I passed a Filipino boy.

"Looks hopeless, Missy."

"I guess we'll all be going over to Corregidor," I replied.

"That will be hell," he said. 'It's like committing suicide to move inside those tunnels. The Japs will pound the hell out of the Rock."

If we couldn't go to the Rock, where would we go? My chest squeezed with anxiety as I thought of Geneva.

I spotted Major Hubbard. His clothes were covered in dust, and his face unshaven. "Sir, are you wounded?"

Barely able to stand, he shook his head. "Been walking for two days without food or water. The frontline has collapsed. Those Japs will be marching this way soon."

With fear in my heart, I walked faster toward our bus.

At the common house, Lieutenant Nesbit was passing out bands of red flannel. I took one unsure what they wanted me to do with it.

"Write your Red Cross number on it, then make an arm band," Josie Nesbit ordered. Next, she passed around an indelible ink. The number was an international code, cleared through Switzerland.

"I have to report to the ward," I said.

"Give it to me. I'll make it for you," Earleen offered. "What's your number?"

I handed her the red flannel, bleached muslin cloth. "It's P-11188. Thanks. I'll get it from you at dinner."

That evening, Earleen gave me the armband. "Thanks."

"What does the P stand for?" Earleen asked.

"Philippines," Whitlow replied.

"Prisoner is more like it," I said.

They laughed. "Let's hope not," Earleen said.

Excitement grew as the frontlines broke one by one allowing the Japanese armies to move forward. I've always heard God doesn't give you more than you can handle. Well, I beg to disagree.

At 6:00 p.m. Mrs. Cruz left me with three wards of hysterical patients to care for. I only had three corpsmen able to help. A sense of urgency to see to all their needs overwhelmed me, because it was impossible.

You couldn't compare our mental patients' overall conditions to mental patients in stateside facilities. They suffered from a higher level of hysteria and cried out from all over the wards. The continuous heavy artillery fire shook the ground with constant concussions and reverberations. The coveralls hanging on the clothesline shook and appeared to be dancing. Sometimes, my teeth chattered, and my ears deafened by the sounds, making it difficult to hear.

"Nurse, the Japs are here!" one shouted. "They're hiding in the jungle."

"You're hallucinating. Stay calm." No sooner than I'd said stay calm, a swish of shells flew over. I laughed. "Just pretend it's Fourth of July fireworks, boys."

My nerves twisted more with each shell that flew over, yet I had to pretend not to be terrified. I had to keep up a façade of all is well. But several times my smile faded from the terror that consumed me. These boys had enough problems without me going into hysterics.

When a large bomb shook the ground, one screamed and rolled beneath his cot.

"What do you want me to do with him?" the corpsman asked.

"Leave him." I pointed to another patient. "Strap him down. He's escaped for the last time." It wasn't uncommon for a patient to make a run for it.

"Yes, ma'am."

No sooner than we had him under control, I turned in time to see another one dash into the jungle. The back of his gown flapped open, showing everyone a full moon. Despite my situation, I couldn't help but laugh. "Go after him before he hurts himself or someone else."

The corpsman grinned. "I'll get him."

By seven, I feared I would collapse from the mental pressure of my job. Captain Gonzales came through.

"Captain, please don't pull these men. I need them. Without them, I'd be alone. I can't do this. I need help."

"They can stay," he said, seeing the panic in my eyes.

"Thank you, sir."

A soldier passing by stopped and motioned me over. "Japs are already at Cabcaben."

Not long after that, Josie Nesbit dropped by, and I repeated what I was told. "Think it's true?"

"Probably. Don't you dare repeat that to anyone. Think of the panic it would cause." Her tone seemed harsher than I'd ever heard her speak. Her face turned ash white, and wrinkles creased her forehead. She hurried off.

An hour later, I had just finished my records when Jean Kennedy came to relieve me. The night shift started at eight. "Boy, am I glad to see you."

"That bad, huh?"

"It's been rough. Other than the corpsmen, I've been alone since six this morning. Anyone coming to help you?"

She shrugged and glanced around. "Doesn't look like it."

Jean Kennedy was our youngest nurse serving with the Army in the Philippines.

"You have three wards. About seven hundred patients. I don't know what idiot believes one nurse with a few corpsmen can handle so many."

"They know it's physically impossible," Jean said. "These boys deserve better. It's just that we're spread so thin."

I didn't want to leave her. I truly wanted to help, but not only did my entire body ache, I was hungry. I hadn't eaten since early that morning.

"Go. I'll be fine." She motioned for me to leave. "I've got this."

I glanced back several times. "Good luck."

She'd need more than luck.

As I left the ward and headed for my bus, a runner came through announcing Cabcaben had been taken by the Japs. I remembered Josie telling me not to repeat it. I guess the cat was out of the bag.

Soldiers and doctors coming from the frontlines passed me as I walked in the dark toward my bus. No one spoke. An eerie silence prevailed. Everyone seemed wrapped up in their own problems, coping with defeat.

I stopped by the mess and ate before walking to our quarters. When I stepped into our bus, Geneva and Earleen stood in the glow of candlelight, repacking their bags. The time would come when we would be evacuated. We wanted to know we had everything.

"I'm taking a bath," I said. "I haven't had one in days."

"Knew I smelled a polecat," Geneva said, smiling.

"I'm sure a polecat smells better than I do." I drew in a deep breath. "The Japs are at Cabcaben?"

"We heard," Geneva said on a sigh. "Can't figure out what's taking them so long to get here."

"I don't think I can take the stress of knowing any minute they could pounce on us." Earleen continued packing. "The tension is driving me batty."

"Me too," I admitted. "I'm wired tighter than a guitar string."

Earleen laughed. "You'd better go take that bath. Chances are you won't get a chance again for days."

I gathered my things. "I'm out of here."

I walked to where the women bathed in the stream. I wasn't the only one taking a late bath. I slipped from my clothes and stepped carefully into the water. The water cooled my body but did little to ease my tension. After getting out, I opened my canteen for a sip of water and found it empty. Then I picked up my flashlight only to discover the batteries were dead. For a moment, I panicked and ran down the dark path heading to the lister bag. I stumbled over a tree root and landed on the ground, dropping everything.

I have to calm down. After a few moments, I was able to stand, gather my things, and walk back.

Our quarters buzzed with activity. We were all busy little bees knowing at any moment, we'd have to leave the hive.

I passed the bus occupied by Adele, Whitlow, and Nancy.

"Hey, Jenkins," Adele shouted. "You and Geneva disposed of your things yet?"

"No, we're going to."

"We buried our stuff in the jungle behind our bus," Adele informed. She pointed to the Japanese helmet someone had given her for a souvenir that she wore. "Gonna bury it too. Might not be good for a Jap to find me wearing it."

I laughed. "Probably best to destroy it."

"They said not to get caught with any valuables," Whitlow added.

"Money too," Gillahan said. "I buried my rings."

I glanced at my rings and hated the thought of leaving them. But it would be worse for the Japs to get our valuables or journals.

I filled my canteen with water and turned to head back to our bus when a shattering blitz hit. I dove in the nearest foxhole and dropped my canteen. For ten minutes, I stayed in the hole while overhead all hell broke loose. I prayed that Geneva and Earleen had left the bus and taken cover. After it was over, I felt around the foxhole searching for my canteen. I finally found it. I climbed out, brushed the dirt from my coveralls, and continued down the path.

"Come see this," Frankie Lewey said, grabbing my arm and pulling me toward a shell that had fallen near them in a foxhole. "That could've killed one of us."

"Thank goodness no one was in it," I said.

I thought of how many times Mildred Dalton and I had dove into that same foxhole. I reached our bus only to find hysteria.

Inside, Earleen paced back and forth in a tiny space. She prayed out loud for the safety of her husband. "Dear sweet Jesus spare Garnet. Please keep him safe." She turned to me. "He could be dead right this minute. Oh, God. I'm so terrified for him."

The three of us held hands and prayed for Dr. Francis.

Finally, she calmed down. We walked into the jungle and buried our things. I couldn't bear to part with the pearl ring I'd purchased on our outing in Manila. I slipped it into my pocket.

Parting with rings, jewelry, and our money was one thing, but burning our diaries and mail from home was another. Reading our letters over and over kept us sane. Crying could be heard all over the camp. I found destroying my memoirs a painful task. I wanted to write a book once home. I would try to keep every event and date in my mind until I could reach a safe point to write it all down.

GENEVA
April 8, 1942

The monsoon season in the Philippines usually consisted of heavy rains. This spring, we had been pounded by a deluge of rain, sweat, and drops of blood. We were flooded with patients. That day we heard the Japanese had pushed our allied lines and marched very close to the new Hospital No. 1 near Little Baguio. I feared for all the patients, nurses, and staff in that area.

A group of soldiers retreating from the frontline staggered toward us.

"Oh my God," Ressa whispered. "They look like a brigade of walking skeletons."

She had described the seventy new arrivals perfectly. They labored with every ounce of strength they had just to put one foot in front of the other. We nurses started assessing their needs and injuries.

"I'll take temperatures and start checking their vitals," I said.

"I'll get the meds." Ressa quickly returned and started dosing the worst cases of malaria with atrabine and dysentery cases with sulfathazole.

Fortunately, medicine from Corregidor had finally reached us. Corpsmen took the few men who were able to the stream to bathe, then to the mess hall. We did our best to make the others comfortable. What these men really needed was food. Sad to say, we had none in our ward to give. Finally, around four, portions of rice arrived.

We took a needed break. Nancy, Whitlow, Ressa and I went to the mess hall. The food was unusually good. Instead of being thrilled, it made us apprehensive. We received the tasty food as a bad omen.

"I wonder what's going on?" I questioned.

A corpsman close by answered, "Word is the Canopus was scuttled. Most of what they saved went to Corregidor. We got what was left. Might as well enjoy it while you can."

My heart ached for the crew of the Canopus, but I was relieved it wasn't the Pigeon. Commander Davis and his boys had a special spot in my heart. Things accelerated after that. Bombs and shells bursting close by kept everyone on edge. It didn't comfort us to learn most of the explosions were from the guns on Corregidor shooting at the Japs.

Captain Katz stopped at our table. "Ladies, the word from the brass is you won't be here much longer. Preparations are being made for an evacuation."

Beds with wounded or sick covered every open spot on the jungle floor. I didn't see how they'd move all of them.

"But sir, a lot of our patients aren't up to that," Nancy stated.

"I'm not talking about everybody. This move is only for nurses and patients able to go. Doctors and corpsmen are staying behind to care for the boys left. Hopefully, we will join you later."

"I feel like a traitor leaving all these men here to die or to be captured." Ressa pursed her lips.

Whitlow slapped her fist on the table. "Me too."

Nancy and I sat stupefied. I couldn't stop worrying about Jerry and all the other brave men being left.

The news devastated us. We were ordered to abandon the men we had worked with in the worst conditions imaginable. Doctors and corpsmen regardless of rank had become family. The thought of leaving them left us weary. We learned they had planned to leave the Filipino nurses, until Josie Nesbit refused to leave without them. Her demand was met.

RESSA
April 8, 1942

During my short break, I quickly fell into the old routine of packing my bags, then unpacking, and re-packing. It had become a nervous obsession.

"Hey, Jenkins," Helen Summers yelled from outside our bus.

"Yeah, what's going on?"

"Are Geneva and Earleen awake?"

"Earleen is, but Geneva's sleeping."

"Wake her up and grab your things." Helen came aboard our bus. "We're leaving."

"Good gravy, they give poor notices. What about Jean Kennedy and the ones in the wards?"

"They're sending a boy to round them up." She held up a bottle of whiskey. "I can't take it with me. I figured we should have a nip."

"Open it. I could use something to dull my nerves," I said. I placed a hand on Geneva's shoulder and shook her. "Wake up. We're pulling out."

Her eyes blinked and finally opened. "When?"

"Now!"

She jumped from the cot and grabbed her bag.

"Where do you think we're going?" Earleen took a sip from Helen's bottle and passed it to me. I took a swig and passed it back to Helen. "I'm betting on Mindoro. A lot of our patients are already there."

Corregidor also remained a strong possibility. We had heard from day one the Rock was a fortress that couldn't be taken, no matter what was thrown at it.

"I'm packed and ready." Geneva sighed. "Nothing to do now but wait."

"Right you are, sis." I waved several pairs of stockings in the air. "Hey, girls, does anybody need extra stockings? I have no way to take them."

Geneva laughed, "I'm not sure of our destination, but one thing I am sure of, we won't need nylons."

"When you put it like that, it does sound silly. I just hate wasting them."

Somebody yelled from the back, "Hell, leave them for the Japs. They're so proud of their silk worms it might give them something else to worry about."

"Amen to that," Earleen said.

I packed several pairs of white stockings, two civilian dresses, underwear, and some odds and ends I had collected. Like the others, I left my white uniforms.

"We should make scarecrows out of them. Maybe they'd scare the Japs," Geneva said. "They could round them up and put them in a prison camp."

I suddenly remembered Lieutenant Childers, an officer with the 57th Infantry of Filipino scouts. I had promised him some cigarettes. I still had several packs left. Infantry scouts had brought him in yesterday, seriously wounded and missing his clothes.

Now, I won't be able to give them to him. He'll think I forgot.

We all had a good laugh. Laughter could both calm and heal us. Sometimes, it's what kept us stitched together. Without it, we would have mentally been ripped apart.

GENEVA
April 8, 1942

While waiting to leave Hospital No. 2, Ressa stood by Earleen. She gave the weeping nurse a reassuring hug and whispered, "I'm sure he's safe."

"God, I hope so. I'd give anything to see Garnet," Earleen responded.

Everyone who knew Earleen shared her anxiety. It made me think of Jerry. If I had the chance, I'd give him an opportunity to explain his proposal to the nurse.

Earleen leaned forward. Her gaze seemed to intensify, "It's him! It's really him." She hurriedly left the bus and ran into Garnet's outstretched arms.

Tears of joy flowed freely from all of us.

There wasn't a dry eye among us. Thank goodness they were able to have this reunion to say goodbye, no matter how brief.

As Helen left, Captain Francis entered our bus to help Earleen with her luggage. He studied us fretting over the things we had to leave and appeared amused. "How you fuss over trivialities and worry about a handful of belongings that don't mean anything at a time like this is beyond me."

"It's a woman's thing," I said. "Hey, this solves our problem of what to do with some of this stuff."

"I'm not taking nylons back to the men," Captain Francis said. "How about cigarettes?"

"They'll always take smokes."

We loaded him down with cigarettes and soap. I found a bucket to put everything in. "Take anything you see that's not packed."

Helen looked at him. "Where do you think they're taking us?"

"Corregidor."

My heart sank. I had mixed feelings about going there.

"It won't be long before you're joining us," Ressa said.

Earleen had tears seeping from her eyes. "I hope so."

"Time to head out," someone shouted.

After slipping on my Army helmet and raincoat, I strapped my barracks bag to my back and grabbed my musette bag, suitcase, and gas mask.

"You know these buses we've been living in will probably be used to take you men to the dock when the time comes," I said.

"Why else would they leave them," Ressa said. "Well, goodbye, Dr. Francis. I'm sure we'll be seeing you soon."

I said goodbye, and we left the bus to give them a few minutes alone. We joined the others running down the dark path, moving as a disorganized mob. People bumped and stumbled over each other. Bags slung into the people who stopped to get their bearings in the night. In our stampede, tempers flared, and people cursed, but somehow, we managed to arrive at the pick-up point. "That was brutal."

"Tell me about it. My feet were stomped on," Ressa said. Nancy and Earleen joined us just as Colonel James Gillespie called roll.

"What now?" Earleen asked.

"Now that we almost killed each other to get here, we'll sit on our bags and wait for no telling how long to be picked up," Nancy responded. "It's the way the Army rolls."

We laughed because it was true.

While we waited, many of the soldiers who had been patients came to say goodbye. I couldn't explain how sick I felt leaving thousands of them behind. I pitied them so, because I knew many of them would be killed or captured.

Ressa wiped tears away. "It's not fair that they stay, and we leave just because we're women. And some day they'll be calling us heroines."

I cleared my throat. "We all feel disgusted about it. There's not a one of us who wouldn't stay, but our leaving is an order. So, pull yourself together."

Around ten that night, a garbage truck, laundry truck, and several cars pulled up. Each car had been assigned a soldier.

"Come with me," the soldier ordered.

We followed him to Colonel William North's car parked at the front of the line and slid across the backseat. We scooted over and made room for Anna Williams, Lucy Wilson, and Helen Hennessey. The five of us crammed into the car. We hated being separated from Earleen and Helen Summers.

Sergeant Zimmerman the old corpsman drove us.

As he drove away it seemed like we were heading straight for Jap lines.

"Where are we going?" I asked.

"To the dock at Mariveles."

"That's at the end of the peninsula," Helen commented.

"Corregidor is the closest," Ressa stated.

I remembered that's where Dr. Francis thought we were going. And he probably had intel our driver didn't.

"Yeah, but from Mariveles, we can go to a number of places," Anna added. "Are you gonna stay with us?"

Our driver shook his head. "Nope. As soon as I drop you ladies off, I'm heading to the frontlines."

No sooner than we had gone too far to turn back, I thought of something terrible.

"Ressa, I left something."

"What?"

"My bras and underwear are hanging on the line. If that doesn't beat all."

They laughed, but I didn't see the humor in it.

"I doubt he'll turn around and go back," Ressa said, a smirk on her face.

"Well, I know that."

"If it'll make you feel any better, I'll share my underwear with you."

Lucy laughed. "That's what sisters are for."

Our laughter stopped when some bombs dropped nearby. No longer did we ask when we'd make it to the dock; instead, it became a question of if we'd make it.

The Rock
Part Five

RESSA
April 8, 1942

The roads gave us a rough ride since most of them had been hit by bombs.

"I don't think this road can get any worse," Helen murmured.

"Never say never," I reminded. "You don't want to jinx us."

My nerves danced like Mexican jumping beans. The others seemed as edgy as me. Dread filled me even more when I realized we were the only car that left the hospital and took this route. We drove without lights so not to alert any Japs.

I glanced back trying to see the jungle hospital, but we'd already driven too far to see its lights.

A loud clunk hit the front of the car. Our bodies slammed forward against the front seat. My heart leapt. "Lord-a mercy."

"My God!" Helen shouted.

Anna gasped.

"What just happened?" Geneva asked.

"I thought a bomb got us," Lucy Wilson added.

"Ladies, we just drove into a bomb crater. Don't worry, we'll get out of this," Zimmerman said.

"This is all your fault," I said to Helen. "You jinxed us back there."

"That's ridiculous. I don't believe in that crap."

I rolled my eyes. "We'll never get out of here."

"Let me get out and assess the damage," he said, gleefully.

We waited with our bags and our helmets in our laps. I thought how insufferable it'd be if we had to walk all the way.

Zimmerman slid back behind the wheel. "It was absolutely nothing. I'll see you ladies get there."

"It sure didn't feel like nothing," Geneva mumbled.

He shifted into reverse and gave it gas, causing dirt and gravel to spit out from under the wheels.

I held my breath hoping he could drive the car out of the crater. When he pulled out, we all sighed with relief.

"Thank you, sweet Jesus," I whispered.

Rather than continue on the road riddled with bomb craters, Zimmerman drove into the rice paddy. "Hang on ladies. Short cut."

The car bounced over the pitted field and tossed us around like rag dolls. Our bags rose from our laps over each bump. It amazed me we didn't clobber one another with our helmets.

"Holy smoke," Helen shouted. "This is worse than the road."

Once out of the rice field, Zimmerman joined a long line of trucks, tanks, caissons, guns, and jeeps, all going to Mariveles. The traffic crept along. Sweat rolled down my neck. *Hurry, hurry, go faster.*

"This is a never-ending Hell," Anna said.

When gunfire whizzed over the car, we screamed and ducked.

"Who's shooting at us," I asked, as we put on our helmets.

"Guns from Corregidor," Zimmerman replied. "They ain't aiming at us. Relax."

"Those misdirected shells are coming a little too close for comfort," I said. "I don't want to die from friendly fire."

We drove by a group of haggard, worn soldiers. We could not bear to look upon their distressed faces. None of the people from home would ever understand this kind of defeat and heartache. The suffering. The desolation of mind, heart, body, and soul.

I wouldn't complain anymore about the slow pace we drove, not while so many were making the trip on foot.

Then it happened. The car sputtered and died.

"Didn't the Colonel always claim this was the best little car in Bataan?" Helen asked.

Zimmerman grinned. "It's the one."

Smoke steamed from the hood, and we ended up stopping again. The evening was hot and sticky. We climbed out and stood while Zimmerman raised the hood. He jumped back as he released the steam. "Bone dry. You ladies hand over your canteens."

I unscrewed the cap and took a swig before handing it over.

Anna Williams started the engine while he poured our precious water into the radiator. The car started but took us only a short distance before it stopped again. Anna steered while Zimmerman pushed. She drove over ruts, making us bounce up and hit our heads on the car's roof. Since we didn't have any lights, it wasn't exactly her fault.

"That hurt," Helen said, gasping.

"Just think how it would've felt without the helmet to protect your noggin," I said.

Zimmerman stopped pushing. "Hold up. This isn't working."

My stomach twisted at the thought of being stranded in the middle of a convoy in a car that had driven its last mile.

He spoke to some of the men in the convoy. When a large truck came up behind us, Zimmerman moved back behind the wheel, and Anna sat beside him. "Here we go. Hang on," he said. "Hope this works."

The truck moved the colonel's car forward pushing it down the road.

The blinding lights from shells painted us gray. I stared at Geneva's face in the pale light and fear gripped me—the fear of us someday being separated or worse. Killed.

In my petrified mind, the same line played over and over in a beating rhythm.

Hell, but the torment of the soul on fire.

Around 2:00 a.m., we reached Little Baguio. About the same time, the convoy line stopped. Zimmerman sighed. "Stay here. I'll get out and see what's happened."

Shortly, he returned. "Bad news. We have to stop."

"How come?" Helen asked, sounding frustrated.

"They're blowing up the ammunition dump ahead of us."

Another knot formed in my stomach. "Where exactly?"

"Just below Hospital No 1."

Concern for our friends at the hospital engulfed us.

"Do you think they've been evacuated?" Geneva asked.

"Surely, they've been moved," Helen suggested.

"Where would they go?" Anna asked.

"Probably the same place as us," Lucy Wilson suggested.

The convoy pulled to the side of the road. Being cramped in the backseat, we climbed from the car and stretched our legs. We continued to talk about the friends we'd left in Hospital No. 1. We'd been on duty since eight that morning, so we were tired and hungry.

A loud explosion rocked the ground as if the Earth had split in half. For a moment, it threw me off balance. My heart raced as a flash of blinding light seared my eyeballs A deafening roar seemingly shook my eardrums. The air was sucked out of my lungs, and I stood trembling and gasping for breath.

It happened again and again.

Anna and Lucy cried.

We all prayed our individual prayers, all asking God to protect us and get us out safely.

"Oh, God, help us," I said. "God, keep us safe. Damn, Damn. God, spare the boys, and keep our patients safe." Another dump exploded. "Damn. Oh, God. God!"

Hopefully, God understood about the prayer mixed with profanity. My mother would've been shocked by my cursing. We stood trembling from fatigue and shock.

A soldier came up carrying canned milk. "Ladies, a milk truck turned over, and I salvaged some of it. I figured you might be starving."

"Yes, we are." My stomach ached from hunger.

"Famished," Helen said. "Thanks."

He tipped his hat and left.

Geneva frowned. "This is just dandy. We've got milk but no can opener."

Anna beamed. "I have one in my suitcase."

"A can opener?" I asked.

"Why yes," Anna replied as if everyone should carry one.

"Praise the Lord," Lucy said, joyfully.

We all laughed. I'm sure those standing around us thought we'd gone mad.

"Seriously? Who thinks of packing a can opener in the middle of an evacuation?" Helen asked.

"You must've been very optimistic that we'd see a can again," I said.

"Let's just be glad she did. Now stop flapping your jaws and open that milk," Geneva said.

Anna nodded. "Let me get my can opener." She returned with it and began opening the big can. We all retrieved our mess cups from our belongings and let Anna divide the milk between us. "Drink up, ladies."

Despite the chaos around us, we drank and didn't say a word. I thought of the good-natured, generous boy who would be thrown into battle maybe facing death. By sharing his milk with us, his act of kindness lifted our spirits.

"Excuse me ladies," said a soldier approaching us. "I've been ordered to stand guard by your car. With this much going on, something could go astray."

Nothing did. So, God had heard our prayers.

Having nowhere to sit, we climbed back in the car and waited.

Though it seemed like days, it had only taken four hours to blow up all the ammunition. Time had almost come to a standstill. We'd already been on the road for six hours. It angered us that Zimmerman had taken us on this route rather than follow the others.

"Be back in a jiffy, ladies. I'll ask when we get to leave," Zimmerman said.

"I want to hit him upside the head," Ressa said. "He's too damn happy."

"I've never seen anyone like him," Lucy added.

"I bet the other nurses are already there," Helen added.

"They'll cross the bay without us," Anna said, on a sigh.

Geneva massaged her temples. "We'll be stranded."

Helen rolled her sleeves down. "Why would he take us this way?"

Zimmerman returned, so we stopped griping. "Ladies, got some bad news."

I didn't know if I could take any more *bad* news. "Just tell us."

"It's making the rounds that in the morning, Bataan is throwing up the white flag." He left and rejoined some men.

The stress from the news showed on our faces while our shoulders slumped in defeat. A calm numbness filled me as though I'd been hypnotized. The noise around me seemed less threatening. I was no longer afraid.

I glanced at Geneva. "What's wrong?"

She couldn't speak, but folded over, clutching her stomach.

"Let her stretch out a moment," I barked at the others.

Helen and Lucy left the car and stood just outside its open door.

I stroked Geneva's forehead. "It's all right, sis. Close your eyes and rest."

Terror heightened our emotions and now this incident had us over the edge. Geneva couldn't cope with it. Somehow my mind had protected me with an almost catatonic trance-like state.

It didn't help when two boys passed by. One asked, "What will they do with us if they catch us?"

The other one replied, "Put us in concentration camps and work the hell out of us."

Once Geneva's dizzy spell subsided, she sat up. Lucy and Helen climbed back in the car.

Around 6:00 a.m., the sun's light shined on us. None of us had slept a wink. "This is it girls. The Japs should be coming by any moment to pick us up," I said.

"We have our Red Cross arm bands on," Helen reminded. "That should count for something."

"Perhaps they'll send us back to our patients," I suggested.

"They'll need us more in the camps to nurse the sick," Geneva said.

I thought of Geneva being overcome by stress earlier. She'd never survive a concentration camp. I silently prayed that if either of us were captured, it would be me. I could cope with imprisonment better than she could.

Zimmerman returned. "Trucks are moving out."

Surprisingly, the rest had done the car some good. It started up.

"Good old baby," Helen said. "She's a good little car."

Zimmerman eased into the long convoy of trucks. We rode a few hundred feet before old baby conked out again. We ended up being pushed by another large truck.

The car bumped up and down the road. Dust came through the windows, and the intense heat caused us to sweat profusely. We came to the dumps that had been burned out completely. The heat and flames had seared all the trees. The air remained hot and acrid with the scent of gun powder. Shrapnel still exploded and pieces flew through the air. It was a dangerous spot.

As we drove past the dump, we wore our helmets and crouched low in the car. God was with us, not a single person was hit. Still the bombardment continued over our heads.

We finally reached Hospital No 1. To our surprise, Phyllis Arnold stood along the roadside, glancing up and down the road.

"Hey, Phyllis," I shouted. "Whatcha doing? Hitchhiking?"

"Our car broke down."

"We could squeeze you in. Wanna ride?" I asked.

She shook her head. "A few of us are over there resting. Lieutenant Nesbit hasn't passed yet. We're waiting for her."

"What happened to the rest of your group?"

"They didn't want to wait and walked."

Once we left Phyllis, I looked at the others. "We're not last."

"Who would have guessed?" Anna asked.

"Not me," Lucy replied. "I thought we were dead last."

"Maybe we were lucky after all. The colonel really does have the best little car in Bataan," Helen said.

We laughed, and for a few minutes, we forgot about our current situation.

But after another hour, we hadn't gone much farther. Soldiers held to the car to be pulled along. Some tried to catch a ride on the bumper. All the boys hanging on made the little car groan and creak.

I was completely exhausted and started dosing off.

Soldiers struggled past me. Line after line walked by.

As I drifted off to sleep, they marched through the trees. Marching…still marching. I opened my weary eyes and squinted. There weren't any soldiers in the trees. For a moment, I thought I'd gone mad, but realized I'd been dreaming.

When we were three kilometers from Mariveles around 7:00 a.m., old baby broke down for the final time. Zimmerman got out, removed his hat, and wiped his brow. "Help me push it to the side."

The young officers came over and pushed old baby off the road. Then they rolled it over and set it on fire.

"If Colonel North saw this, he'd probably cry," Geneva said.

"She was a good little car," Helen said. "Too bad we couldn't take her all the way."

We stood around until the car had burned completely out, then we headed off on foot following soldiers down the dusty road to Mariveles. We had one more ridge to conquer before the steep road led us downhill to our destination.

Someone came upon us very quickly, and I jumped.

"Carry your bags, ladies?" a young soldier asked.

He and several of his friends took our bags from us and carried them. I felt almost guilty, because we had ridden most of the way while they had walked. After several yards, they dropped our bags. The soldier carrying mine turned to me. "Sorry, ma'am, but I can't carry it. You see, we haven't eaten in three days, and I guess I'm a little weaker than I realized."

I hated I didn't have any food to give them.

A short time later, a large truck lumbered up the road. With a smile Zimmerman motioned it through. Did this man ever frown or become discontent? His constant cheeriness in this glum situation annoyed the hell out of us. Perhaps, he kept up the façade for our benefit. The truck stopped, and the driver glanced out the window. "Hop in. I'm sure we're all going to the same place." He glanced at the soldiers. "Y'all hop in and help the women folk."

With talk like that, I figured he was from Tennessee.

The soldiers helped us climb in the back of the truck. I didn't feel so selfish riding since the young men got to also.

As we rode along, bouncing all over the back and doing our best to hold on, the driver stopped to pick up more soldiers and officers.

"Welcome aboard," I said. "It beats walking."

"Sure does, ma'am," a young soldier replied.

Upon the last high ridge, we stood in the back of the truck and stared down on the panoramic view of Bataan. Fires burned everywhere; it looked like the entire jungle was ablaze.

"My God, that's unbelievable." Lucy stammered.

Anna nodded, looking almost too stunned to speak.

"I wonder if Hospital No. 2 is burning," Helen murmured.

"It has to be with those blazes spreading across the land," I said.

"Surely, they got everyone out of there," Geneva said, her voice trembling.

The thought of our brave soldiers being trapped in that inferno gave me chills.

The truck gunned its engine and started down the winding and steep road that led to the Mariveles docks. I studied the mountains around us. Some had cliffs that dropped straight down into the water. The forest gave way to the scrub growth as we neared the lower half. Once down on flat ground, our truck joined a line of soldiers on foot, and other trucks and vehicles heading to the docks.

We moved slowly in one massive exodus from Bataan. Like the Hebrews leaving Egypt, I knew God was with us.

When our truck stopped and the driver climbed out, I wondered what was wrong. Then Zimmerman took off to see why people were literally standing around. Nothing moved. He returned. "They're about to set that truck on fire."

All the vehicles would have to be destroyed to keep them from benefiting the Japanese.

"Ask if we can pass first," I suggested.

Zimmerman checked with the man in charge, then returned. "He agreed." He hopped in the truck. The driver revved up the engine, hit the accelerator, and drove on.

GENEVA
April 9, 1942 (early morning)

Finally, we arrived at the dock. Zimmerman hopped from the truck and helped us down. "End of the line ladies, everybody out."

We said our goodbyes to the soldiers and wished them the best of luck. We gathered our bags.

"My bag—it's not here," Lucy Wilson said with a gasp. "Oh my God, I must've left it on the side of the road. Everything I own was in it."

Anna turned to Zimmerman. "Can we go back for it?"

"There's no way to find it," he said. "I'm sorry."

We all agreed to share our things with her.

Corregidor loomed ahead of us in the early morning light like an ominous fortress. It was about three miles from where we stood on the dock. Zimmerman, who had watched over us like a shepherd protecting his sheep, left us. We were on our own.

A tug boat waited with its engine humming. Our little group approached it.

"Are you waiting for us?" I asked.

"I'm taking this bunch to Corregidor," the tug's captain replied.

"No one has told us what we're supposed to do or where we go now," Helen stated.

"There's already been some nurses go over," he said. "The white flag is about to go up over Bataan. You'd better take the chance and come with us."

We climbed aboard the crowded vessel.

"Ladies, put these life vests on," a man ordered.

They smelled stale and damp, but we didn't have a choice.

"I can't get this on without taking off my helmet," I said, almost too tired to attempt it.

"Same here," Ressa said. We finally got situated. As we left from the dock, Japanese planes swooped low over Bataan, bombing the roads we had just traveled. I worried about the ones still trying to make it to the dock.

Relief ran through me at the sight of the Pigeon afloat with Commander Davis, still in charge.

Sadly, many of the men tried to swim across the bay. Some would all of a sudden go under and not come back up. We knew they had either drowned or a shark had attacked them.

The captain in command of our tug spotted a sinking rowboat, through his binoculars and quickly made way to intercept it. "It's taking on water. Looks like there are three or four people aboard."

"It's Ruby Motley!" Ressa shouted.

Ruby and three men sat in the boat. She was a dietician we'd worked with before. As she came aboard, her appearance shocked us, definitely a major weight loss. Truth be known, she probably thought the same of us.

Ruby joined us. Her eyes appeared dull, lifeless, and her face pale and pinched.

"Ruby, are you okay?" Ressa asked.

"Tell us what's wrong," Anna said.

Slowly her eyes opened. Tears ran down her cheeks.

"Take your time. You're safe now," I said to reassure her, knowing it was a lie. Japs flew above us, and sharks swam below. We were anything but safe.

Her eyes cleared a little, as if waking from a deep sleep. Her grief-stricken gaze moved slowly from face to face. Finally, she took a deep breath and exhaled. "I'm better now," she whispered, 'It was so ghastly. They evacuated us through the Navy tunnels. The Japs pounded us hard. We couldn't get through, we were blocked, God, we were blocked by..." She closed her eyes and grimaced.

I patted her hand. "Take a deep breath."

She inhaled deeply. "We were blocked by piles of dead bodies, so many men. We were helpless to do anything. The wounded that were able moved them out of our way and stacked them to the side of the road."

"That's dreadful," Anna said.

Ressa nodded, agreeing. "It's devastating."

Ruby grimaced. "It seemed as if they were logs of wood and had never been living beings. I'll never get that image out of my mind if I live to be a hundred years old, horrible, just horrible!"

We comforted her as best we could. We could sympathize with her, because all of us were burdened with images of war no one should ever have to witness.

Halfway across the bay, someone yelled, "It's time. Well, folks the show is over. The white flag is going up."

Planes still flew over bombing causing the smoke to thicken.

We stared back at Bataan. It had finally fallen. The surrender was official. We stood in silence praying for the safety of so many friends left behind.

General Wainwright's announcement read as follows.

Bataan has fallen. The Philippine American troops on this war-ravaged bloodstained peninsula have laid down their arms—with heads bloody but unbowed. They have yielded to the superior force and numbers of the enemy.

But the decision had to come. Men fighting under the banner of an unshakable faith are made of something more than flesh, but they are not made of impervious steel. The flesh must yield at last, endurance melts away, and the end of the battle must come.

Bataan has fallen, but the spirit that made it stands—a beacon to all the liberty- loving peoples of the world—cannot fall."

Smoke from the mainland drifted across the bay. The oil stench blended with the sea smells. The unforgiving rays of the sun beat down on our boat as it plodded toward the Rock. With every beat of the tug's engine and the motion of it rocking on the swells, I felt worse and worse. My stomach churned.

Ressa placed a hand on me. "Geneva, are you all right? You don't look well."

I started to respond, when a wave of nausea hit. I immediately leaned over the rail and thought I was going to vomit. Dry heaves racked my body with painful spasms. I didn't have any food in my stomach to throw up. I finally straightened up and took a couple of deep breaths. My head throbbed with excruciating pain. I massaged my temples trying to ease it.

Ressa hovered like a mother hen protecting her chick. She gently massaged my shoulders and neck. "You'll feel better once we get you on land. A warm shower and food will perk you up."

I knew she meant well, but I didn't want food or a shower, I wanted to collapse in a bed and sleep. I was exhausted, mentally and physically.

GENEVA
April 9, 1942

We set foot on the shore of Corregidor at ten a.m. I felt better once I stepped off the boat. People milled about the dock, staring towards Bataan. Hortense McKay saw me and waved.

"Where's your friend, Beulah Putman?"

She shrugged. "I'm not sure. We got separated on the trip over. There's one other nurse from Hospital No. 2 here. Jerry brought us over in a row boat. He's gone back for more."

I tried not to worry about him, but I did. I blew out a frustrated breath. "With the five of us, that means there's only six who have made it so far."

We stared back at the flames and black smoke shooting up from Bataan.

"Do you see any more boats coming?" Helen asked.

Ressa shook her head. "No."

"At least I'm alive." Lucy sighed. "I feel so selfish for worrying about my bag."

Cars picked us up on the dock, and we arrived at the tunnel ten minutes later. A camouflage netting covered the entrance of the tunnel in an effort to conceal it from Jap bombers.

People we didn't know stood outside the tunnel. None of them offered to help us and only stared as if we were from Mars.

"My, what a nice reception committee," Lucy said.

"Don't take it personal," the corpsman escorting us replied. "We just learned about Manila surrendering."

Though Ressa had described it after her September visit, the size of the tunnel was larger than I expected.

As a raid started, everyone ran inside the tunnel. Overhead, red lights came on.

"It's a raid warning," he stated. We walked farther inside the well-lit tunnel. Electric lights glowed everywhere. It seemed strange after being in the jungle so long. And I liked it much better than the blue lights we lived with at Sternberg and Hospital No. 1.

After receiving directions and thanking him, we made our way to the lateral with the nurses' quarters. As we pushed back the curtain used as a door and entered, Maude Davison greeted us. She and some others had come over during the night.

"How many came over with you?" she asked.

"Five of us, I believe," Anna answered. "And Hortense was out front."

"Were there others behind you?" Maude asked, apprehensively.

We sadly shook our heads. Our co-workers and friends stranded on the mainland weighed heavily on us. No one took it harder than Maude Davison. She considered all of us her girls.

Nurses from the new Hospital No. 1, and Hospital No. 2 had been evacuated to the Rock.

"All we can do is pray, wait, and hope they all make it out. Let's take care of first things first." Davison pointed at the opening of a lateral. "At the end of that one, you'll find beds. Until they can get more beds, it'll be two to a bunk. Set up in your quarters. Try to get some sleep, God knows you need it."

We didn't waste any time following orders. Each lateral had bunkbeds running against the outer walls on both sides. Even though they were built for single occupancy, they looked luxurious to us. After claiming a lower bunk, we started setting our bed up. To keep our minds off of what was happening around us, we talked about irrelevant things. Things that wouldn't remind us of our friends still trying to make it over or the thousands of patients left in the jungle.

"The Filipino nurses," I said. "I've never seen anything like them. No matter how bad it gets they sing happy songs and giggle like kids at a birthday party."

"I know. It bugged me at first. I finally realized the wisdom of it. We worry constantly. All our worrying won't do one iota of good. Those giggling Filipinos are a hell of a lot smarter than we are. Stress wears us out while they sing."

"Many a night their songs have put me to sleep. Better than any sleeping pill," Anna admitted.

"Same here," Ressa added. "Let's keep our things beneath the bed until we're assigned a locker."

The minute the essentials had been taken care of, I collapsed on the bed.

"Geneva, want me to get you something to eat?" Ressa asked.

I didn't answer, but merely shook my head.

"You sure? It might make you feel better to have something in your stomach."

"Food is the last thing on my mind. I think if I tried to eat, it'd just come back up." I covered my eyes.

"Suit yourself."

RESSA
April 9, 1942

I decided to try out the showers. The nurses' lateral had two showers, two basins, and two toilets. I stepped in the clean shower and let the hot water run over me. I loved the sheer physical pleasure of standing in a clean shower. I hated it had to end, but we'd been warned to use the water sparingly.

I found Geneva in bed, still in agony. Her nervous condition wouldn't allow her to sleep. I figured her headache and nausea could be from hunger, but I couldn't convince her to eat. She wasn't the only one with these symptoms.

I was lucky. I didn't feel sick, just numb all over. Though I moved, it seemed more like I was watching someone else move.

"You're all getting a dose of luminal to help you sleep," a nurse shouted.

When it was my turn, I inquired about Winnie. "Is she still here?"

"She's on duty. You can see her tomorrow."

Knowing Winnie was there and safe, I finally surrendered and stretched out beside Geneva on the bed. I soon dosed off. I woke with a start from a dream where I was running and falling. *It's a nightmare.* It required a few minutes to realize I was safe.

RESSA
April 10, 1942

"Wake up, ladies. Lunch is ready. If you want to eat, you need to jump out of those beds and head for the mess."

"I haven't heard anyone use the word lunch in a long time," I said to the others.

"It's music to my ears," Nancy said.

"Meals are served in three shifts," the lady shouted. "You're on second shift. You have to be done before the third shift begins."

"Has our shift actually started?" I asked.

"Starts in ten minutes when first shift ends."

I jumped up and found Geneva already showered and dressed. "I'm glad you're better."

"My headache is gone. Hurry, I want to eat."

I nodded and made my way to the bathroom. After getting dressed, I took time to apply a little red lipstick.

Helen applied hers as well. "We haven't given up yet. We're still able to apply our red badge of courage and prepare for another battle."

We entered the officers' mess, a room approximately eighteen by forty feet in size. Tables seating eight to ten filled the room.

While sitting with our friends, we scarcely spoke more than a greeting. We were still too tired to make the effort. I ate my hot soup and savored the touch and taste of real homemade white bread. After we ate, we returned to our beds and many fell asleep. Unfortunately, I wasn't one of them. I stared at the ceiling. I thought of Robert. I was always afraid I'd see him being brought in by a medic. Then I wondered if he had been among the bodies Ruby had seen piled up on the road. My heart squeezed at the thought.

"More nurses coming in from Hospital No. 2," Ethel shouted. "A bunch are here from Hospital No. 1 also."

I placed my hand over my heart. "Thank God, they finally made it."

"I'd almost given up on them," Lucy added.

"I was starting to think the worst," Helen Hennessey admitted.

We walked out to greet them. Lieutenant Josie Nesbit looked worn out and tired. She'd been in charge of the entire group. If anyone deserved a medal for courage, good humor, and ability, it was her.

Helen's hands rested on her hips. "What took so long?"

"Our truck broke down," Josie sucked in a breath.

"The road was repeatedly bombed," Minnie added. "On top of that I have malaria. I was so sick I just wanted to die."

"We ended up sleeping in an old Navy tunnel," Hattie Brantley told us.

"Thank God, I managed to find a phone and called Corregidor," Josie said. "They sent a boat for us."

217

"Better hug those boys who fetched you in the boat," Geneva said. "That was a suicide mission if there ever was one."

Juanita Redmond, who'd been with them, joined us.

"When the boat first arrived, it had engine trouble. Once we got under way, they had to zigzag through the water to avoid the bombs and aircraft over us," Josie said. "Boats of every kind and size filled the bay, trying to make it to Corregidor."

"On the wings of angels," Harriet Lee said, a Boston girl.

"Right after they dropped us off, they headed back to the mainland to pick up more Army personnel," Juanita said. "Word is they didn't make it."

"Any survivors?" Geneva asked.

Juanita shrugged. "We don't know yet."

"Lord be merciful to them," Maude Davison added.

"I'm afraid our angels were bombed by the Japs and sank," Josie whispered. "We saw Ruby Motley. But instead of waiting with us, she left with some men in a little boat. Do you know if she made it?"

I nodded. "Our tug picked them up. She was a nervous wreck."

"She's resting now," Maude Davison stated.

"It shows how God was watching out for us," Juanita said. "We all docked here safely."

Helen Summers, who had also arrived late, being Catholic made the sign of the cross.

"It's funny how religious war can make you. You won't find any atheist here," Harriet said.

"That's for sure," added Nancy, another one who'd finally made it.

"Well, last night our guardian angels were watching over us," I said.

A colonel passing by saw Harriet's swollen legs and feet. "Ah, a toe dancer no doubt."

We laughed. After hearing what these ladies had gone through, our trip didn't seem so bad. Like us, they arrived nauseated, in shock, and with severe headaches. After they finished eating, they would sleep all day.

That night, I couldn't sleep. It was hot and stuffy with no air circulating. After living out in the open for so long, this air seemed heavy. It made me feel like I was gasping for breath. An image of the fish my father would catch came to mind. A box full of fish gasping for a breath. That's how I felt.

Our bed and everything around us shook as bombs exploded overhead like thunder. During raids, the blowers stopped allowing the smells of the hospital to fill every inch of the tunnel.

"That's a hit on top," Helen Hennessey said, from a nearby bed.

I was glad the shells were muffled by being underground and only echoed along the laterals.

"I almost jumped out of bed to dive into my foxhole," Harriet said. "Then I realized I'm in the tunnel."

We laughed softly.

Using a map, Geneva, Jean, Helen, Nancy, and I explored the tunnel familiarizing ourselves with the different laterals.

The main tunnel, Malinta Tunnel, ran though Malinta Hill, running east and west. Trolley car tracks ran through it. A trolley had run from the eastern entrance to Topside, but unfortunately, the Japanese put it out of commission early on.

Twenty laterals, used for storing supplies, ammunition, and food, and the offices of the quartermaster, the Signal Corps, Anti-aircraft, and Harbor Defense as well as others branched off from both sides of Malinta Tunnel.

The hospital operated in its own laterals. Where the hospital branched off were the anti-aircraft post and the offices of the United States Armed Forces in the far east. USAFFE. Our hospital tunnel known as the Army Dock area had an entrance on the north side of Malinta Hill, and the laterals in the hospital contained numerous wards such as the mess hall, nurses' quarters, and supplies. The soldiers' mess was located outside our entrance.

The Navy tunnel had an entrance on the south side and was connected to the Quartermaster Department. On the south shore in a small cove, a hangar for Navy planes, a few houses, and a barracks sat nestled away.

Malinta Hill rose six hundred feet above the shore with a narrow and steep road leading to the top. The shore entrance to the tunnels were located on Bottomside. Halfway up to the main plateau of Topside, a section with barracks, some houses, and schools for the children who lived on the island was called Middleside.

While I found it confusing, I marveled over the sheer cleverness of its design. The entire system showed a brilliant work of superior engineering skills. I told the nurses from Sternberg how beautiful it had been before the Japs bombed it, making it look like a desert. "It doesn't even look like the same place."

One rule of Corregidor. No smoking. I would have a difficult time doing without my cigarettes. Geneva hoped I'd use this time to quit them all together.

About four O' clock, we walked to the mess hall and sat at our table. The people who'd just arrived still appeared groggy. I recalled how I had felt after that first night.

The corned-beef hash and potatoes tasted wonderful. I took my time savoring each bite.

"More stragglers arrived," Harriet said.

"I heard the firing on Bataan stopped this morning and hundreds of people used it as a chance to escape," Geneva said. "They'll have to swim. It's hard to find a boat."

"Build a raft," Mary Lohr added, who'd joined the group.

"In these shark infested waters, I wouldn't chance it," Jean Kennedy added. "But I guess it beats swimming."

"There's supposed to be more than a thousand-people crammed inside this tunnel tonight," Josie added. "I'm not sure where they'll put us all."

"I'm glad we had first choice of the bunks," Nancy said.

Helen Hennessey nodded. "I bet they run out."

"Someone can bunk with me," Lucy added.

We were lucky to have a bed. The people arriving would have to sleep on the floor.

At last most of the nurses serving in the Philippines had arrived. It was nice being reunited with our old friends who we hadn't seen in a while.

On the way back to our quarters, Geneva and I stopped at the bulletin board to see what ward we were assigned to.

The next morning at 7:00 a.m., I reported to the surgical ward, and Geneva to the nurses' quarters where many of the girls were ill with malaria, dysentery, and colds.

The hospital consisted of six laterals. The fair-sized surgical ward held thirty patients. Some boys were seriously ill, while others wore casts. Three or four beds stacked high lined both sides of the tunnel.

Beulah Putman, along with a Filipino nurse, and I would work this ward today. I turned to Beulah. "It's wonderful having medicine and bandages again."

She smiled. "You can sure say that again. I got really tired of washing bloody bandages and reusing them."

I started right off bathing patients and administering medicine. The cleanliness of the ward with shining white porcelain and plenty of clean linens made me almost giddy. I stayed busy all day, feeling like we could really make a difference for these sick and wounded men now that we had adequate medicine and supplies.

I looked at Beulah. "I can't believe our shift is over."

"This working half a day is going to spoil us."

"Well, there's not enough jobs for all of us. How many nurses do you think are here?"

"According to Josie, all eighty-five of the American Army nurses are here. Then you add the one Navy nurse and forty Filipino nurses."

"That's amazing." I twisted my pearl ring nervously. "I really hate most of the Navy nurses were captured. It's heartbreaking."

Beulah sighed. "They should've gotten them out of there."

"Geneva thinks in the long run we'll all in up prisoners."

We stared at each other lost in our thoughts. I thought of poor Mary Harrington and the others being held prisoners.

At lunch, Winnie caught up with us. We hugged for several minutes before we could speak. "Believe you me, I've been getting white hairs worrying about you two."

"We made it. Now if we can adjust to being inside," I said.

"I'm used to it. It's safe here. I figure I'll live to tell another tale," Winnie said.

"We're so use to the open sky above us, that this is like being in a gym with all the dirty smells circulating. I don't think I'll ever get used to it." Geneva flashed a sly look my way. "I know why you don't like it. You can't smoke."

"I could but going out and shining the tip of a cigarette up to the sky might make me a prime target."

We laughed.

"Most people find it easier to quit," Winnie said. "I did, and if I did, you can too. I really don't miss it."

"I'm not believing they give out a carton every week," I said, knowing I'd never quit if they were plentiful. "If we had had this many cigarettes in the jungle, we would've been millionaires."

We explained how we paid for everything with them.

"So, they were a luxury item?" Winnie asked.

"Yep. You could buy just about anything with them," I said. "Ironic that now I have plenty of cigarettes, but nowhere to smoke them."

"Being down here, you tend to forget Corregidor is more than the tunnel. It's an island four and a half miles long. The Marines never come inside. The fourth Marine division stay dug in at the beaches," Winnie stated. "Believe you me, those are some brave men."

"How are the sick nurses?" I asked Geneva.

"Having a difficult time staying on a liquid diet. Most of them are suffering from starvation. They know they shouldn't try eating, but their stomachs don't."

Dorothy Scholl joined us not looking very pleased. She flopped down with us. "I didn't get a bed. There's none left. I'm having to sleep on the floor."

"I'm sorry." I thought of something. "You can sleep in our bed until tonight. Maybe by then, you'll have your own bed."

"That's mighty sweet of you."

"You lugged my radio for me into the jungle."

"Check with Lucy Wilson and see if she has a bunkmate yet," Geneva suggested. "Last I heard, she didn't."

"Denny Williams beat me to it."

"Check with Dorothea Daley. Have you heard from Arnold?" I asked apprehensively.

She shook her head, appearing worried. "Not a word."

Later, I came across Eleanor O'Neill, chief nurse from Fort McKinley.

"Eleanor, it's me Ressa."

"Why, Ressa, you're looking good. How long have you been here?"

"A few days. We came in from Hospital Ho. 2 What are you assigned to?"

"I'm Miss Davison's assistant now. I help with supplies."

I was glad she had a somewhat easy job. She'd lost a lot of weight, and something in her eyes gave me the impression, she wasn't well.

GENEVA
April 11, 1942

In a short time, we were back to doing what we did best, caring for the sick and wounded. Great therapy, if you're focused on the care of others you forget about your own hardships. Most of us adapted to tunnel life quickly. Our duties didn't allow much time for contemplation. Living in Malinta Tunnel created a new scenario of pros and cons.

We no longer had to dive into trenches. But in exchange for safety, we had to surrender the warming rays of the sun and the feel of a breeze against our skin. The part of jungle-living we liked.

No matter how large the tunnel was, it still felt confining.

Slightly damp clothes hung all over our quarters since it required hours for anything to dry. It looked like a Chinese laundry.

If I died and went to Hell, an eternity spent in Malinta Tunnel would suffice nicely.

Dorothy Scholl came toward me. "They moved in more beds. I managed to snag a bottom bunk."

"Good. Heard from Arnold?"

"Not yet. I spent half the night praying for him."

Explosions and gunfire erupted near the tunnel's entrance. Bits of dust floated down coating us in a thick gray dust. I brushed it off. "I've got to go."

"Same here." Dorothy walked away, heading in the opposite direction.

In the ward, we quickly made accommodations for mangled boys being carried in. There would be men with the Army, Navy, and Marines. Most had been assigned to the gun emplacements. So many direct hits could mean only one thing.

Traitors lived among us.

Signals had been set off, designating targets for Jap bombers. The thought they were people who lived with us and witnessed on a daily basis the suffering they caused infuriated me. I can't imagine any punishment too severe for them.

The blowers stopped, and I choked on the scent of death and blood.

"Get ready! Wounded are coming," Harriet shouted.

At the sound of the horn's blast Ressa, Rita Palmer, and I prepared for their arrival.

Three boys, the youngest being sixteen, suffered a direct hit from Bataan. The battery they occupied had been destroyed.

"Try not to move, private." I said as I stripped his clothes off and cleaned him up for surgery.

"How bad is it?" he asked.

I wiped blood off his cheek, "Don't worry, you'll make it, but you won't be shooting Japs any time soon."

It burdened my heart to lie. He and his friends appeared in critical condition.

Captain Nelson, a very competent Navy doctor, quickly took charge. Ressa and I had worked with Rita's fiancé on several occasions.

"Doc, do you have any news about my buddies?" the injured soldier asked.

Captain Nelson sighed. "I can tell you they are in good hands."

After putting him to sleep, Doctor Nelson worked diligently on the young soldier cautiously probing and removing shrapnel. "There, that should just about do it. I've done all I can for him.

Hopefully his friend will join him soon. I'll check on him when he wakes up."

"Yes sir. I noticed you said friend, not friends," I said.

"The sixteen-year old didn't make it," Dr. Nelson admitted. "When I said they were both in good hands, I told him the truth. One is in the hands of a doctor and the other in the hands of God. When he's a little stronger, I'll tell him the truth."

"Yes, sir." I recognized the wisdom of his diplomacy. Actually, everyone on this island was in God's hands.

"Miss Jenkins. Get him to recovery."

"Yes, sir."

With the help of an aide, we were able to move him to recovery. Fortunately, his comrade was already there. At least when he came out of it, his buddy would be close by. A nurse hovered over his friend wiping his face with a damp cloth. He groaned softly but didn't wake up.

"How bad is he?" I asked the nurse working behind me.

"Pretty banged up, but he should pull through."

I recognized Ressa's voice. "I didn't realize that was you back there."

"I'm so busy I didn't notice you being there. How's yours doing?"

"About the same. It's a miracle these two survived."

"Yeah, they're tough guys. Too bad their buddy wasn't as lucky. Francis told me he died within minutes after they started to operate."

"I know, but at least Nelson saved two out of three," I said.

Ressa wiped her tears. "If you're trying to make me feel better, don't. It's not working."

"You're right, sis. Sorry. Some dark clouds are just black with no silver linings."

"No, I'm sorry, I shouldn't snap at you. It's just that everything seems so hopeless."

"They'll never take Corregidor," a young orderly said, rolling in another patient. "We would never permit the Japs to take it. Think how we'd lose face."

Others made similar remarks as we worked on patients.

225

I hated to tell him, we'd already lost face. Japan kept coming and still coming, pushing us back even more. Where were the reinforcements President Roosevelt had promised?

Some faced the reality that help might never come. As for Ressa and I, we had reconciled ourselves to the fact we'd never return home.

"All the talk about Corregidor being safe sounds good, but I'm not buying it. What do you see in regards to our future?" Ressa asked.

I stared at her a moment. "Honest answer?" She merely nodded without uttering a word. I sighed. "We will be back in Manila soon."

It was a matter of time before we were taken as prisoners, transported, and placed in an internment camp.

"How are these boys doing?" Agnes Barre asked as she entered the ward.

Ressa glanced up from washing her hands. "They aren't out of the woods yet, but they're tough."

"We got Second Lieutenant Bliss here," an orderly shouted. "He's got shrapnel wounds on his head."

"Get him to surgery," Francis Nash yelled.

"What happened?" I couldn't imagine how he'd been wounded.

"He went Topside to get a view of Manila. Japs spotted him and let a shell go that hit near him."

Going Topside was risky. The Japanese knew most of what went on. They had a clever method of observing us. They would attach a balloon to a truck with a camera mounted on it, then patrol up and down the Bataan airfield. It was obvious to everyone saboteurs on Corregidor gave signals since too many direct hits were made to be considered just coincidences.

Later Captain Fox received shrapnel wounds on his arms and legs. He'd been treating some men at a battery on Topside when they'd received a direct hit.

By the end of the day, Nelson grinned. "Ladies, it's time to swab the deck."

We knew it was his humorous way of telling us to mop the floor. We giggled and found our mops.

While we mopped, General Wainwright, who was idolized by everyone on Corregidor walked through the ward. From having beriberi, he walked with a cane. He often made the rounds, speaking to the doctors and nurses, stopping to chat with the soldiers at their post, and visiting the wounded in the wards.

Major General George F. Moore, who commanded all of the batteries on Corregidor, accompanied him as he did so many times.

A soldier lying on a stretcher raised his head as General Wainwright walked by. "Don't worry, General. The folks back home wouldn't let us down. They'll come over any minute and knock the hell out of these Nips."

Another soldier sitting off to the side frowned. "What in the hell is taking so long?"

Neither commanding officer's expression gave away what they knew. They didn't commit to promises they couldn't keep.

It had been General Wainwright, who had given the order to bring us out of the jungles of Bataan. He had not wanted us to fall into the hands of the Japs.

The man knew every battery, and he could tell which was firing from the direction of its sound. We used to be amused when they were shooting, and he would listen for a moment, and then say, "Give 'em hell, Battery 59 or whatever battery was firing."

RESSA
April 15, 1942

I spotted one of my patients who'd been suffering with malaria coming down the hall. He wore a new cast on his leg.

"Stop right there," I ordered. "What happened to your leg?"

"Well, ma'am, it's like this. I snuck out of bed to grab a smoke outside. I got caught up in the shelling."

I pinned a stern look on him. "What a lame thing to do. You risked your life for a cigarette. The next time you want a smoke, you ask permission. You do not leave that ward without it. Am I clear?"

"Yes, ma'am."

"Now get back to bed and stay there."

He appeared sad, and I immediately regretted my harshness. My mood lightened when I came upon Colonel Chet Elms, our quartermaster. We truly adored him for bringing us little things he hoarded.

"Got any more of that soap?" I asked.

"Ressa, darlin' for you I have the moon."

I smiled. "Soap is fine."

He pulled out clothes and other odd and ends before handing me a small bar of soap. I couldn't have asked for a better treat. In the jungle, the soap would have slipped into the stream and disappeared. A lot of what we had in the jungle had done us little good. Like our stockings and white uniforms, but here in the tunnel, we could've used them. Too bad we'd left them.

I hated wearing the brown Army fatigues and boots. I only had one tan dress left and one pair of stockings. I wanted to kick myself for getting rid of everything.

"I got more than soap, cutie pie."

He motioned to a table with neatly pressed skirts and shirts. "Help yourself."

Helen Summers joined us. "Where'd they come from?"

"Had a couple of Chinese tailors whip them up for you. Now the shirts were GI shirts cut down to fit you ladies."

Several of us hugged his neck. He held out a bag. "Got some white ladies' loafers. Let me know if you can't find your size."

I grabbed clothes and shoes for Geneva also. It felt as if Christmas had just arrived.

At dinner, I sat with Dorothy and Madeline. Miss Nau, the Red Cross representative, sat with a little boy at the far end of the table.

"Hey, where'd the cute kid come from?" I asked.

Madeline replied, "The sergeant found him wandering around Mariveles. His parents were killed."

I salted my food, then glanced back at the boy. "Poor little guy."

Major Latimore, who'd been our Bataan Ordinance officer, joined us. "Ladies, good seeing you again."

"I wasn't sure you'd make it out. How'd you manage that?" Dorothy asked.

"The night Bataan fell, a group of us made it to Mariveles, found a boat, and came over." He described his adventure more.

I had worried about him. The man had five children back home. Actually, his trip sounded as stressful as ours.

With few supplies coming in and so many people to feed, our meals had been rationed to two meals a day. I tried to eat every bite of my soup and crackers. Sometimes, we'd make peanut butter and jelly sandwiches to sneak to the guys.

That night at seven, Commander Al Heady came around with a silver pitcher of lemonade. He'd hidden it under a pillowcase. "Ladies, thought you could use a little refreshment tonight."

"You got that right," Nancy said.

We joined the group of nurses and followed him outside. The moon hid behind clouds, making it harder for the Japs to see us. We sat and drank the sweet liquid. It tasted so good and refreshing, I almost felt guilty the others didn't get any.

"Can you believe I've actually gained weight?" Nancy asked.

"Me too," I admitted, while sipping my drink.

We all confessed we'd gained weight on the small rations we received.

"When we were in the jungle, we walked from one end to the other and we had so little to eat." Geneva set her glass down.

Nancy shifted her stance, placing her weight on her right hip. "Not to mention the food was dreadful."

Whitlow nodded. "You've also got to consider, here we do very little walking and have shorter shifts."

Jean Kennedy grinned. "Besides that, the food is really good."

"And we have a lot less anxiety here," Nancy said. "We're not jumping in and out of foxholes."

"There's not a one of us who didn't need to gain some weight," Geneva reminded.

We laughed, but we all knew if we were captured by the Japs, we'd need every pound to stay alive if they starved us.

One of Jean's officer friends joined us. "Ladies, nice evening."

"Any evening is nice if I can sit outside without being bombed," Helen Summers said.

"So, what's the first thing you'll do when you get home?" he asked.

"I want to attend the Newsreel Theater," Helen Summers said.

Jean's hand shot in the air. "Me too."

"I'd want to open a dance club." I pushed my sleeves up. "I'll call it the Bataan Club."

Helen laughed. "Everyone would have to wear helmets."

"Paint the girls' helmets pink," Geneva added.

We laughed.

Jean smiled. "Decorate the club in bamboo with foxholes."

"And we'd only cater to Philippine veterans," I added.

"What do you think you'll be doing forty years from now?" Helen asked me.

"Why in forty years, we'll be walking down some street at home still wearing our tin hats, and someone will say oh look at those strange women and someone else will say oh let them be. They're harmless. That's those shell-shocked nurses from Bataan."

We laughed again. It was easy to discuss time when you knew you might not have even forty days to live. Our conversation was all in jest. Weary minds were easily entertained.

When the moon escaped from behind the clouds, we returned inside.

That night, we couldn't sleep. "I hate this tunnel."

"Me too," Geneva whispered. "I can never get a good breath of air. I always feel like my lungs are only half full."

"It gives a false sense of security that's unhealthy."

"Remember how jittery Winnie and the others were when they visited the jungle?"

"Also, they took short, little breaths of air almost like panting."

Geneva pulled the sheet up over us. "Are we doing that?"

"Not yet. That's why we have to make ourselves go out when they're not bombing."

Many of the girls never went out. They stayed in their bunks and stared at the ceiling. I didn't want to end up like them.

I worried the most about Dorothy Scholl. She had withdrawn a great deal. Maybe because she hadn't heard from Arnold.

The next day, we played cards with a group, then we all went outside during a lapse in the bombing. The air smelled wonderful. A nice breeze blew across my skin. We sat on the hill and stared out over the harbor. The Pigeon floated in the water below.

Helen Summers, Nancy, Whitlow, Geneva and I talked some, but mainly we were quiet. We'd said everything that could be said. Why repeat it? Though, we never tired of laughing about Geneva leaving her underwear.

Geneva pinned her gaze on me. "Do you have my Bible?"

"No, didn't you pack it?"

"I thought I had."

Nancy glanced up from her cards. "What does it look like?"

"White with little pink roses. I've had it since I was a kid. I must've left it on the bus."

Ressa frowned. "Well, I'll be. I really hate that. I know how much it meant to you."

Boom!

The sky lit.

Boom!

I scrambled to my feet. Another blinding light flashed. "Run, Geneva!"

"I can't see the door," Helen shouted.

Bam, bam, bam. Shells sprayed around us.

I tripped over something and fell. My brain sent orders faster than my body could react. *Get up. Run. Hurry.* I managed to get to my feet and charged toward the door. We lunged inside the entrance and leaned against the wall, panting, hearts beating rapidly. It took another five minutes before our heartrates returned to normal.

I wouldn't dare mention our experience to anyone, especially Dorothy Scholl. Later, I saw her in her bunk, staring up at the ceiling. Her face revealed her depression and sadness.

"Hey, Dorothy, want to play cards?"

She didn't answer.

"If I can't beat them. I figure I might have a better chance beating you."

Still no answer. Her eyes remained glassy and blank of emotion.

I gave up and went to bed. I'm sure she was worried about Arnold.

My spirit lifted the next evening when Commander Davis visited from the Pigeon.

"What brings you our way?" I asked.

"I brought my men over to sleep in the tunnel, but they said they'd rather take their chances outside than to suffocate in here. I don't see how you ladies do it."

"What choice do we have?" I asked.

We walked to the mess hall and grabbed a cup of coffee, then sat at a table.

During our conversation, he described the night Bataan fell. "I went with some officers to Hospital No. 2 to try and save some nurses, but the holes gutted the roads making it impossible to travel on."

I set my cup down. "The night we left was chaotic. There were so many soldiers who could barely stand trying to make it here."

"There's nothing worse than an army retreating. We ran into soldiers only dressed in shorts. They had scratches where thorns had shredded their legs when they crossed through the thick jungle." He sipped his coffee, then cradled it in his hand. "It made us sick to think of you ladies in the hands of those devils. I'm glad you got out."

"I'm glad you didn't make it there. You would have made the trip for nothing."

"I'd also been ordered to blow up the docks and Navy tunnels and scuttle the Canopus. She'd survived the attacks on December twenty-ninth and January first only to be destroyed by us. I hated to do it, but April tenth, we destroyed her."

"Sad to think of the Canopus demolished. The night we left people were trying to swim across the bay."

Davis nodded. "The Pigeon was ordered on a mission to accompany a submarine. People filled the bay, trying to swim to Corregidor. I had my orders. I couldn't stop to pick them up. It would've sunk us. But swimming it is impossible. With that strong current, I'm afraid most were washed to sea or killed by sharks."

I shuddered. "Were any saved? Do you know?"

"I had some tugs go out. They saved men who were clinging to the mines."

"I know of one man who swam it," I said. "Captain Benson of the MPs stripped down and swam. He even swam against the current. He told us it was an atrocious experience he'd never do again. He was exhausted to the point of passing out when he walked up on the other side."

"He must've been a hell of a swimmer."

I smiled. "And lucky the sharks didn't find him."

"Are you one of the nurses Captain Benson sent whiskey to?"

I laughed. "Seems I remember that. Tell him we all appreciated it."

"When I asked him about it, he told me those nurses deserved a little fun."

"Well, we had fun and also headaches the next day."

I left him and joined a group determined to sneak outside. An order had come earlier not to leave the tunnel. In our defense, the bombing had stopped several hours ago. I'd never been one who skipped school and went places I'd been told not to go, but tonight I was suffocating.

We slipped outside and smoked, keeping a hand in front of the glowing tip, so it wouldn't be spotted. Our outing only lasted a few minutes. It wasn't until the next night that I learned the importance of following orders. The building that we had sat by was blown to pieces that day. It was the only time, and the last time, I disobeyed orders.

Geneva hadn't been with us, and I was glad.

The next day, we used our medical skills for a new problem. Food poisoning had been reported on the island and victims came to us. Over a hundred people were vomiting. I kept looking for emesis pans and ended up using buckets or whatever I could find. No one died, but the ungodly stench left in the poorly ventilated laterals was indescribable. Fortunately, Geneva had been off and missed it.

As I was leaving, I noticed how thin Captain Maude Davison had become. She worried about us constantly and never herself. She busied herself doing reports. She fussed over us all the time, making sure we were cared for and had the proper clothes. She had been in the Army about twenty years. Though tough as nails and proficient, we could tell living on the Rock was getting to her. Thank goodness, she had Lieutenant Nesbit to help her. Josie had been a godsend.

On the way to my quarters, I passed Chaplain Wilcox, the protestant chaplain on Corregidor. He treated the boys well, and everyone respected and liked him.

"Hey, Miss Ressa Jenkins. Where you heading?"

I told him about the food poisoning. "I need a shower. I'm surprised you can't smell me."

"I don't. Stay and visit."

He appeared lonely, so I sat down. "How's your family?"

"I haven't heard anything in a while." He pulled out a folded letter. "I've read this one over fifty times. Want to hear the poem she wrote when we first married?"

I nodded. "Sure."

He read the poem, and it touched me. The poem showed how much his wife loved him.

And for a few minutes, the poem made me forget the horrors of war. I finally parted from him and headed toward the ward.

Winnie stopped me. "You's going to the dance tonight?"

I laughed. "Where are they holding it?"

"In one of the laterals. It's cleared out for a new ward to be set up. But that's not until tomorrow. I even heard some of the guys scrounged up some instruments."

"Geneva's off. We'll be there." I couldn't imagine there being room to move much less dance.

GENEVA
April 18, 1942

That evening, Ressa and I stood in the lateral along with so many others that it made dancing impossible. Music played from somewhere in front of us. The strumming of guitar strings and the blare of a horn filled the area.

"Some dance this is?" I shouted to Ressa.

Winnie stood across a sea of people from us and waved. We couldn't reach her. As more people piled into the area, the air became hot and unbearable.

"I can't breathe in here," I confessed.

"Me neither," Ressa said. "Let's go before we get trampled to death."

Still feeling like we were suffocating, we stepped outside from the entrance near our lateral. I breathed in the fresh air replenishing my lungs. "Better?"

Ressa nodded. "Much."

A group of soldiers greeted us. One of them started singing *Danny Boy*. His warm soft tones eased the tension running through me.

"I enjoyed your song. You have a lovely voice. Have a nice evening," I said.

"Thanks. Night, ladies," he said.

We slipped back inside our quarters and prepared for bed. While lying in bed that night, continuous shelling kept a constant rumble going above.

Ressa cleared her throat. "I overheard three nurses arguing today. I'm not sure who started it, but Dr. Nelson ended it."

"It's hard to keep our tempers in check under these conditions."

"Filipino nurses manage. I know there are several who can't stand each other, but they never speak a cross word."

"No, they just avoid one another," I said. "But they always manage to stay upbeat and hopeful. I don't see how they do it."

Not long after we stopped talking, Ressa snored softly.

I longed for home and family, for the things I didn't believe I'd ever see again. I also thought of Jerry and what the young nurse had told me.

The next day, I stopped with a group of nurses admiring the layette a young civilian nurse held up. She'd made the infant clothes from old linens and sheets. I didn't know her only that she was married to an Army lieutenant. She'd been stationed in Manila. Once it had been declared an open city, she traveled by boat to Corregidor to be with him. It hadn't sounded that daring until I learned the boat's cargo was a load of dynamite.

Susan Downing Gallagher, who had married Lieutenant Robert Gallagher, also announced they were having a baby. She sent a letter telling him the good news with a group heading out to join the troops in the jungles.

RESSA
April 24, 1942

Geneva slept soundly beside me, but I couldn't sleep. Instead, I stared at the ceiling, wondering how much longer before we were captured.

Bam, bam, bam. Shells hit in rapid succession. A deafening noise caused confusion and panic. We screamed and climbed out of bed, stumbling over each other in the dark. It had come from inside the tunnel. *How? Where?*

We ran toward the commotion to see what had happened. Immediately, the Japs fired into the west entrance. Three shells fell into the soldiers' mess hall.

At the tunnel entrance the impact of the bomb had been so great, it had closed the iron gate. People clung to it trying to get back inside as shells plowed them down and shredded their bodies.

It wasn't until we moved closer that we realized body parts and flesh stuck between the bars. I gasped as my stomach churned, threatening to bring up my dinner.

Bodies lay scattered all over the ground. We stepped over severed body parts and torsos that had once been men. Men we recognized from the hospital and clubs.

Blood covered everything.

Cassie stood in shock over the head laying at her feet. I placed a hand on her. "Don't look."

She nodded.

We were ordered inside to assist the men who'd been in the mess hall and their quarters. Fear and panic spread through the chaotic tunnel.

A doctor pointed at a soldier. "Get him on a stretcher."

"Yes, sir." I called for a corpsman to help me. "I'll get his feet."

We carried him, weaving through disoriented men stumbling about while bleeding. Some cursed while others screamed in intense pain louder than they ever had in the jungles.

I stared at the commotion unable to react. I felt my emotions and fears giving way. I wanted to scream and give in to what I was feeling. How much longer could we be expected to hold it together? I calmed myself down, gritted my teeth, and went to work.

Every nurse had been called to duty. There had been sixty casualties. Much more of this and all our training wouldn't do us any good, because we would eventually break down.

"I was in the shower," the boy said. "The man next to me was blown to pieces."

"Just try not to think about it. Let's get your injuries tended to."

I washed all the blood, brains, and guts off of him, and oddly, he didn't have a scratch on him. It had all been from the man killed beside him. Still, he had to be treated for shock. With so many, we worked fast. Geneva and many of the others worked around me, moving from patient to patient.

The most we could do for some was make them as comfortable as possible until a doctor could get to them. I administered shots and first aid, undressed them, and put them into bed as quickly as possible.

The operating room worked at top speed until 2:00 a.m. We continued working to save these men. Sticky blood covered the operating room floors. I had to empty a bucket of toes, fingers, hands, and flesh, and I thought I would surely be sick. But instead, this senseless loss of life made me angry.

Seventeen of the severely wounded men died. The fact that shells had reached inside the tunnel shook us to our core. This attack showed us our sense of safety was an illusion.

Though we had ended up in different wards, Geneva and I went off duty about the same time. Strangely enough, we were hungry, but there wasn't anything to eat. I had given an officer my bread earlier, and just this once, I regretted my generosity.

"How bad did it get in the operating room?" I asked, trying to keep my mind off my hunger.

Geneva wiped her hands on her pants. "Mangled legs and arms. A lot of head injuries."

"I'd really like to find the traitor and perform an emergency castration," I said.

The other nurses around us laughed.

Helen Hennessey added, "Once he's caught, there's no telling what they'll do to him."

"Nothing could be harsh enough," I added. It terrified me, we had stood in the very same area on several evenings. It could've happened to us.

GENEVA
April 25, 1942

Ressa climbed out of bed, looking crestfallen. "I've seen too many deaths. It's such a waste. I'm not sure I can face it today."

"Well, you don't have a choice," I said. "Jose, that nice Filipino major, paid us a visit. He left our favorite cheese."

Her eyes showed a spark of excitement. She hurried to the table and nibbled at the dried cheese crumbs. "I needed this."

I laughed at the immediate change in her disposition.

Cheese wasn't easy to come by, and this was store cheese. Even though it was dried out crumbs, we loved it. Most of our food was bland, so to have a few bites of something flavorful sent our taste buds into overdrive and lifted our spirits.

At lunch that day, I met up with Winnie and Ressa. "I saw Miss Nau. She looks so overworked."

Miss Nau was our Red Cross worker.

"There's just too much for her to do. She's up against a psychological barrier. So many are suffering with mental issues."

"She said what we need is a recreational program." Ressa scraped her fork around her plate, trying to get the peas on it.

Winnie pointed her fork at us. "Here's the issue with that. There's not room for any kind of program. You betcha, it was perfect here until you guys showed up."

I scowled. "Just what does that mean?"

Winnie lowered the fork. "It's overrun with people. Not only are most of the medical personnel here and soldiers, we have tons of civilians. There are people sleeping on the floors in every hallway. Not to mention, we're running out of food."

"It's not like we had any other place to go," Ressa said, in a defensive tone.

"I'm not blaming you. It's just that claustrophobia is getting the best of me."

Ressa and I returned to the ward and worked the rest of the day. We had little chance to talk. While I worked, I thought of what Winnie had said, and I wondered how long the food would last. We no longer had horses, carabao, or monkeys to eat.

Agnes and Earleen entered the ward. Earleen signed in. "We came to relieve you. I guess they figured even the Jenkins girls need a break every now and then."

"I don't know about Ressa, but this Jenkins girl definitely needs a hot cup of coffee."

"Sounds good to me, sis." She turned her attention to Agnes and Earleen, "These young men came out of surgery less than twenty minutes ago, so they should be out for a while."

"Sounds like easy duty for now." Earleen took a stack of gauze from me. "Around here you never know when all hell will break loose."

"What time have you got, Geneva?" Ressa asked.

I glanced at my wrist. "Six-thirty-five."

She reset her watch. "Thanks. We've got just enough time for that cup of coffee."

In the mess, we grabbed our coffee and found a seat. I sipped the hot brew.

Ressa checked the time. Every day, two important events happened at 10:00 a.m. and 7:00 p.m. *The Voice of Freedom* broadcasted—our only connection with the outside world. We finished our coffee and hurried to a lateral that had a radio.

I glanced around us. "Wow, Ressa, this place is packed."

"Like they say, standing room only."

People huddled together and generated enough body heat to make the area uncomfortable. Sweat beaded on my forehead. I could still taste the coffee in my throat.

At the first crackle of the radio, people grew silent and waited.

This is the Voice of Freedom coming to you live with the latest news from the home front. Every recruiting station in the country is experiencing patriotism at its finest as lines of brave young men wait their turn to enlist.

Women, formerly called the fairer sex, will not be out done as thousands converge on war plants throughout the land. Planes, tanks, and guns are being produced at a record pace.

We listened intently. Eyes sparkled with enthusiasm. My heart beat with pride. The news we had been praying for should be coming any moment now. Troops were coming to save us. I wrung my hands together as I waited to hear those words.

President Roosevelt has ordered forces to Ireland.

In that chamber, a soft moan resonated. I heard sobbing. We all felt the same emotion—betrayal, not from our enemies, but from our own country.

Someone turned the radio off, and we slowly made our way back to our quarters. It was heartbreaking. Yes, they considered us the red-haired stepchildren of the war. That night, rumors of Roosevelt's Rainbow 5 plan leaked out. It only involved Europe. We weren't a part of it.

I turned to Ressa, "I wish the politicians behind Roosevelt and his war strategy could have seen the expressions on people's faces in that room. It would give them something to think about."

"I bet the folks at home don't even realize there's a war going on over here."

To the Washington politicians, we were no more than game pieces in their war game to be pushed back, because they had a more important play to make.

As we walked through our quarters, someone in a nearby bunk sobbed hard with disheartened disappointment.

Abandonment is a formidable thing, much worse than fear. We kept telling ourselves that we served a small purpose in a large plan, but it didn't make us feel any less abandoned.

Cassie had said earlier that we were expendable. And I agreed with her. No one was worried about coming to our aid. We were not important. I wonder how Roosevelt and the others could sleep at night. Apparently, just fine.

A submarine hadn't come in since Bataan had fallen. We were convinced none would, so the fact that no one was coming didn't shock us as much as it had the others. Our deaths wouldn't affect Roosevelt's war plan. Besides if ships came, it would mean horrible slaughter to more young men. I couldn't bear to think of more of them being maimed and killed trying to save us.

Regardless of our apparent abandonment by our government, the soldiers continued to talk about being saved. They'd always start with *rumor has it* and end by asking our opinion. I didn't dare share my opinion, because hope was all they had.

The next evening, we peeked in on a wedding being held in one of the laterals. Candlelight glowed softly as Mary Brown and Colonel Menzie stood before the chaplain.

Mary had come from the states to Manila to marry Colonel Menzie, who was stationed there. She'd barely arrived when war broke out. She joined the Army Nurse Corps. The colonel had been stationed on Corregidor, so she finally came over when Bataan fell.

After they'd been pronounced husband and wife, Mary smiled. "It's about time we got married. I wasn't willing to put it off another day."

Ressa hadn't heard anything about Robert. She had grown fond of the young pilot. He'd last been seen in the jungles. She had always warned that matters of the heart were best avoided in wartimes. The chance of separation or the loss of your spouse was a daily risk.

That night, Ressa slept soundly while I remained awake, my mind spinning with fears and doubts. The day had been long and overall depressing with the exception of Jose's cheese. There had also been news of the Filipino nurses being inducted in the Philippine army as lieutenants. They worked hard and deserved the promotion and honor.

Finally, I thought of Jerry. Had he died back on Bataan?

GENEVA
April 27, 1942

The following morning, a rumor that some of us were being evacuated dominated our conversations. Ethel Thor, Millie Dalton, and Anna Williams debated on whether it was true. Neither Ressa nor I believed it. It was too good to be true.

I sighed on a long breath. "Not happening."

Ressa shook her head. "I'm not buying it either. And if they did rescue us, where would we go?"

"Exactly." Dorothy finished off her coffee. She had heard from Arnold and was much happier these days. "There's nowhere that doesn't have Japs."

Helen Summer's face tightened. "Still, it's a possibility."

"But they can't take us all," Ressa reminded. "How do they choose?"

"You're becoming about as negative as Geneva," Ethel said. "You're usually the positive one."

Ressa laughed. "True, but so much of what we hear turns out to be nothing. So, why get our hopes up?"

"I can't argue with that," Millie Dalton said.

Anna Williams shook her head. "This one is true, but how will they decide who leaves and who stays?"

We all stared at one another. Who would get the opportunity to leave and return home? Whatever happened, I knew Ressa and I would stay together.

"Believe you me, I'm going to ignore these outrageous rumors until we hear it from the brass," Winnie said. "Until then, we'd better get to work. You betcha more wounded are coming in this morning."

Peggy O'Neil folded her arms in a defiant way. "I still think they're moving some of us out."

I glanced at Peggy and Winnie. "Just because it's so crowded here, don't think you'll get rid of us that easily."

We all laughed and agreed not to discuss it. Instead, we talked about the wedding and those who were thinking of getting married.

Something had changed. The Japs kept guns aimed on the tunnel's entrances. No one could go outside for a breath of fresh air.

We were trapped like mice waiting for the cats to leave. But they didn't. They shelled the Rock even harder. We all feared a Japanese invasion into the tunnel at any time. Finally, they let up. How many more bombings could the tunnel withstand?

Later that morning, a call of alert went out. We made our way to our stations. Colonel N.C. Pilet made an inspection. His visit terrified us. Were we being prepared for a Japanese invasion into the tunnel? We all knew it was inevitable unless troops came.

I hadn't heard any bombs or planes for a while, so I decided to get some fresh air. As I walked to the tunnel entrance, a truck pulled up. They had brought more wounded soldiers here from Bataan.

I gasped when Jerry climbed from the truck, looking dirty and exhausted. When he turned around, he saw me. "Geneva."

"Jerry. I'm glad you're safe."

"I was hoping I'd get a chance to see you."

"If you still want to talk, I'll listen."

"I need to clean up and eat something. Can we talk tonight?"

I nodded and told him when and where to meet me. Though I fought feeling anything for him, I did. I tried to make myself angry with him, but I wasn't.

Later that evening, we met in one of the new wards being set up. No one was there. Rarely, could you find a spot where you weren't surrounded by people.

I sat on the edge of a cot across from him. I decided not to mention what the nurse had said. "Go ahead. I'm listening."

He explained about his insurance and the benefits that came from being married to a service man who dies in action. "I didn't think we'd make it back. I had this dread hanging over me like I knew I wasn't ever making it home. I thought it was sad that no one would benefit from my death. So, I asked her to marry me. I didn't love her. We're just friends."

"But you did survive. Are you two getting married?"

"No. She turned me down."

"So, are you here because she turned you down?"

He appeared to be thinking. "No, Geneva. I was happy when she turned me down. I had changed my mind also. You're the one I care about, the one I love."

There it was. That word. I'd been raised smart enough to know men threw it around like paper airplanes.

He sighed. "Say something. Because I sure can't tell what you're thinking."

"I'm speechless."

"But are you still mad?"

"I should be."

He grinned. "Does that mean you're not?"

I gave a surrendering sigh. "No, I'm not. But that hurt, Jerry. And I was humiliated on top of it."

"I'm sorry. I panicked when I thought I was about to die."

I glanced at my watch. "I've got to go. How long will you be here?"

"I'm not sure. There's a lot of wounded still out there we need to get to safety."

We stood. Finally, I walked toward him and wrapped my arms around him. "I don't want you going back."

"Trust me, I'm not crazy about it. It's a war out there, sweetheart," he said, trying to sound like Bogart.

"It's not funny," I said.

He kissed the crown of my head.

I lifted my face and kissed him lightly. "You pull something like that proposal again, don't even bother talking to me."

He grinned. "Can I see you tomorrow?"

"I'll be in the mess hall tomorrow morning around seven."

"See you then, Geneva."

RESSA
April 28, 1942

I bumped into Commander Davis in the hall. "What brings you our way?"

"Came over to visit my buddy, Hap Goodall." He motioned me closer. "I've got some items on the Pigeon you ladies might be interested in."

I nodded. "You have my attention."

"An officer was sent back to the states. He left everything. Seems he'd been buying things for the folks back home and then had to leave it. I'll bring them over to you first chance I get. So long as those little yellow devils don't start back shelling."

"That's been pretty much a constant lately."

"Where's that gorgeous sister of yours?" Davis asked.

"She should be getting off duty about now."

"Why don't you gals join me at mass tomorrow? I'll bring those things with me."

"We'll be there."

RESSA
April 29, 1942

The next morning, Nancy, Geneva, and I attended mass in the Malinta Tunnel. A good size crowd entered in front of us. Once inside, we didn't see Commander Davis. Had something come up? Right before the service started, he came up the aisle with a bundle in his arms.

During the very early morning mass, everyone sat quietly. The gloom of capture loomed over us. Each prayer was heartfelt.

After the service, Commander Davis unfolded the bundle and revealed his loot. "You ladies take what you want."

Geneva picked through the items. "You're positive he's not coming back for any of this?"

"Positive. Help yourself, Geneva." He smiled at my sister with admiration.

We each selected a new pair of Chinese tailored silk pajamas, a can of talcum powder, and a deck of playing cards. Other nurses came over to investigate and took what was left.

I winked at Commander Davis. "Thanks for thinking of us first."

He grinned. "Got to keep the Jenkins sisters happy."

We walked out the entrance for some air. Fortunately, there hadn't been a bombing or shells hitting us that morning. I inhaled long breaths of the fresh air, cleansing my lungs. The sun shined on my pale face and warmed me.

We found Josie Nesbit and Miss Putnam sitting outside. We joined them. It was very tranquil and peaceful. No one spoke. We sat soaking up sunshine while lost in our thoughts.

It ended when Commander Davis joined us and paced up and down nervously. His distress was apparent. Looking like he'd explode if he didn't speak, he turned to us. "At communion I prayed you both would get evacuated to Australia."

I smiled. "Thank you for your prayers, but we won't retreat this time and leave the other nurses and our patients."

Geneva nodded. "Where'd you get the funny notion that some of us would be leaving?"

"You've heard the rumors."

"We have, but that's all they are—rumors," I said. But if anyone knew the truth, he would. So perhaps, the rumor was true. I turned back to him. "We're completely resigned to the inevitability of our fate. We're prepared to stay."

Geneva nodded. "Like always, she speaks for both of us."

His expression grew stern. "If you girls have a chance to leave, promise me you'll take it."

I sighed. "I can't make that promise."

"Think long and hard about it before you decide," he advised.

We both agreed we'd give it careful consideration.

Our time outside ended when the Japanese started bombing. They bombed the tunnel all day until 4:00 p.m. At dinner, one of the doctors looked at us. "The little yellow devils are celebrating Hirohito's birthday today. That's why they haven't let up."

An officer spoke up. "Relax, they can't penetrate the tunnel."

We relaxed and sang *Happy Birthday* to Dorothy Scholl, who shared the birth date with the Japanese leader.

The Japanese celebration caused many casualties from all the batteries. This was the largest number of wounded yet.

The corpsmen delivered four of them to my ward. The soldiers had been horribly burned when a shell made a direct hit on a gasoline drum.

I worked on a captain for over an hour. I gave him a shot for the pain, then painted his burned skin with gentian violet. I fought the urge to vomit from the smell of his burnt flesh. The poor man died. I closed my eyes and grimaced. Death never became routine.

I moved on to the next wounded man, hoping to save him. While I smoothed my hair back from my face, an officer stepped up to me. "There will be nine cars entering the tunnel tonight around 10:00 p.m. It's my guess that some of the nurses will be driven out."

After he left, I shared what he'd said with Beulah and immediately regretted it. Her face filled with joy. "I'm going to pack."

I grabbed her arm. "Wait. There are eighty-six nurses. They won't take us all. Don't get your hopes up until you know for sure if you're one of the ones chosen."

Though I was determined not to retreat which I had proclaimed often, I had to admit the chance of freedom, of being away from this island and this stifling tunnel, made my pulse pound. I had to be honest. All my brave talk of remaining behind had been just that—talk. It had been my way of protecting myself from false hope. But now that the possibility existed, I wanted to leave, so long as Geneva could also.

An hour later, Lieutenant Josie Nesbit stopped me in the hall. "I wish to see you in the mess hall at 6:00 p.m. Make sure you're there."

"Yes, ma'am." I knew something was up. My rapid heartbeat made it difficult to think. This didn't mean anything. Or did it?

I made my way to the room where we were to meet. Around twenty nurses waited. I spotted Juanita, Sally, Whitlow, Rosemary, Mary, Eunice, Sue, and Harriet but not Geneva. What if I had been chosen and she hadn't?

GENEVA
April 29, 1942 (6:00 p.m.)

I glanced up from my reports.
A young corpsman stood before me. "Miss Jenkins?"

"Yes, may I help you?"

"You're to report to the mess hall. Colonel Pilet and Captain Davison are expecting you."

I didn't question him on what it was about. I nodded and left. A part of me knew it could be about the evacuation, and it surprised me I was selected. Then I had a foreboding thought. Had something happened to Jerry?

He hadn't shown up for breakfast. I learned he had been sent back out on another detail before daybreak. But if something had happened, I'd be reporting to a chaplain instead of a colonel.

By the time, I reached the dining area, at least sixteen or more nurses and officers had congregated there. I sat somberly, then studied the surrounding faces. A stream of anxiety flowed through me until I finally saw Ressa. A sigh of relief passed through my lips. Now whatever this was about didn't matter as much. I always felt a sense of security with her nearby.

She waved, then came over and sat beside me. She squeezed my hand. "I was terrified when you weren't here."

"That's how I felt when I didn't see you." I turned to the other nurses. "Anybody know what's going on?"

Sally Blaine responded, "Not really. Josie pulled me off duty and told me to report here."

"Same here," Rosemary Hogan added. "I guess we'll find out soon enough."

Deep down, I think we all suspected what was happening but were too afraid to feel even an ounce of hope.

For months we had been moved from one location to another. Setting up new facilities to care for the wounded and comfort the dying. Always one step ahead of an advancing yellow wave of death. The Empire of the Sun consumed everything in its path. We sat right in that path.

"Ladies, please, I need your attention." All eyes focused on our leader, Maude Davison. "First, let me say what an honor it has been to serve with all of you. There isn't a finer, more dedicated group of nurses to be found anywhere." She stepped aside and let Colonel Pilet come forward.

"What I'm about to say cannot be repeated outside this assembly. Those are strict orders." He stood with a rigid spine and stern expression. "You twenty are being evacuated tonight."

A low moan resounded from the entire group. My emotions overwhelmed me. Feelings of relief collided with guilt. Everyone had dreamed of nothing else for months, but we never considered the possibility of leaving friends behind.

The dream was shattered by the reality of so many others left at the mercy of Japan. As a group, we had formed a bond and shared experiences no one should witness. Every one of us had changed. Mere words, no matter how well written could describe the horrors of war we'd experienced.

Pilet allowed a few minutes to pass until we came to terms with the news. "The planes will be numbered one and seven. Each of you will be given orders that will include your plane and your position on the aircraft."

Maude Davison handed out our orders. I put mine away. Ressa stole a peek and looked at me. "We're on PBY 7. I'm position ten. You're probably nine."

I nodded and didn't think any more about it.

Colonel Pilet cleared his throat. "When you leave here, go directly to your quarters and pack. Leave anything you can live without. You are limited to carrying less than ten pounds. I can't stress this enough, it is imperative for you to keep this meeting confidential. You may only bring your musette bag. Destroy any letters or diaries. Return to your duties. Then gather your things and make your way here. You'll leave at 2145 hours."

I touched Ressa's arm, "I've got to find Jerry."

"I thought he met you for breakfast."

I shook my head. "He was sent out early, and he still hasn't returned. I'm worried sick about him." My concern had turned to panic, but I did a good job of hiding it. I kept telling myself any moment he'd walk up.

"You don't have long."

"I know."

"I'll pack your bag. That will give you more time."

"Thanks." I hugged Ressa and left to check on Jerry.

If he didn't return in time, I would leave a letter telling him how I felt. I should've told him in the ward, but my pride still suffered a little from his proposal to the young nurse.

RESSA
April 29, 1942

If was difficult to be around the nurses who hadn't been included. It was even harder to be with the nurses I knew were going and not able to say anything. Even though rumored earlier, our news would cause a panic.

In my quarters, I tried to pack without being noticed. I didn't dare look up at anyone because they would see it in my eyes. They would guess my secret.

Geneva hadn't found Jerry. I had gone twice with her to find him to no avail. Finally, she decided to write him a letter while I finished packing. My sister's face couldn't hide her heartache and frustration that she wouldn't be able to tell him goodbye in person and might never see him again.

She glanced up. "Come with me. If I can't find him, I'll leave it with one of his friends."

I nodded and stood. "Lead the way."

Geneva checked in two places where she thought Jerry might be.

At the lateral where Jerry reported for orders, I waited to the side while Geneva asked different ones about him.

I wondered what had become of Robert. But then my thoughts returned to leaving this island. It all seemed like a dream, and I moved in a haze of uncertainty. I had closed my mind to ever getting off the Rock, which made it hard to grasp the significance of leaving.

My mind kept turning over and over wondering why we were picked over others who seemed so deserving. Many had heavy responsibilities at home. Winnie, Cassie, and Dorothy, our dear friends wouldn't be going. It broke my heart to leave them.

As Geneva left the desk where she'd asked about Jerry, a medic who worked with him approached. "Miss Jenkins."

250

She turned to him. "Y'all are back. Thank goodness. Where's Jerry?"

"No ma'am. I didn't go out with them."

"Do you know where he is?"

"A rescue party was sent out to find them. They just returned. Ma'am, I hate to be the one to tell you, but everyone on that mission was killed. Jerry included."

Geneva's face withered with sadness and tears ran down her cheeks. "God, no. Please check. Maybe they're wrong."

"Ma'am, his body was brought back. I'm sorry."

I gripped her arm to support her. "I'm so sorry, sis."

Grief and heartbreak showed on a face that had always been good at concealing emotions. She gasped for a breath.

"Let's get you out of here." I managed to get her back to our bed, then I left her alone with her grief. I used the time to carry some of my cigarettes to men in the ward.

A Marine grinned. "Hey, kid. You're going out tonight, aren't you?"

"I'm not going anywhere," I answered, realizing my voice had been gruff. "You know no one can get out of here. It's orders."

Rather than accept my reply, his grin grew in size. "Aw, you're going."

I wanted to run and hide. I didn't want to leave, but that feeling of self-preservation, the desire to save yourself at whatever cost, is very strong in all of us. There are few people who wouldn't want to be saved under such conditions. So, I was torn about leaving, but I had to think of Geneva. If I refused to go, so would she. I owed it to my younger sister to take this chance to get us home.

Captain Benson, who knew I was leaving, handed me some letters. I nodded and tucked them away quickly.

When I returned to our quarters, Geneva wiped her eyes and sat up. "You know leaving can be as dangerous as staying, don't you?"

I nodded. "I'm sure it is, but there's a chance we might make it. If we stay here, we will be handed over to the Japs."

"What's worse? To be captured here or in some jungle alone?"

I shrugged. "We have to chance it."

"Colonel Stuart Wood has tried twice to leave and hasn't made it yet."

Stu as we called him was G-2, military intelligence and very valuable considering he spoke fluent Japanese. His first plane split open at one of the seams and made an emergency landing. Then his second plane was forced down.

"Well, let's hope his third time is the charm," I said.

"Why's that?" Geneva asked.

"He's being sent out with us."

"You don't say? Well, I hope he doesn't turn out to be a Jonah."

I didn't mention Jerry's death. I knew if she wanted to talk about him she would.

When the others entered, we stopped talking about leaving and just looked at each other. They stared making me uncomfortable. Somehow, they knew.

I had to get out, so I paid Commander Goodall a visit. He was aware we were leaving, and I needed to be with someone who I could speak with openly. "It's so hard not talking about it around the others. It's not like they haven't figured it out."

"Ressa, my girl," he said, "life has never been fair and never will be. Tell me this, what's the first thing you plan to purchase in Australia?"

I thought for a moment. "The biggest bottle of Paris perfume I can buy and an outfit with lots of lace. I want to feel feminine again."

He smiled. "You do that. I wish you and Geneva the best."

I nodded, shook his hand, and left. The visit uplifted my spirits until I entered the nurses' quarters. The guilt of knowing I would be leaving and many wouldn't put a tremendous pressure on me.

Everyone gawked with fascination, but no one spoke about it. Their eyes followed our every move causing me to fumble and drop things.

Geneva once again had an onset of tears for Jerry.

At that moment, I wished a bomb would come right through the Rock and get this sorry mess over with.

In my hand, I held a deck of cards Commander Davis had given me.

"You're not taking those, are you?" Adele asked in a flat voice.

I didn't answer, but I handed them to her.

She knows.

Everyone knows.

The silence that followed seemed more like a sentence of condemnation.

In those moments, I thought of General MacArthur. Was this what he experienced when he was ordered out, knowing he was leaving so many people who needed him? I thought of him with a kind of kinship. Was he feeling what I'm feeling now? I'm sure he felt worse since we had all depended on him to save us.

I remembered our money and turned to Geneva. "Go with me to the finance department to see if they'll exchange our Philippine money."

Afterwards, we bumped into Nancy Gillahan and Whitlow. They both appeared upset.

"What's wrong?" I asked.

"I'm going," Whitlow said. "She's not."

Nancy rubbed her eyes. "I feel like Evelyn and I are sisters and should go together. We've been together for so long why separate us now?"

We didn't say anything, but somehow, they knew we were going. Maybe, because I had exchanged my money—a dead give-away we weren't staying.

"I'm sorry," I said.

Whitlow glanced at Geneva. "I heard about Jerry. I'm sorry."

Geneva drew in her bottom lip and nodded.

I placed an arm around Geneva and hugged. "Let's go."

All we could do was go back and wait until 9:45 p.m. and wait with women who had figured out that we were leaving and they weren't.

My emotions were an insane mix of joy and misery.

THE ESCAPE
Part Six

GENEVA
April 29, 1942

We met at 9:45 p.m., then waited. Finally, the time arrived to depart from the tunnel. Though my heart was still breaking over Jerry, I had to pull myself together and prepare to leave. Leave our friends and patients to whatever fate had in store for them. We were given strict orders to keep our mouths shut—no goodbyes, no explanations of what was happening—just go.

I walked as if in a dream. I felt dizzy and nauseated. Ressa stumbled beside me.

"Are you all right?"

She turned toward me with tears in her eyes. "No, I'm not. This is the worst thing I have ever experienced. We should he happy to leave this place but..."

"I know, Ressa. Trust me, I know."

We plodded along slowly, making our way through Malinta Tunnel. As we approached the exit, people stood on both sides.

Ressa reached out and squeezed Dorothy's hand. Dorothy gave her a tearful smile. "I'm happy for you and Geneva."

Everybody knew we were headed home. Winnie held out a letter. "Mail this for me when you get back."

I couldn't answer. With a trembling hand, I took it and nodded. Several others handed us letters and notes with phone numbers and contact information. I know they had to be wondering *why them and not us?* I wanted to scream, *we don't want to leave. They're making us go.*

We had been officially relieved of duty in the Philippines and ordered to report in Australia. But the word had leaked out. Many were angry. They didn't hide their frustration and said harsh things as we passed. Some of the things Cassie and Denny said I found hateful, and it disappointed me.

It wasn't necessary. All knew orders were orders. We did understand the human emotion of resentment at being left behind. If the shoe had been on the other foot, I would have felt exactly the same. We finally emerged past the friends and patients we were leaving and gathered to wait at the end of the tunnel for further orders. We said our goodbyes to Josie Nesbit, who had refused to leave when given the chance. We thanked Maude Davison.

"God, I'm glad that's over," Ressa said.

"Me too. I'll be seeing those faces in my dreams forever."

Ressa sighed. "Me and you both."

After being loaded into cars, we were driven out of the tunnel. For the first time, I pulled out my orders. I frowned. "What plane did you say you were on?"

"PBY 7. Same as you."

I showed her my orders. "PBY 1, position six."

We stared at one another with a look of horror. Neither of us had considered the possibility we might be separated.

"I wished I'd opened it sooner," I said.

"This has to be a mistake. We'll get it corrected."

I could usually read my sister like a book. She didn't fool me one bit. Beneath the calm exterior there was an undertone of shock and panic. I had a bad feeling about this.

Once we arrived at the dock, we hurried from the car and searched for someone of authority.

"There's Colonel Pilet. He'll fix this, come on Geneva, follow me."

Ressa flagged him down. "Colonel Pilet."

"Yes, Lieutenant."

"Sir, there seems to be a mistake. My sister and I have been assigned to different planes."

"That's not a mistake. Those are your orders."

"But, sir, please. We've been together since we arrived and before that. We depend on each other."

"Please, sir. Let us stay together," I pleaded. My tears flowed freely. The entire day had been surreal. I had been at the breaking point for hours. First Jerry's death, then friends handing me letters for loved ones back home. The only thing that kept me sane was Ressa and now they were taking her away.

No, please God not this.

Pilet tried to console us. "Listen to me and try to understand. We didn't separate you on a whim. This is a lesson learned from experience. Hopefully, both planes will make it to safety, but in war anything can happen. One plane might make it and not the other. If you are separated, the chances are better that one will get through. If that happens at least your parents will have one daughter coming home, opposed to losing both of you."

I thought of another solution. "Sir, could we give our places to others. I would rather stay on Corregidor with my sister than be separated for any reason. I'm sure she feels the same way."

Ressa nodded in agreement.

"I'm sorry. My hands are tied. I couldn't change your orders, even if I wanted to. We all have to do our duty."

"But, sir, please do something," Ressa begged.

"This is for the best. I'm not changing it," Colonel Pilet said. This time his face grew stern to let us know to stop crying and follow our orders.

I wiped my eyes and sighed. I finally glanced at Ressa. Tears continued to roll over her cheeks and fall. We held hands as we walked back and rejoined the others.

Two groups of nurses had assembled on the dock. General Wainwright and Colonel Charles Savage were both present to wish us all safe passage.

Juanita wrapped her arms around General Wainwright and kissed him. "Oh, thank you, General."

"Well for crying out loud. If that's not the boldest woman," I remarked.

"She just wants him to know how appreciative she is," Ressa said.

To make it worse, we learned passengers on plane 1 and plane 7 would be leaving the dock on different boats. We were instructed to form two lines.

I turned to Ressa and broke into a sob. I wrapped my arms around her and hugged with all my might. My tears fell on her shoulder while I cried. "I don't like this. I'd rather stay if it means we could stay together."

"Me too," she whispered.

"Jenkins girls. Time to go," someone shouted. "You'll see each other on Mindanao."

I forced a smile. "Love you, sis."

Ressa didn't smile. Instead, she nodded. "I love you. See you soon."

Unable to say anything else, I turned and joined the line. But my heart was breaking. It was as if the ground had fallen out from under my feet and left me suspended. I wouldn't regain a sense of wholeness until Ressa and I were reunited.

I slipped, but Sally caught my arm to steady me. "I've got you."

"Thanks, Sally."

"Don't want to lose you. We've got to get you home."

Soldiers assisted me into the boat that rocked in the rough water. While waiting for everyone to be loaded, I said a little prayer that we'd all make it home.

Our PT boat bounced over the waves, tossing us a bit. Searchlights raked the shoreline from Corregidor in an effort to distract the Japanese from us. The night was calm. For some reason, the Japs had let up on the attacks.

I finally noticed those around me. Rita Palmer, Sally Blaine, Peggy O'Neil, Earleen Allen, Helen Gardiner, Lois Auschicks, Agnes Barre, Evelyn Whitlow, and Rosemary Hogan stared at me with sympathetic eyes. I'd been with some of these ladies since first arriving in the Philippines. I respected them and considered them friends. I also noticed Colonel Stuart Wood and remembered what I'd said about him being a Jonah. I forced myself to think more on what Ressa had said. *Third times the charm.* So maybe Stu would bring us good luck.

A mere nine months prior, this bay had served as a welcome mat to adventure. My tired brain reviewed the date. Yes, it had only been nine months since our arrival. I felt as if I had aged ten years in that short span.

Rosemary turned toward me and gave a weary smile and a slight nod. A small gesture of recognition saying I know how you feel.

Evelyn Whitlow squeezed my hand, reassuring me.

Earleen Allen probably identified with what I was feeling more than the others, since she was separated from Garnet.

The slapping of the water on the hull and the men conversing about the trip made it difficult to talk loud enough to be heard.

They transferred us over the side into a smaller shore boat. We traversed the dark water, constantly searching for the plane. In the distance the hum of a plane's propeller could be heard, a low rhythmic swoosh, swoosh. Finally, I could see the outline of it.

We waited patiently as the crew unloaded medical supplies for Corregidor. Whitlow whispered, "What's going on? Why is it taking so long?"

Sally Blaine responded, "They're bringing in supplies."

"I didn't know. Tell the boys to take their time and be careful. God knows they need them."

Finally, the task of unloading crates of desperately needed medical supplies was done. The boat moved into place beside the floating plane.

A crewmember spoke, "Please keep only what's needed. Throw all other items over the side. We're taking on extra people and sheer body weight is going to push our capabilities to the limit."

Men stood in the open door with their arms outstretched offering assistance. "Take my hand. Easy now. There you go."

One by one, they quickly transferred us into the belly of the plane. He hadn't exaggerated; the plane was packed. Counting the flight crew, nurses, officers, and family members, the headcount was at least twenty-nine. There were no chairs only three bunk beds along the wall. We sat side by side on the floor.

"We're pulling out, ladies. Sit tight." Thomas Pollock, our pilot wasted no time getting airborne. PBY 1 rapidly gained altitude. Our heading was due south to Mindanao, then onto Australia—close to two thousand miles. Most of it would be flown through enemy territory. If things went according to plan, we would land on Lake Lanao to reunite with the other plane before completing the trip. I would be reunited with Ressa for a short time.

I wasn't prepared for the sensation of being cold. After months of living in the tropical heat even fifty degrees felt frigid. I wrapped my arms around myself. "I'm freezing."

The other nurses nodded. Helen and Lois motioned for us to huddle together.

Seeing us, the crewmen offered their jackets. Their act of kindness and gallantry was greatly appreciated.

RESSA
April 30, 1942 (early morning hours)

It wasn't until PBY 7 was in the air that I stopped crying over Geneva. I'm sure I looked a pitiful sight with swollen eyes. Finally, my eyes adjusted to the darkness, and I was able to see the other passengers clearly. The plane smelled stale like a mildewed tent, but it beat the stench of the tunnel.

Gwen Lee, Florence MacDonald, Mary Lohr, Sue Downing Gallagher, Eunice Hatchett, Juanita Redmond, Harriet Lee, Dorothea Daley, Willa Hook, Catherine Acorn stared at me with empathy. Two civilian women, Mrs. Luther B. Beweley and her daughter, Virginia, about ten Army and Navy officers, and a Catholic priest, Father Edwin Ronan, flew with me.

For the first time, I noticed Juanita looked as disheartened as I felt. "Are you all right?"

She sighed. "It got a little nasty before we left."

"I heard what Cassie said. I doubt that's why you were chosen to leave."

Juanita Redmond had the looks of a Hollywood starlet.

"People I thought were my friends turned on me," she said.

"If it makes you feel any better, they were saying the same thing about Earleen Allen. What they need to realize, there are a lot of pretty nurses left behind."

Jose, the Filipino Major, and Major Latimer sat to my right. I smiled at Major Latimer. "I'm glad you're returning home to your family."

His eyes appeared sorrowful. "I'm not. I'm only going to Mindanao." He pulled out some letters to his family. "Take these and mail them for me."

"I'll take some," Mrs. Beweley said.

"He handed her several."

The moon shined brightly through the plane's windows.

Jose pointed out the window.

I leaned forward. My heart warmed to see the other plane. Geneva was safe. For a short time, we flew low. From the window, I could see the water below and the mountains in the distance. The sight was both beautiful and eerie in the moonlight. Below, I could see fires in the jungle. If all the fires continued, there'd be no jungle.

"Are those flashes guns shooting at us?" Juanita asked.

The crewmen shrugged. "Could be."

The possibility of being shot down by a Japanese Zero hung over us. If a plane was shot down, I just hoped it wasn't plane 1 carrying Geneva.

The pilot took the plane higher. The inside grew colder. My teeth chattered.

"Get out your Army capes," Willa shouted.

I pulled mine out and draped it around me but still shivered.

A crewman entered with his arms full. "Ladies, you can slip these flight suits on. They might help."

"Thank you." We huddled together and wasted little time putting on the one-piece suits, then wrapping our capes around us.

One by one, the nurses dozed off, all but me. I couldn't sleep or relax. I worried about Geneva and considered a lot of what ifs. My nerves kept tingling with anxiety.

Our pilot flew into a blanket of fog, and I lost sight of the other plane. Where was it? Had something happened to it?

My stomach coiled in a knot.

At some point, I fell asleep. The plane jarred me awake as it hit the water. It bounced the plane up about twenty feet at least three times before we coasted to a stop. Then our pilot taxied in.

"For Heaven's sake, that was rough," I said.

Catherine gasped. "I thought we'd crashed."

"You think they could've made that any rougher," Mary said, sarcastically.

"What time is it?" I asked.

"0400," a crewman replied.

I couldn't see anything for the thick fog. My mind drifted to when Geneva and I were little girls. She'd always been my little shadow. I remembered teaching her to tie her shoes and braiding her hair. We'd always been close. I loved all my sisters, but Geneva held a special spot in my heart.

I'd never be able to forgive myself if anything happening to her. Though, I wasn't in the clear myself. The men who had volunteered for this mission said it had been described as a suicide mission. I appreciated the sacrifice they were willing to make.

The plane bobbed over the waves as we sat in a sea of fog.

"What's wrong?" Eunice asked.

"I'll find out," Major Latimer offered. He returned shortly. "Emergency landing on Lake Tarac. There's a hole in the plane. Once it's fixed and this thick fog lifts, we'll take off and join the others."

We sat lost in our own thoughts. My concern was Geneva. What if her plane had landed in Mindanao, refueled, and left for Australia before we arrived? I wanted to see her.

"I'm going to throw up," Virginia said.

"Actually, I'm sick too," Eunice added.

Both women made it to the open door before throwing up. The constant movement had made them ill.

My mind wandered to Robert. I wondered if by chance I'd see him on Mindanao. Then I thought of Geneva alone and still grieving for Jerry.

"All done. Ready to take off," shouted the pilot. "Sit tight."

Since we were packed like sardines, we didn't have a choice but to sit tight.

GENEVA
April 30, 1942

The plane carrying us landed smoothly on Lake Lanao, so far so good, one step closer to home. I exited the craft and boarded a boat. I didn't see the other plane. Fear rippled through me. Had something happened to it?

"Excuse me, can you tell where the other plane is?" I asked one of the crew.

"They put down on Lake Tarac. Something minor. Word has it they'll be here soon. Pretty standard, nothing to worry about."

I thanked him and breathed a sigh of relief. It would be short lived at best. Total relief wouldn't come until Ressa and I were standing on American soil.

The boat took us to shore. From there, they escorted us to an old hotel for breakfast. It seemed a pleasant break to finally sit in a chair that wasn't moving.

The aroma of hot coffee and pancakes filled the air. Fresh pineapple and coconut tasted sweet to the tongue. Simple things of life taken for granted before now had become luxuries. I made a vow that when I got home I would never complain about anything trivial again. Ever.

A crewman shouted, "Time to move!"

Once we boarded the bus, it drove toward the Del Monte Plantation to pick up several others joining the evacuation. At this juncture, we learned the Japanese forces were only forty miles away. It seemed as though they were always close by. Like a deadly reoccurring disease that kept spreading.

We heard the Zeros coming toward us.

"Get off the bus!"

We hurried out and took cover in the thick brush and trees. As the planes flew over they riddled the bus with bullets.

"Why would they want to waste ammo on the likes of us," Rosemary Hogan asked.

"Sport. It's all for the hell of it," Rita said.

"All clear," Colonel Stuart shouted. "Back on the bus."

We boarded our bus and continued. Several times along the way, Zeros dove and strafed us. After what seemed a long journey, we arrived at the Army headquarters unscathed to find another meal of fresh eggs and coffee prepared and waiting.

I had every intention of waiting to greet Ressa, but I decided to lay down for just a second. Before long, I dreamt of being at home with the entire family, laughing at something funny. Univieve and all the family members were there. Only one of my siblings was missing—Ressa.

263

RESSA
April 30, 1942

By 9:00 a.m., we came down in Lake Lanao, deep in the Moro country in Mindanao. These were the natives who'd made my pearl ring.

"How long will we be here?" I asked.

"All day while the planes are being serviced," Major Latimer said. "Besides, we can't take off until it's dark. Even then, it's not safe."

Navy men waded out carrying bamboo branches and palm leaves to camouflage the plane. They didn't stop until the entire craft had been covered.

When I stood, I groaned. "Oh my. I'm stiff."

"I've seen dead people who weren't as stiff as I feel," Harriet said.

We groaned as we stretched our bodies after sitting for so long in one position. With help from the crew, I stepped out onto a platform, then crossed over to the rocks on shore. I glanced around looking for Geneva. Her plane was there, so I knew they had arrived safely. Relief rushed through me.

"Where are the nurses from the other plane?" I asked an officer.

"They've been taken to Army headquarters. You'll be joining them."

"Thanks." I joined the others in my group.

"Ladies, I need you to climb in the banca tied at the shore," an officer said. "We're taking you around to the others."

Once we were in the boat, the driver steered us around to the other side of the lake. A half a mile upstream, we transferred to a houseboat. We were avoiding a Japanese scouting party that had been spotted. The other nurses had gone straight from the plane to the bus.

Being the largest lake in Mindanao, we traveled for two hours in a scenic setting with dense, undisturbed jungles. The ride relaxed me. If not for my excitement of being reunited with Geneva, I would've fallen asleep. People talked and laughed, but it came across as a distorted mumble. It seemed more like we were out on a day's outing rather than escaping the Japanese.

We disembarked at a small barrio. Villagers stood around wearing their native garb. Many of the children didn't wear clothes. Wild chickens ran up and down the road. The scene would've made a great postcard to send home.

After a warm greeting, Army officers directed us to a bus. We rode deep into untouched jungles thick with vegetation and vines. This is how Bataan had probably looked before the war.

We reached an Army camp and were served hot cakes and coffee that made me feel a lot better. I gulped both down all the while feeling guilty. I knew the soldiers would come up short on rations from sharing.

"Back on the bus," an officer shouted.

"How much farther before we arrive at Dansalan?" I asked.

"Thirty-five miles inland to Army headquarters," he replied.

My heart sank. With these roads, it could take hours.

Harriet, Mary, Eunice, and Willa motioned for me to join them.

"Just relax," Mary said. "We'll be there before you know it."

Willa placed a hand on my shoulder. "Just be glad she's safe."

"I am. Everything seems to take so long," I complained. "It's like walking through quicksand."

They laughed, and we merrily joined the others on the bus.

But our merriment ended quickly.

"Holy smoke," Willa gasped.

My heart sped up when a Zero flew right over us. I kept thinking we'd have to climb out and run for cover, but we didn't.

"Why didn't he shell us?" Mary asked.

Major Latimer turned to her. "I'm not sure."

The bus trip through the jungle bounced us up and down on the hard seats. I kept trying to grip the seat in front of me. If not for the constant struggle to stay seated, the ride would have been lovely.

The bus stopped, and I glanced up to see if we had arrived. "What's going on?"

Juanita peered out the window. "I don't know. I can't see."

"I hope it's not the Japs," Catherine murmured.

The driver stood. "Bus no go. Busted."

I couldn't believe it. By the time we reached the others, it'd be time to take off. Of all the rotten luck. Geneva's group seemed to have had the smoother trip.

"I have a headache," Virginia said. "I feel sick from all the bouncing."

The ride had left many of us feeling queasy. Seems I was destined to always be in the vehicle breaking down. I recalled baby, the little car that took us part of the way to Mariveles.

Major Latimer and Jose climbed out and helped the driver push the bus aside. When a truck passed us, the driver flagged him down. "Ask them to send another bus."

We sat on the hot bus waiting for a replacement. Finally, it arrived.

At Army headquarters, Whitlow waved. "It's about time you got here."

"We had plane trouble and our bus broke down. It was a hell of a trip. Where's Geneva?"

"Resting in the bunk house." Whitlow pointed to it. "After all the candy they gave us, I'm surprised she can rest. Geneva was sick from the bus ride."

"That's understandable. A lot of us are queasy too. How long have y'all been here?" I asked.

"We landed around 5:00 a.m. Your sister's been worried about you."

"I was worried about me. Actually, about all of us."

"Glad you finally made it."

The scent of flowers filled the air. Mary Lohr and I walked toward the bunk house. They had gotten there early enough to be given bunks to rest in. Several nurses including Sally, who was sick, rested quietly. Geneva slept soundly. She wore a beautiful, large red rose behind her ear. My heart warmed with love for my little sister.

Mary giggled. "My, she went native fast."

I laughed. Though I hated to wake her, I did. I wanted time to visit with her before we all had to leave again. "Geneva, wake up."

She opened her eyes and smiled. "I was worried sick. I'm glad you're here."

"We had plane and bus issues. Where did you ever find a rose that big?" I asked.

"They're growing all around the grounds. It reminded me of home, so I couldn't resist picking it. It was like receiving a message from Momma, so I stuck it behind my ear to feel closer to her."

"She's always loved roses."

"I begged Colonel Wood to wake me when you arrived."

"Stu probably didn't have a chance. We came straight here." My stomach growled reminding me how hungry I was. It surprised me since we'd eaten pancakes earlier. "We're starving," I said. "We'll let you rest while we go eat."

Geneva nodded. "The mess is inside the main building."

I leaned and hugged her. "We'll come back as soon as we've eaten something."

Mary and I left Geneva and used our noses to find the mess hall. It smelled wonderful. We ate perfectly scrambled eggs. I was a glutton and ate at least six. Several officers brought out glasses of champagne to toast us.

Happiness ran through us, but then I remembered all the nurses who had remained behind in that suffocating tunnel. They would end up being captured by the Japs. Again, I experienced a deep guilt sensation.

After our enormous feast, we showered and changed into clean clothes. Later, Geneva greeted us. Apparently, she didn't feel ill anymore. We sat and talked for hours. I told her about our dreadful luck with the hole in the plane and the broken-down bus.

"For once, I'm the lucky one. Our plane didn't have one problem," Geneva said.

"And here you thought Stu might jinx you."

"Rita Palmer and Rosemary Hogan are on my plane. Rita hated leaving Captain Nelson."

"There's no telling how long before they'll be together again."

"Wartime is a horrible time to get married," I said, wondering what had become of Robert. I secretly hoped I'd see him at this camp.

"See if you have room in your bag for some of my stuff." Geneva shook her head. "Never mind, I forgot. We won't be together."

I forced a smile. "We will be in Australia."

"I might come up needing it before then. I'll just pack a little tighter."

An officer joined us. "Ladies, time to move out. The Japs are only thirty kilometers away and advancing. Gather your things and join your group."

Our tears returned. Once again, we had the heartbreaking task of saying goodbye. Geneva and I hugged for a long time and kissed cheeks and foreheads. Good thing we hadn't been wearing lipstick.

I squeezed her again. "It's harder to let you go this time."

"I know. I feel the same way. And I'm worried about that plane you're in," Geneva said. "You had a dreadful time getting here."

"Just pray that we make it. What else can we do?" I finally let her go and gathered my things. "Bye, sis. I love you."

"Love you more." Geneva offered me a sweet smile. How absolutely beautiful she appeared with the large rose still tucked behind her ear. After one brief hug, Geneva left to join her group.

Mary handed me my bag. "We really need to go."

I walked from the quarters with a lump in the pit of my stomach. I wished I could find a way to stuff her into my bag and take her with us. Of course, she seemed to be on the better plane. Perhaps, I should go with her. I disregarded the ridiculous notion.

As we walked through the camp, I inhaled deep breaths to hold myself together. The scent of roses reminded me of Geneva.

Sue Gallagher sat in an open area, writing quickly.

"Sue, it's time to go," Mary Lohr shouted. "Come on."

Sue shook her head. Her eyes revealed she'd been crying. "This is where Robert is stationed. I had hoped to see him before leaving." She sobbed more. "They sent him to the frontline yesterday. I'm not even sure he received my letter about our baby."

"Are you almost finished?" I asked.

"Almost." She broke down, gasping and sobbing. "I just wanted to see him. I wanted to place his hand across my stomach and let him feel the baby." Once Sue folded the letter, Mary and I helped her up.

She left her letter with an officer who promised to get it to Robert. We headed toward our bus. "I just have this horrible feeling I'll never see him again."

"Sure you will," Mary said. "Don't talk like that."

I didn't comment. I wouldn't give her any false hopes. The Japs left very little in their path alive. "Let's go. It's almost three."

We passed through a barrio and came to the clearest water I've ever seen. The local people formed a line along the path and studied us with interest.

"I guess they've never seen so many American women before," Juanita said, who had joined us.

"I hate to think that we represent what a well-dressed American lady should look like."

We laughed, because we looked terrible.

We stopped by three buses and listened for our names as roll was called.

A soldier motioned us over. "Four lines, ladies. Make it quick."

An officer walked up. "Throw down anything you have with you that is not absolutely needed. It might mean the difference in life or death. We can't overload the planes."

We dug through our bags looking for things to part with. The local people gathered around. As someone dropped something, they grabbed it. I handed a man my soap and cigarettes. I kept one change of clothes and a pair of shoes along with some items I hated to part with. All of it together shouldn't be over the ten-pound limit.

While waiting, we filled up on bananas sold by local vendors.

"If we keep eating, we'll weigh the plane down," Mrs. Beweley said.

We loaded onto the first two buses and left the third one empty. It would follow in case one of the buses broke down.

After the long bus ride, we waited for boats to take us to the planes.

"Wait up!" a young American soldier shouted.

"We're supposed to leave with you," his friend yelled. "We have orders."

Appearing edgy, they stopped in front of one of the officers.

He sighed. "Sorry, guys. This plane is full. There's not room for another person. You'll have to leave tomorrow. There'll be another plane."

Disappointment showed on their faces. Crestfallen, the young soldiers walked back toward the barrio. Their fate sealed.

I felt so sorry for them, because with the Japanese advancing, the Army camp could be taken over by tomorrow. If they had waited, perhaps one of them could've gone. At the last minute, Commander Teasdale decided to stay with his men.

When we arrived near the shore, it surprised me to see Geneva's group. I quickly scanned the nurses. She stood in line having her bag inspected and weighed.

At this point, I had to give up the knife I'd been carrying since being in the jungle. I gave my last bar of soap to a soldier. Ahead of me, Dorothea voluntarily surrendered her jewelry.

When it was my turn, I kept my hand at my side, so he wouldn't notice the small pearl ring. Normally, I wasn't a selfish person, but I couldn't part with it. I had purchased it while shopping with Geneva in Manila. It reminded me of happier times.

I kept hoping I'd have one last chance to say something to Geneva. But for the moment, we had to stay with our groups. I sat beside our pilot, Lieutenant Deede.

"I hope I never have to go back to Corregidor," he said.

"Me too," I agreed.

"That damn emergency landing made me angry. I swear I'm gonna get you girls to Australia if it's the last thing I do."

I offered him a smile. "Thank you."

Geneva ran over and joined me. "I just have a minute. Did you get some of those bananas?"

I nodded. "Too many."

Though she pretended to be happy, I knew better. My heart ached to stay with her and not be separated. I know she felt it, but she was trying to keep up a good front.

"I'd better kiss you goodbye one more time, because I might never see you again." She hugged and planted a solid kiss on my cheek. I couldn't laugh. All I could do was sob, so I held her a minute. After one last hug and kiss, she rejoined her group.

The lump returned to my stomach, that knot of uncertainty, doubt, and anxiety.

I didn't dare look at her. I knew I'd break down.

A lean, tall soldier tried to crack a joke, but I wasn't in the mood. My heart was breaking, and I was struggling not to show it.

Finally, it was dark enough to leave. My group left first. As we loaded in the boats, I glanced at Geneva. She waved. I forced a smile and waved back. "See you in Australia."

Soldiers stood in the water removing the branches that had hidden our plane. With their assistance, we boarded the plane and waited for Deede to take off.

GENEVA
April 30, 1942

I anxiously waited with my group.

Though I'd never met some of the people, I knew who they were such as Brigadier General Seals and his wife. Commander F.J. Bridgett. Lieutenants: Weschler, Long, Erickson, Dennison, and Colonel Stuart Wood. The nurses were Earleen Allen, Lois Auschicks, Agnes Barre, Rosemary Hogan, Rita Palmer, Peggy O'Neil, Helen Gardiner, Sally Blaine, Evelyn Whitlow and me. Mrs. Virginia Bradley, the wife of an Army officer and Mrs. Ryder, the wife of a Navy officer, and a lieutenant colonel from the finance department also boarded along with some civilians and Filipinos.

I nervously shuffled my feet in the loose sand as we waited to be loaded on the ferries and transported to our plane PBY 1. Ressa's plane had had several problems getting to Mindanao, so I worried it wouldn't take off let alone make it to Australia.

PBY 7 carrying Ressa's group taxied down Lake Lanao. Engines revved up as the propellers spun faster. The aircraft rapidly traversed the water, but then slowed down and circled back. Their pilot tried again to no avail. After lining up again, the pilot revved the engine even more. The aircraft skimmed across the lake and slowly rose into the air.

"Whew, third time is the charm. Thank God," I whispered. "Thank you, Jesus."

Several of the others let out a sigh of relief when PBY 7 finally made it and headed toward Australia. Now it was our turn. We stepped aboard the ferry in the order we would enter the plane. It'd make it easier taking our assigned seats.

While waiting for the other plane to become airborne, the wind increased, causing white caps to form on the dark lake.

The pilot addressed us. "Please leave anything you can do without. I know some things might have sentimental value, but trust me, all that stuff won't be worth a plug nickel if we crash."

We complied willingly. I left everything but a change of clothes and shoes. After months of performing our duties under harsh conditions, making sacrifices had become second nature. Strange how little objects mean when your life is in the balance.

The pilot and crew left watches and coins behind, setting a good example.

They ferried us to the plane using several boats. As we crossed the rough water, lights shined on it, allowing the crewmen to remove the palm branches that camouflaged it.

Once there, soldiers helped us cross from the boat to the plane. We had our assigned positions. Rita Palmer and Rosemary sat together. Sally Blaine had malaria and dengue fever. The twenty-four-year old's weight had dropped to one hundred pounds. Evelyn Whitlow sat with Sally, trying to make her comfortable. I was happy being in the middle. A few new people joined our flight, mainly evacuees leaving Mindanao. The two men with wives aboard sat with them.

The white caps sloshed against the plane, making it rock.

I tried to relax as we sat snuggled shoulder to shoulder inside the packed plane.

Almost over. Thank God. It's almost over.

I stiffened involuntarily as the aircraft moved ever so slowly. I wondered if the others shared my same emotions—exhilaration, apprehension, optimism, but overshadowed with a dark cloud of disbelief in a successful rescue. We had all been through so much, there had to be an end to this.

Something seemed wrong.

"What's happening?" I asked.

One of the crewmen answered me. "Waves are pushing us into shallow water."

"What will he do?" Rita asked.

"A man who has a boat is going to pull us to deeper water. Don't sweat it."

Our plane continued to sway back and forth in the choppy water, moving even closer to land.

"Nothing to worry about, ladies. We'll get under way shortly," an officer assured us.

A vision of reuniting with Ressa in Australia played in my mind. What a celebration we would have. The image crumbled when the plane's wall shook with a spasm and made a thunk sound. The motion hurled us forward, slamming us together like dominoes. We gasped and screamed. Fortunately, the colonel's wife sat beside me and cushioned me.

"Remain calm and stay seated. No harm," Pollock, the pilot, shouted.

His reassurance and confidence eased my tension a little. He tried to turn the plane slowly to get into position for takeoff, but the wind and rough water continued to wreak havoc.

Whitlow whispered reassuringly, "Oh well, it took the other plane a couple of tries before lifting off."

In the process of taking off, it happened. This time, the aircraft shook violently. A metallic rending scream of skkuurrrrunk echoed through the hull, and the outer skin of the plane ripped open.

"We're taking on water!" Sally Blaine shouted.

The civilian ladies and wives panicked and cried.

As nurses we remained relatively calm. We had been through so much that little surprised or excited us. Still, we all prayed for a miracle.

"Hand me any jackets you're wearing," Lieutenant Dennison shouted.

People started tossing clothes and blankets his way.

He stuffed the hole to slow the water's entry. Rosemary Hogan moved toward the hole and stuffed her terry cloth jacket in the gap. "Well, I've owned that a long time. That's how life goes."

None of the items stopped the lake water from coming in.

When Pollock turned the plane again and tried to taxi it deeper, even more water gushed inside.

"It's up to my ankles and rising," I said. "I could swear I saw a fish."

Gassett, the radio man, contacted officials. "A B-17 is heading our way."

"When?" General Seals asked.

"Sir, they didn't say. But it's coming from Australia, so I gathered it'd be tomorrow."

"Evacuate the plane," Pollock ordered.

"If you have any rations aboard bring them with us," General Seals said.

"Come on, Sally. Let's get off," Rita said. They made their way to the door and climbed out on the wing.

"Geneva, give me your hand," Agnes said. "I'll help you out."

"Thanks." I turned back to Earleen. "Follow us."

I stepped out onto the slippery surface trying not to fall. "I don't want to go for a swim."

"Me neither," Agnes replied.

I held my bag in one hand and tried to balance. "I'm not leaving it."

Lieutenant Erickson frowned. "So long as you can carry it."

"I can."

The men maneuvered the wounded aircraft to a small wharf. We crossed over onto it and waited for the others. The old wooden platform wobbled and swayed. I thought it might give way with all of us standing on it.

"Let me by." The officer's wife pushed through us, almost knocking everyone down. "I don't like all this motion."

Up until then, she had needed assistance claiming she suffered from acute arthritis.

Whitlow joined us. "This didn't go so well."

Helen Gardiner stood next to me. "I hope the other plane arrives tonight."

I nodded and walked to the end of the makeshift wharf. "Same here."

At any time, Zeros could fly over and shell us.

If any of us had been alone, we might have fallen into a crying hysterical breakdown. We had all gone through unimaginable hardships together. We were a chain of ten links, all of equal and enduring strength.

Without the weight of human cargo, the plane could be maneuvered more easily. The flight crew stayed determined to save it. If in the end they couldn't, it would be destroyed. No way would this plane fall into enemy hands.

"Do we wait for the other plane?" Rosemary asked. Despite the fact she'd been wounded, she remained a powerhouse.

"This isn't any place for a beach party. We're sitting ducks for Zeros," I whispered to Whitlow.

"We can't stay here. The Japs will find us," Colonel Stuart Wood said. "We'd better head into the hills for the night."

Colonel Stuart Wood, the senior officer, had been put in command. "Even if they repair the hole, I don't believe that seaplane is safe." Stu glanced toward the mountains and jungles. "But we can't go too far or we'll miss the plane they're sending. I've decided we'll return to the hotel we stopped at yesterday. We can hide there until MacArthur sends the plane. Let's head up that hill to the bus."

"We have to walk?" the officer's wife inquired, with an expression of disbelief.

Stu removed his hat and wiped his forehead. "That bus can't come down here."

"But I have arthritis."

"It didn't seem to trouble you getting off the plane."

"Yes, but…"

He walked away, smiling.

Our pilot, a Naval officer, some crew members, and a young soldier stayed with the plane in hopes of repairing it. Some of the soldiers who had been there to see us off were sure it could be fixed. But Colonel Wood, Commander Bridgett, and Major Seal didn't believe they had the needed equipment to repair the damage. Stu tried to get the pilot and others to come with us and hitch a ride on the B-17.

We stood on the shore and looked back at the plane. It leaned precariously, sitting low in the dark water.

For the time being, we were on our own. All we could do was wait, survive, and dodge the advancing Japanese.

RESSA
April 30, 1942

After an hour of flying, a stowaway was discovered. A young private around seventeen years old had hidden on the plane. And here, I'd blamed my ring for the rough takeoff. I put my conscience at ease.

The plane flew extremely high, and I shivered until one of the crewmen gave me his flight suit. Later, he sported my Army cape, wearing it like a true nurse.

"Would you like your flight suit back?" I asked.

He grinned. "Naw, I'm not proud. I'm warm enough."

"Okay. Thanks."

"We'll bring around some hot soup. That should warm you up."

And it did. We all enjoyed the chicken and vegetable soup. As predicted, my chills had gone.

"Jenkins, it's your turn on the bunk," Willa shouted.

I didn't think I could sleep but stretching out for a short period sounded good. I made my way to the cot and plunked down. Surprisingly, I must've fallen asleep and slept for a full hour.

Around midnight while flying over Timor, I heard another plane. My heart leapt with joy. It had to be PBY 1. I tried to peer out the small window to catch a glimpse of it.

"Sir, is that our other plane I'm hearing?" I asked, praying he'd say yes.

"No, it's a Jap plane. Deede will take us up higher to lose it."

Disappointment plowed through me, leaving me in a state of despair.

GENEVA
April 30, 1942

The officers, the civilians, and the ten of us made the climb up a narrow, winding trail to the top of the hill. The muddy ground made in even more difficult. Whitlow helped Sally, who still ran a fever.

I almost regretted taking my bag. I switched it from one hand to the other. "These mosquitoes are relentless."

"I'm covered in bites," Rosemary complained. "We'll all have malaria."

The mosquitoes were a constant nuisance. Discomfort had become the norm. I couldn't remember the last time I had felt clean and comfortable.

"I can't do this," complained the officer's wife.

"You're doing fine," Colonel Wood said. He and the other men assisted the sick and weaker women up the hill.

"Hallelujah. I see the bus!" Whitlow shouted.

"The sick and weak get on first," Colonel Wood ordered.

As before, the officer's wife pushed ahead of Sally and the others who were ill. "My arthritis is killing me. I've got to sit before I pass out."

If we were captured by the Japanese, I could imagine their reaction when this woman demanded to go first or wanted them to move out of her way. She would be in for a rude awakening.

I climbed aboard the bus and took a seat by Rosemary. Our driver drove to Dansalan. We arrived around 2:30 a.m. at the hotel where we'd stopped before. It had been deserted due to the Japs moving in. The place had been ransacked. It was difficult to believe this was where we'd enjoyed a wonderful breakfast upon arriving.

"I'm wet and hungry," I said to Earleen. "I hope they left some food behind."

"I'm hungry and exhausted. This has been so discouraging."

Fortunately, canned goods had been left. We ate beans and peaches and not a one of us complained. There was plenty of hot coffee. Being here gave us a chance to dry our clothes and rest. While we ate, the men discussed our next move.

"Since we haven't heard from Pollock, I'm assuming he didn't get the plane repaired. We won't waste time going back to Lake Lanoa."

"We need to head to the closest airstrip," an officer said.

"There are several in the area," Commander Seal said.

"What if Pollock gets our plane repaired and then he can't find us?" Agnes Barre asked, interrupting them.

Everyone laughed, because the thought was ridiculous. We'd all seen the enormous hole.

General Seals sighed. "I think by now they've destroyed the plane and joined the other soldiers fighting."

Colonel Wood set his plate down. "Our best bet is to return to the Del Monte pineapple plantation."

"It was used as a temporary headquarters for Allied forces on Mindanao," one of the lieutenants added. "MacArthur even stopped over there last March."

"Sounds like a good choice," Commander Seals commented.

We found the hotel more comfortable than sleeping on the ground. I found an old mattress and shared it with Earleen and Helen Gardiner.

The officer's wife frowned at us. She had been busy eating and hadn't claimed a mattress. She had no choice but to sleep on the floor. She huffed and walked around us. I think she expected us to surrender our mattress. Despite being tired, we couldn't help but laugh.

Whitlow stayed by Sally's side, making sure her fever didn't get too high. Sally moaned through the night.

On May first, our bus drove over rough roads to the pineapple plantation and arrived around 10:00 a.m. Our bodies had stiffened, so we climbed from the bus and stretched our legs.

The plantation manager greeted us with hostility and argued with Stu and the other men. It didn't take long to figure out he didn't want the Japs finding military personnel associated with the place.

Nevertheless, he allowed us to rest and gave us lunch. After eating, we wanted to brush our teeth. It'd been days since I'd had an opportunity.

Myself and others, with toothbrushes in hand, headed for an outdoor faucet.

Sally turned the handle. "Oh no! I don't believe it."

"What?" I asked, trying to see around her.

"This." She stepped back so we could see there wasn't any water just the sound of gurgling air "The water has been cut off."

"It could be worse." Agnes Barre added.

"How?" Sally and I asked in unison.

"We could be back in the tunnel on the Rock."

We both sheepishly grinned knowing Agnes was right.

Rita Palmer came in. "I guess you heard about the water."

"We found out the hard way. I was looking forward to washing up and brushing my teeth."

"Like they say back home, you never miss the water till the well runs dry." I added.

They laughed.

"Never knew how amusing you can be," Rita said. "Usually, Ressa is the funny one. Brush and rinse with pineapple juice. I did. It works, and there's plenty of it."

Later, we bathed in a nearby stream that offered us privacy. Afterwards, we took naps and lounged around.

The tension between our officers and the manager grew more intense.

Wood mumbled a few obscene names referring to the manager under his breath.

We giggled totally agreeing with him.

"Ladies," Wood said, around two. "We're not welcome here. We're not staying. Make your way to the bus." We moaned and groaned, but stood, gathered our things, and boarded the bus. We headed out looking for another place to hide.

"I can't imagine where we can go," I said to Rosemary.

"Me neither. There aren't a lot of choices left."

RESSA
May 1, 1942

At 7:30 a.m., we landed safely in Darwin, Australia at the Navy base. It wasn't until we landed, the crew discovered a second stowaway. They had been the reason our plane had struggled to take off and wasted so much precious time. The moment I stepped from the plane, I searched for PBY 1 that carried Geneva, hoping it had landed before us, but it was nowhere in sight.

My heart squeezed at the horrible possibilities. I reminded myself that we had left before them. It only made sense that we landed first. They should be landing any time now.

A soldier pointed us in the right direction. "Ladies, restrooms and water fountains are over there."

We walked toward the facilities together.

"Lieutenant Deede," I said. "I'm going to give you the Navy cross."

He grinned. "Save it. I've already got one."

"Think there's an alert on," Harriet asked.

I glanced around and didn't see anyone. "Sure looks that way."

"Bombed yesterday," an Australian officer said. "It's been evacuated. I'm afraid we're the only ones still here."

He and others escorted us to a nearby hospital. Several of the wards had been bombed. The Army used the ones that remained.

They assigned us rooms and even passed out clean pajamas.

"I feel like a princess," Virginia, Mrs. Beweley's daughter said. "And all of these wonderful Australian men are here to serve me."

She turned to see a handsome Aussie standing in the door, and her cheeks turned red.

We all laughed.

"Your highness," he said. "Lunch is served. Follow me."

We smiled and filed behind him

Real meat, butter, and sweet milk. I devoured the wonderful meal with my eyes before eating it. I placed a little butter on the tip of my tongue and savored it. Since my stomach had shrunk, I nibbled little bites of my pork chop and the fresh bread. But the acid of guilt kept me from enjoying it fully. I couldn't help but wonder if Geneva and the others had food.

"All this food and I can barely eat it," Eunice complained.

"Same here," Harriet added. "My stomach can't handle it."

Every time I heard a noise, my head jerked up hoping to see Geneva. Surely by now, her plane had arrived.

But despite the thrill of the delicious food and my apprehension for Geneva's arrival, my eyes kept closing. The trip had left me exhausted.

GENEVA
May 1, 1942

The Philippines had been a place of promises. Promises that were never kept.

But at least the chance of another plane coming served as a reprieve for us. Sort of a plan B. The downside to all of this centered on an advancing Japanese army getting closer by the hour.

Returning to Colonel Sharp's headquarters wasn't an option. They had evacuated and more than likely, the Japs had taken over the camp.

Mindanao, the southernmost island, had two main highways: Route 1 and Sayre Highway. A new highway Route 2 was under construction. This island had no trains. The beach areas, for the most part, were flat. Two large river valleys helped making it across this island easier. The Diuata Mountains ran east.

Traveling the main roads would almost certainly lead us into the hands of the Japanese. Nevertheless, we drove to a nearby deserted airstrip and hoped a plane would arrive.

The officers spoke with some villagers near the airstrip, but none of them had seen a plane other than Japanese.

Helen Gardiner sighed. "We can't hang around here waiting for a plane."

"The Japs have control of the highways," Lieutenant Dennison stated.

"I think we should give the plane more time," Sally Blaine said.

"Me too," Rosemary Hogan added. "It could still show up. And this is the closest landing strip to Lake Lanao. It'd make sense they'd come here."

We waited, but no plane came.

I hated being right about the plane. I didn't gloat for we were all heartbroken one hadn't come.

We looked at Colonel Wood for an answer. He placed his hands on his hips and shook his head. "I'm not sure. It could be the Japs have the entire area secured. Any aircraft that tries to reach us would be shot down as soon as they attempt to land."

"This place is swarming with Japs," General Seals stated. "I'd like to get you nurses to safety."

Mindanao had two rivers, the Agusan and the Mindano. The Mindano ran parallel to Highway 1. They discussed the best route to take including river routes.

"Can we find someone with a boat willing to take the risk?" Seals asked Wood. The men debated on whether river travel might be a possibility.

Stu shook his head. "I hate giving up the bus. Say we get someone to take us down the river, what then? We wouldn't have any transportation."

My mind drifted to Ressa. Where was she? I prayed to God they had made it. If she had made it to Australia, she'd worry herself sick over me.

We talked and bickered among ourselves. Rather than leave immediately, we lingered in the area hoping the second plane would arrive, but all the while the sky grew grayer as dusk set in.

We heard a plane and became giddy. We stood prepared to wave, but then recognized the sound of a Japanese Zero's engine.

"Get down!" General Seals shouted.

Other officers shouted similar orders, and some of the women screamed. We scattered and slid into gullies and ditches until the plane had passed.

Rosemary said, "We don't have any foxholes. I don't want to take another hit from shrapnel."

"How will they react coming across us in the jungle?" Rita said. "They may kill us right there on the spot."

Again, the debate of where to go and how to get there started back.

"We can't stay here. If the pilot saw us, he'll report it," Seals stated.

"What if a plane comes, and we're not here?" Virginia Bradley asked.

Wood sighed. "I'm not sure. Perhaps, they'll search for us."

"And perhaps, they won't see us and leave us behind," Virginia countered.

"For now, we have to get somewhere to rest and hide," Seals said.

One of the soldiers knew of a Philippine military hospital in the jungle and offered to guide us to it.

Regardless, I thought we were doomed. Whether, we stayed or went. Whether, we drove down the highway or marched through the jungle.

We came to the Mindanao Hills. Our vintage bus couldn't make it up the steep road.

"Climb out," ordered the officers.

"If you're able, help us push the bus!" Colonel Wood shouted.

Sally and the other sick and disabled people walked up the hill.

Rosemary, despite her injuries, jumped in and put herself wholehearted into pushing. She grunted and grimaced.

I did what I could but doubted my little muscles could move that bus. We managed to get it up the hill and finally, made it to Force Hospital around 6:00 p.m. It consisted of two long buildings and a few other structures scattered about with thick jungle surrounding it. The facility lay under tall trees offering shade with lush flowers growing everywhere. It reminded me of Sternberg when we'd first arrived in Manila. Like all wartime hospitals, wounded soldiers filled every bed.

Recognizing we suffered from dehydration and exhaustion, the Filipino nurses gave us water.

"Come, I'll take you to your quarters," a very pretty nurse with a beautiful smile said. "You can clean up before dinner."

We bathed at the bottom of a waterfall that was off limits to the men. The Filipino nurses shared their clean clothes with us.

"I've never met nicer people than the Filipinos," Rita said.

"Me neither. They amaze me," Sally replied as she rinsed her hair.

"This feels heavenly," Whitlow said.

"You can say that again," I added.

That night we feasted on rice and fish with fresh bread. We had cots to sleep on and were thankful we didn't have to sleep on the ground.

GENEVA
May 2, 1942

The next morning, we ate eggs and fruit. I didn't waste any time gobbling mine down, then I sipped the hot coffee slowly.

Colonel Wood stood outside studying our jungle surroundings. "If there's a plane, it'll never find us here. I think we need to head for the Valencia Airstrip."

I actually felt sorry for Stu. He appeared disoriented and uncertain about his decisions. I remembered thinking of him as bad luck. Maybe, I had been right.

We traveled across the Ormoc Valley and headed toward the Valencia Airstrip, hoping to find the B-17.

Finally, the bus ran out of gas. I closed my eyes and released a sigh of discouragement and despair.

"Can't they find some gas?" Rita asked.

"I don't think so. I don't see any service stations out here," I said. "Hope you've got your walking shoes on."

"But my arthritis," the officer's wife said with a moan.

"Then stay here and surrender to the Japs. Maybe they'll give a damn," one of the men shouted.

She glanced around trying to see who had said it. "Why I never."

Major Seals faced us. "This bus can be spotted a mile away by the Japs. It's best we leave it anyway."

We walked all day, all the time moving away from where our plane had crashed. That night, we slept fully dressed ready to move at a moment's notice.

"Do you really think a plane is coming?" Rita asked.

I shrugged. "About as much as I think troops are coming to save the Philippines."

Rita frowned. "You are so negative."

"I'm one of the most positive people you'll ever meet. I'm positive this won't end well." I didn't like sugarcoating anything. Why say things we knew wouldn't happen just to make ourselves feel better?

"Now we wait and pray," Whitlow responded.

"I don't have a problem with praying," Rosemary announced. "It's the waiting that has me on edge."

"It's the not knowing that scares me," I added. "I just hope PBY 7 made it to Darwin." I found a place to lay on the ground and used my bag to rest my head on. Still, I couldn't sleep.

Had Ressa made it to Australia?

Please, Lord, get Ressa there safely.

Lois whispered, "All this time you were worried Ressa's plane would be the one that didn't make it."

"I know. And I still have no way of knowing she's safe."

Earleen sniffed and sighed. "I just hope Garnet is all right."

"I'm sure he is," I said. "Just keep praying."

Everyone grew quiet, but wearing damp clothes and feeling dirty, I couldn't sleep. Perspiration beaded on my forehead and added to my discomfort.

I peered through the canopy at the night sky, a beautiful panorama of stars shined brightly. From here, the full moon seemed so large. I knew somewhere Ressa was under the same moon. Perhaps, right now she too was staring up. I breathed in the jungle's pungent scent with every breath. It seemed as if all my senses had shifted to a higher level of awareness. Insects provided a chorus of rhythmic sounds.

I had told Ressa that I thought we'd end up in an internment camp in Manila. Unless the plane arrived soon, that's exactly where I'd find myself.

RESSA
May 2, 1942

"Has the other plane landed? I asked, fear gnawing away at me. I held my breath while I waited for an answer.

Before the answer came, I already knew it hadn't. The officer's eyes revealed regret. "Not yet. Stop worrying. They'll show up."

I tried to calm myself, but fear ripped through me, causing me to fall apart. Everything we had gone through came cascading over me. All the young men we had watched die. The knowledge that if the other plane didn't make it, Geneva and the others would be at the mercy of the Japs, who had no mercy. On top of this, we had learned the previous evening, Lieutenant Deede, our pilot, had been killed.

I couldn't stop the tears that clogged and burned my throat.

Willa, Harriet, and Eunice gathered around me and comforted me. "Don't do this to yourself," Willa said. "You don't know anything for sure. Stop imagining the worst."

Little did I know, one of them had a syringe until I felt the slight sting of the needle. I gasped. "You sedated me. Why you sneaky little bitties!"

They offered me apologetic looks.

"For your own good," Harriet said.

"If you keep this up, you'll make yourself sick," Willa added.

But the sedative didn't calm me. I continued to weep for Geneva. I didn't sleep that night. I listened for planes. Not hearing anything and unable to sleep, I jotted down notes about our experience. I wanted to write a book once I returned home. I wanted the world to know what we had gone through and possibly what my sister was still going through.

RESSA
May 3, 1942 Darwin, Australia

"Ressa, PBY 1 just landed," Willa shouted into my room from the doorway the next morning.

"Thank God! I'm coming."

After dressing, I hurried down to see the plane for myself. Seeing PBY 1, my heart filled with joy. I couldn't wait to wrap

Geneva in my arms and hug her. I didn't think I'd be able to let her go.

Lieutenant Tayler, an Australian Navy doctor joined me. "I'm sorry, but the nurses aren't with them."

"But it's their plane."

"Only the pilot, a Naval officer, and a kid made it out."

A pressure pushed the air right out of me, and I thought I'd pass out. My head spun in circles as my heart fired rapid beats.

"The young man might be able to tell you what happened."

I hunted the eighteen-year-old kid down who had red hair and freckles. He suffered with a nasty case of malaria.

"Do you remember me?" I asked, in a demanding tone.

"Yes, ma'am, I saw you on Mindanao."

"Do you know what happened to the nurses?"

His eyes dulled with sorrow. "We tried to take off right after your plane, but the wind kept blowing us into the shallow water. We hit a rock, and water poured into the plane."

My breath caught in my throat. "Go on."

"They were ordered back to the shore until the plane could be repaired or one could be sent to get us. I was too ill, so they just left me at the beach."

I couldn't believe what I was hearing. "Continue."

"When the plane was fixed, the pilot sent the Naval officer into the hills to get them."

"And?"

"There wasn't a trace of them. He sent out a second search party with some other soldiers who'd shown up, and they couldn't find them either. Pollock was going crazy not knowing what to do."

"He left them behind?"

"The Nips were closing in, ma'am. He couldn't let them get the plane."

My hands trembled at the thought of those women and my sister being deserted. "He left without them. There's no excuse for it."

"It wasn't his fault. I tell ya, the man was sick with grief. We were all sick over it. If they'd just hung around. The commander assured us another plane was coming."

As I considered what this meant, my stomach churned, and I grew dizzy. I was sure I'd faint. This news had left me devastated.

"Ma'am, the nurses probably went back to headquarters. They'll get here."

"Thank you for telling me. Excuse me." I stumbled to my room and fell into bed. I thought I'd die. Die from guilt and heartache.

I thought of what the Japanese did to the Chinese women. Why Geneva and not me? Why?

I cried and cried until my eyes couldn't produce anymore tears and had swollen shut. Pain radiated in my head and chest. I had sobbed so hard that my ribs were sore. My darling Geneva was left for the Japs to capture. An image of her sleeping with the rose behind her ear came to mind, sending an excruciating pain through me.

Geneva had said if we leave Corregidor, we'll end up in the hands of the Japs. Had it been a premonition on her part?

I prayed they made it safely to Colonel Sharp's headquarters until another plane arrived.

Once I confronted the truth and faced the reality Geneva would be in enemy hands, I reached the point of hysteria and cried aloud until sleep wrapped me in a blanket of darkness and peace.

GENEVA
May 3, 1942

"Finish up," Colonel Wood said. "We're traveling by foot. We got to stay one step ahead of those Nips."

None of us argued. I figured he knew the area better than any of us. But several of us suffered from malaria or dysentery. If we didn't have either, we'd end up with beriberi.

We headed out on foot farther into the interior through mountainous jungle, but the walking caused blisters on my feet. When we stopped, I switched shoes. I had an extra pair in my bag.

Lieutenant Dennison and the other men picked up a small amount of food from locals, mainly pineapples and bananas. There was only enough for each person to have one small section of pineapple and half of a banana.

I eagerly ate mine and licked the juice off my fingers. My stomach still ached for more, but I didn't complain. Some of the men had gone without so we could eat.

Eventually, we encountered two men from our flight who'd been sent to find help. They'd come across Major William Sharp and his Army forces. We piled into the back of one of their trucks. Of course, riding on a Japanese controlled highway with a group of soldiers made us a prime target. Though it was an illusion, I felt safer with the extra soldiers.

"Scoot down," Rita shouted to the colonel's wife. "All of us are tired. Make room for us."

Whitlow and I climbed in last. We sat almost on top of each other. "You smell almost as ripe as I do," she said to me.

"Back home, our pigs would smell better than us," I replied.

We headed toward the hospital.

"If they stop this truck, they'll search it," Rosemary Hogan shouted over the noise.

Rita laughed. "They'll be in for a real shock finding this many American women."

We chuckled softly, but the idea of being caught by the Japanese was anything but amusing. The possibility terrified us.

Riding in back of the truck was hot and uncomfortable, but it beat hoofing it.

They drove us to the edge of the jungle. All of us along with several soldiers who hoped to catch a ride on the B-17 climbed from the truck. On our walk to the airstrip, my feet started aching.

After arriving, they gave us foreshadowing news. No one had seen an American plane. The airstrip was located in the open and easily seen from the sky. Jap planes flew over, and we ducked in ditches on the airstrip's outer perimeter, hoping not to be seen. When dusk set in, we moved back into the hills under thick canopies to spend the night.

RESSA
May 3, 1942

On the trip to Melbourne, thoughts of Geneva and the others left behind haunted me. While many around me celebrated their freedom, my freedom came with guilt. Geneva had been my responsibility. I'd promised our parents I'd keep her safe.

We arrived at an American airbase near the Adelaide River under the supervision of Major Bradford of the Air Corps. That evening, they treated us to a steak dinner, and an orchestra played for us. But my shredded nerves made it impossible to relax and forget Geneva. Not a single bite did I take that I didn't wonder if she had eaten.

That night we stayed in an Australian field hospital. They assigned us to barracks equipped with bathroom facilities.

"I plan to wash everything," Mary Lohr said. "Hair, clothes, and me."

I chuckled. "It will be wonderful to stay clean for once and wear clean clothes. We'd better hurry. I heard we're moving to Batchelor Field. We'll be there a couple of days."

"I hope the food is as good there as it has been here," Willa said. "I bet I've gained ten pounds."

I glanced at her. "No, maybe five. We could gain forty pounds and still not be overweight."

"Once I'm back, I'm shopping for all new clothes." Catherine ran her hands over her tattered clothes.

"Boots won't recognize me," Doreatha added.

I realized all their chatter was to cheer me up.

At Batchelor Field, we ran into a number of pilots we'd known in the Philippines. I stopped before two guys who'd been friends with Robert. "Do you have any idea where Robert Robbins is?"

Their faces grew grim.

"If he's alive, he's still somewhere in the jungle," one said.

At least neither were aware of him dying. There was still hope he was alive.

"It'd be sad to think he survived the crash with Colin Kelly only to die in some godforsaken jungle." I drew in a breath. "He was one of my patients at Sternberg."

They nodded. Had my eyes revealed my fondness for him?

"She used to sneak him candy bars and food from the mess," Juanita said.

My cheeks warmed. "Look, he was quite a bit younger than me."

"And a flyer," Mary said. "Geneva mentioned you have a thing for pilots."

We chuckled. The lightness of conversation made me feel a little better.

Around 3:00 a.m., we continued on to Melbourne. We landed at Alice Springs the following morning around 11:00 a.m. to pick up some passengers and refuel. After leaving the plane, they served us tea and toast.

"It's hot here." Mrs. Beweley fanned herself with her hand.

"And dusty." Mary shook her shirt, and dust flew up.

"It's the flies that bother me," Catherine said. "They bite."

During the rest of our flight to Melbourne, the pilot flew at high altitudes to avoid any other aircraft. Once again, we shivered and had to wrap up in whatever we could find. Many of us fell asleep. I used the quiet private moment to pray for my sister.

I couldn't stop my heart from aching. It was just as great a loss as an arm or leg. I couldn't function as well without her. How was she doing without me?

GENEVA
May 4, 1942 Mindanao

Boom. Boom. Boom.

We woke with a start from the pounding of bombs.

Once the planes had gone, we made our way to the airstrip only to find it totally destroyed. If a plane came, it wouldn't be able to land.

We piled back in the truck and headed for Force General Hospital where once again the Filipinos greeted us with open arms. We showered and ate a good dinner.

Rita glanced at us. "I heard the officers talking."

Rosemary glanced up from her breakfast. "What about?"

"Getting us out of here. There's not a plane or boat anywhere that can make it past the Japs."

Whitlow appeared gloomy. "You know what that means."

"It means that at some point, we'll be captured and sent to an internment camp," I said.

"Think they'll send us back to Manila?" Peggy asked, fear showing in her eyes.

Lois shrugged. "There's plenty of internment camps right here in Mindanao."

"Davao and Bacolod," Rosemary said.

I glanced up. "Well, I guess we have no choice but to take it one day at a time and enjoy what we have for the moment."

They stared at me as if I'd turned pink with yellow polka dots.

"What?" I asked.

Rita smiled. "You're always so quiet."

Helen sighed. "And negative. It's surprising that you're little Miss Ray of sunshine today."

"Well usually, I don't have to give an opinion. Ressa has always been vocal and opinionated. I just listen."

They laughed.

For the next few days, we did what we'd been trained to do. We took care of the patients. Though supplies were limited, we did the best we could. Hemp made a good substitute for sutures. With a shortage of bandages, we had to boil the ones we used, then dry them to reuse.

I had no complaints, though the officer's wife did. So long as we had food and a place to sleep, I couldn't have been more content. But this couldn't last. I wasn't a negative person as the others saw me. I was a realist. I knew it was just a matter of time before our luck ran out. Eventually, capture was eminent with the exception of death in the meantime. I didn't dwell on a dismal future, there wasn't time to wallow in self-pity I now had patients to care for. My attention stayed on the sick and wounded.

GENEVA
May 6, 1942

Today the Japs bombed the small hospital. Thank God the damage was minor only destroying a few storage buildings.
Several people had been injured, but all would survive.

RESSA
MAY 6, 1942 Melbourne, Australia.

We arrived in Melbourne around 4:00 that afternoon. A handsome officer approached us, "Where are you ladies from?"
"Corregidor," Willa and Mary shouted in unison.
His face paled, and his eyes widened in disbelief. Stunned, he didn't speak. He turned and walked away.
"That was some welcome," Dorothea Daley said.
"I think he was flabbergasted that we made it off the Rock," Mary added.
"Let's find headquarters," I suggested. We received directions from soldiers in the area and made our way there.
Floramund Fellmeth greeted us warmly and introduced Captain Jane Clements. They had come over with the officers earlier on the Mactan. After talking briefly about our experience, she told us how close they had come to being bombed and destroyed. She took us to Captain Carrol's office. He'd been our commanding officer at Sternberg. He'd been the one who'd told us *War is a terrible thing.*
His speech given when the Japanese had first bombed Clark Field seemed like ages ago. We had all stood around in our crisp white uniforms. How young and innocent we were. At that time, none of us had an inkling of what he'd said. Yes, we knew war was terrible, but we had no idea how terrible until we had lived it, seen it, and smelled it. We were full of hopes and dreams. There weren't

any doubts at the time that President Roosevelt would send troops and the skirmish would be brief.

Now we too knew how terrible a thing war is.

His wise eyes studied us carefully, his face stern. "Ladies, it's good seeing you. I'm just sorry more of you didn't make it out." His eyes grew sympathetic. "Your sister?"

I shook my head. "No one knows what happened to them."

He nodded. "I'm sorry. But there's a good chance she'll show up." He stood. "Let's talk over lunch at the cafeteria. You girls look like you could use a good meal."

After lunch when we were leaving, I touched his arm. "If you hear anything about Geneva's group, you will let me know?"

"I will. They'll find a way out," he said. Later that evening he dropped off some vitamin supplements for us.

GENEVA
May 7, 1942

The bombing left Colonel Wood uneasy. He ordered us to move out on foot. We made our way to Force-tech Ranch. The people welcomed us graciously.

The next morning, the officers approached us at breakfast.

"Ladies, you're to stay here while we search for the plane," Colonel Wood said with authority. "We can move more quickly and go unnoticed without you." They walked away and prepared to leave.

I smiled. "I started to argue with him, but then I remembered her royal highness slowing us down."

Lois laughed. "Hell, I can keep up, she should be able to."

"We've got a good thing here," Whitlow said. "Food and beds. Life can't get any better."

"Amen," Peggy O'Neil said. "I was so afraid they'd want us to go. Let's just hope they find a plane."

"In that case, we'd better do a lot of praying," Rosemary stated.

RESSA
May 8, 1942

The devastating news finally reached Melbourne.

May sixth, Corregidor had surrendered.

In only six months after bombing Pearl Harbor, they had already taken the Rock. An energy draining wave of despair washed over me. For now, all hope seemed lost. At first, I didn't want to believe it, but it made the headlines of every newspaper.

A pain ripped through my chest. I didn't know Geneva's fate. Was she alive or dead? Had she been captured? Not just her, but all the ones we left behind at Corregidor. I made a mental note of all my friends who would be sent to an internment camp.

Rumors floating around said Colonel Milton A. Hill, Colonel C. L. Irwin, and Colonel Charles Savage had left Corregidor on the Quail and were taken to a submarine. They also took twelve nurses. I could only hope that some of my friends were among them.

It had been reported that they had to remain for twenty-four hours submerged in Manila Bay. I can't imagine the stress they must've endured.

I sat quietly writing my family a letter when Eunice joined me. "I heard they sent planes to look for the nurses left on Mindanao." Her face grew solemn.

My stomach coiled. "What happened?"

"It crashed before finding them. Then they sent a second plane, and it was captured, and they haven't heard from the third plane yet."

"You got any more good news?" Catherine asked. "Maybe, you should've kept that bit of information to yourself."

"I thought she should know they are trying to find them."

"It's all right. It does make me feel better they haven't given up on them."

Dorothea joined us. "Well, what I heard was just as depressing."

"I don't want to hear it," Catherine said, placing her hands over her ears.

"I do. We can't hide from it. Eventually, we'll hear about it," I said.

"Shortly after the fall of Corregidor, the Pigeon sank, and Commander Davis and his men were captured."

My fortitude fell as the news hit me hard. I placed my face in my hands and cried for a moment.

Catherine rested a hand on my back. "You'll live through this."

"I know I will, but will Geneva, and what about the others? I feel so damn guilty that I made it out."

We all shared a sense of guilt. Mine was greater because of Geneva. For days afterwards, nothing could cheer me up until I had a visitor.

"Ressa Jenkins, I heard you were here," Captain Richard Taylor said. He had been a pre-med student when I was in nursing school. Seeing a friendly face was wonderful.

"I'm surprised to see you this far from Tennessee."

We talked for several hours of home and happier times. His visit left me feeling better. He said all the right things to cheer me up.

Juel Nramor, Jeanne Haas, and Mary Boyle, three American nurses at the hospital were very kind to me. They brought me some of their clothes and even their precious stockings. I found myself feeling like I had forgotten something. I glanced around a moment before I realized it was my gas mask and helmet. They were no longer needed, but they had become such a part of my life it seemed strange without them.

I dropped in on Colonel Carrol. "Sir, do you have a minute?"

He glanced up and smiled. "Yes, come in."

"I don't want to go home. I want to stay in Australia, so I'll be closer to Geneva. I want to be here when our troops regain control."

He sighed. "Ressa, your orders are to go home. You need the rest."

"But, Sir…"

His stern expression let me know there would be no argument.

Later that day, we were issued nice fitting official uniforms for the first time in our military career. It consisted of an A-line skirt and blazer. It gave me a spark of interest in clothes. Despite things being strictly rationed in Australia, they issued us shoes to go with our smart looking navy colored uniforms.

We paraded in front of the mirror. "Thank goodness they put bustlines in and tailored the waistlines," I said. "I'm tired of dressing like a man."

"Same here," Mary said. "They reveal just enough of our legs to look good."

Eunice smiled. "We're supposed to wear them at the ceremony today."

We were being honored, but without Geneva, all the glory seemed empty.

That day, we received praise and awards for our heroism. I tried to keep a smile, but it was difficult. My heart wasn't in it. It was back in the Philippines.

They didn't restrict us to the hospital, so the other nurses and I went shopping. I purchased all new under garments and nightgowns. We were finally recapturing our femininity and feeling like women again.

RESSA
May 9, 1942

The next day I stared at myself in the mirror. My reflection surprised me. My eyes seemed larger than I remembered and around them were deep dark sockets. I was thin and my bones seemingly poked out all over. "I look appalling."

Mary laughed. "Don't we all."

I picked at my hair. "It's horrible. All straight and stringy. I can't let my family see me looking like this. I need a perm."

"My hair is dry. Probably from washing it with soap," Mary Lohr said. "There is a place in town. Let's get our hair done."

I nodded. "I want the works. Cut and permanent wave. Facial. Manicure. It has to be an improvement. I need to look like a human in a hurry."

Two days later, I sat in the chair getting my perm. The smell of the chemicals burned my nose, but I kept reminding myself how great I'd look afterwards.

The girl working on my hair couldn't have been any slower. Mary had her hair done and had returned to the hospital. The beautician slowly twisted my hair with the little papers and clips. Finally, she had my hair wrapped and the perm solution applied. I was ready for the dryer.

"You, Ressa Jenkins?" a lady at the front desk asked.

"Yes. Why?"

"You've got a call."

She handed me the phone. "Hello."

"It's Catherine. You've got to get back here now."

"Now?"

"Yes, our ship leaves in an hour for home."

"An hour? Heaven's sake. They don't give very good notices." I explained about my hair.

"We'll pack your things. Hurry."

"I will." I handed the receiver back to the lady who'd stretched the phone too me. "Here." I shoved some money in the beautician's hand. "Thanks. I've got to go."

"But your hair."

I wanted to say, *who's fault is that, slow poke*.

I rushed back to the hospital and found the others had packed for me. I ripped the papers from my hair and rinsed it. I didn't have time to style it, because I had to make it to the bank and exchange my money for American currency.

"Have you seen Florence MacDonald? She left and didn't tell anyone where she was going. She may miss the boat."

"I haven't seen her." I grabbed my purse. "I'm heading for the bank."

"But your hair," Eunice said.

"I know. It looks worse than before. My parents will think I was tortured."

They laughed at my attempt at humor.

Mary's hair looked great. She smiled. "Your hair will look better once it dries. I think you'll have a little wave to it."

"If I see Florence while I'm out, I'll tell her."

The others chuckled at the sight of me running around like one of mama's chickens after she'd cut its head off.

I made it to the bank only to wait in line. My blood pressure had to be rising with every second I had to wait. By the time I got back, it was time to leave for the ship.

Florence still hadn't been found, but they had packed her bags and were carrying them to the boat. I grabbed my new suitcases.

Colonel Carrol, Captain Jane Clements, and Ann along with others saw us off.

"Godspeed, ladies." He turned to me and took my hand. "Ressa, Geneva is going to be all right. Don't worry about her and take care of yourself."

Tears clouded my eyes as I nodded.

We boarded at 4:00 p.m. and waited and waited. I could have finished my perm. Florence made it in plenty of time. Finally, around 10:00 p.m., the transport ship pulled out.

A number of civilians, several Australian flyers, and five American war correspondents traveled with us on the enormous ship. John Lardner, Allen Raymond, Ralph Jordan, H.R. Knickerbocker, and Merrill Rueller would get an ear full from me. I hoped they'd go back and report the horrors I planned to tell them. And if they continued to hide what was happening in the Philippines, I'd share our story with as many people as possible.

I wouldn't be quiet about how our government had deserted us. I wouldn't be quiet about the nurses, doctors, and soldiers left in the hands of the Japanese. I planned to talk and talk loudly to anyone willing to listen in order to raise awareness. If I made enough noise, maybe our government would rescue the ones the Japanese held prisoner. I could only pray that Geneva would be rescued.

While quiet and shy on the outside, my sister could be a volcano on the inside. Maybe, it would help her survive the ordeal she faced. I would have felt better if I were there looking out for her.

I ended up taking care of Gwen Lee, who had malaria. I also helped Captain Samuel Elor, the medical officer. We stopped over in New Zealand and visited Wellington where they fed us wonderful food and entertained us. My two new suitcases bulged with new clothes. While there, I asked to see if anyone received any news on Geneva and her group. No one had.

GENEVA
May 11, 1942

Colonel Wood and the other men returned to the ranch with bad news. Only one plane had taken off. It had been a P-40 aircraft piloted by a Filipino pilot heading to Leyte. "Ladies, I'm afraid there's not a plane coming. There'd be no way to land it. We also looked for a boat to no avail."

"Corregidor fell May sixth, and General Sharp is surrendering Mindanao today," Commander Seals announced.

"We are returning to the hospital, and it is there where we will be taken into captivity," Colonel Wood said. "I'm sorry. I feel like I have failed you."

Many of us cried because it sealed our fate.

"Some of the men retrieved our bus and filled it with enough gas to drive us back to the hospital. They will accompany us to make sure we make it. Any mail you are carrying for those you left at Corregidor must be destroyed. Burn it now."

"But I have a stack of letters," Sally said.

"I'm sorry. It can't fall into the hands of the Japs."

She removed a silk handkerchief that held the letters. We pulled out any money from them and kept it, hopefully to return it someday. With heavy hearts, we helped her burn the letters.

Once back at the hospital, we did what we did best. We helped with the sick and wounded. I worked in a ward bandaging a young soldier who'd been brought in the previous day. Many of these men were missing arms and legs. I offered them smiles trying to reassure them, but I knew many would die or be captured by the Japanese and then die.

"They're here. The Japs are here!" Sally Blaine shouted.

"God, why?" Evelyn Whitlow whispered. "This is it, ladies."

"Just keep working, until they order you otherwise," the doctor said.

Our patients saw the fear in our eyes. Many tried to sit up. I pushed one back down. "Stay down."

Within seconds, Japanese soldiers entered the hospital. Their boots pounded the floor in a regulated rhythm, and the rattling of their swords at their sides put our nerves on edge. Their faces appeared stern as they stormed past us.

My heart leapt. I recalled all the stories of how they had treated the Chinese women.

The soldiers herded us outside where we were lined up. As they walked down the line looking at us, I stared straight ahead not blinking an eye. I had heard stories of them chopping off heads of people who were disobedient.

The doctor who ran the facility had served in Japan and spoke the language fluently. He also had a better understanding of the culture than most. He greeted the officer in charge exhibiting proper respect for his rank. He then was ordered to escort the officer on a tour of the hospital. We were ordered back to our duties.

They walked the halls from ward to ward. Occasionally, the Japanese officer would stop and question the doctor about a patient or a procedure. When the officer had seen every inch of the hospital and appeared satisfied, the doctor returned to us.

We quickly gathered around him to learn of our fate.

"Ladies for the time being we will continue our duties. Your daily routine of caring for patients won't change. The only change will be the freedom to come and go. We are officially prisoners of Japan. I will speak with the officer in charge and work out the details of hygiene breaks. So far, he seems a reasonable sort."

"By the injuries these boys have, I see just how reasonable they can be," Rosemary said.

"Many of them speak good enough English to know you are smarting off about them or making fun of them. That will get you in trouble. I'm giving you a lesson in proper Japanese etiquette." He demonstrated the *all-important bow*, a display of respect. "Now you try it."

"I'd rather kiss a fish," Whitlow whispered.

Even under stress, we smirked.

I wanted to pick up something and throw it at the Japs for what they'd done to all these people, for Jerry and all the others who'd died. My common sense kicked in, and I practiced my bow.

While doing so, I fumed with rage. "I can't believe these bastards have the nerve to talk about respect. From what I've seen, respect is the last thing they deserve."

Heads nodded in agreement with my statement.

"I understand how all of you feel," the doctor said. "Hell, I'm with you. I've lived with these people, and I know they're big on honor and respect but that seems to differ from Jap to Jap. So, my advice is to bow and stay out of their way."

Later that day, the Japs loaded the doctor and the other men, then drove them to a male prison camp.

At least we'd had a few days at this beautiful hospital to rest.

For the next few days, we worked under extreme duress. The Japanese came and went as they pleased. It didn't matter if it was in our quarters at night or while we were bathing.

They seemed to always have their eyes on us. We made sure we stayed in pairs to avoid being alone with one. But most Japanese men considered themselves superior and too good for American women.

Supplies became scarce. Food also became an issue. I knew they'd feed themselves and let us starve.

Someone who'd been captured and brought here had heard a group of nurses from Corregidor had landed in Australia. Knowing my sister was safe lifted a weight of despair off of me.

RESSA
June 11, 1942

My heart leapt when we entered San Francisco Bay as the Golden Gate Bridge loomed ahead of us. We were finally home. "Mary, I think I'm going to cry."

"Me too."

"If only Geneva were with me. Then this would be the greatest moment of my life."

"And all the others we left behind," Juanita said. "It breaks my heart that they're still there facing all the horrors of war."

"This is definitely bittersweet," I said.

"May God bring them home safely," Father Edwin Ronan said.

We were given some good news. My good friends, Ruth Straub, Helen Summers, Grace Hallman and Nancy Gillahan had been on the submarine and had landed safely. Also, with them were Beth Veley, Lucy Wilson, Leona Gastinger, Hortense McKay, Mollie Peterson, Ann Bernatitus, a Navy nurse, and Mabel Stevens. All ladies I had worked with. It saddened me that Winnie and Dorothy Scholl hadn't been with them.

We were told we would be picked up and carried to our hotel. Seems the government and city wanted to shower us with attention. And I would use every bit of that attention to demand help and relief for the Philippines.

As we grew closer, I thought of the sacrifices we'd made, the sacrifices of so many who had died, and the ones we had left behind. This is what it was all about. Freedom. Freedom from tyranny and oppression. This was the beautiful land of the free. To keep it this way, we all have a duty to fulfill whether on the home front or on the battlefield. A duty of honor that preserves humanity.

GENEVA
June 1942

At dinner, the Japanese guards watched us closely, making it difficult for us to speak. Several of the girls had been reprimanded for letting their expressions show what they thought. As for me, I had always been a hard one to read. In just this short time of being separated from Ressa, I quickly discovered I'm strong and able to fend for myself. I wished I had a way of telling her so she wouldn't worry about me.

"I heard they're moving us," Whitlow whispered. "They have a bunch of missionaries in Cagayan. From there by boat, they'll move us to Davao."

"Holy smoke," Agnes said. "That's on the coast on the other side of the island." She continued eating.

"It's an old pineapple plantation," Whitlow whispered.

"One of the Filipino nurses knows some Japanese. She heard them say the actual camp is overcrowded. They've started using buildings in the town like the old school house," Rosemary said.

"I doubt they'll keep us there long if it's overcrowded," Peggy added, while scraping every crumb off her plate.

"Nope, we'll end up in Manila," I said, being my usual gloomy self.

Rita fanned a fly away. "I'm not sure which is worse, being in Manila or being isolated in some little coastal town."

"At least being in Manila, we might get Red Cross assistance," I said. "We might even be able to get letters home."

"True," Peggy agreed.

Rosemary brushed a line of ants from the table. "Do you have any idea when they'll move us?"

Whitlow shrugged. "I'm not sure."

"Well, I like it here for the most part," Peggy said. "It's been a nice break from the tunnel and the air raids. Too bad we can't ride out the war here."

The guard glared at us and shouted in Japanese.

I flinched. We didn't have to speak the language to know he was telling us to stop talking.

That night in bed, I couldn't stop thinking of Ressa.

If I knew anything about my older sister, she would bring a lot of attention to those of us imprisoned in the Philippines. So, God made the right choice in which sister to send home.

We would be rescued.

And I was sure God would give me the strength needed to survive the hardships and imprisonment ahead of me as I waited in the shadow of the sun.

The End

RESSA JENKINS—born November 2, 1908

Ressa left the Philippines determined to bring attention to what they had endured. Once they arrived in San Francisco, the nurses had their hair done and were treated to a shopping spree. A formal dinner followed with a special showing of Disney's *Fantasia* as the people opened their arms to these nurses. For some reason, Ressa didn't want her name mentioned in one of the articles at that time. I'm assuming it was because Geneva was still missing.

Once back, she was stationed at the Army Air Field in San Bernardino, California and was chief nurse at the San Bernardino Army Air Depot. While she was approved for active duty, she decided to remain stateside to share their story with as many people as possible.

In early June, a reporter named Hayes interviewed Ressa. She acted as a spokesperson for the Red Cross, but she didn't miss an opportunity to tell the people about her experience and the ones still in the Philippines under Japanese imprisonment. She also did a program with Frank Sinatra as he promoted war bonds by singing *The War Bond Man* and other government written songs.

In June, Lieutenant Ressa Jenkins was the guest of honor at an outdoor auditorium at the Douglas Aircraft Corporation in Santa Monica, California. She stood in the center of the auditorium and told their story to a large, attentive audience.

June 16, 1942, 2:00 p.m. Juanita Redmond, Dorothea Daley, and Ressa spoke on the KGO Coast Blue and East radio talk show.

June 23, 1942, the Red Cross held a rally at a junior college recruiting nurses.

June 24th, She and other nurses who had escaped spoke at a county council business session to the Veterans of Foreign Wars.

June 29, 1942 Juanita Redmond, Eunice Hatchet, and Ressa met with mothers of men who were prisoners of war.

On July 1, 1942 at 4:30 p.m. Dorothea Daley, Susan Downing Gallagher, Eunice Hatchett, Junita Redmond, Harriet G. Lee, Mary G. Lohr, Florence MacDonald, and Ressa were invited to the American Red Cross Nursing Services held in the Red Cross Garden in Washington D.C.

The attending nurses received purple citation ribbons and pins. First lady, Eleanor Roosevelt praised them for their bravery, comparing them to the country's greatest heroes. The audience consisted of military, Red Cross nurses, radio broadcasters, news cameramen, reporters, and photographers. The Army band played for the occasion.

In the first lady's speech, she gave the presidents regards and gratitude for all they had done and his promise that liberation would be coming for those captured. Later they had tea with Mrs. Roosevelt. One thing that was pointed out in *We Band of Angels* was that she referred to them as Lieutenants rather than Miss.

July 28th, 1943 Big Army Show in the Bowl. Ressa spoke to thousands.

On Friday, Sept 10, 1943 Ressa spoke at a breakfast and helped promote the Victory Parade. It was a tribute to all the soldiers who had fought. The parade displayed military bands, equipment, and soldiers.

Ressa continued to accept speaking engagements to bring attention to the people held prisoner in the Philippines.

She never saw Robert again.

Ressa Jenkins found her pilot, Captain Donald T. Curry from Montana. He was an engineer. Though he was much younger, they married, but never had children.

Years later, she finished her career at Franciscan Conventional Hospital. After forty-six years of nursing, she retired. Her husband preceded her in death, and she remained a widow. Donald died on October 23, 1957.

Ressa Jenkins died August 15, 1986 and is buried in the Golden Gate National Cemetery in San Bruno, California with her husband.

GENEVA JENKINS—born October 31, 1910

Some of this is based on an Interview with a Tennessee magazine called *Now and Then* published by the Tennessee State University in 1987.

From May through July, the nurses remained at the small jungle hospital and worked under Japanese supervision.

August 21, 1942 Geneva and the other nurses and civilians were sent to Davao Internment Camp on the coast. It was a five-day journey in a filthy freighter. They were forced in a hold and the hatch closed with no ventilation. Rats and cockroaches ran freely in the enclosed space. Geneva later said her two main memories of it after arriving in Davao were sleeping on the floor of a schoolhouse where some of the internees had been taken and being accompanied by Japanese soldiers on a shopping spree for food.

On September 5, 1942, she and the others were transported by a freighter to Manila. The sea voyage from Davao over the Sulu and the South China Seas to Luzon and Manila was dangerous.

They were detained at the campus of Santo Tomas. She was later quoted saying, "At the camp, no provisions were made for us. No beds or anything, no place to take a bath."

Here she was reunited with Josie Nesbit, Maude Davison, Dorothy Scholl, and her good friend, Winnie Madden, along with other nurses she'd worked with. They entered the camp with no money that could buy things. Fortunately, everyone shared.

Mrs. Hube, a German citizen, a naturalized American who wasn't imprisoned, brought the nurses food and supplies for making clothes. Also, the Red Cross sent in supplies.

Geneva stated in an interview that the nurses' conditions were much better than some internees. The one thing they would have liked more of was privacy. She said, "We had to shower with everyone without hot water. But the climate was warm. So, that was okay."

"Army nurses were treated better because of our roles as nurses. We were not mistreated or abused. They respected our position, and even on road trips, we weren't bothered."

Like all the nurses, Geneva had a job. Her job consisted of taking care of the civilian patients with tropical diseases like malaria. Some nurses were even assigned to raising vegetables. Santo Tomas had become a small city. Earleen Allen and Peggy O'Neil were not assigned to work. Everyone knew Peggy had very high blood pressure.

Nevertheless, they lived in fear. Especially, when there was an escape attempt. The Japanese soldiers could come in at any time and search them and their belongings. They would ask us for medicine, but we would always reply, "We don't have any medicine."

In the article, she describes having to take care of a high ranking Japanese officer. "I didn't like it one bit, but what could I do."

On one occasion, she was ordered to report for duty after a typhoon. She waded through water making her way to the hospital while dodging poisonous snakes.

While at Santo Tomas, she discovered the library and borrowed books. "I read a lot. It helped me pass the time and to forget about all of my problems." She was quoted saying her reading books and faith in Jesus Christ were the mainstays that got her through her imprisonment.

She lived on rice and a fish that smelled like skunk. After the battle of Midway when the tide turned against the Japanese, not only did food became harder to come by, their treatment became harsher.

"If it had gone on a few more months, I wouldn't have lasted," she told the interviewer. She continued. "Near the end, you only got one cup of rice twice a day. That was all."

In February of 1945, General MacArthur and the American soldiers retook control of Manila. The nurses were finally liberated.

"I shook hands with him," Geneva said, "and thanked him."

At the time of her release, Geneva who was five-foot, four weighed only one hundred pounds. Once freed, she stayed and continued nursing in the Philippines until relief arrived. The Japanese continued to shell the university. The hospital where she worked escaped damage but not her living quarters. During these raids, many of the recently released POWs were killed.

On February 28, 1945, Geneva returned stateside. Ressa was there to greet her. The hug that should've happened in Australia finally happened. A parade was given in the POW's behalf. Geneva rode in a convertible with actress, Patricia Neal, and a soldier.

No sooner than she'd arrived, she suffered an attack of bronchitis and was hospitalized in North Carolina. After her discharge, she was sent to live at the Grove Park Inn and even had a chauffeur to drive her around. Flowers and fruit baskets arrived often to pay respect for her sacrifice. But the frills of her heroism came to an end when she was ordered back to work.

"No one cared about what we had gone through," she told the reporter. She's quoted as saying, "No one knows what being a POW is like unless you have experienced it yourself. Still, they should have retired every one of us. We were in no physical condition to work. Three years of starving under such harsh conditions affected our health and our life."

While walking down the street, she ran into the Methodist minister who had found her missing Bible. As he returned it, he told her how he had read it and used it.

In 1947, Geneva retired on disability with severe chronic bronchitis. After caring for her father in Tennessee for several years, she returned to the warmer climate of Los Angeles, California not far from Ressa, who lived in San Francisco.

In 1983, Geneva and thirty other nurses were recognized for their wartime service. She was flown first class to Washington D.C. where she met President Reagan and Tennessee representative, Howard Baker. The women were presented medals and awards by both gentlemen.

Geneva never married or had children.

She said, "Going through that kind of experience makes you understand many things. It makes you appreciate what you have and to understand people who don't have anything."

The magazine reporter asked if she suffered any long-term trauma.

Geneva denied that it had caused any permanent damage. "No. We're normal. I want to forget it. I don't want to relive it. It's like a bad dream I had long ago."

Geneva died on February 8, 1988 and is buried at the Knoxville National Cemetery in Tennessee.

What about the fate of the others? This is what we know.

Donald Robert Robbins of the 14th Bomb Squad was taken prisoner of war and while being transported on the Arisan Maru on October 24, 1944. Robert died when the U.S. opened fire on the Japanese vessel not knowing it carried our POWs. Along with Robbins, 1,752 other Americans lost their lives. These ships were referred to as Hell ships.

Lieutenant Commander Frank A. Davis was interned as a prisoner of war where he ran an underground operation to sneak food and medicine in. He died December 14, 1945 on a Hell ship. He received the Navy Cross of Valor for commanding the Pigeon and the Purple Heart. (see the letter from his wife to Ressa in scrapbook.)

Earleen Allen Francis's husband, Garnet Francis died in the Philippines.

Rita Palmer's Dr. Edwin Nelson died on one of the Hell ships. Later, she married Lloyd James and had four children.

Sue Downing Gallagher returned home and had a daughter, but her husband Robert Gallagher never made it home.

Dorothy Scholl married Arnold, and they had four children.

Denny William's husband, Bill, also died on one of the Hell ships.

Josie Nesbit married POW Bill Davis after they were freed. She died in 1993 at 99.

Frankie Lewey married Lt. Francis Jerrett.

Mildred Dalton was the last Angel of Bataan to pass away at 98 in 2013.

Helen Cassiani (Cassie) was freed and returned home. Her mother had died three days before her return. She later married and had children.

Madeline Ullom continued in the military and then served two terms on the Congressional committee of Veteran Affairs.

Hattie Brantley married another POW she met after the war.

Ruby Bradly became the most decorated woman in military history at that time. She received the Florence Nightingale Medal.

310

The Ralston boy from Tennessee also died on a hell ship.

Juanita Redmond married Hipps in 1946 and died at the age of 66.

Mary Harrington (Red) Spent her imprisonment at Los Banos where she met POW, Page Nelson. After liberation, they returned to the states and married. She had four children and five grandchildren.

Jean (Imogene Kennedy) married Richard Schmidt and settled in California where she continued in nursing. She died at 88.

Evelyn Whitlow married a former POW from Santo Tomas and also ended up in California. She died at 78.

Maude Davison at sixty married Charles Jackson. She died in 1956.

William J. Latimer never made it home to his wife, Mary. After enduring the Death March of Bataan, a 60-mile march of 60,000 to 80,000 Filipino and American soldiers. It was a known fact that anyone who stumbled or hesitated were immediately killed. Latimer survived the march and was placed in POW camp 2 in Davao, Mindanao, Philippines. He died being transported on a ship on January 23, 1945.

Major William Keggie was in the cramped hold of the POW ship, Taga Maru in semi-darkness and with only a razor performed a successful appendectomy on a soldier. There was no evidence that this ship sank like many of the Hell ships. We hope Keggie made it home to his family.

Lieutenant Colonel Stuart Wood (Stu) was imprisoned but survived the war and returned home where he received the Army Distinguished Service Medal for his service in the Philippines.

Author's Final Note:

Personally, I pray these nurses we've written about are in Heaven, because they had already experienced Hell here on Earth.

Geoffrey Meece

Scrapbook

Orders for Geneva and Ressa to report to Sternberg

R E S T R I C T E D

HEADQUARTERS PHILIPPINE DEPARTMENT

SPECIAL ORDERS.   Manila, P. I
No.........177.   E X T R A C T   31 July 1941
              X   X   X

    4. Second Lieutenant Winifred P. Madden, (N-703029), Nurse,
Army Nurse Corps, due to arrive in the department on SS PRESIDENT
COOLIDGE, on or about 1 August 1941, is, effective upon arrival assigned to Harbor Defenses of Manila and Subic Bays, with station at
Fort Mills, P. I., and will report to the commanding general for duty
with the Medical Department. The Quartermaster Corps will furnish the
necessary water transportation. The travel directed is necessary in
the military service.

    5. Each of the following-named Nurses, Army Nurse Corps, due
to arrive in the department on the SS PRESIDENT COOLIDGE, on or about
1 August 1941, is, effective upon arrival, assigned to Sternberg General Hospital, with station in Manila, P. I., and will report to the
commanding officer for duty with the Medical Department.

        Second Lieutenant Geneva Jenkins
        Second Lieutenant Ressa Jenkins
        X   X   X

    By command of Major General GRUNERT:

                         A. W. HOLDERNESS,
                Colonel, General Staff Corps,
                      Chief of Staff.

OFFICIAL:

    G. W. CHRISTENBERRY,
Lieutenant Colonel, A. G. D.,
    Adjutant General.

DISTRIBUTION:
Ea. Nurse   (3)   CO, Sternbert Hosp.   Dept. FO.
Dept. Surg.   Off. Div.   Ret. Div
Surg. Ft. Mills.   G-1.   MRS.
CG, Ft. Mills.   QM Transp.   File AGO.

313

Nurses' Quarters at Sternberg

Jungle Hospital   **Malinta Tunnel**

Ressa Jenkins

Orders to the nurses who made it to Australia to return to the states.

```
Symbols:    WP   Will proceed to
            TDN  The travel directed is necessary in the military
                 service
            TSNT The Transportation Service will furnish the neces-
                 sary transportation
```

                    HEADQUARTERS
        UNITED STATES ARMY FORCES IN AUSTRALIA

Special Orders)   A.P.O.501,
)   21 May,1942.
No.........127)

              - E X T R A C T -

        3. The following nurses ANC now patients in the 4th Gen Hosp,
Camp Pell, Vic, are reld fr asgmt with the 4th Gen Hosp and WP by
first available Govt T to USA for further observation and treatment.
TSNT TDN. FD Xl P4-06 A-0410-2. QM Xl P57-07 A-0525-2. (210.31
(AG-0))

            2D LT JUANITA REDMOND, N-702902
            2D LT DOROTHEA M. DALEY, N-703056
            2D LT SUSAN K. GALLAGHER, N-763001
            2D LT RESSA JENKINS, N-736170
            2D LT FLORENCE MACDONALD, N-700335
            2D LT HARRIET G. LEE, N-703313
            2D LT MARY LOHR, N-702907

      By command of Major General BARNES:

                              F. S. CLARK,
                    Brigadier General, U. S. Army,
OFFICIAL: Chief of Staff.

        GEORGE L. DUTTON,
        Lieut. Colonel, A.G.D.,
        Acting Adjutant General.

CERTIFIED A TRUE COPY:

        Samuel J. Klor
        SAMUEL J. KLOR,
        1st Lieut., MC.

Letter received by Ressa's father stating that she has arrived in Australia.

IN REPLY REFER TO S.G.O. SPMCN

Jof/ea

WAR DEPARTMENT
OFFICE OF THE SURGEON GENERAL
WASHINGTON

May 31, 1942.

Mrs. J. S. Jenkins,
Route 6, Box #85,
Sevierville, Tennessee.

Dear Mrs. Jenkins:

This office has been notified of the safe arrival in Australia of your daughter, Ressa Jenkins, and our gratitude for this information is, I believe, second only to your own.

We are indeed proud of the heroism and devotion to duty which the nurses in the Philippines have displayed and our hopes and prayers are for their safety and well-being.

Sincerely yours,

Julia O. Flikke,
Colonel, A.U.S.,
Superintendent, ANC.

Letter praising Ressa's work with the Red Cross.

April 7, 1944

Colonel Maynie McCormick, Commanding Officer
San Bernardino Army Air Base
San Bernardino, California

Dear Colonel McCormick:

We would be most ungrateful indeed if we were to neglect
reporting to you what a splendid contribution to the Red
Cross fund raising drive Lt. Ressa Jenkins made during her
visit here last week.

She gave four stirring addresses before our employes at
El Segundo. She spoke at five employe gatherings here at
Santa Monica plant, appeared as guest of Sam Hayes, distinguished news analyst of the Blue Network, and recorded
an interview with myself which is to be released to about
125 radio stations throughout the country, through one of
the radio news syndicates in New York.

We know definitely that many of our employes increased
their subscriptions to the Red Cross after they heard from
Lt. Jenkins what the Red Cross is doing for our boys. And,
we are convinced that her account of the hardships which
our men and women at the front endure without complaint has
had a most stimulating effect on the morale of our people.

With greetings and regards, I am

                                  Sincerely,

                                  Otto Horace Kiser,
                                  Industrial and Public
                                                Relations

OHK:mah

**Ressa
July 28, 1943**

317

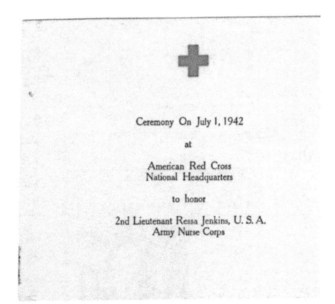

The American Red Cross Nursing Service invites you to attend a ceremony in the Red Cross garden on July first at 4:30 o'clock

to honor

the nurses serving with the armed forces, represented by

Dorothea Daley   Ressa Jenkins
Susan Downing   Harriet G. Lee
Leona Gastinger   Mary G. Lohr
Eunice Hatchett   Florence MacDonald
           Juanita Redmond

who have escaped from Corregidor

Please present this card

Ceremony On July 1, 1942

at

American Red Cross
National Headquarters

to honor

2nd Lieutenant Ressa Jenkins, U. S. A.
Army Nurse Corps

Invitation to the Red Cross ceremony in Washington D.C.

Letter from Sue Davis, wife of Lt. CMDR Frank Davis of the Pigeon.

San Diego 11, California.

May 12, 1946.

Dear Miss Jenkins:

Not having heard anything definite about Frank, I hesitated writing to you. However, Dr. Carey Smith returned from the Bilibid Prison Camp, and called to see me at my old address. The neighbors over there told me about it, and gave me his telephone number, so I called him on the telephone. Wasn't your sister at Bilibid? Did she know Dr. Carey Smith?

It was Dr. Smith who operated upon Frank at Bilibid in October 1944, and was on the first ship which our forces torpedoed. He and Frank were rescued and placed aboard another ship leaving from Lingayen Bay. They left about December 26, 1944, and the ship proceeded to Takao Harbor, Formosa. The ship tied up at the pier there for ten days, and during that time our forces bombed the Japanese shipping in that harbor. On January 9, 1945, there were between 40 and 50 Jap ships in that harbor and the only one our forces bombed was the one that carried the P.O.W.'s. They didn't even sink the ship - just a hole in the side of the ship where Frank was standing. Frank was struck in the chest and died immediately. Some of the boys lost arms and legs and lived in agony for a week or ten days without medicine or drugs. I asked what was done with the bodies and Dr Smith said they were cremated. I feel dreadful that my darling should meet such an end. I am thankful though that his body was not abused over there anyway. Dr Smith said that Frank remained in perfect health and the very highest spirits all through his captivity, and always talked about coming home. He just knew he would be home soon. Frank was awarded the Legion of Merit Medal for his activities in camp while a prisoner of war. Did I tell you he was awarded two Presidential Citations along with the Navy Cross? I know I told you about the Navy Cross, but I can't remember if I told you about the two Presidential citations. He was awarded the Purple Heart, too. I haven't received the Legion of Merit medal yet, but the Purple Heart and Navy Cross are beautiful. Would you like to have a copy of his citations? Let me know.

I sent a little package to you at Xmas time. Hope you received it and could use it.

How is your sister now? Hope she is well and happy and does not have any ill effects from her ungodly captivity in the P.I.

Hope you are well and happy. Do drop a note soon. I know you are busy, but I do like to hear from you,

Sincerely,

319

Geoffrey and Elaine Meece

Letter to Ressa inquiring about Bob Levering.

DEPARTMENT OF COMMERCE
BUREAU OF THE CENSUS
WASHINGTON

November 5, 1942.
114 C. Street, S. E.
Washington, D. C.

Second Lieutenant Ressa Jenkins,
Sevierville,
Tennessee.

Dear Miss Jenkins:

I hope you will pardon, and understand, my writing you. I have read in the newspapers you were on Bataan and Corregidor.

I have a friend, Robert (Bob) Levering, who was employed in a legal capacity by the War Department, Office of the Engineer, Procurement Section, Manila. His home was in Ohio.

Often in his letters home he spoke of a nurse in Manila, whose home was in Tennessee. Could you possibly be that nurse? About all we know of her is her age, 34 years, that she was attractive and athletic, and that she was wanting to get back to the States.

Bob's mother has officially been notified that he is missing as of May 7, 1942, and naturally she is very worried. We haven't heard of him for eight months. We thought there was a chance you might be the nurse he spoke of ... and if so, could tell us how he was when you last saw him. I realize you probably have been beseiged with similiar letters ... but know you would understand our anxiety, and our grasping of any "straw" to hear of him, even a presumption like this.

May I bless you for your courage and care of our boys.

Respectfully yours,

(Miss) Wilda Way

320

Letter from Josie Nesbit stating their dislike for the movie,
Women of Valor.

From: Josie & Bill Davis   8-18-86

TO: Ressa Jenkins Curry

Dear Ressa,

Enclosed is a copy of Hattie
Brantley's letter, which we received on
8-15-86. It describes the showing of the
CBS film, "WOMEN OF VALOR," to 5
former military POW nurses in late July,
1986 in Washington. The premiere showing will
be at the Kennedy Center for Performing Arts on
Sept. 24. It will be publicly shown by CBS
on Oct. 5, 1986. If CBS tries to contact
you, the decision to attend or not will be
yours, of course. As for Josie + me,
we don't want to attend the Sept. 24
premiere of such gross distortion of ANC
POW history. We will watch the Oct. 5,
1986 CBS airing on our home TV screen.
        With our love,
            Josie + Bill Davis
Encl: Hattie's letter and our reply.

Geoffrey and Elaine Meece

Geneva Jenkins

Notification of Geneva missing in action. The second letter validates she's missing in action.

WAR DEPARTMENT

THE ADJUTANT GENERAL'S OFFICE

WASHINGTON

May 10, 1943.

IN REPLY
REFER TO
AG 201 Jenkins, Geneva
(5-7-42)PC-S

Mr. John Jenkins,
Route #6,
Sevierville, Tennessee.

Dear Mr. Jenkins:

The records of the War Department show your daughter, Second Lieutenant Geneva Jenkins, N-736,283, Army Nurse Corps, missing in action in the Philippine Islands since May 7, 1942.

All available information concerning your daughter has been carefully considered and under the provisions of Public Law 490, 77th Congress, as amended, an official determination has been made continuing her on the records of the War Department in a missing status. The law cited provides that pay and allowances are to be credited to the missing person's account and payment of allotments to authorized allottees are to be continued during the absence of such persons in a missing status.

I fully appreciate your concern and deep interest. You will, without further request on your part, receive immediate notification of any change in your daughter's status. I regret that the far-flung operations of the present war, the ebb and flow of combat over great distances in isolated areas, and the characteristics of our enemies impose upon some of us this heavy burden of uncertainty with respect to the safety of our loved ones.

Very truly yours,

J. A. ULIO
Major General,
The Adjutant General.

322

WAR DEPARTMENT
SERVICES OF SUPPLY
OFFICE OF THE ADJUTANT GENERAL
WASHINGTON

JAU

IN REPLY
REFER TO

AG 201 Jenkins, Geneva

May 18, 1942.

John Jenkins,
Route 6,
Sevierville, Tennessee.

Dear Mr. Jenkins:

According to War Department records, you have been designated as the emergency addressee of 2nd Lt. Geneva Jenkins, Nurse, A.N.C. who, according to the latest information available, was serving in the Philippine Islands at the time of the final surrender.

I deeply regret that it is impossible for me to give you more information than is contained in this letter. In the last days before the surrender of Bataan there were casualties which were not reported to the War Department. Conceivably the same is true of the surrender of Corregidor and possibly of other islands of the Philippines. The Japanese Government has indicated its intention of conforming to the terms of the Geneva Convention with respect to the interchange of information regarding prisoners of war. At some future date this Government will receive through Geneva a list of persons who have been taken prisoners of war. Until that time the War Department cannot give you positive information.

The War Department will consider the persons serving in the Philippine Islands as "missing in action" from the date of the surrender of Corregidor, May 7, 1942, until definite information to the contrary is received. It is to be hoped that the Japanese Government will communicate a list of prisoners of war at an early date. At that time you will be notified by this office in the event his name is contained in the list of prisoners of war. In the case of persons known to have been present in the Philippines and who are not reported to be prisoners of war by the Japanese Government, the War Department will continue to carry them as "missing in action," in the absence of information to the contrary, until twelve months have expired. At the expiration of twelve months and in the absence of other information the War Department is authorized to make a final determination.

Recent legislation makes provision to continue the pay and allowances of persons carried in a "missing" status for a period of not to exceed twelve months; to continue, for the duration of the war, the pay and allowances of persons

This letter is stating Geneva is a prisoner at war.

HEADQUARTERS ARMY SERVICE FORCES
OFFICE OF THE PROVOST MARSHAL GENERAL
WASHINGTON 25, D. C.

14 June 44

RE: Geneva Jenkins,
United States Civilian Internee,
Santo Tomas Camp,
Manila, Philippine Islands,
Via: New York, New York

Mr. John Jenkins,
Route #6,
Sevierville, Tennessee.

Dear Mr. Jenkins:

The Provost Marshal General has directed me to inform you that the above-named civilian has been reported transferred and is now interned by the Japanese Government.

You may direct letter mail to this internee by following instructions in the inclosed circular.

Sincerely yours,

Howard F. Bresee

Howard F. Bresee,
Colonel, C.M.P.,
Assistant Director,
Prisoner of War Division.

Incl.
Mailing Instructions
Info. Cir. 11-C.

Santo Tomas Interment Camp where Geneva was held.

Telegram stating Geneva had been freed.
Bottom picture Geneva riding in a parade with a soldier and actress, Patricia Neal.

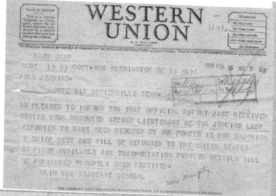

Sevierville Nurse Who Trained at General Is Among 'Angels of Bataan' Freed at Manila

Joyous news raced up a muddy mountain road to a little home out from Sevierville early today. Mrs. Ina Seaton, Sevier County Red Cross Chapter head, carried it, and it was for Mrs. John S. Jenkins. It was:

"Your daughter, Nurse Geneva Jenkins, has been rescued from the Jap Prison Camp, Santo Tomas."

Word of the rescue of Nurse Jenkins, along with many others of these "Angels of Bataan and Corregidor," came to The News-Sentinel by the United Press. It was relayed to Mrs. Seaton who got out of bed for the arduous drive up the mountain road to the Jenkins home.

Mrs. Seaton said the mother had not heard directly from her daughter since before the fall of Corregidor in 1942.

Another daughter, Nurse Ressa Jenkins, also was on Corregidor but was in a group of Bataan nurses flown out to Australia by a bomber. It was understood that Nurse Geneva was stranded in the path of the invaders when another large plane, outward bound with her party, was ground by en-

WAVES. Mrs. Seaton planned to get word to both of these sisters today.

Miss Ressa and Miss Geneva Jenkins took their training at General Hospital here. They enlisted in the Army Nursing Corps in 1941.

Rescued Nurses Go Right To Work

By FRANK HEWLETT
United Press Staff Correspondent

SANTO TOMAS, PRISON CAMP, Manila, Feb. 4—(Delayed)—The long ordeal of the "Angels of Bataan and Corregidor," the American Army nurses who cared for American and Filipina wounded in the black days of Japanese invasion, is ended at last and all are accounted for.

By way of rejoicing, they received in again having clean bandages and an abundance of drugs brought to them by cavalry units to work with in the care of the wounded in the fight to free Manila.

Imprisoned in these islands since early 1942, they knew nothing of...

(Turn to Last Page, Col. 4)
GENEVA JENKINS

LT. GENEVA JENKINS
gine trouble in the lower Philippines.

Nurse Ressa now is on duty in an Army hospital at San Bernardino, Calif. A third daughter, Seaman Sara Jenkins, is in the

'Home Never So Wonderful'

Lt. Geneva Jenkins Comes Home From Jap Prison Camp

Sevier County Nurse Saw No Atrocities, but Heard of Plenty in 2 1-2 Years in Santo Tomas

Geneva writes to ask for a replacement for her Red Cross pin she lost in the jungle.

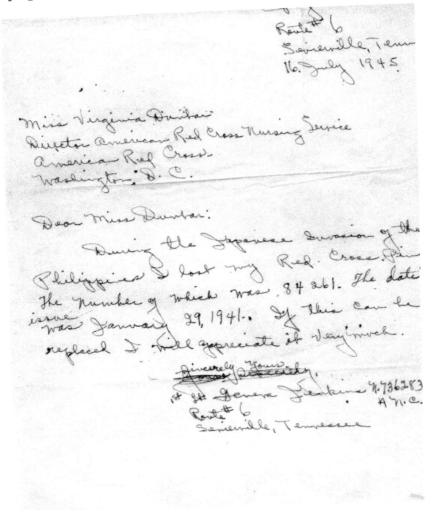

The Silver Lining
From
The First Methodist Church
St. Cloud, Florida

The following is a true story.

Once upon a time, about twenty-five years ago, somewhere in the United States on one Sunday morning a Bible was presented to a little girl.

In due time, she grew up and became a nurse in the United States Army. This nurse was on duty in the Army Hospital at Clark Field in Luzon before World War II began, December 1941. During the Battle of Bataan, she was moved to a hospital on Bataan having been bombed out of Manila Field. The nurse was assigned to the hospital in the jungles of Bataan where I was stationed. Bataan capitulated to the Japanese and in the middle of the night the nurses took what belongings they could easily carry and evacuated to Corregidor.

The next day while looking through their empty quarters, I found a Bible that belonged to this nurse, Lt. Geneva Jenkins. I took the Bible, not that I needed another, but it seemed wrong to leave it there in the jungle and it did have references and maps that were not in my Bible. During the next 3 1/2 years, it was of great service to me in the preparation of Easter – Christmas, and burial services not to mention ordinary services. The margins and fly leaves were crowded with notes and references which I had written for my own use. We were quite good friends, that Bible and me!

Upon arriving in San Francisco, November 1945, whom do you think I met, Geneva Jenkins – and she wanted her Bible. I gave it to her.

Dr. J.C. Rinaman.

(After seeing his notes and how he had come to love her Bible, Geneva returned it to him.)

Geoffrey and Elaine Meece

Note from Geneva to her sister.

Philippine money from WWII.